PERSEPHONE'S
TORCH

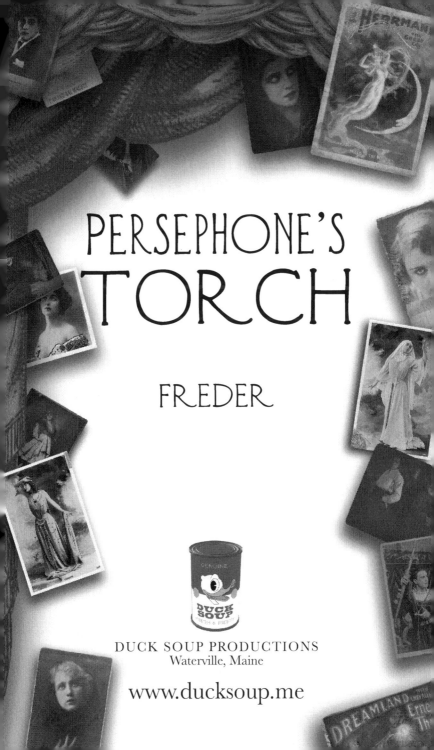

PERSEPHONE'S TORCH

FREDER

DUCK SOUP PRODUCTIONS
Waterville, Maine

www.ducksoup.me

Persephone's Torch © 2013 Douglas Thornsjo
All rights reserved.

ISBN: 148250667X
ISBN-13: 978-1482506679

Also available as an eBook
ISBN: 978-0-9884140-0-6 (ePUB)
ISBN: 978-0-9884140-3-7 (Kindle)

Portions of *Persephone's Torch* first first appeared in the following
magazines: "Hare", "The Houdini Challenge", "Roustabout" and "The
Unbroken Line" in *Kinesis*, "Blocking" in *The North American Review*,
"Heiress" in *Three Speed*, "Casting Shadows" in *The Pikestaff Forum*,
"The Paper Age" and "Star Witness" in *Millennium*.

***This extensively "remastered," revisited and rewritten edition of
the novel should be seen as the definitive text, superseding any
and all previous versions no matter where they may be lurking.***
— Freder.

Artwork, art direction, book layout and design
by Doug Thornsjo, Duck Soup Productions.

For my Grandparents.

JONES
TRANSPORTATION
COMPANY

Classic and Contemporary Plays
Commedia dell' Arte entr'actes
Fantastic Tableaux • Festival Spirit

PERFORMANCES NIGHTLY AT 8:40
Prices $.75—1.35—1.85
THREE NIGHTS ONLY.

"Ah! they would be content with a sawdust Pierrot with the long-awaited word to act as the cue for their well-rehearsed roles, so that they could at last speak the lines, full of a sweet and terrible bitterness, that crowded to their lips exciting them violently, like some novel devoured at night, while the tears streamed down their cheeks."

Bruno Schulz,
The Street of Crocodiles

"A theatrical piece ought to be written, mounted, costumed, furnished with musical accompaniment, played, and danced, all by one and the same man. Such a universal athlete does not exist, and the next best thing is to replace the individual by what is most like an individual: a friendly group."

— Jean Cocteau

14 W. Seventh Street
New York, New York
12 October 1958

Mr. George Spelvin
St. John Publishing Company
545 Fifth Avenue
New York 17, New York

Dear George;

Sorry for the delay. When you asked for an introduction to the new volume I'm sure you had no idea it would take this long. Let me assure you that I have been working at it steadily all this time, though it feels rather more as if I've been away on a long drive through a country that I left behind years ago. Now I guess the joke is on both of us: on you because the "introduction" has grown to nearly four hundred pages, and on me because I had to write the thing.

I believe you know the basic facts: in June 1939 I was working as a secretary for a local businessman in St. Paul, Minnesota. One of his properties was a little theater downtown that had seen better days; my responsibilities included dealing with the touring companies that played there, getting contracts signed, getting them all settled in, that sort of thing.

That was how I met Margaret Darwin.

ACT ONE: THE FOURTH WALL

(JUNE 1939)

MRS. LYNGE:
And there was even a theater company on
tour here, I've heard.

MRS. RUMMEL:
Yes, that was the worst of all.
— Henrik Ibsen,
The Pillars of The Community

BREAKING CHARACTER

UNDER the marquee the footprints of passersby blurred into a broad trail of wetness running from puddle to puddle across the bare concrete. Inside, where the alcove was lined with yellowing posters from the season before, bits of rubbish and crumpled newspaper had gathered at the foot of the rustcolored doors. It took a moment or two of searching through my pockets before I could find the key; as I fitted it into the lock, a hulking grey truck with a grey canvas tied over its back end came lumbering across the frosted glass, throwing motor noise against the building. Waterstreaked faces peered out at my back; the truck gave a mechanical whine, slowed, then rolled on and turned at the end of the block.

It was cool inside the lobby, and perfectly still but for my own shuffling echoed back to me from the emerald walls. I came in and stood dripping on the tile, still catching my breath from the run across town, waiting now for the players to come. Out beyond the marquee cars splashed up waves in the growing sunlight. Moments later, another truck just like the first drove by, blinking its taillights. That will be them, I thought. Wake up.

Beyond a low archway the building opened out into a twilit cavern, thick with the smell that grows on old places when they have been closed up for a week, or a season, or more. I went past fading murals of willowtrees in their frames of painted tile, past the rows of leather-clad seats. Empty during the long winters, they held a hundred and fifty whispering townies nearly every night from June through August, when the touring companies came around and the playhouse breathed in sweltering air from under the moon. Now Mr. Deighton was talking about refurbishing the place, turning it into a movie house that could be open year 'round. I understood his pragmatist position, but the Romantic in me didn't like the idea; I worried about what the building would lose. "It will chase away the ghosts," I said, trying to make a joke out of it even though I knew Mr. Deighton was himself a firm believer in the supernatural. "Perhaps," he would say, giving me his best sly smile from across the desk. "But at least the building will survive, hmm?"

The first of the trucks had already parked by the time I came into the back. It was standing with its nose almost touching the building and a cluster of strangers posed alongside, two men and two women who seemed to have nothing in common other than distance traveled, mileage accumulated along steaming, endless roads. Three of them were standing out under an awful old batwing of an umbrella; a couple in their fifties, obviously married though they were shaped differently, as graceful in their manner as royalty fallen on hard times, and a man with the look of a mechanic about him, lots of pale flesh piled onto a frame slightly smaller than the truck's and an expression on his face as if he didn't like his cigarette but was going to keep on smoking it anyway. The fourth was a girl no older than myself, perched on the running board in the shelter of the others. Blonde curls bordered the edge of her face; she was dressed in what looked like a parody of Victorian mourning, black blouse, black embroidered vest, a lacy black skirt with a hint of slip showing at the hem, and high-button shoes.

They looked up as I fumbled with the lock. One by one they each took up a dented suitcase or a basket or a rose-colored bundle and came in under the dripping overhang. They waited patiently, but the stage door was so badly swollen from the spring humidity that I could not get it to open, and at last the big man came through from behind, put his palm above the handle and shoved with such force that I nearly lost my balance. Then the sound of their laughter and the sound of the rain pushed away the dead calm. With their arms full of color the company brushed past me in single file, a damp, tatty little parade, smiling politely, whispering their hellos.

"Would you be the manager?" I said as the big man entered. He was carrying a trunk that might comfortably have held the girl, but he paused in mid-step, squinted at me and nodded back towards the alley. Around the cigarette, his lips were set in the faint beginnings of a grin. "You want Jones," he said. "Back there."

The second truck had just pulled in from the alley beyond. Steam curled off of its hood, all four doors stood open above the wet gravel. Two troupers in raincoats and hats were already working at the old rope holding the canvas fast. I was about to call to the nearest of them, "Mr. Jones?" when I saw a booted foot coming down from the passenger side. "You were right," a woman's voice said behind the windowglare. "It's clearing now."

She came around the front of the truck, not looking where she was going and apparently not needing to, lean and tall in a man's jacket and silver-grey slacks, a tie knotted loosely through the collar of a dark blue workshirt. Her hair was not quite black. She had a manner of assured and relaxed authority that I had never seen in a woman before, and a face that wouldn't blur no matter how poorly you focused on her. One hand was cupped over her brow. Her gaze followed along the building as far and as high as it went. She didn't notice me until she had come halfway across the yard.

"Miss Jones?" I said.

A silent laugh rose up behind her eyes, and was caught before it could escape. "Just Jones," she said, offering her hand. "You look like something out of Horatio Alger."

"Mr. Deighton doesn't get around much," I said. "I'm his, his agent. Winslow Howe. I've got some papers for you to sign."

Jones only smiled. This was enough to knock my legs out from underneath me. High up on the truck, the canvas cover had come away, its underside flaked with the remains of a painted scene, a still-blue sky dotted with battered cotton shapes. "Lead on," she said.

The largest room I could offer them was a place wedged in close beside the stage. Its walls were of cream-colored tile, well lit from a slanted tier of windows. A row of tables held up a parallel row of empty mirrors. It already seemed crowded; in the constant motion of the company, ironing boards, clothes racks and other, more unfamiliar things were appearing, boxed all around by an infinity of trunks. My briefcase was hiding in the corner where I had left it; Jones and I found a quiet spot at the end of the tables, and I opened it against a backdrop of black glass.

Inside was a mess of hand-and-typewritten pages, few of which hand anything to do with business. They were stuffed all anyhow into the pockets, spilling over into the main compartment. The contracts should have been on top, but were not; Jones waited with her elbows on the chair back and her chin resting in the palm of her hand while I rifled through the stack. "Kind of a swamp," I said. My motives in piling the case up this way had not been entirely innocent. I shot her a sideways look to see if she suspected.

She seemed to be paying no attention at all, but then: "So I see. Do you mind...?"

Without waiting for an answer she lifted out a paperclipped wad of sheets and held them under the windowlight. She studied them without a trace of surprise or even interest, her eyes dark and perfectly steady, almost unmoving. "What's this?" she said.

I lied to her. At least, I lied insofar as I was concerned. "Nothing important," I said. "Mr. Deighton lets me use his typewriter after hours. Here, here they are." With some urgency, to show her that I hadn't planned it this way, I shoved the contracts under her nose.

Jones set the other pages aside, drew a beautiful silver-capped fountain pen from her jacket pocket. "Where do I sign?"

"There. There. And there. Um, I'd read them first."

"I trust you."

"That's as may be, but Mr. Deighton..."

"Is a man of honor, I'm sure." She bent and signed three times:

Margaret Darwin

Then with the pen still scratching and her face still turned down to the paper, her voice as full and as still as the empty theater beyond, she said, "I knew what inspiration meant..."

A cool breeze blew in from the yard. It came from behind her, pushing the scent of the open road into my face. Jones capped her pen, straightened, and looked me in the eye. "I knew the charm and magic of quiet nights," she said, "when you sit at your desk from dusk to dawn and indulge in flights of fancy."

I said, "I beg your pardon?"

One corner of her mouth turned itself up, so faintly that I wondered if I was imagining it. "It's Chekov. Slightly altered. You reminded me of it. You and your boss's typewriter. These." And at that she took up the pages that she had set aside a moment before. I stopped breathing. She folded them lengthwise, tucked them together with the pen back into her breast pocket, then closed and latched my briefcase for me and nodded toward the stage. "Go on," she said. "I'll get some order here and then you can give us a guided tour, yes?"

Yes, I said. I laughed almost convulsively and did as I was told. On my way out to the stage I passed the little blonde in her Victorian black, carrying what looked like a basket of laundry. She had pulled off her shoes and stockings; dust curled around from the soles of her feet, a wavering line of footprints followed her across the tile. "Got your business done?" she said as she went by. And she gave a funny smile, a sideways look, a look that said she knew it all.

{THE SCENE}

THE Depression affected my family only as a backdrop might color the action onstage. Once that I know of, a tramp appeared at our kitchen door. My mother handled it well. Outwardly calm, she simply shut the door and turned away. Then in silence, her mouth set in the same outraged straight line that she wore whenever my father or I disappointed her, she went to the icebox, came back and made two sandwiches. The first one she gave to me. The second, wrapped in palpable hate, she took to the door.

The tramp was still waiting outside, stooped with his back to inside of the house. His nose turned towards the magnetic attraction of the sandwich and pulled his face around after it, followed by his upper body and then his hips and finally his shaggy feet; his gaze flicked expectantly around the doorframe, passing over me to quickly take in the spotless room in which I sat, white tile floor, white oven, white icebox, white walls, a white towel draped over the edge of the sink. My mother shoved the sandwich rudely at him. "Go away," she said.

The door opened just a few inches, then swished shut. From our places on either side of the impromptu proscenium that it had created, just for a moment, the tramp and I had both experienced a glimpse into another world. "Filthy," my mother said bitterly. "They should all be made to get a job."

When my father heard of the visit, he said nothing, but immediately went outside and drew a bucket of soapy water. He scouted around the outside walls of the house until he found the mark that the tramp had made; and he washed it off.

"No respect," my father said. "Not for other people's property. Not for themselves."

My father, who was a lawyer for a local manufacturing company, bought the house on Hampshire Drive in 1921 for ten thousand dollars, and paid for it in cash. It had concrete steps running down to the street (I sprained my ankle on them once, running down them two at a time), a finished basement, a small back yard with shed and a detached garage. Its stucco walls were well-covered with ivy; a single maple in the front yard had by the early thirties grown tall enough to provide some shade. We lived across the street from a small park with a wading pool and a swing-set, but on Saturdays it was just as much fun for us children to ride to the end of the block and play in the empty lot.

Most Sundays after church (tolerated at the time, but in later years regarded as my first exposure to theater), the extended family, including my father's beloved aunt Min and my cousins on my father's side and both sets of grandparents, would gather for an afternoon meal around the picnic table. My father and mother provided and prepared all the food; in those days I thought nothing of this, or the reasons why no one else contributed to the meal. I played with my cousins, or sometimes with the neighbors' children, and ate with them at a child-sized table set well apart from the adults.

The atmosphere in the house the rest of the week was one of distant courtesy. If my parents harbored any hostility towards each other, it was silenced by an unwritten contract that could not be violated. When disagreements happened, my parents would withdraw to their separate corners.

For my mother, this was the kitchen. Magazines and the telephone took her away.

My father would walk out through the kitchen door to the little shed in back, which he called his workshop. Indeed it was fitted out with a full set of carpenter's tools and a bin filled with scrap wood and shavings. But there was never any sign of productivity from the workshop. Never a sound. Only a man who came by once a week with some bottles covered in straw.

I know that it grieved my mother, but so far as I know, my father's drinking did not affect our relationship as I grew older. What affected our relationship was that I disdained the study of Law, and wanted very much to be Something Else.

BREAKING CHARACTER

THAT night I took my parents to see the Jones Transportation Company give their first performance in our town. We arrived at the theater five minutes before the curtain, after a long uncomfortable ride with the three of us crushed in the back seat of a yellow cab. My father would not allow me to pay the fare; once inside the lobby, he pushed past me and made for the ticket booth, though I had told him more than once that they were to be my guests. "The name is Howe," he said with his face almost touching the glass. "Mr. and Mrs. Carroll Howe." But the girl beyond had already spotted me, had already pushed the tickets through in a dusky red envelope marked PAID below my name. By the time he turned away from the window, the lobby lights had begun to flicker. "I'll pay you back," he said. Without taking another step, he opened his coat, and vanished his hand inside.

As from a great distance, in the shadow of the darkening theater, someone began to raise a graceful, beckoning series of notes from the strings of a dulcimer. "Forget it," I said. "Please. Let's just go in." But he paused still with his fingers touching the wallet, the ticket envelope still unopened against his lapel, until my mother pretended to notice the music for the first time. "Listen," she said. "They've started." So at last he gave in. The usher took our tickets, ripped them in half envelope and all, and waved us through. As we passed under the archway, a black swirl of draperies closed at our backs.

Down before the stage, a cracked canvas was dangling in a haze of orangecolored light. Its left half was dominated by a skeleton, twelve feet tall and shrouded in rags, facing a half-naked woman on the right. She had the moon at her back and willow leaves for hair. The two giant figures were lifting the corners of a starry curtain to expose a scene beyond like something out of a picture book. In it, a cast of painted actors performed *Romeo and Juliet* to a small painted audience made up of kings and queens; behind them, a canvas backdrop hung from the rafters featuring Earth and Death parting another star-patterned curtain from across another performance, another audience, another curtain, an endless infinity of Giants, actors, kings, from where the music of the dulcimer at first seemed to come.

There were no more then twenty people in the house. We settled into the middle of the third row, into seats that were so thickly upholstered that we sank slowly all through the show. "Why are there so many titles?" my mother said. She had opened the program in her gloved hands, a single parchment-like sheet of paper folded into eight different sections, one for each performance of the week. "Here," I said in a whisper. "This is tonight's."

It was to be *The Lady From The Sea*, followed by an intermission with music, then a "panorama" called *The Twilight of The Gods*. "How long does this thing go on?" my father said as the last of the overhead light dropped away. "Do they plan on keeping us here all night?"

In the stillness that followed I caught a hint of kerosene fumes drifting from behind the stage. For one moment it seemed as if the skeleton and the goddess had actually begun to draw the curtain apart, until they were themselves gathered into folds of colored cloth. They opened onto a stereoptican vista that shot back and back beyond the walls of the theater. A globe of sun climbed out of the distant sea, rising in a lazy dreamlike arc, so real that it drew applause.

Ten minutes passed before the dulcimer spoke again, to mark the entrance of The Lady from The Sea. I was sitting so close to the stage that I could hear her breathe. Her hair was wet. It was Jones.

Then I thought I could hear my father whispering something in the dark at my side. *Hsst*, I thought he said. *Listen... time.* But when I turned, his face was as expressionless as if he had covered it with a blanket. He did not notice me, or pretended not to. Thick squares of light had fallen across the surface of his glasses; I could see the play reflected there, a double image of luminous figures in motion before his eyes.

It was a strange, alchemic sort of drama, about a woman with a choice to make and the older man she has married, who grants her the freedom to make it. I had never seen an play by Ibsen before, and so had no idea what to expect, how much of the mysticism came from the author and how much from Jones's distant presence. As Ellida Wangel she carried herself in a state of distracted grace, her voice more fragile than it had been in the afternoon, though still clear, with an evocative edge that caught at her words and carried weight into the rafters, the dusty corners, the bones of the theater. Alone in the garden, she was haunted by a stranger from the past, a man with a dark face like a wedge lurking in the shadow behind the gate. It was a dreadful choice that he offered her, a choice that could turn the past into the future, and myth into reality...

When it was over I could hardly believe that they had enough left in them to give us more. But the house lights lifted only halfway. In the ten minutes that they allowed, I went through the playbill section by section while from the stage above a woman played to the hall on an instrument that she held in her hands. There were only seven names, appearing again and again, oftentimes within the same show; I could not even match them with the faces of the actors, though I had met them all earlier, in the light of day.

The "panorama" turned out to be a tragedy without dialogue, in which the pagan Gods, some Greek, some Norse, and some more ancient to whom I could not give names, all met at the Gates of Death. Faced with their own extinction brought about by the refusal of modern man simply to believe in their existence, the Gods descended one last time into the world of the mortals, to make themselves known once again, to plead their case before cab drivers and construction workers, doctors and university students, only to be exorcised, or dissected, or ignored, anything but believed, as one by one the golden threads of their lives are snipped by the remorseless Norns. The performances were as broad and as passionate as anything I had ever seen, led by the man I had mistaken for an elder statesman, Wangel from Ibsen's *Lady*, who played Wotan. The Jones woman, Margaret

Darwin, played four parts: Artemis, Hela, Persephone, and Verdande, who cut the thread of the Allfather's life. Together with the others of her company, her pantheon, she moved in a fanciful world that must have been all wires and clockwork behind the grandeur: demons appeared and circled in the clouds; the heavens opened and delivered the Gods to the mortal plane; images of the Great Myths paraded across the skies, and the floorboards of the theater itself rumbled with the passing of the ancients.

By then I had forgotten all about my parents, my concern for whether or not the show was understandable to them, or even tolerable. I was the only one standing when the canvas of Earth and Death closed upon the body of Wotan; as the players filed out from under Death's raised arm I felt my mother's fingers closing at the hem of my jacket, trying to pull me back down into the chair. She succeeded once, only to have me rise again. Did the Jones woman notice? She bowed from the edge of the stage, her face spattered with paint just like a crazy Indian, her hair all wild, her eyes like dark glass never turning down. She looked straight past me, into the back.

"Well," my mother said when the house lights came up. She drew her wrap close around her shoulders, latched it, then lifted her hat from the empty seat at her side. It had birds wired into an arrangement of cloth flowers above the band; they wobbled and fluttered as she set them back up on her head. She said nothing more. We waited in our seats, my father craning his head to see if the departing audience had thinned out enough to please him. We were just about to leave when a little blonde head appeared around the edge of the curtain, and said, "Winslow...!"

It was not her calling to me but the way she used my first name that made my parents look around. The girl grinned at us, thrust her hand through and waved, then motioned for us to come up out of the aisle. "Winslow!" she said again. "Come on! Jones wants to see you!"

There in back, in the warren of musty, propfilled rooms and cramped hallways, my parents waited like frightened tourists in the bowels of a South American police station. They would not take off their hats, they did not intend to relax; we stood in a corner outside the green room looking earnest and polite as the players came and went with pieces of the scenery in their costumed arms. When Jones came out at last she was wearing an apricot robe, perspiring some under the remains of her facepaint. She towered over my parents, shook their hands, asked if they had been comfortable during the length of the show.

"Oh yes," my mother said. "It was very nice. Very colorful."

Jones gave her that same indulgent twisting of her mouth, that same smirk she had used on me earlier in the day. "Well it's not Sabbattini," she said. "At least not entirely." Then she turned her face to mine. "I read that tall tale of yours. I liked it."

"Thank you," I said. "Which one?"

"You haven't made up your mind. 'The House of Marvels' is crossed out at the top. 'Whispers' is inked in the margin. I like your second idea, it has mystery. The other is just descriptive."

I said I would keep that in mind, then, foolishly, asked if she had the manuscript close at hand. "It was my only copy," I said. "I never thought I would need another, so I never made one."

If I had stepped outside of the scene as she had planned it, Jones gave no sign. "I'll tell you what," she said, quite convincingly, as if the thought had just come to her. "Why don't you stop by tomorrow morning? I'll have it for you then. You can stay and watch the rehearsal. We like to play with dialogue; maybe we can learn you a trick or two, hmm?"

I could feel my parents watching me. Nothing but a simple "no thank you" would have suited them, but I could not bring myself to say it, any more than I could bring myself to say yes in front of them. It would be a Saturday   I did not even have Mr. Deighton to use as an excuse. Jones was waiting. In the end I blamed the rails. "Well, the trains are always late on the weekend... I doubt that I could get here on time."

"Perfect," Jones said. For the first time her manner seemed genuinely friendly. "We don't get started until late, except when we're driving. I'll see you then, around ten-thirty?"

She took my hand and was gone before I could reply. My parents and I were left standing alone in the wings, in the steady flow of busy, whispering actors. No one took any further notice of us.

We went out through the front into the quiet city, walking along with our shapes lengthening and falling away from under us until I could hail a cab. Something on my mother's wrist jingled as we climbed inside; in the blue light from the street I could just see the shadow of a robin's felt wing as it dipped above her left shoulder. She sat without speaking, but with the intention of speaking bubbling up more and more as the car rolled along a mile or two under the moon. Then, with her face downturned, her voice as cool and as inevitable as she could make it, she whispered, "How do you know *her?*"

I was still awake, unable to reconcile my own House of Marvels with the marvels I had seen, the motions she had made, when the four-thirty train passed by on its way to Minneapolis. Its cry came to me from across the night. When I was a child the train whistle rarely wakened me, but once when I was twelve I heard it and conjured a vision in my mind of a ghostly woman dressed all in spiderwebs, wailing from the edge of town, not over a loss or for an unborn baby, but as a calling-on song, for me. Seeing her so far off, wondering what was really out there, I turned in my bed to look out through the window. It was a bright night, the edges of the yard standing out as if in the glow of a faraway light, gelled blue. Across the drive I followed the undergrowth in the direction of the railroad, as far as my eyes could see before my breath clouded up the glass.

I was nine years older now, remembering her for the first time in half a decade, lying there in the same bed with a tightness in me that I had never felt before. "Hold your breath," I said aloud. "Hold your breath, and it will go away."

INTERVAL: WHISPERS
A STORY BY WINSLOW HOWE

ON Friday nights I would crawl out of my window and walk along the empty road to the edge of town, where a small weatherbeaten building crouched against the evening sky. From a distance the house always looked dark and empty; if you came around often enough, as often as I did, you learned that it was because the windows had all been covered over with black cloth. It was to give the place a more sinister look, as if it was not sinister enough all by itself with no grass and no trees nearby, only dirt all around and a single iron post out front with a lantern that cast just enough light to read the sign:

DOCTOR VITAE'S HOUSE OF MARVELS.

On the far side of the house was a secret door that led into a storage room lined with black curtains...

...where sometimes the professor would pull open the skylight with a handworn boathook he kept for the purpose; there with the moon shining down on a decaying row of old mannequins, down on pulleys, tools, mechanical gadgets, lightning rods, cogs, he would work alone with the exhibits that had yet to be perfected: the jars filled with celluloid things that did not quite pass as the embalmed lizards, the dinosaur fetuses or extinct birds that they were supposed to represent; the electric mule, resting lifeless in an out of the way corner, waiting to receive the charge that would fill it with fire, and send it bucking and jumping with its eyes wild, to kick the dust off of its back in the center of the room; the super-dynamo, all wire and ancient generator parts mounted close around a bulky metal drum, that looked convincing but worked only in my imagination, where nightly it coruscated with living power drawn deep from its brightly painted nucleus.

It was something wonderful to come in that way, with the room starlit and motionless, the house so still that it seemed for that short time as if I was the only person inside. But I didn't know any of that until later. At first for the longest time I waited on the path with the other rubes, country men with their dates plastered to their sides, a few teenagers, a stranger or two from the next county. They came to check out the latest exhibit, or to fulfill the conditions of a dare, or just because they knew that the town council was trying to close the place down. They laughed and smoked and sometimes drank from pocket flasks until at last the bar across the door lifted itself, allowing us through into the dark unadorned hall beyond. In one wall a curtained window opened into a small booth, where a woman named Constance always sat, nearly invisible in the green glow on the other side of the bars. She would take your fifty cents or a dollar (the price depending on age, and whether or not there was a special new exhibit) and give you back the ripped corner of a yellow ticket, without ever speaking or looking up, no matter who tried to get her attention or what they said.

When the hall had filled as far as it was going to, the curtain would close without the girl ever moving to touch it. Then a soft voice would say from behind us: *Good evening*, and we would turn to see a tall man of no specific age, standing alone in an old dark suit and a top hat: the professor himself. He had grey eyebrows that didn't match the color of his hair; I learned later that neither were false. His manner was almost gentle, with none of the greasy overplay of the carnival huckster, yet his first words to us were always a warning as to the horrors, the dark mysteries that were to follow, and a disavowal of any responsibility for heart attacks, fainting spells, fits or seizures. Laughter inevitably followed on that little speech, though he didn't seem to mean it as a joke. The tour could not begin until the last echo of it had died away; then it was off through one twisting corridor after another, from room to room to absorb the sights that waited, moth-eaten and grey, for our perusal and our judgment.

In every room Constance would be waiting. It was never clear how she managed it; there were no doors other than the ones we used, and she was never seen in the halls. Together, Constance and the professor conspired to unfold the House of Marvels for a nervous and tittering crowd, offering up the cheap, the sordid, the decayed and the sensational as if they were the secrets of Time and the Universe, as if they were enlightenment itself. *Behold*, he whispered so softly, and beware, while beyond the silken cord that separated us, Constance alone could approach the displays. Silent, somehow protected, she was the one who appeared to have the real knowledge where the professor could only guess: it was she who ran her fingers down the row of jars, or fed the hideous, snakelike monster that writhed under the floorboards...

My favorite was the Egyptian Room. Inscriptions and arcane paintings adorned its walls, telling tales of Gods, cataclysms, palace intrigues, and predicting more to follow: the hopeful, shrouded future that was in turn our own past. In the shadow of a stuffed crocodile hanging from the rafters were glass-enclosed shelves lined with row after row of mummified things: cats, bats, severed hands, frogs, salamanders, exotic plants that had never been seen in our town or anyplace near, all dried and shriveled as if groping for long-lost life.

When Constance appeared in the Egyptian Room she was not Constance at all, but Isis herself, made real in mist and ectoplasm, as dreamlike in her amber gown and jeweled tiara as an image projected on smoke. She showed us water, REAL water from the Nile itself, the lifeblood of Egypt, its gift from the blessed Moon. She showed us a black alter laden with scrolls bearing all of the arcane knowledge at Egypt's command. She showed us the tools of the high priest's trade, a silver-handled dagger, a crook and flail, a golden scarab and an ankh made from stone. She showed us an empty casket from the tombs of the pharaohs, with the face of Rama painted onto the lid. And last of all, best of all, she showed us the thing at the end of the room, mounted on a narrow pedestal and encased in glass.

It was the head of a Sphinx. Its skin was the texture of pulp paper, as brown as the sunburned dirt behind the House. Its withered lips were slightly parted; the nose rotted half away, the lashes like ancient thread a quarter of an inch long, the eyes always closed but somehow alive with the hint of a movement that was never really there. We were told that she, it, was not dead but merely sleeping, that it had not moved in hundreds of years except in the right balance of the stars, to shiver at the cold of Eternity or to whisper some half-audible secret or question from the depths of its slumber. At some future time, so the legend foretold, if ever a person of pure innocence were to come into its presence, then its eyes would flutter open once again and flood the penitent with clear light. Perhaps, if the stars ordained, tonight...

But whenever I visited the House of Marvels the stars failed to align themselves properly, or else some member of our group made too much noise, or believed too little. The head of the sphinx never so much as twitched behind the panel of glass, never whispered, never winked. It didn't matter much, not to a boy who was as willing to believe as I. In silence, it was somehow more convincing to me than any display, more dreadful in the distance of sleep, if only because it was impossible to be certain, or because I wished it so much...

One night, when the head had failed once again to come alive, I held myself back as the professor began to herd us along to the next exhibit. The flow of the rubes passed and closed around me. Left almost alone in the sacred room, I turned back, and there, for the first time, I spoke to Isis.

It was perhaps my fifteenth or twentieth visit; it took that long for me to get up the nerve. I don't know why I chose her instead of the professor, for she frightened me more, the goddess of a forgotten time in the body of a beautiful, tired-looking woman. I said to her: "Please let me stay. I'll be quiet."

She looked down at me. Her lips moved just lightly, and her eyes (of the palest blue) widened with a mixture of surprise and interest and laughter. She was trying hard not to smile. She said nothing.

That was for the professor. He came around the crowd and nudged me gently back into their midst where I could not escape again. "I'm glad you believe," he said, kneeling so that his eyes were almost level with mine. "But there are too many grown-ups."

The people all laughed, and the professor rose and took us off to see the lightning machine. He kept an eye on me all through the rest of the tour. It was not necessary, I would not have tried to sneak back. I had done so on three separate occasions, and knew that the door to the Egyptian Room would be locked from the inside.

The professor ended every show by ushering us into a narrow cul-de-sac in the back of the building, from which he would promptly vanish. The door at our backs that led from the body of the house would be closed by unseen hands, and another one in front of us would open. Beyond this there was only the starry night, and a broad path of beaten dirt leading down to a gravel parking lot below the house. That night was no different. One by one the visitors went down to their cars, climbed in, and either drove away or sat for a while revving their engines, spilling light over the tall grass. It was past eleven o'clock. I started out on my shortcut across the fields, my head ringing with the echo of dusty wonders.

I had just come out of the shadow of the house when I heard a footstep in the weeds behind me. "Little boy," said a faint, exhausted voice that seemed to come over the wind from the next county. When I turned, I saw Constance standing alone against the grey shingles. It was the first time that I had ever seen her out of costume, out of make-up, though in the moonlight it seemed that she was still in character, still playing the ancient. She came from the side of the building and loomed over me, so pale that she did not seem quite solid. She was wearing slacks and a long coat that she held closed in front with both hands. I could see only the left half of her face. "Would you like to come in and see the real head of the sphinx?" she said.

It took me a while to make out her words. I was too busy looking at her, wondering whether or not I should run. She had to repeat herself three times. When at last I understood, the only answer I could give was to take a step closer.

"Good," she said with the hint of what might have been a wistful smile. "Come on." Then she pulled a lever that had been disguised as a knot in the siding, and the wall began to open up.

I found the professor making shadow puppets on the walls of his cramped, yellow office. His top hat was crushed flat on the desktop at his elbow, his moustaches were gone. He looked up as I came in, and for a moment I thought that his gaze had somehow passed around me. "Has Constance gone?" he said softly. "She didn't even say good night."

Then I missed her for the first time: she had not been beside me in the halls, she had not even come back inside. I said, "I guess so. I mean I guess not," and his face took on the strangest, most mournful look, one that even I was not too young to understand.

"It's no wonder," he said into his hands. "She has two little boys just about your age. She waits tables in town during the afternoon, does two long shows here at night. Assuming the mantle of Isis is the least of her problems."

He rose from behind the desk and blew out the lamp. Now the only light in the building was a distant blue glow that filtered from a narrow corridor I had never seen before. "Come on," he said to me from out of the dark. "I'll show you the secret."

We went up through a slanting hall that was no more than three feet wide. At times it twisted and doubled back upon itself; it ran up stairs and around the edge of the little house, through patches of total darkness where lines of red light cut through the inside wall. "What's your name?" he said at last.

"Winslow," I said.

We stopped just above one of the cracks of light. There was a number stenciled on the plaster in chipping, luminescent paint. Under the professor's hand it split into two equal halves. The first thing that I saw was a closed and bolted door on the far side of the room beyond, then the silken dividing cord, then the alter, covered over with a dirty sheet, then the mummy case, the displays, and the Sphinx's head, facing away. It was the Egyptian Room.

The professor led me along behind the exhibits. We went carefully past shelves laden with dusty jars, sidestepped around urns and braziers, until at last we stood at the case with the head inside. I had never been so close to the thing. From there, it was clear that the face was not golden at all, but carved wood covered with a layer of gold leaf that had already begun to flake away. The eyes had been repainted recently; it was a poor job. They were hinged at the corner with nearly invisible wires. The lids were made of canvas.

There was a catch on the back of the pedestal, below the case. The professor opened a panel there that I could never have known about; no moths flew out, there was no gust of ancient air. Instead, the interior was lined with a thick cast-iron casing, housing a complicated arrangement of rotten belts and rustcovered crankshafts, with a brittle cylinder set in under the business end of a needle, all wired to a battery that had long since corroded beyond any usefulness. "That's all it is," he said. "Flywheels. An infernal machine. I bought it twenty years ago from a man who used it in a traveling sideshow. It hasn't worked since he sold it to me. I've tinkered with it over the years, but I never have been able to figure it out. Some of it doesn't make any sense at all. See that camshaft, there? It doesn't seem to drive anything. Perhaps that's the key. I'll never know. I've given up."

I did not try to hide my disappointment at the shabby reality I was beginning to see behind the House of Marvels. "Is it all fake?" I said. "Is everything fake?"

The man who called himself Vitae looked young and pale and sick in the fire-colored light. "Oh, no," he said. "Some of it's real. Much of it's real. Even this is real in its own way." And I remembered the strange irritation I had sometimes seen on him, the disappointment that crossed his features when the head refused to waken. I thought, *he believed in a story, too. It was just a different one.*

Then the professor began to shrink. His long coat gathered itself into a little black puddle, until at last he sat back on his heels, took hold of his lapels, and began to look, even without his moustache, like the strange man who guided us all through the house. "You see it is all head," he whispered to me. "It has no heart, at least not one that works. But, if you would ask your parents' permission, perhaps you could come to work for me. Not every day, but two or three afternoons a week. If we worked together, maybe we could learn what she has to say. The cosmos in their proper alignment, yes?"

I remember how he stressed asking my parents, and I remember knowing that I would pretend to forget. "Yeah!" I said. "Can we?"

The professor raised one finger and pointed at me like Uncle Sam. "It will take some doing," he said, "but you and I, together, will make it come alive..."

THE HOUDINI
CHALLENGE

MR. Deighton had only to come down a narrow, whitewashed flight of stairs from his apartment above the office; even so, most mornings I still managed to arrive before him and get through much of the first mail before I heard the distant creaking from between the floors that let me know he was on his way. Age had slowed him down some, but he still insisted on making his own breakfast and dressing himself in the ancient three piece suits that he wore, fully pressed and tightly buttoned even in the hottest weather, that made him look like a tintype from the century before. And so I was surprised that morning when I came up from the street and found him already settled behind his desk, cutting open a letter with such enthusiasm that he nearly spilled his coffee. "Winslow," he said, raising his eyes so that I had just a flash of grey before they turned back to the contents of the envelope. "You look tired. Did you go down to the theater again?"

"Yes," I said, unable to look at him, as if under the force of his will I could tell no lie. "But it's not that. I didn't sleep well. I think..."

For a moment the office was as still as if we had never entered it. Then Mr. Deighton sat back in his chair. The leather breathed out a long sigh under the shifting of his bones, his face came half into the pale windowlight. I was flattered once again, as in so many other times, to have his full attention. "What?" he said. "What do you think?"

How could I say it?

That first sweltering afternoon, when at any other stage in my life I would have been at home mowing the lawn or reading a book, Jones invited me to watch a performance from the other side of the proscenium. It was the most exotic thing, the players rushing in silence through the darkness of the wings, their faces painted so that they might have been illustrations come to life, halfway familiar creatures with bright eyes and expressions like masks from the other side of sleep. They were nothing but polite, when they noticed me at all. Pausing with their profiles against the curtain, they would adjust some portion of their costume, or close their eyes, or whisper something secret to themselves before being drawn out into the folds of the play, from where their voices might echo for an hour or more before the blackout that followed on their final, whispered lines.

The mechanics of what they did amazed me: alone behind the painted scenes the big man, whose name was Lon, worked the lights from a luminescent switchboard, turning away now and then to hoist a glass globe filled with water that represented the moon, or to crank a barrel-shaped machine that made cloth waves roll by in the distance. He howled banshee-calls through a cardboard megaphone, pounded on thick sheets of metal to send a convincing thunder rolling through the stalls all the way out to the lobby. With the help of the actors, he raised entire buildings and peeled away their fronts, erecting room after room for the characters to settle into, while on the other side of the curtain, the invisible fourth wall, the audience glanced at their programs or whispered to each other, knowing nothing of the work being done just out of their sight.

I did not know what I was supposed to listen for, to learn, but I stayed with them all the way through their final performance of the day, which ended just before midnight. With some guidance, I helped them pack the plays away into night-colored trunks; in return for that, or out of simple politeness, Jones asked to see some more of my writing. So I must have looked a bit shell-shocked, riding home alone with the streetcar rattling almost empty on its long trip out into the suburbs. It was the first night of the full moon, the first cool night in more than a month of wetness and heat, and I took no notice of it.

I went back the next day and the day after that, and for two weeks thereafter, the entirety of their stay, I gave them all my free hours, my weekends, my nights. Until that time, Mr. Deighton had been used to finding me at work as late as ten or eleven o clock; now I left at the stroke of five. In the six blocks that separated the office from the playhouse I had just enough time to tempt myself, to wonder what I would walk into, what I would see, what play they would offer, and especially to worry if this would be the day when their indifference towards me turned into open hostility, if this would be the day when Margaret Darwin looked up from whatever she was doing with an expression that asked, What are you doing here? *Hurry up*, I would say to myself. *Hurry*, walking so fast that my legs began to ache, working myself into a breathless, boyish state of unrest, as if I was going to be late for them, as if they needed me.

Two days before they were due to move along to another town, I was approached by Mary Eckert. I had noticed her in a number of small parts, but it was offstage that she did her most important work, playing mandolin or dulcimer to accompany the action of the play, or singing lovely ghostlike ballads in the intervals between acts. She was taller than she seemed, with a long, delicate face and hands that moved when she spoke. Though fair, she seemed as much a gypsy as any of them, in her second-hand dresses so faded and patched as to be tramp-elegant. On the stage her best quality was a wistfulness that was not too cloying, something that I took to be a professional facade until I saw that it followed her nearly all the time, even when she was alone, like a memory of melancholy so distant as to be almost forgotten.

She took me aside during *The Twilight of The Gods*. In a little dressing room that I had never seen before, far back from the stage, she drew a thick, well-traveled folio out from under the satchel that came with her every morning from the hotel. Its edges were tied up with lengths of black string; inside, there were pages and pages of intricate drawings, all splashed with color, marked over with arrows and penciled notations. "I thought that you might like to see these," she said softly, standing so that I could look over her shoulder as she spread three of them out under the dim light. They were set designs for a series of sinister rooms, all laced with spiderwebs and filled to brimming with arcane memorabilia set out on moonlit shelves. I saw jars with deformed fetuses floating in the depths of penciled muck. I saw an empty casket leaning so that the figure painted onto its lid caught just the farthest edge of light. I saw a wild-eyed horse made of metal, with a lightning rod for a tail; and, on a velvet-covered pedestal at the end of the room, gleaming with golden skin, its eyes half open like a dead thing, I saw the head of a sphinx.

How, then?

It seemed foolish to me now, in the dry air of Mr. Deighton's office, solid wood and leather all around, the supreme egotism to say *I think they are going to produce a play from a story of mine*, that assumption based on a furtive peek at some drawings a stranger had shown to me in an off-moment from the fall of Zeus and Wotan. How could I tell him?

Mr. Deighton sat with his fingers folded, his eyes bright and alert, his ears like a bull elephant's jutting out at right angles from his head. He looked at me with what might have been wry amusement. "Not to act, I hope," he said at last. "Never to act..."

"Beg your pardon?" I said.

He took up his pen from the the blotter, dipped it, and brought out a single sheet of his personal letterhead, the kind with just his name at the top, none of the pictures of steaming pies or sweet rolls dripping with icing that adorned his business stationery. Without any pause to search for words, he began to fill the paper with handwriting as graceful as a woman's, the letters growing tails that dangled well into the characters of the line below. "You look all right, I suppose," he said as he wrote. "But your face is too open. You haven't forgotten the portion they still owe? I know you think well of them, but I'm not inclined to give them a two hundred and fifty dollar gift..."

His name appeared an inch from the bottom of the page. He blotted the note, turned it in his hands, and passed it across to me. It began:

This is to introduce Winslow Howe, a fine...

I held the paper out almost at arm's length. It quivered in my fingers like the wings of a moth. "You've made a mistake," I said. "I'm not leaving. I'm..."

"All right then," he said. I could not tell whether or not he thought I meant it, or if he thought I had made a good choice. He took back the note and folded it twice, then tucked it into the bookshelf that stood at his side, so that an inch or so of paper stuck out from between *The American Boy's Handy Book* and *The Plays of Christopher Marlowe.* "But you must be a strong man. Stronger than I ever thought. Or else just dull. Because if I was your age, I would already be lost."

And he turned back to the mail, working down through the stack with that old appearance of satisfaction settling back into the corners of his face. "Interesting batch," he said when he had dealt with it all. "Not a sign of bad news."

I was on the road from ten until noon, traveling down to the capitol plant and back in Mr. Deighton's own silver Packard. For the sake of the interior I drove with the top up and fastened tight, even in the heat of the morning; by the time I reached the factory I was as breathless as if I had run the whole way. I spent half an hour acting as Mr. Deighton's eyes and ears, trying to sort the real from the hopeful in the supervisor's talk as he walked me through the building. At last I was led upstairs to a cool yellow office. They gave me the week's paperwork all done up in a bundle tied with string, and a pie just off of the line. It was so fresh that I could feel its warmth through the box bottom. From its place on the seat beside me it filled the old car with the smell of cherries and heat, soft at first from around the corners, then rising up under the windshield until I knew it had settled even into my clothes.

I still smelled of cherry pie when I came in through the front of the theater and saw Jones alone on the open stage, setting up Prospero's sanctum for the first act of *The Tempest*. In the ungelled light her face and hands were pale as limestone, her hair tied back carelessly, dotted with flecks of color from the night before. "You're early," she said when I had come halfway down the aisle. Far behind her words, I could hear what sounded like an army drilling in the wings at her back.

"It's a business visit," I said. "I'm on another mission for Mr. Deighton."

The stage floor, like her work clothes, was smudged with a fine white dust. In places around where the action was to take place, crosses and stars had been chalked onto the boards. "Well?" Jones said. "That's no crime."

When we passed through the green room I saw what the racket was all about. The company was packing, setting their trunks in a neat pile by the stage door. Lon and Moscow had already started to lift them out into the yard. "Everything that we don't need for tonight," Jones said from over her shoulder. "It's all going onto the truck."

"When are you leaving?" I said.

"Right after the curtain. As soon as we get Father William put away. We'll drive all night."

Jones had set up a kind of office in a corner of her dressing room. It was nothing more than a black box, a ledger book and some papers spread out any which way under a tiny lamp that made as much shadow as it did light. In the pages of the open book I could follow the flow of the company from city to city, through cramped hotel rooms, truck repairs, food and supplies and paint and the price of a hall. "Here," Jones said, as I studied the numbers. "I've got something of yours..."

She lifted out a small sheaf of yellow paper. It was my stack of foolish stories, *Whisperings*, *In The Dream House*, *Heirloom*, and *The Funeral*, set down in the wavering characters of the office typewriter, marked by my many scratchings-out. The pages opened in my hands. There was new writing in the margins, a decisive, almost mystical hand that matched the notations of the ledger, black ink that now and then crept between the typed lines.

They were long, thoughtful comments, snatches of dialogue that I had only hinted at, questions about the characters, and hints at how the events could be turned and expanded on the stage. "Thank you," I said, trying not to read them at once, not knowing whether it was the notes or the thought of the company leaving by night that kept me from saying the thing that I had come to say. I had formed the words more than two hours before. It should have been easy to say them. But I could not.

And so we stood in silence for more than a minute, Jones with her eyes perfectly still and her face framed in blackness. Then she said, so quietly that it was almost a whisper, "If you make a change like that you will have to do it fast. Sometimes not making a decision is the same thing as making one."

I folded the pages away carefully into a pocket of my briefcase. "Yes," I said at last.

Still, I could not make up my mind. It was easy to feel one way in the heart of the theater and just as easy to slip back when I was safe in my own chair on the far side of Mr. Deighton's desk. In the office I had nothing more demanding to do than answer the telephone, or double check the sales figures from the capitol plant. I had no questions that could not be answered by a simple trip to the filing cabinet. I would have only to deal with my failure to collect the rent. I could live with that; I had even saved enough money to cover it, if that was what he wanted.

I had just decided that I would not go back down to that place, that nightmare theater, when the bell that Mr. Deighton had himself hung over the door, the one that hadn't worked in more than a year, gave a good loud ding-a-ling in the next room, and Jones stepped in from the landing outside. She came straight through without bothering to knock, looking more like a lady pilot than an actress, nodding at me in passing as if we had never met. "Margaret Darwin," she said with her hand extended above the desktop and her head slightly cocked so that she could meet his eyes. "Up from the Jones Transportation Company. I'm your tenant player."

"Nelson Deighton," he said, and there again was all of his old strength, his old charm. He came out of his chair with such ease that I began to wonder if he was not a pretty fair actor himself. "Tenant player, hey? What can I do for you?"

Jones held his hand in hers, and caused her face uncannily to mirror his own, as if she had managed to syphon a bit of his personality up the length of her arm and onto her features: the impersonal smile that was nothing more than a slight curling of his upper lip, one eye burning just a touch more brightly than the other. "To start with, I'd like it very much if you would show me your library."

She had seen the third room, where beyond a tall arch the walls were lined with leather-bound volumes. Later, she told me that it seemed the perfect place to fight it out: she would have all of history at her back, a conquering army of print and myth. "Of course," Mr. Deighton said. "After you. I think I might even have some things that would interest a, um, a 'Tenant Player'..."

They moved slowly along the stacks, appearing to read the embossed spines, occasionally taking something down. They acted like old friends. *Try not to look up,* I said to myself. *Work.* But the numbers no longer made any sense; I pushed them around on the page and got different totals every time. Now and then a whisper would filter out to me, shapeless as smoke, too fragmented to understand. It was worse than not being able to hear anything.

They sat together in the library for nearly forty minutes. Across town, her company would be readying *The Tempest*, raising banners, brushing off costumes, checking the lights. In another half hour they would open the doors; it might take her that long just to get back to the theater. Mary Eckert could cover for her with a patriotic tune. Perhaps I should call them, I thought, and warn them to play for time.

"Ask Winslow," Jones might have said, when at last they came around to the reason for her visit. "He saw my books. I made a point of it."

Mr. Deighton would only have folded his hands, leaving two fingers up in the shape of a steeple. "Yes, that's what I hear. And yet he tells me that for the better part of your stay you've been playing to houses that were very nearly full."

"More nearly half full. Winslow is such a boy in a candy shop."

Records could be checked, but Mr. Deighton would not have asked for that. It could not have been a pleasant moment for him; he disliked being railroaded as much as he disliked a fight. He had no qualms about locking horns with a woman, but it must have bothered him that they were circling about a thing as important to him as the little theater. "Just how good are you, Miss Darwin?" he might have said. "How deserving of my charity? That I would like to know."

"You can come down and see. You could have come down at any time."

He wouldn't bother to answer, that was not any of her business. He might even have known it was not meant for an answer, that he had lost ground by letting her say it. And so the corners of his mouth would have turned down sharply by the time he spoke, and then he would have said only: " 'Tenant player...' "

That was when he might have seen the idea: his own voice echoing for the third time that thing she had planted, and the roadweary Jones sitting opposite with her unhuman calm, her hands resting motionless one over the other just above her knees, her eyes never wavering, never leaving his. "Tenant player," he would whisper again, thinking *I've skunked her. And yet she seems to be asking for it...* before adding at last: "Winslow tells me that you work magic on the stage. Sorcery. He used that word."

The smile again. "Such a boy."

Circling each other, as they sat motionless. Mr. Deighton stroking his chin. "Could you work it here?"

"   In this building?"

"In this library. In this room. Let's say that you need to give one more performance to cover your rent. Could you and your company work your, your sorcery without props? Without scenery or trap doors or costumes? Without tricks?

"Could you *move* me, Miss Darwin?

"*That* might be worth two hundred and fifty dollars to me..."

I imagine her taking a quick survey of the room and everything in it, every door that led in, every window looking out. She'd have studied the rafters and the distance between the cases; she wouldn't have missed a single frayed edge in the rug, a single knot in the wood. When she met his eyes again it would be with one eyebrow cocked, and an expression that had just enough assurance in it, just enough doubt. "All right," she would say. "Name the play."

"What's in your repertoire? Shakespeare, of course..."

"Of course. Even *Titus Andronicus*, if you like that sort of thing."

"Marlowe?"

"Second rate. But we know them."

"Moliere? Ibsen?"

The softest of smiles. "Ah, now you're playing into my hands..." Ask on, she would say. But by then the dusk would be coming down in the corners of the room, and the bargain would have to be closed. Perhaps it would be "Surprise me," or perhaps "You'll think of something," in a lowering voice with just a hint of its full carrying power. "I'm late. It will be eleven thirty before we've finished over there. Is that all right?"

At a quarter to six they rose together and again shook hands across the map-covered table. They were still talking about books when they came out, Jones grinning at a comment I hadn't heard, buttoning her jacket though it was not cold outside. She slapped me once on the back the way a man might have, the way my father had done sometimes when I was a child. "Don't go away," she said as she passed. When she had gone Mr. Deighton came and stood looking past me, all black and white with a face like a man who had no choices left. "It's not decided yet," he said. "But it will be."

I called my parents ten minutes later to tell them that I would not be home for dinner. "It's to do with that Jones woman, isn't it?" my mother said from down the length of the wire, her voice made flat as tin by the ancient office receiver.

"Yes," I said.

"Well be careful."

I said I would, and then ran down to the diner at the end of the block to get some sandwiches. It was going to be a long wait.

The clock-hands had almost touched.

"How many names does she have?" Mr. Deighton asked for the second time, and at that moment we heard soft sounds drifting up from the street below. He turned his face owl-eyed up to mine. "Can it be them?" he said; without answering, I went through into the office to wait alone. It will never be the same place again, I thought, switching out the lights on the mantel, wall and desk. A distant glow had laid itself against the frosted glass that squared the main door. I sat in the dark, in Mr. Deighton's own chair, and watched as it gathered itself and began to grow murmuring shadows from the bottom of the frame.

At first I thought they were wearing masks. But it was only their make-up left over from the evening show, their skins an unnatural orange, hard black lines drawn into the crevices below their eyes, along their cheekbones. They came one by one in their travel-worn coats, each with a flashlight or a candle or a kerosene lamp in their hands. The seven of them filled the outer room. Then Jones came forward with the lamplight flickering yellow across her face, and said, "Is he here?"

"He's inside," I said.

She turned under the arch, leaving a streak on the air, a tail of light in her wake. The company followed without a word. They formed a glowing line across the center of the library, shuffling some, their tiredness showing, their lamps floating waist high. It was Lon Burden, their Man Behind The Curtain, who paused with his flashlight making a pool at his feet, and found me in the dark. "You coming?" he said softly.

I said I guess I am, and he motioned me ahead with the light. Inside, the library looked like some archaic throne room, with Mr. Deighton in the seat of power, his back up against the east wall and the low table like a dais at his feet. He sat uncomfortably as if he were the one on display, slightly hunched with his right hand covering his mouth. "Winslow," he said. "Perhaps you should do the introductions."

I came around the line. It was the first time I had ever spoken before the group; my voice sounded hollow. "Folks," I said, "this is my boss, Mr. Deighton. Mr. D., this is the Jones Transportation Company: Sylvie Lindstromm, Ruth Templeton, Peter Moscow, Margaret Darwin, Claude Templeton, Mary Eckert, Lon Burden."

Everyone bowed. At last Jones took one step forward out of the line. "Well," she said. "What's it to be?"

We waited in the wavering light, the growing stench of kerosene. Then Mr. Deighton coughed. From the look in his eyes I thought he would let them go. I thought it right up until he opened his mouth.

"*Saint Joan*," he said.

Jones said nothing. She looked back over her left shoulder, then over her right. A faint smile crept into her eyes. She bowed her head over the black chimney of her lamp, and slowly vanished.

Late in the second scene, Joan lifted her eyes to mine. Her face had been recently washed, and had something in it that I could not bear to look at. We were alone and not alone: the men and women of the court had left the scene, but I could see them there still at the farthest edge of the candlelight, watching silently with their arms crossed, their faces thoughtful and low. *"Art afraid?"* Joan said.

Had I imagined it? *"Yes: I am afraid. It's no use preaching to me about it..."*

It was the little blonde, Sylvie, in the part. It did not even matter that she was playing a man: her voice was just right for his undetermined character; it made him seem younger than his years. It answered for us both.

"Blethers!" Joan said. She used a simple, artless voice that could have commanded the moon, yet there was something coaxing in it as well, something that hinted of the black current that ran in her veins. She lifted her hands as if to receive his heart, then closed them into fists. *"We are all like that to begin with. I shall put courage into thee."*

Now the Dauphin turned his face away, exactly as I had done a moment before. *"But I don't want to have courage put into me. I want to sleep in a comfortable bed, and not live in continual terror of being killed or wounded. Put courage into the others, and let them have their bellyful of fighting, but let me alone."*

"It's no use, Charlie," Joan said, so that now in the straightbacked chair against the books I felt the same chill that had come to me in my own bed on the night I first met her. *"Thou must face what God puts on thee."*

It was Jones, as much as the spirit of the martyred farmgirl, who ended by asking God when the world would be ready for saints. "How long, 0 Lord, how long?" standing alone with the light dying behind her until all we could see was a glimpse of her silhouette against a patch of blue-black, windowframed sky. At last even her shape faded away, leaving only a perfect silence, in which I could have believed that the library had been emptied, that I alone still occupied it.

Then Mr. Deighton coughed in the dark beside me.

"Thank you," he said. "I guess that was the best bet I ever lost. I have to say that I don't mind it a bit."

An answering laugh and a spatter of applause went around the room. Lights snapped on in the outer office. The actors came out of the corners and stood in a broken row. They looked tired and relieved and a little happy. They looked as if they had fought a hard battle and won it, none more so than Jones, who took a long, low bow at Mr. Deighton's feet, straightened, gave him an off-hand salute, and grinned. "I hate that play," she said. "Only Shaw could write Joan as a supporting part in her own story. Whatever made you choose it?"

"I wanted to win," Mr. Deighton said.

He stepped down and was surrounded by the company. He shook their hands and patted them on the shoulder and said the things that they deserved to hear. He spoke to each one of them in turn, asking about their backgrounds, their favorite parts, and the parts that they would someday like to play.

I waited around on the edge of the group until I thought it was safe. Then I slipped away. The outer office was cool by comparison, and almost still. I could breathe again. As I put on my coat their voices came through so distant and glad, like a party in the next room. It reminded me of Christmas.

I was just leaving when I saw the letter sticking out from the middle of the third shelf. I had never really forgotten it; it was there every time I raised my eyes, crowding out the diploma, the photo and the dollar bill that hung on the wall beyond. *Strong*, he had said. *Or else just dull. Very dull indeed.*

It made the softest of hissing sounds coming out from between the books. I was going to put it in my pocket, take it home, maybe frame it. I was tired of looking at it there. At least that was what I told myself.

"Well, matey. You haven't said a word." It was Jones leaning in from the library, her weight against the frame, her arms crossed. She looked like every part I'd seen her play. She looked like a horrible, beautiful blur.

"Goodbye," I said.

Jones almost laughed. "Now that was good," she said. "Perfectly simple, but loaded with subtext. I like that."

I didn't answer. The paper was crisp and sharp in my hands. I thought that she would just take it. But she made me hand it to her.

She opened it with a simple flick of her wrist, read down through to the signature at the bottom of the page, then handed it back without ever changing her expression. "I don't need this," she said. "But bring it along anyway. You might want it someday."

Mr. Deighton was still visiting with the others in the next room. He must have felt me watching him; he lifted his eyes, gave me a soft, tired smile. It was the last time I ever saw him.

14 W. Seventh Street
New York, New York
12 October 1958

Mr. George Spelvin
St. John Publishing Company
545 Fifth Avenue
New York 17, New York

Dear George;

...

...I think you understand now why I still can't decide whether I joined the Transportation Company or was swallowed by it. By her. "That woman," as my mother called her, for the final time, while I packed my bags with those two huge trucks idling at the curb in front of the house. Those trucks were a great aid to me that night! My folks were so concerned about waking the neighbors that my packing and leaving was almost a secondary concern.

Throughout the summer of '39 we toured down through the Midwest, into the South, then headed back the long way northeast to Philadelphia, where the company kept its winter quarters in a run-down theater house that Jones called Valenciennes, after the birthplace of theatrical spectacle. All that time I ran errands, hefted scenery, brewed coffee, cooked meals, loaded trucks, unloaded trucks, raised sets, struck them, fed lines to the actors, gave out handbills, hung posters, sold tickets, laundered costumes, and oh in my spare time yes I scribbled away at new plays for the company, taking a lot of abuse for my efforts from pretty much everyone, but also learning a lot about the craft — and the people I was traveling with. Just so you understand — I don't dwell on details of that sort, but it was going on like that all the time.

I know you wanted to learn more about how the plays came into being; their 'gestation' to use one of those overripe arty words that some of you folks favor. I know you're interested in the 'Creative Process,' but honestly, George, it's boring. I never was a process-minded person. Looking back on it I suppose that caused me no end of difficulty in those days. Maragret... never mind.

Just take my word for it. I promise you that making the plays was the least interesting part of that whole astonishing season...

ACT TWO: THE ARCADIAN TUNNEL

(JUNE – SEPTEMBER 1939)

"undermen... dragging shrouded treasures which they had filched from the uncatalogued storehouses of Man's most ancient past."

> Cordwainer Smith
> (Paul Linebarger),
> "Under Old Earth"

ENTR'ACTE: WHISPERS
PART TWO

THE House was not nearly so fearsome by day　just a featureless old box of a place that had been plunked down in the middle of nowhere and allowed to decay past recovery. On the east side, facing the road, were the flaked remains of a Coca-Cola sign, invisible at night. It would have been easy to find the door there, perhaps under the flaring tail of the big C. On the west side there wasn't any paint at all. I had to search for fifteen minutes, running my fingers over the broken boards, before I found what I was looking for.

For three days that was all I had thought about, in school or at home, that hidden door which would admit me into my first real job, the magical job of helping the head to speak. In my sleep I could hear its voice, an awful, cracked, distant sound, whispering the secrets of men's hearts, secrets that I could never manage to carry with me into wakefulness. It no longer mattered that the head was just a machine; it was a machine that had once learned words, and that was almost as good.

I came into a long empty hall flooded with light from the open office at the far end. The walls had been painted green, once. I picked my way down along its length, calling "Perfessor? Perfessor? It's me, like you asked.   Um, Perfessor?"

The office was not like one that I thought a professor should have. There were no books, no papers, no maps, only an old issue of *Photoplay* and some copies of *The Black Mask* spread out across his desk. On the floor in the near corner was an antique toolbox almost like a doctor's bag, lying open with the handle of a hacksaw sticking out at a strange angle. The ceiling, which had been solid the last time I saw it, now had a hole gaping from where a flight of stairs had been lowered. It fell so that the steps crossed just below the window. From the foot of them I could see up into an attic space filled with webs and clutter. A faint rustling came from somewhere in the back. "Perfessor," I said. "It's me…"

"Catch this," he called from above. A hand in an oily sleeve appeared over the edge and tossed something, some metal contrivance, down at me. It was a pedal with a long piece of fencing wire hinged to it. "You like to drive?" the professor said. He came around the top of the stairs with his arms full of iron junk, some of which had leaked black soup onto the front of his coveralls. "Your pappy ever let you run a tractor? Now you will learn to run Oracles."

His hair might have been dressed with motor oil; tufts of it gripped his forehead or stuck straight up in the air. He had the look of a blissful archeologist who had been digging for too long and had come up with some great stuff. "You're just in time. I've got the answer, I have. It's just a matter of hooking it up." He stepped around me and then turned back, pulled a low stool out from under the desk with the end of his foot. "Bring that," he said, "and come on…"

We went through the wall passages all the way to the Egypt room, where he had been working all morning, laying the guts of the sphinx machine out neatly across a dun-colored dropcloth. There were twisty bits of steel and clockwork that had all rusted solid; I watched and helped, handing in tools now and then, as he removed a dirty speaker from under the head and began wiring the pedal into its place. I supposed that he was wondering what use he could get out of the pieces, if they could be assembled into something good enough for his Technological Wonder Room, or if it would all just end up in the pile in the back yard. I knew that he wouldn't throw any of it away. Perhaps, if I did a very good job, he would give some of it to me.

"The important thing to remember is not to offer them too much," he said with his thin ropeveined arms pushed under the machinery, his face turned up and away as he groped for some unseen bolt. "They'll ask questions and you just try your best to answer them without really saying anything. Ehh. There. You won't be able to see them, so we'll have to figure on some code system for Connie to help you. She's good at that, she's got an eye for the different types of people. You'll know some of them, being a local boy; that's even better. Don't worry about embarrassing anyone."

"Where did you meet Connie?" I said.

The professor craned his head around and flashed his teeth at me. "One day I had enough change in my pockets to buy me some lunch. And there she was. Isis bussing tables, hey? Sounds kind of funny. But that's what it was. I came back here and right away knew what the show was missing. But it was more than month before I could get up the nerve to offer her a job."

I found a piece of an old spring and pressed it between my hands, imagining the professor in his costume, his frock coat and top hat and the false moustaches in the corner booth of Weston's Diner, downtown. I imagined Constance whispering between the tables, nearly invisible in that blue uniform, ignoring him, marking the pad and pushing it back down into her apron without ever looking up. I believed him about the month.

I was studying the little rusty circles that the spring had left on my palms when the professor at last finished his work inside of the machine. Very gently, as if he were trying not to wake anyone, he cleared away the pieces that he had removed and the nuts and bolts that had held them in place, until all that remained on the floor behind the pedestal was the foot pedal and two things like handles from a cellar door, wired into the neck of the Sphinx. He set the stool a foot or so back from the gutted machine, sat me down on it, and disappeared around the front. "Don't do anything yet," he said. He bent this way and that; he craned his neck and walked around a bit and squinted. "Nope," he said when he had finished. "We'll have to set you back more, get you a curtain. I can still see you. Now pick up those hand controls and give them a squeeze. The left trigger operates the right eye and the right trigger operates the left eye. Foot pedal should operate the mouth. See what you can do."

The pedal worked quite easily; when I pressed the triggers in my hand I could hear an ominous scraping sound from deep inside the machine, and the leathery creak of the eyelids beginning to move. "That's good," the professor said. "Try making faces." And I hunkered my head down, squeezed the controls and said, "Nyaa nyaa nyaa..."

The professor only laughed. "What should I do about my voice?"

I said. "If I just talk like me they'll know who I am. How about if I talked like this?"

I made a voice like my father gargling, and another like my grandmother waking me in the morning. The professor smiled and shook his head. "Why don't we take our clue from this," he said. From a ledge on the front of the machine he lifted a small, covered box. Inside, wrapped loosely in tissue and straw, was the silver cylinder that had been mounted beneath a useless needle. "Careful, now," he said as he lowered it, box and all, into my waiting hands. "The mummy's voice, every word and whisper scratched into these grooves. I've got just the machine to play it on. Connie will want to hear it, too."

I never did get a chance to listen; there was no time, that day. When the professor and I went back down to his office I noticed the sun riding big and low along the edge of the sky, and knew that my parents would be wondering where I was. "Come back again tomorrow afternoon," the professor called as I ran out past the roadsign. "Connie will come in early. We'll work up a routine..."

But I came back that same night, along the path I knew where the night flowers bloomed under the moon. I had a big handful of them by the time I came into the shadow of the building. Far above, I could hear the house complaining under the weight of the guests. The professor and Constance would still be caught up in presenting the first show; I hurried straight to the little office, placed my bunch of flowers at the end of the passage where Constance would come upon them, and hid in the narrow footspace underneath his desk.

I thought it would be a fearful wait, but it wasn't at all. I sat in the absolute dark with my knees pulled up close under my chin, wishing that I had brought along a flashlight and a comic book. There was no sound when Constance came bearing her lantern through the wall, just an angle of light cutting across the floor and a female shape rising up inside it until the room was held in a flickering blue glow. She set the light down just over my head, and gave a sigh in the empty room.

"I told you no more flowers," she said when the professor came in from the hall. It was the same emotionless monotone she had used in the night behind the house, the only other time I had heard her speak. "I thought we talked about that."

"I don't ——" the professor said.

Connie cut him off, lowered her voice to a whisper. "I can't stay here if you're going to keep this up," she said.

"They're only flowers... I don't ——"

That was when I remembered the voice, and used it for the first time. It surprised and frightened me when it came out, a filthy sibilant push of dead air, a creak with words:

... from the boy...

No one moved or spoke in that cramped room for nearly a minute. I waited under the desk with both hands clamped over my mouth. Then the professor turned on his heels so that his boots made a crunching sound in the grit and dust scattered over the floorboards. "Only one place," he said. His face came under the legspace and I held myself like a frightened animal until at last he smiled. "Well," he said. "Looks like you're ready after all..."

{THE SCENE}

SUPPER WITH SEVEN STRANGERS

I remember thinking how quiet they were, picking their personal bags expertly out of the mountains of stage paraphernalia, then crunching their feet across the cold gravel of the courtyard, their voices hushed and soft as breath. There was no light in the alley, nor in the street beyond; I followed them through the dark up along a narrow avenue of houses, wondering if they remembered I was there, or if they cared. Once I heard Mary laugh, softly, in response to a whisper from Jones ahead of her. It was barely audible, almost drowned out in the whisper of crickets, the barking of a dog in the distant yards. Halfway up the hill we turned into a sidestreet and paused like tramps or ghosts before a high grey building with a sign planted below the steps. A sad old iron fence circled the yard. There was no gate; Jones stalked through, her shoulders set hard under the weight of her black coat. She went straight up the walk and entered the front of the house without knocking. I remember climbing into sudden light, into an entry hall that was much too small to hold all of us. "Jones Transportation Company," I heard her say to the man behind the desk. "Oh, and there's one extra."

It had been uncomfortably like regressing into childhood, sitting again in the back seat with my forehead pressed against the glass, watching the land roll by, not knowing how far we were going or when we would arrive. In the front passenger seat Jones passed the trip with a nest of paper spread out across her lap, her face downturned, her features cloaked by spirals of black hair. She kept a running conversation with Lon, who was driving, but their voices were inaudible to me over the noise of the engine, the hum of tires on the road, and the sometimes alarming sounds of the contents in back shifting as we lumbered on down the road. I wasn't sure that it would mean anything to me even if I could make out their words.

We had gone nearly forty miles before I dared ask Mrs. Templeton if she knew where we were going.

"A place called 'Dexter,' " she said, brightening a little, as if she were glad to learn that I had a mouth. "It's some distance yet. I've never played there before. Let's hope they have running water."

"Have you played in places that don't?"

Oh yes, Mrs. Templeton said. She told me about horrible boarding houses with stairwells that were a threat to life and limb, about rooms that allowed wind to rush in through cracks in the walls, about vermin under the floorboards chattering and scrabbling, about frozen mornings when the rugs crunched underfoot, and what it felt like to meet a stranger on your way down to the bathroom in the middle of the night. She spoke with her face perfectly composed, almost serene, as if the subject was nothing more ominous than pickled herring. After a time I thought I saw the faintest hint of a twinkle behind the oval frames of her glasses and thought, She's trying to frighten me! Testing the new kid. I turned my face away, hoping that Jones would break into the conversation. But she never looked back.

Mrs. Templeton was still talking, quite on her own hook, when we drove into Dexter. It was a little river town built into the side of a hill, the high windows of the houses above looking out over the roofs of the main street. We passed a general store, a diner, two banks and a barber shop that looked like a place people had been avoiding for a long time. Coming in past the theater, with its empty marquee and the cardboard posters Jones had sent ahead tacked up in the shade, I had the awful feeling of having switched places within my own memory, so that as we came opposite the lobby doors I half-expected to see another young man just inside, looking back through the glass. He'd be waiting in the yard behind the building, wearing a clean new suit, clean shoes, a businesslike tie with blue polka dots. Jones would climb down from the truck once again, and again he would not know what to make of her...

We followed Moscow's truck onto the first side street and then into an alleyway so narrow that I could hear the rasp of canvas against brick as we inched our way through. At the far end the stage door was standing open with a stocky greyhaired man inside, sweeping dust out into the yard. He frowned and poked at the sill. "Surprised you didn't draw a crowd," he said in the alien quiet that rushed in when Lon cut the motor. To me it sounded like he was shouting. "We could hear you coming ten miles away."

Lon and Moscow climbed up in the sun and started to untie our load. "Ah, that's part of our advertising," Templeton said from the other truck. He came out of a sliver of shade behind the cab. "Can't afford advance men. So we've modified our trucks to blat out a fanfare."

"Heads up," Moscow said. He lifted a canvas sack out under the yellow glare and threw it down at me. It hit me in the chest, harder than I thought was absolutely necessary, but I caught it, and I didn't drop it.

It took an hour and a half to unload the trucks and get a start on raising the set for the evening show. By then everyone was tired and cranky, but resigned to the longest part of the day that remained ahead. Watching them rehearse from a musty seat far back in the stalls, I imagined that they must have felt like paper figures fading inside a sand toy, following through the repetition of ceaseless motion as grains of silver fell through the chambers of a watermill connected to their joints. Their words came up to me in sighs and mumbles from the stage below, and when I could make them out it was a strange mixture of dialogue and stage directions, questions and insults, fragments of incantation and baseball gossip, so that nothing made sense to me except that they were rehearsing some new kind of play, something discordant and European that would never have gone over in Saint Paul. In time I realized that they were not so much rehearsing the play as *fitting* it to the new stage, changing a mark here, compressing a bit of action there. Jones, circling the scene like a predatory animal, was the only one of the cast who spoke all of her lines. But her mind was on other things; the words came in a monotone under her breath, drifting without form or meaning down over the clouded footlights.

Just before dark I went out alone to stand in the cool air that blew down from the end of the alley. All that remained were a few unnecessary things still wrapped in sackcloth, frayed ends of rope dangling in silhouette; from where I stood, in the shadow cast by the lowering sun against the crest of the town, I could hear water rushing close below the theater. Inside, Lon was testing the thunder machine. It started with a rumble like the beginning of an earthquake, then let loose with an authentic wallop that I could feel through the stage door. At the peak of the blast Sylvie came stumbling over the threshold as if she had been thrust over by the storm; her bare feet hit the ground hard enough to raise a cloud of dust that reached to the hem of her skirts.

She took a long stretch at the edge of the yard, then began to pace aimlessly in and around between the trucks, her toes pointed in the air, her legs trailing black lace. She pitched her shoes so that they landed and tumbled in the bed of the truck. She made a point of showing me that she didn't know I was there.

At last she turned her face sidelong up to mine. "You know it's never too late," she said. "All these places have train stations. You can always change your mind."

I watched her poke at the dirt with her foot. "You've got me wrong," I said. "I'm not having any second thoughts. I feel a little guilty about that."

Sylvie pulled herself up and sat above the tailgate, looking through parallel slats out over the long, low hill that ran to the edge of town. "Well, I knew it was something. Just look at you. Ugh, are your palms sweaty as well?"

I said no, held them out for her to look at, and was surprised when she took them into her own. She ran her thumbs across my open hands, studied my fingers as intently as if she were staring into a bowl of clear water. "I read palms," she said, "but yours would take hours, all the little lines. That means you're indecisive. Look at how they all run cross-ways to each other. You could use a manicure, too. I don't do those."

She hopped down and danced away across the gravel, swaying inside of her skirt. Watching her, I wondered how she could travel and work in such fragile clothing without tearing it to shreds. "What will your first play be about?" she said. "Jones wouldn't tell."

A cool breeze had come up from the river; it was hard to keep from shivering. "I don't know. Not about actors. And not about runaway clerks."

Sylvie allowed her last spin to wear itself out. She stood with her weight on one leg, her arms crossed, and looked at me with a sad little frown. "Well, we'd better go in," she said. "Jones will have missed us by now. She'll cut off my head. She'll disembowel you."

Now bent over the the front desk of the little boarding house Jones signed the register for everyone, dipping the pen, writing out her stage name, then dipping it again and drawing an arrow down along the edge of her finger, five, six lines. In her black jacket, her hair as wet as if it had been rained on, she reminded me again of a lady barnstormer coming in off the tarmac with the engines still roaring in the distance and the night air breaking around her, closing at her back. I remember the scratching of the pen, and the sound it made when she laid it flat in the book. Of the six keys the night man had set out, only two remained; Jones scooped them up, tossed one at me without looking at it, and turned into the stairwell after the others.

She climbed up ahead with a paper sack in one hand and a clothes bag draped over her shoulder. At the landing she looked down at me over the rail, gave a tired laugh at something that she saw, and went on. The stairs ended in a little hall not more than three feet wide that wound all through the center of the building. It was lined with misshapen doors that didn't entirely fit in their frames. I found my room number in a blue triangle of light and was fitting my key into the lock when Jones looked back again. "You can if you want," she said. "That's your business. But aren't you the least bit hungry?"

"What's open at this time of night," I said. "In a town like this?"

Jones made a come-on motion with her head. "Chateau Eckert."

She raised her chin and in her best, modulated stage voice called out "Where sall we gang an' dine the day?!"

"Number five," the voices called back.

We stepped through into a crowded, blue-papered room that already looked as if it belonged to another building entirely. There was no sign of the bed, if there had ever been one; instead, an oriental rug covered the floor with a puddle of maroon and blue. Mary knelt at one end, dealing out cardboard plates and silverware and parcels of food wrapped in foil and waxed paper from a wicker basket at her side. I recognized Happiness Home Apple Pie and Happiness Home Molasses Doughnuts, and felt guilty about not having thought to provide them myself.

They had coffee warming on a hotplate in the corner, also a thermos and a wine bottle three-quarters filled with dark liquid slopping around inside. As we came in, the company was just beginning to settle down. Moscow had taken a place in a chair before the window, his frock coat spilling over the sides like black ink. "Penalty for late arrival," he said.

"Well damn," Jones said. "Hope you didn't eat all the fish eggs." She lowered her face without looking at me and said, just as if she were blocking a scene, "Look around: stocking the basket will be your job from now on."

She took the place that had been saved for her at the foot of the rug. "How's everyone doing? Ruth? Doctor?"

Templeton shook his head. He had changed into a clean summer suit; though their faces were drawn, the Templetons still made the rest of us look like tramps. "I think we're all wishing that we'd listened to our parents," he said. "But that's not your fault."

"No," Moscow said. "That Shylock pie man."

Sylvie was busy setting a row of empty cans across the east windowsill, lighting candles one from the other and then burning the bottoms so that they would stand free. It was Mary who asked if I was going to sit down; even then, I could not shake my awkwardness until she indicated a spot next to her.

Jones poured a little wine into the bottom of a glass, passed it on to Moscow at her left, found another and poured again, and the glasses made their way around the rug. At the same time, Mary and Mrs. Templeton were opening the parcels and setting their contents out. There was cold chicken and ham, two kinds of grapes, sourdough bread sliced into heavy slabs, and a gooey jar of apricot preserves. Everyone was helping themselves. I waited.

At the head of the table, Jones downed her glass, poured herself another and smiled through tired eyes. "Our new addition looks as if he's holding up all right."

"Hah. And Mr. Deighton said that I couldn't act."

No one laughed.

"What shall we call him?" Mary said, laying down a swath of jam onto the bread and biting into it, all in one motion.

"Hey, you," Moscow said.

Templeton snorted.

"Well if his name won't do," Jones said, chewing.

"Oh, it won't," Mary said.

The "table" fell silent, but it seemed hardly anyone was concerned with the topic. It had become heavily uncomfortable and I was wondering how to possibly move things onto another track when Mrs. Templeton looked at me pointedly and said, "Is there a proper name for 'waif?' "

This did bring some laughter, though not from the men.

Still Jones chewed. At last she looked up, her eyes lit; she had it.

Proud of herself, she angled her head alarmingly like a flirt.

"Penfold," she said.

Sylvie said, "Can I keep him, Mommy?" and popped a purple grape into her mouth.

"He … Penfold … in addition to his other duties which he will learn about as we go along…"

Jones canted to her right as she said this, and in response to the signal Lon looked up from his meal. His eyes met mine with a hard gorilla stare that said, *Oh yes you will learn, I will see to that.*

"…will be working with all of us, individually and collectively, to develop new material for the fall season."

"He's our new Marlowe, then?" Moscow said cynically from his chair.

Jones drew a lot of air in through her nose. "Less than a writer and more than a typist," she said, and once again I felt deflated. "This is a group thing just as it's always been. We're all learning. Even you my dear."

Silence. She turned back to the company. "What I want to do, we can't do without someone like him. What he wants to do, he'll never in a million years be able to do without us. We brainstorm together as a body. We work under the assumption that all ideas are good until proven otherwise. We do the repertoire at night, and we work all day on the new stuff. I don't know what it's going to be yet. He sure as hell doesn't. But I know that everyone sitting here has ideas."

Templeton, Mary and Lon all nodded silently. Light and candlesmoke moved on every face. Our shadows touched the wall, bound on both sides by patches of luminance reflected from off of the wine. Jones raised her glass. "Here's to a perfect little season," she said.

We drank to that, and then it was just as if the ice had cracked; the company all began to talk at once. Leaning over the rug, balancing his food, Lon poked through the remains of the chicken as though trying to find the wish bone. "She always asks for the same thing," he said. "Just like a broken record."

Jones smiled. Her fork arced down towards the plate from her left hand. "I'll keep asking for it until I get it."

Templeton came back from the sink with his glass full of tap water. He sank back painfully again into his place on the other side of the rug. "You're joining a long tradition of hack playwrights," he said. "It's real seat of the pants work. A lot like yellow journalism, I'd guess."

"Making it up as we go along?" Mary said. "How exciting!"

"Does that mean I won't have to learn any lines?" Sylvie said.

I felt myself give out a sigh. My thoughts dropped away from the scene. Not for the first time that day, I thought *What am I doing here?*

Looking one by one at their tired faces, I began to wonder how I could imagine them. A protestant miller and his wife. A farm family, mother and daughter. Most everyone here is of a piece, I thought. Most everyone here is clay. I can imagine nearly all of them taking shape in some role, out there, in the real world. But how in hell do I conceive *her* as anything other than what she is?

I kept my silence the rest of the evening, only listening to see how they interacted with each other, how their relationships played out. Mary helped; her face was easy to read, watching her was like having a translator who could not resist adding her own opinions. After a while it became evident that there was only one member of the company that she actively disliked: and this was Sylvie.

It was uncomfortable sitting on the floor. I began to feel as if home had never existed, as if the whole world was sleeping, but for us.

At a quarter to two Jones looked at her wrist, folded her napkin into a careless V; and the company let out its breath all in one exhausted sigh and prepared to withdraw. Plates were wiped clean, the remaining food wrapped up tight, the rug rolled tightly and nudged against a blue-painted radiator. There was a lot of shuffling about and brushing of crumbs, but no one left the room until Templeton opened a mahogany door in the back wall and pulled the bed back down out of it, feet first. He took off his jacket, sat at the foot and pointedly said, "Goodnight folks."

Mine was a corner room, close by the stairs. It was a hot airless box with a window that couldn't be opened and a bed that looked as if it was made of lumpy oatmeal. There was a single lamp with a shade that had yellowed so that it almost matched the color of the wallpaper, a clean sink sticking oddly from the middle of the wall, a closet wedged in where the stairs bent around the outside of the room. I waited half in the yellow light, in the faint creaking that rose out of the floor as the company spread out along the length of the building. I was just turning to close the door when I saw that Moscow was standing there, still in the frock coat, blue faced, his hair all uncombed, his cheeks darkened with stubble. He looked me in the eye, then moved his head as if to indicate the room. "So?" he said. "This is what you bought."

THE PAPER AGE

WHENever Mrs. Templeton traveled there was always a rolled tube of paper sticking three or four inches from the top of her carpetbag. She would sit with the bag on her grey-coated lap, the tube almost touching the back of the seat ahead, and on bumpy roads or on crowded streets she would cradle it protectively against her broad body, lowering her shoulders over the paper to see that it would not get crushed. Once, sitting too close beside her in the stuffy cab, midway along the drive from Nashville to Tell City, I got a good look at the paper and saw for the first time how old it was. It had been rolled and unrolled so carefully and so often that it had taken on the suppleness of leather, had turned under her fingers into something more permanent than paper: aged oilcloth at its wrinkled edges.

I never did find the courage to ask what it was. It was for the same reason that I could never call her by her first name, always Mrs. Templeton when to everyone else she was just Ruth, who never played a leading role with the Jones Transportation Company, though she carried something of the Leading Actress about her, some of the quietude, the authority. She was a small woman who had filled out with age, who favored plain blue dresses and who managed to keep her dignity without also being aloof. Oftentimes, when the cast met in the shreds of their make-up for a late-night dinner in some cafe, I would sit beside or across from her and listen to the steady turn of her voice, and think: *she is friendly enough. Maybe I can ask her now.* But she would never meet my eye when I thought I had screwed up enough nerve; instead she would start in with Lon or Mary or Jones about baseball, her favorite subject, or about radio dramas, which fascinated her, or movie dramas, which didn't. That would draw me into the conversation just as she intended, and before long she could look at me again without risking any more serious question than her opinion of Laurel and Hardy. Then she would sit back and grace me with the faintest smile, and make her harmless reply.

And so the Jones Transportation Company had played in more than fourteen little towns before I had a chance to see the poster, or learn about it, and the man it pictured her with. It was in that quiet interval following the afternoon sessions when everyone, even Mr. and Mrs. Templeton, went their separate ways, to read, or sleep, or drink, or just to be alone. Mrs. Templeton came out of character into the cramped room behind the stage, where I waited alone with two trays of cold food and the echo of their voices rising and falling from the stage beyond. "Penfold," she said, not looking at me, as she put the water on for her afternoon tea. One by one the others spilled out on her heels through the stage door. "Could I have a word with you?"

It had been a good reading and spirits were high; for a time all but Lon stood by in a close, informal group, laughing and working on the stack of apple danish that I had brought from a local bakery. Then Mrs. Templeton set out a prop teatray, filled the company's battered old silver pot almost to the rim, and added some pastry to the setting, enough for two. She took the whole arrangement into her hands, and pointed at me with her nose.

Her dressing room was a few steps down the hall. I held the door open and she went rattling through into a cramped, sunlit cubbyhole with off-white paint peeling from the walls; once inside, I saw the poster for the first time. It was hanging where the wall jutted inward to make room for a small closet, close by a plant stand supporting a fluted vase filled with the petunias she had picked a few days before, along the road. Unrolled, it was at least four feet tall, reaching almost to the floor so that the figures inside might almost have been life-sized: the youth in military clothes hunched in the dark grass with a yellowing skull cradled in his lap, in his long fingers; a wisp of humanshaped fog circling up from behind him, eyeless, one bony transparent hand caressing the youth's shoulder; and beyond them both, far across the field under the black arms of a dying tree, mad Ophelia crushing flowers to her breast, her purple gown whipped up in the grip of the night air. Above, in liquid letters woven into the sky, it said:

The Montgomery Playhouse
THEODORE BAXTER

And below the youth's bended knees, simply:

—HAMLET—

and the playdates, hand-lettered in black there along the bottom edge of the paper:

August 20, 21 & 22, 1910.

Mrs. Templeton set the tray down gently on her dressing table, stood with her back to me and filled one cracked cup and then the other. "This new play," she said, lifting the tray again, offering it out until I had taken a cup and one of the pastries. Her eyes were wide and she was nodding repeatedly as she spoke, as if to convince me that she meant no harm. "Very much 'Big Picture.' Very much 'The Great Illusion.' Oh, Margaret loves that sort of thing."

She sat in the room's only chair and took the remaining cup, sipped from it, then broke her danish into three crumbling pieces over a paper napkin that she had laid out on the dresser top. "Mmm. Good central vision. That's your strength; a real sense of the mystery of life. But for some of us in the supporting roles…"

I stood with the teacup in one hand and the apple filling dripping onto my fingers. There on the poster, the printed brushstrokes under cooling blue leaves were so graceful, a single line shaping the youth's jaw, his golden hair rising like vapor, like undersea grass, his dark eyes almost like Saint Jones' looking out past my shoulder. But it was Ophelia, far off behind the central image, the lurking, salacious ghost, who held my attention: her face was not as round, her neck thinner and longer somehow, her cheekbones just a bit more prominent, but it was still her, wearing the same expression even that I had seen under folds of fat as she stood out under the light, on the stage. It was the owlish brown eyes that gave her away.

Mrs. Templeton sat looking up through her glasses, her legs crossed at the ankle. "I'm not trying to pad my part," she said softly. "It isn't that. There was a time when I would have mounted an elaborate campaign to get a juicier scene, or a good line. But that isn't me, now."

"It's you," I said at last, not looking at her or even at her likeness of twenty-eight years before, but at the youth, the Hamlet with the face sculpted from fairy tales. "But I don't know him. A man like that can't have existed; he's too pure; he's impossible."

There was no sound in the little room but the touch of china to china. Mrs. Templeton sat up in the chair and looked over at me with the most intent expression; then she settled back and smiled, and made a pantomime of throwing aside an invisible script. "Mr. Baxter did look like that," she said, "once long before. He always looked well. But by the time I took Ophelia, when Olivia Baxter got too old, he was nearing sixty, he hadn't looked like that for two decades, and the picture had to be idealized some. It wasn't lying, exactly. His Hamlet was beautiful, even then."

She drew herself so close to the dressing table that her legs disappeared as she slid open the topmost drawer on the right side. There was an old book of poems bound in marbled paper with leather along the spine and across the corners, a sad, dogeared copy of *Measure For Measure*, and a brown envelope large enough to hold legal papers, but now nearly empty, nearly flat. It was held fast with a strip of black cloth looped around rusting clasps; she lifted it out under the light, uncurled the cloth ribbon to its full length, and reached inside.

There were three photographs, printed on thick yellowing paper, the size of lobby cards. She propped them up on the teatray, against the pot, the cup, and the mirrorglass. "There," she said, lifting them one by one so that the lightglare rode down the figures and then vanished. "Here I am as Medea. My first leading role. And Olivia and Theodore Baxter both here in *Macbeth*, and Mr. Baxter and I in *Hamlet*. That was our last production."

It was like looking back into another age, into some frozen pre-history of the theater, all ancient yellow figures posed in the most piercing harshness of light, haloed with their faces painted and lined, black lipstick on their mouths, kohl smeared around their eyes. There was Mrs. Templeton, so much younger, her body thin as rope, standing bloodless and terrified over a rag-covered corpse. There was a tall, vague woman dressed in black silk; she might have been better suited to a Titania, Queen of The Fairies than to the spitting, snarling Lady Macbeth she played here, a Lady Macbeth who could not even be troubled to wash. And the Hamlet, Theodore Baxter, the face from the poster all right, huge and fervent, but spreading out now into a man no amount of make-up could have made young again. Though still handsome in his long military coat, he had gone harsh, the skin more like wax than ivory beneath the curl of golden hair that was not even his own anymore, and the black lines painted onto his eyelids only added to the touch of the unnatural that rose from off of him.

"What made him stop?" I said. For the man in the picture, though old enough to be ridiculous in the part, looked as if he would be content to play Hamlet forever, well on into his nineties.

Mrs. Templeton gave me a look from over her shoulder that was not quite bitter and not quite amused. "It was the poisoned sword," she said. "His wife. She couldn't stand to be alone, and she would not abide the nurses. He went back to the house to care for her, and he closed the theater down.

"The next day I came down for work as usual, all in my hat and scarf. I had forgotten about it, or put it out of my mind. I came under the marquee and didn't even see that the signs had been taken down. I didn't remember until I gripped the doorhandle and pulled. And I felt so cheated. No final moments, you see, no last walk out onto the stage. Just a door that wouldn't open.

"Wistfulness," she said, and without looking at them Mrs. Templeton snapped up the photographs and tucked them into the envelope again and then into the drawer. "It's not the approved method of building a character, but it will do in a pinch, it's better than nothing..."

"Mrs. Templeton?" I said. My hands were empty now but for the empty cup. My fingers were sticky with the remains of apple filling; I stood and tried to keep from wiping them on the back of my pants.

"Your play. It's true that we are an improvisational company, we do work without a net sometimes. Most of the time. But you will be a better playwright if you think some more about the small characters. Round them out, or, if they must be flat, give them sharp edges. Especially for poor Mary, she's a singer you know, she isn't used to coming up with her own dialogue. Just hold them in the back of your mind; don't force anything on them that they don't seem ready to take. And if you can't work them into anything more than props with mouths and legs, then get rid of them. Better not to be on the stage at all than to be there and have nothing to do."

I looked into Ophelia's painted eyes, into the bottom of my cup, and then back. "Why is she having you tell me this?" I said. "Why doesn't she tell me herself?"

But Mrs. Templeton only turned her face down and away. Her eyebrows climbed well above the rim of her glasses; she asked if I would like some more tea. As she was filling me up she gave me a look that suggested she had once played Lady Macbeth herself. She topped off her own cup, set the pot back in its place. When she had taken a sip and swallowed, she said without looking at me, "Do you know, I never was the sort of girl who took things quietly, who stood around mooning and looking out of windows."

"I didn't think you were," I said.

"No? Well, I did that for a week. I did a lot of mooning and looking out of windows and that sort of thing. For the first time in my life. And I decided after... well, soon enough that it didn't suit me. There was nothing else in town, no other company at all, much less one that needed an actress. The nearest other big town was, oh about fifty miles away. I could not think about moving. I had family, then. Well, in the end I did the only thing that was open to me, the only thing I could think of to do. I borrowed my brother's car and I drove out to the old Baxter house, and I begged him to re-open the theater.

"Oh, I thought it would be horrible. It was, at first. The Baxters had retired to a beautiful Victorian mansion, of course it *had* to be, didn't it, a place right out of a book, surrounded by about twenty acres of gardens. In earlier years when they could afford it there were men who cut the hedges and mowed the grass and made all sorts of buzz as they went out over the grounds, but when I came up for the first time there wasn't a soul about. It was the dead of winter, all of the little pools had been drained, everything lay still, white and grey along the pathways. They'd had it fixed so that guests had a long silent walk that ended under a crumbling archway at the bottom of the lawn, with a fine view of the house. It had great grey windows like those on a greenhouse. When I came up closer I could see inside. It was all dark and empty, stone floors, sheets thrown over every scrap of the furniture. But there was one lighted room far in the back. So I put my feet very close together, squared my shoulders just as I always did before the curtain swept open. And I gave a tiny little knock.

"All the time that I waited I worried about my costume. I had chosen a colorful paisley dress with a rust-colored belt and a matching hat with a flower in it, much brighter than anything I was used to, but nothing too grand. I had taken particular care to look modest without being drab... now I wasn't certain but that drab mightn't have been the better way to go. Because I knew what I was going to be asking for, and, now that I had seen the house, from whom.

"Before very long, and without any sort of approaching sound from inside, the door was opened, and there was Mr. Baxter himself. It had only been a month since I'd seen him, but he had so changed... his hair was snowy white now, and uncombed — he had just stopped dyeing it, I suppose, though I didn't think of that at the time. He was wearing spectacles at the end of his beautiful nose, and an old, tweedy sort of suit, like a little professor-man. And he was so happy to see me. He held out his arms to me and took my freezing hands in his, and I was drawn inside.

"It was a cozy, low-ceilinged living room deep in the house. Mr. Baxter had a fire going, which was very nice because of the way it lit some of the small pieces of his collection, his theatrical bric-a-brac, masks and prop swords and a few exotic, jeweled costumes that were set about there. We sat together and talked for some time over tea, just as you and I have done. And he never said no when I asked him, which was more than once. But after twenty minutes or so there came an awful rattling, banging sound, and when I looked up I saw that Olivia had come into the room.

"She had been strapped into an awful old wooden wheelchair, and was pushing herself along on the bare floor. She had lost quite a lot of weight, her arms were so very thin, yet she managed the chair well enough. But I believe the worst of it was the wig and the make-up. She mightn't have seemed so pathetic if she hadn't insisted on that. Well, she made no great secret of the fact that she was not happy to see me. 'Ruth,' she said, and put out her hand like this. She would not look me in the eye. She sat and shook, and worked her mouth silently, as if she had bitten into something awfully sour and could not politely spit it out.

" 'You see how it is,' Mr. Baxter said to me, quite softly, as he led me back out along the dark hall. 'You see it cannot be any other way than this.' And I agreed as well as I could, but I was feeling sorry and blubbery for myself and it came out as something like a stage whimper. We had reached the front hall. It was time to say my goodbyes. But when I looked at him I found that I could recognize his ruined old face for the first time, even under that lot of white whiskers. He said, 'Perhaps there is something I can show you.' And he turned away.

"I followed him through into the east wing of the house, where everything was closed off and unheated. Throughout the afternoon I had done nearly all of the talking, he had hardly spoken, but now as he went he called back to me from over his tweedy shoulder. 'Of course it won't take the place of the real thing. No applause, for starters, but no booing either. And it might keep you in practice until something better comes along. I can't think of any other way that a man my size could have got to play Puck.'

"I thought, 'Puck? *Puck?*' And I was led through a white doorway into what must have been the largest room in the house. There were great, sheeted dinosaur shapes huddled together from wall to wall, so close that we had to turn sideways to pass between them. When he pulled back the curtains from the east windows, a shower of dust fell into the sunlight and floated in the beams.

"Under the sheets there were long rows of worktables, and on the tables were dozens of antique toy theaters. Some were quite large, made of wood and metal, but most were of paper or cardboard lithographed with the brightest, purest colors imaginable. I looked in through their roofs, down behind their shrunken prosceniums. They were perfect in so many ways, to the smallest detail; it was like looking into a forgotten age. There were models of the great houses of the world, and wholly imaginary, fanciful houses with cloth curtains and gargoyles above the stage. All were frozen in mid-act. They held orange-and-yellow jungles that seemed to go back and back, and cold palaces, and marketplaces and ships at sea, balconies and peasant cottages, and more than a few of the darkest dungeons I had ever seen. They were set out with hundreds of little flat figures, so expressively drawn, frozen in moments of passion and folly and danger. There were harlequins and beasts, maidens with the whitest skin, magicians of all types, blue knights, pirates, winged fairies, royalty and common folk. They loved and postured, murdered and bowed as Mr. Baxter and I passed along before them. We saw tableaus from *Red Riding Hood* and *Beauty and The Beast* as well as *Julius Ceasar* and *Othello*. The characters could be moved with wires or sticks; my favorite was the house playing *The Casket of Elaine*: the figures had metal bases, they could be moved with magnets from under the stage, so that no control rod would be visible to an audience.

"There were more than eighty houses, each playing something different, each with a full script laying out in front. I said 'Puck?' again, and Mr. Baxter took me to a model of the Globe Theater. As I watched, he lifted a back painting, added three sets of wings; the house in Athens was transformed into a dark, enchanted wood. At the end of a wooden stick, a little, leafy creature entered, and spoke:

How now, spirit! wither wander you?

When I looked up there was Mr. Baxter with a Puckish grin on his face, holding out a green-printed fairy on the end of another stick. So I took it. I made it enter from the tiny stage right, and I said,

> *Over hill, over dale,*
> *Thorough bush, thorough briar,*
> *Over park, over pale,*
> *Thorough flood, thorough fire,*
> *I do wander every where,*
> *Swifter than the moon's sphere;*
> *And I serve the fairy Queen,*
> *To do her orbs upon the green.*

and I clutched my sides and laughed and laughed.

"And that was all. I came out to the Baxter house, not every day, but once or twice a week. Mr. Baxter had complete sets, actors, scripts for all of the great plays, and many not so great. I would take entire productions — not just the leading roles; I would be them all, men and women, children, animals supernatural beings, the entire cast — there in that big quiet room with only Mr. Baxter listening, and sometimes the family dog. 'There was I, and little John Doit of Staffordshire, and black George Barnes, and Francis Pickbone, and Will Squele, a Cotsol man: you had not four such swinge-bucklers in all the Inns o' Court again; and I may say to you, we knew where the bona-robas were, and had the best of them all at commandment.' "

Now Mrs. Templeton put her head down and laughed so hard that she shook. She rubbed the bridge of her nose with two fingers, turned and laughed sideways at me; her eyes were wet, her lips pulled back so far that I could see where her teeth ended. She was sitting in shadow now; the sun had passed around the building long before, and I remembered how she waited in costume at the edge of the stagelight, in the shelter of the wings. She never looked at a script, yet always in those moments offstage she would stand in silence, moving her lips so that the voices of Jones or Moscow or Templeton seemed to come out of her as they spoke their lines under the light. Then she would see me and smile, and touch her breast, whispering: "I carry them all. In here. Every word," just before she darted out onto the stage.

"Mrs. Templeton," I said, and she faced me now with that same embarrassed smile.

"Ruth," she said. "Please."

"You never played another lead again? I mean a real one, out there?"

"Oh no," she said. "My parts are just paper." She lifted a spoon in the tips of her fingers and maneuvered it lightly like a control rod dancing in the air. "Only paper."

She sat for a moment mopping the stray crumbs up into a little pile with a napkin and the edge of her hand; then she took the tea-tray by its handles, stood with it and turned away from the mirror. "There's one of these rolls left," she said. "Would you like it? One was more than enough sweetness for me..."

FOUND OBJECTS

THAT week we played in a pretty, sweltering university town, where every night the brick theater-house cooked us under lamps that burned away whatever coolness the dark brought along. Costumes would not keep their shape in that heat; make up would not stand, always melting into a pasty mud that made the actors look like something out of Flash Gordon. Alone in her chair behind the scrim, where the mountains billowed if anyone walked by, or sitting out in the evening sun before the show, Mrs. Templeton managed to stay dry. I thought she must have found a pocket of night air, a ventilation shaft pushing arctic breezes from some unknown source.

When I told Mary about my theory she laughed. She had not yet made her entrance in act two, but already she'd soaked through the extra padding sewn into her costume. The layers of pancake and rouge on her face were beginning to run. Out in the muggy stalls, where the air stirred hardly at all, I could hear the audience shifting in their seats. "That's just Ruth," she whispered, lowering her face sideways to mine. "She's always composed. You wait. There's the softest breeze out there now. By eleven thirty it'll be perfectly still."

She was right. In the boarding house after midnight I propped my writing board up under the window and sat there half naked, chin in palm, trying to stir the air with the pages of a play we were calling *The Funeral* that week. It was one of several projects that we had going all at once, and it was turning into a nightmare. Oh, everybody had ideas all right, mainly having to do with their own characters, but I was the only one who seemed interested in giving it a shape, though I dared not speak my mind on the subject; meanwhile Jones was determined that it should have moral impact, that it deliver a real hard-nosed punch, which was difficult because it didn't have any special target to poke at. Everybody in the company could work up some anger about *something*, myself included; but more often than not the anger was directed inward. It was very frustrating, and I confined my input to these solitary sessions in the early morning hours. If she liked what I did, which was maybe a third of the time, Jones had the company circle around the pages, and they became a springboard for that day's work. By mid-morning anything I'd done would be unrecognizable; and so every time I slid a piece of paper under my nose it seemed that I was starting over again.

It was too hot to work that night, but I kept at it out of guilt, thinking of what they endured to perform. A little after three-thirty I gave in and collapsed across the middle of the bed. It didn't matter that the spread was damp, that it smelled of mold. All I cared was that it felt cool against me.

I was wakened by a familiar weight, down at the foot of the bed. In a groggy sort of way I knew that it had been there for a while. I knew who it was. The question was what did I want more, to see her or to go on sleeping?

I opened my eyes. Jones sat there in dungarees and a sky-colored blouse, sleeves rolled up to her elbows, hair tied back carelessly with a length of twine. I couldn't see her face. She was reading through the work that I'd done, holding the pages slightly out, angled against the morning air. The room was already bright. Below the window a car rolled by on its way down to the main street. She heard it and covered the stack of pages at her side, as if she expected a wind to carry them away.

"Are you awake?" she said without looking around.

I said no. Snuffling like a mule, I sat up in bed and wondered what I'd done with my shirt.

Jones finished a page, set it aside, and read on. "We were just going out to search the town dump," she said. "Custom of ours. You're welcome to come along."

At any other time it would have seemed a thrill to be included in some company ritual, but just at the moment I wasn't sure of what I'd heard. The hall door was standing open. A two-headed shape lurked outside, mumbling to itself. " 'Morning," Mary's bright voice said. I could just make out Lon looking blue over her shoulder. When Mary stepped into the light she looked as fresh as if she'd taken a week off. "Penfold? Will you join us?"

"Did she say 'dump'?"

Jones tossed the pages aside. This meant that I had failed. She kicked my shoes up close beside the bed. "Are you coming or not?"

I grabbed a tie, jacket and hat and followed them down through the building, clumsily buttoning myself into a band-collar shirt that belonged to the company and was at least two sizes too large for me. "No, did you really mean the town dump? The junkyard?" I said. Nobody answered; they were talking about witches and whether or not the heat was affecting attendance, and weren't paying me the least bit of attention.

It was a busy morning. Our boarding house was close to the university; students and professional types alike were criss-crossing the town square. The heat aside, this had been my favorite gig so far. Unlike some of the towns we'd been to, the Depression seemed not to have visited here at all. We were playing in the charming little college facility right in the heart of the campus and drawing a mixed crowd of academics and students and townies alike. Thanks to that, we were able to ditch nearly all of the lower-tone melodramas in the repertoire, keeping only *Dracula*, for a straight dose of Ibsen, some gory Greek tragedies, Moliere and the specialty "panoramas," and we didn't have to worry about the reception, or meeting the bills. Jones was in her element.

We crossed to a tiny park where everything was wilting green and brown in the pelting sun. I counted two benches and a fountain without any water in it. Under the momentary leafshade, Mary began to whisper to herself:

> *I've got the blues,*
> *I feel so lonely;*
> *Oh, when you gone*
> *I'm worried all day long.*
> *Baby, won't you please come home?*

Breaking out again on the other side Lon looked both ways, then lumbered across, face downturned, hands in pockets, to the yellow and red diner sitting aloof on the opposite corner. Our own gaudy handbills stared back at us from the windows. It was moderately busy in there, maybe two-thirds full; without exception the patrons sat with heavy-lidded eyes under the ceiling fans, moving only their mouths and hands.

Absolutely another reason that I liked this gig was that we could walk into a diner without being stared at. If there was something of Barnum in our handbills and signage, especially in the flamboyant rustcolored eye at the top with its lightning bolts radiating from the iris, still and all I disliked being made to feel like a freak. I had felt no such prejudice and so I had not imagined it would exist in others. Yet there it was, in the way they looked at us up and down, as if seeking out the source of a bad smell.

For my part, I still felt more like them than I did a member of the company. Their breed ran strong in me. The townies had their well-written lives just like the people that I had left behind in St. Paul. The fine details may have varied somewhat from town to town, the accents certainly were different, the local foods were a marvel of variety, but I found that the hard bones of their life stories were all very similar underneath. The towns themselves were living creatures that needed feeding, and the same functionaries to make them work. Police were the same wherever we went. The rest, the shopkeepers and the bankers and the power plant managers and the line workers and the street car drivers, all wore a finite set of characteristics that changed from place to place like masks, but they all wanted the same thing underneath, the same thing that my parents had wanted, and that was just to get on. This was my problem with them. This was what I wanted to get away from. I wanted very much more than just to get on.

I was still trying to pull myself together. Mary lagged behind to help me with my tie and collar; even such casual contact as that still left me feeling awkward and embarrassed. By the time we reached the booth Jones and Lon were already ensconced in the window seats, muttering to each other dejectedly. Jones had her chin in her hand and a deep frown on her face. As I settled in diagonally from her (I still could not muster the nerve to sit down right at her side, as if such proximity might burn me to a cinder), she buried her face in her hands, then folded her fingers tightly, rested her nose on her knuckles and stared ahead into the distant nowhere.

"So what have we got with this *Funeral*," she said, "we've got a great big nothing. I'm about ready to put this one out of its misery."

"Well it isn't *about* anything," Mary said, and we all looked up with raised eyebrows, because that was exactly it, only none of us had been able to arrive at that point. We'd tied ourselves in knots over it all the previous afternoon, I'd wrestled with it half the night, and just like that she got to the heart of it.

Lon nodded and Jones, who always talked with her hands, began to gesture wildly. "Right, it's not a play, it's, it's, it's" and I said "It's a backdrop for a play" and she snapped her fingers at me and said "You're learning."

It was always a succession of problems like that. You solve one problem and fifteen more crop up, but the solving of one problem is a good place to stop thinking about the others and just eat your breakfast, so that is what we settled down to do.

Jones, Lon and I received our coffee, Mary her tea; our orders were taken; it wasn't until the waitress left that I noticed how close to me she had been standing, the same way that you don't notice warmth until it's gone. The other three were all looking at each other in silent amusement. "Are we really going to a dump?" I said.

Jones made a cocking motion with her head. "You never know," she said. "You don't look, you don't find. We're not Radio City. Sometimes we can turn a prop or two."

"More than that," Mary said. "You'd be amazed at what people throw away."

"I'm always amazed at what you see in some things," Lon said.

Mary puckered her mouth in feigned embarrassment. "Don't look at me that way," she said. "I don't live in a junkyard."

"No, you just furnished it from one," Lon said.

"Oh, stop! So I have a few shelves with the fruit labels still on them. My kitchen table has some very fancy Victorian legs," she said to me. "But I think the top came from a butcher's."

"Mary's place will confound the historians when they come to catalog it," Jones said.

At that moment our breakfast arrived: one order of wheatcakes, one of toasted bread and apricot preserves, and two of eggs and bacon. When she set my plate down in front of me, the waitress didn't seem to like how it landed. Her hand remained on the dish. She turned it this way and that. I looked up and had just a flash of her pale blue eyes in an otherwise plain, pale face before she twisted away.

To judge from the others at the table this was the height of comedy. Lon and Mary were facing the window and the table respectively, making no effort at all to conceal the smirk on their faces. Jones's mouth was in full sadistic twist as she reached for her silverware.

"What?" I said.

She tucked in happily. "You have an admirer, my dear."

I shot an involuntary look at the waitress, who quickly turned away and concentrated on taking an order from a table on the other side of the floor.

"What, her?" I said; and looking at the three of them enjoying their laugh, I felt a wave of embarrassment and annoyance shoot through me. The tired-looking, common girl in her waitress blue was headed back to the kitchen. She lowered her head and tried an up-from-under glance in my direction, but corrected herself quickly when she saw that I was looking. Jones was watching me, very much enjoying my discomfort. I pushed my plate away untouched.

"Since day one," Mary said. "You really haven't noticed?"

"I think you should ask her out," Jones said. "Really I do. I think you could use the uhm, the uhm…" She looked across the table at Lon and made a sound through her nose. The mirth was building up inside her until I was certain that she couldn't hold it in any longer. "I tell you what, I'll give her a free pass. Then after the show we'll invite her back and trust me, you won't have to do anything. Well, nothing much."

"Stop it," I said. The anger had turned to humiliation and I could feel my entire body glowing with heat. I wanted to hide my face, to crawl under the table. "She doesn't know me." I said. "She doesn't know anything about me. She can't possibly…"

Then Jones smiled with half of her mouth and frowned with the other half and looked me dead in the eye. "Exactly," she said.

Mary kicked me gently under the table. "You're an Exotic now. You just don't know it yet."

The dumpkeeper was a friendly-looking middle-aged man in scuffed blue trousers who seemed not to have the exaggerated sense of self-importance that we often encountered in small-town officials. Lon and I watched from the truck as Jones did her cajoling thing with him, while Mary stood at an angle, peering over her shoulder, trying to see around the copse of yew trees that framed the entryway to the yard. Jones handed over the inevitable pair of free tickets; and then we were in.

I half-climbed, half-jumped down onto the grass and noted that Lon hadn't moved from the driver's seat. Eyes closed, he sank down until all I could see of him was the balding top of his head. A hand like a baseball mitt appeared, scrabbling about in the dust above the dashboard. It found the road map, shook it out and draped it blue and green over Lon's invisible face.

I leaned in at the passenger side. "You're not joining this treasure hunt?"

"No reason why I should," Lon said. The map on his head didn't stir. "If she finds anything she'll let me know. I'm just the chauffeur on this trip."

I wondered what that made me. I stood with one foot up on the running board, watching Jones and Mary poking about on the other side of the shimmering heat. "What's she looking for, anyway?"

"Just what she said. Anything we can use. Anything that might give her an idea. Most times it isn't worth the trouble."

"Then why bother?"

Lon lifted a corner of the map and looked at me out of one eye. "It's Jones," he said as if that explained everything. "Maybe she's hoping for a pony."

Now the map began to tremble all over, a paper earthquake as the man underneath it laughed at his own joke. 'Way off beyond the shack, Jones heard us and lifted her eyes. "Speaking of looks," Lon said, "maybe you'd better go."

The sun was high and diffuse behind a distant haze. We could have been near the town or 'way out past the county line; the amplified crunching of gravel under our feet was the only sound for miles and miles.

The only thing Jones had come across so far was a stick. She was leaning on it as I came up. She had the look of a crazy pioneer woman who'd just tilled ten acres of field, wrassled six bears, fought off an Indian attack and walked away from it all with a healthy glow, ready for more. I looked around us and saw a half of a wagon wheel rotting in the sun, a barrel held together with the remains of a single hoop, a broken crate, and an old-fashioned clothes wringer rusted through in at least six places. "Oh yes," I said. "Wonderful stuff. Just what we need."

"You don't talk to the locals," Jones said.

"No need," I said. I was still smarting from being made the object of her amusement, and would not meet her gaze.

She slid one hand into a pocket and spoke with her face turned up the slope to the edge where a man in striped trousers and a tee shirt was wrestling with a trashcan in the trunk of his De Soto. "Nonetheless, it's good form. And you never know what you might pick up."

She swung about and climbed upward at a pace and I hung back until Mary came along and seemed to swoop me up, netlike. She took me by the hand and drew me along beside her.

"That girl at the restaurant," she said. "We were teasing you, but really it's all right." She smiled in a way that was meant to be kind. "You may have noticed that we don't have any rules against picking up strays."

"That's what I am to her?" I said. "A stray?"

"Except for Lonny I guess we all more or less fall into that category. You're far from the *first*." She emphasized first if that was the thing that mattered most to me, as if being uniquely a stray would have made it more difficult. "In fact, you're not even the first this season. We picked up one and lost her this past May, all within three week's time. *She* wanted to be an actress, though. She had kind of the same problem that you do."

She looked at me in a way that asked if I wanted to know, and I looked away from her in a way that said I didn't.

Mary laughed. "I didn't say with whom! It was *Templeton*, in fact. Can you imagine? She just adored him. Of course Ruth saw to that. In the nicest possible way, mind you."

Jones called for her and I could not have been more relieved. Hands in pockets, I poked about through the dirt and rubbish and rubble, wondering just exactly what I was supposed to make of all this, wondering why she'd asked me along, wondering if she knew. Perhaps, I thought, it was just so that she could get a crack at me about that girl.

From time to time I snuck a glance at Jones and Mary. They seemed to be coming up empty handed. Mary had found the highest point and was standing atop it with one hand cupped over her eyes like an explorer; Jones contented herself poking about in the lower areas with her stick. From the edge of the dump there was a motionless tide of refuse sloping down into the brush about fifty yards away. I saw bedsprings and cracked tires lying in the dirt with extravagant weeds growing up through them. There were old newspapers and bits of glass and metal, but nothing that gave me any ideas.

As I was heading up to join them I spotted a soda-cracker tin of the same brand that my mother favored. She had always had one in her pantry, for as long as I could remember. It was several more uphill steps before the coin finally dropped and I realized that it wasn't the object, the battered-up old tin with its missing lid, but the fact that it had made me think of home.

I slowed down to a shuffling pace, shoved my hands in my pockets, and the thing began to work itself out in my mind. By the time I reached them, my gaze had turned inward and I nearly walked into Mary. Jones grabbed me by the arm. "Watch it," she said.

I said, "I've got it. It's not a funeral. The funeral was weeks ago, and now they're cleaning out the house. And everything, every single thing in that house, has memories and feelings attached. Sometimes the same object means different things to different members of the family. And conflicts come up, because they're fighting over their past, they're fighting over their sense of themselves, and their whole sense of self-worth is caught up in the arguments over these, these knick-knacks… and then, when things are already pretty tightly coiled, one of the family finds a trunk in the attic. And it's bound up in chains. And no one remembers it, but everyone has to have it, because they all imagine that they know what's inside. And you all can come up with those imaginings yourselves…"

At first I thought she was angry. Jones threw down her stick, gripped my face in her left hand so hard that my mouth pinched up like a fish's. She shook me and shook me and said "You. you, you, you…" and then pushed me away so violently that I nearly fell over.

"You just earned your keep for the day," she said. And then to Mary: "Come on, I think we're done here."

We pulled up in front of the boarding house just as the Templetons were crossing back from the diner beyond the park. "Don't have to be a swami to know where you folks have been," Templeton said. He made a show of sniffing the air.

Mrs. Templeton peered into the back of the truck. "Did you find anything at all?"

"Some heirlooms," Jones said. "You'll see."

There were just a few minutes left to us before it was time to head up to the college for the last time. For the most part we lived out of our cases, so packing was not a big production number. Still, some things had a habit of spreading out: brushes, shaving kit, the shoe that I sometimes used as a doorstop. I was closing the window of my little room for the last time when the floor creaked behind me. I turned to see that Jones had materialized there. I'd grown so used to this sort of thing already that I wasn't startled. She had her mailbag slung over one shoulder and her duck traveler's bag in her left hand and an uncommonly smug look on her face.

"Normally it's more tangible," she said. "Still, you never know. You don't look, you don't find."

"All right. I'll grant you that this, this dump-diving could maybe have its uses. But as for talking to the Townies, really there's no need. I know all about them."

Her face darkened, and she turned away. "Where do you think the shirt that you're wearing came from?" she said. "Don't be so arrogant."

And then she was gone.

Lon had come lumbering down the hall. He paused in the doorway, as if he had a question that needed answering. I looked out at him and he stood looking in at me. "What is she?" I said.

Lon only shook his head. He didn't give any other answer.

HEIRESS

ONE afternoon, when she and I were cloistered together behind the green glass of the ticket booth, Sylvie told me that her favorite actresses were Jean Harlow and Fay Wray, because she wanted to be the one, and she identified with the other. And it was true that her hair was colored much the same orange blonde as Fay Wray's, and that, in the small, backward country towns where we sometimes played, hairy young men would whistle or call from the invisible crowd as she posed or giggled on the stage. But Sylvie was not the type to scream. I think Jones would have preferred that; it would have been something the other actors could ad-lib around.

"Why Harlow?" I said. "You wouldn't want to end up like her..."

"She's my ideal," Sylvie said, "because she knew how to handle men." And she reached into what remained of our lunch, pulled out a carrot-stick, bit it down into a stump: *crunch, crunch, crunch.*

This was in Clinton, Iowa; I remember because

our accommodations were nicer than usual: we stayed in a converted brick mansion surrounded by elms whose branches met over the street, tentlike, turning the entire avenue into a kind of green cathedral that covered a generous swath of the town. Even at the theater, the walls of the booth were speckled with emerald light. Where the stairs to the balcony passed overhead, the ceiling lowered into a dusty corner; there, the girl whose job it was supposed to be to sell the tickets sat with her legs crossed, reading funny pages that she removed, one by one, from a cardboard box that someone had left there, sometime before. There was just enough room for the three chairs (mine with the frozen wheels that could not be budged), for Sylvie's legs and mine under the cash drawer and the black marble countertop. Out beyond the window Mary had set up her dulcimer in the slantwise shade. Its clear notes came at us through the grating, a wistful accompaniment to our sandwiches and pretzels. She was playing by the display board just outside the theater, where the names of the plays, the pictures of everyone but Lon and myself were tacked onto a folding signboard: Sylvie at her most winsome, Templeton in a beard that did not belong to him, Jones looking out with her head cocked and her professional smile that was also a challenge. A small crowd had gathered around the dulcimer-table; one of them pointed at Mary's picture, so that she laughed and changed over from ballad to jig.

At last a lady in blue came over, lowered her mouth to the grille. She had shiny black hair and a hat with cuttingly sharp lace upon it, and the bright red lips that I was seeing more often now that color had become a movie novelty. Two dollars each seemed like a lot of money to her, but she ended up buying three tickets. When she had gone back again to hear Mary play, Sylvie turned her face up from the yellow ticket roll. Her brows were high under a fringe of golden curls. "I was the start of a riot once," she said, and though she was trying hard, working at it, she did not now look winsome at all. "The whole dance hall was fighting over me, just a mass of men jumping around and hitting each other. There were chairs lifted up. Billy Nash was knocked cold."

"Two for the seven-thirty show, please." This was a gentleman in brown, with a wide-brimmed hat that covered his eyes, as if he was ashamed to be seen buying theater tickets. Sylvie went on talking. It was hard for me to pay attention to what she was saying and make change at the same time.

She tore off two tickets without looking and passed them under the glass. "There wasn't a thing I could do," she said. "I found a safe corner where there was nothing flying around and watched them all and just laughed. Then a man I'd never seen before took me by the arm. He had a hat and a moustache. Come on, he said. He took me outside around behind the hall. There was a crooked tree growing up right next to the side of the building. He propped me up in the crook and started kissing me on the neck. He smelled like dead corn."

The girl in the corner looked up from *Barney Google*. She had blue eyes set well back into her head. She looked just like a setter with its ears turned forward to catch every sound.

"You're proud of that?" I said. Sylvie didn't answer except to wrinkle her nose, and then I felt foolish for having believed her yet again.

There was a rustle of paper from behind us as the girl pulled her chair up close to our backs. She hung her jaw over Sylvie's shoulder and asked about the man, if Sylvie had ever found out who he was, if he had harmed her, how the brawl had finally died.

But it was only one of Sylvie's stories, without consequence or beginning, that owed more to the stillness of the yellow booths than to anything like simple fact. She had been telling them for days now, since that first time, two weeks after I joined the company, when she came in from the afternoon sessions wearing the most flamboyant sulk, flopped down into the chair next to mine and said, "At least if she won't let me do anything she could let me go early!"

Before that, the ticket booths had been good places to work. They were quiet, though open to the street, there was light enough, space enough for me to spread out my papers. All that I had to do was look up whenever the local girl sold a ticket, and change my notation from H̶H̶ to VI. Now, nearly every afternoon, Sylvie sat in her layers of black and white, in her colorful vests unbuttoned to the waist and her soft shoes almost touching mine. She poured out tales about herself, the unblossomed Harlow waiting to be discovered, until my imagination was no longer my own, until I had no choice left but to set the plays aside.

She was varyingly from Platte, Nebraska or Cheyenne, Wyoming, but Jones assured me that her home was somewhere in New York state. She liked to tell about her escape from the musty plains in a freight car on the longest, black-wheeled train she had ever seen; how she waited in the dark, in the long grass, to wake the next morning beyond Wichita with straw in her hair, smoke and sun in a narrow line along the wooden floor of the boxcar. She told about swimming naked in a wood-shadowed quarry, joined by some local boys who told her that the pool was bottomless, that the bones of murdered children had drifted down and settled into the rocks and silt. She told how they touched her, under the surface of glowing, moon-patched water, how they were caught toweling each other dry when the game warden turned his headlights down into the gully. And I sat in the booth, in silence, and listened to it all, and half believed.

Now Sylvie grew tired of the ticket-girl's questions. She hadn't wanted them in the first place, not from her, not when the answers turned the stories too uncomfortably on their backs. "Five tickets," Sylvie said into the cash box, and the girl must have felt herself vanish, traceless as decomposed ash, into the air. She dug her heels into a crack in the floor, rolled back to the boxes and the blue and red waterstained pages they contained. "Five tickets," Sylvie said again, "in the last twenty minutes. There's hardly any point. Jonesy should have me out there, then you wouldn't even be able to keep track. That music puts me to sleep."

"What would you do?" I said. The only things in my notebook now were scribbles, stick-figures, a few Porky Pigs drawn badly into the margins.

Sylvie tilted her head at me. "Don't you know?" She grinned and stood in the cramped booth, pushed her chair back hard until it bumped into the knees of the ticket girl, who looked up again and glared. Sylvie ignored her. "Watch," she said. "See? This."

Sometimes now I wonder how she saw herself, trying without luck to set her skirts awhirl, raising her hands awkwardly, such an odd youthful figure in her ancient clothes, dancing and failing to dance in that faraway booth. Dust rose into the green light. The ticket girl tried not to watch, and I tried to keep from looking away. From beyond the window the dulcimer music came so sad and fine; Sylvie kicked up her heels out of step, out of time, whispering her own interior tune. She offered me her hands, fingers splayed, elbows straight, and I would have had to join her, but for a man who came to the glass. He bought four tickets, two adults and two children, peered through his spectacles at Sylvie and turned away with his shoulders hunched as if he was pushing down a sudden wave of lust. Sylvie pretended not to notice.

"You'd draw them, all right," I said, when with a show of breathlessness Sylvie pulled the chair back up under herself. "But somehow I don't think they'd be the kind of crowd Jones is looking for."

She had seemed pleased with the dance, the stamp and flourish that had ended it, but now Sylvie colored and turned her chair away. Windowlight fell in triangle shapes across her cheek. The ticket girl rolled her eyes at me. After a time the music stopped outside; we sat in the booth in perfect silence, until a new face came to the grate, then another and another. Beyond where they waited, afternoon shadows moved soft against old brick. At the end of the line Mary appeared, the dulcimer in its case with the strap over her shoulder, the table pressing its folded legs against her skirt. She waved, and pointed at her watch.

"Hey," she said when she had reached the window. "You all look so grim."

The glass twisted her face into green waves. "I was trying to be funny," I said. Sylvie still would not meet my eyes. "I said the wrong thing."

"It couldn't have been that bad," Mary said. "Not from you." She rapped on the window under Sylvie's nose. "Time to go in," she said. "And you,"   to the girl with the Sunday funnies spread in a bright pool across her lap — "Does your boss drive a black DeSoto? He just turned into the alley..."

The girl came to her feet all in a rush, sending a flurry of heroes and clowns into the air. They twisted, danced, and finally fell; Sylvie batted them away. "You two have fun together now," she said, passing under the storm.

The ticket girl only frowned. "Go break a leg," she said.

Mary had already gone. The girl snapped up her scattered sheets from the floor, the desk, the chair, stuffed them away without care, then took her seat at the window, rearranging the cash drawer so that the faces looked down. "Better not turn your back on her," she said. "She'll eat you alive. Eat you up and spit out the seeds."

Only the week before, Lon had taught me the proper way of drawing the moon across the sky. Now in the low haze of blue-and-purple light that filtered back through the scrim, I worked the control lines, marking my time by the voices on the other side, by the stilted music that came from the shadows nearby. It was Mary, sitting in the backwash at the battered upright piano that the theater had supplied us, a thing so badly abused that some of its notes struck uncontrollably two at a time, others sounded off-key, and still others refused to strike at all; even so, Mary still managed to do the music a kind of witched, drunken justice. Soon there would be trolls in the wings, rushing to button the last of their skins. Nothing more to worry about, I thought, until then.

Halfway through the scene she lifted her eyes from the keyboard and gave me a warning look. At first I thought that the moon-globe must have stopped, that I had crossed the lines or allowed it to come out of the light. "*No,*" Mary whispered. "*Sylvie.*" On the downbeat she raised and lowered her chin, pointing that way out across the stage.

I could see what she meant. In the opposite dark, Sylvie floated on an invisible stool, one leg bent, knuckle in mouth, the silver gown hiked up along her calves, waiting for her entrance line. Her face was turned towards the fusebox, her eyes unfocused, as if in her nervousness she could look straight through the wall, into the night beyond.

Mary swiveled in place, changed over to the dulcimer set high against the blue glow at her side. The music snapped back into key, soft enchantment as she struck at the wires. *"Whistlers,"* she said, not looking up. *"She's going to do it again..."*

And as I watched, Sylvie jumped down, took three steps out under the light, and said nothing.

We were all used to the occasional drunks, but this time it was just as if she had worked it out ahead of the show, planted some idiot shill in the middle of the house. Because this time she actually paused, where no pause was called for or desired. She canted forward at the waist, widening her eyes, forming her mouth into a little O. The silver gown rode and clung in the right places. With her right hand she touched her lips; then the whistle floated down high and strident from beyond the fifth row, right on cue; the whistler in this case not even having to be drunk, not having to be full of himself, because it had been invited, it was part of the show now, although someone must have wondered how such a moment found its way into the middle of *Peer Gynt*. It brought some laughter, some whispers, a lot of shifting and craning about in the house. Sylvie grinned. She gave a small movement of her shoulders, a melting, implicit thankyou, before she went the rest of the way and at last said her words.

Mary had closed her eyes. Her hands went on striking automatically at the strings of the dulcimer; she got lost, winged it, twisted some notes around, found her way back. Even then she would not look up. Neither of us spoke.

It was a corker of a scene, once Moscow and Mrs. Templeton got their feet back under them. The show seemed to burn extra bright from that point on, incandescent bright, and everyone in the house could feel it. I should have taken that as a warning. But when Sylvie came back out into the wings I was busy minding the ropes, and so all that I saw was Moscow's hand coming off after her, chasing her, catching her by the arm.

As the glass globe landed cool in my fingers Moscow thrust his face into the dark. He slammed her back hard against the naked brick. *"Forget them,"* Mary said. *"Push."* She came up all in a rush from behind the piano, so that the grey cloth hanging behind her stirred and began to wave. *"Stop it, stop it!"* Templeton said. We counted three, then turned the scenery around one third, melting the forest away, raising mountains in its place. *"Bitch,"* Moscow said. Lon had changed the backdrop and was tying it into place. *"Stop it,"* Templeton said. By the time I turned around it was almost done, it looked as if they were dancing, except that Templeton in the whiskers and coat was still trying to come between them. Then Sylvie got her right hand free. She hit Moscow hard across the face, her fingers closed into a fist, her eyes all pinched and squinty as if she were fighting back tears. Mary flopped back into her chair, didn't waste time trying to get the mallets into her hands; she punched out a chord on the piano instead. Moscow stepped back. The blow had smeared his make-up. He touched his cheek, glowered at Mary, turned away. The following scene had already begun. He went onto the stage without missing a beat, as if nothing had happened.

Sylvie shrank against the wall, ignoring Templeton when he bent to whisper something in her ear. She looked across the burning perimeter of light into the opposite wings, where Jones stood waiting in her usual trance, one arm curled around the awful doll that represented Moscow's bastard son. By then Jones had switched over from company leader to actress; the only words that concerned her were the words of the woman in green. Had she seen it? Had she heard? Jones's eyes were the only part of her that moved. They tracked Sylvie until she passed out of sight, then flicked back to the motion of the play. From her stage face, there was no way to tell.

Midway through the first intermission I found Sylvie sitting half in and half out of the building, her back propped against the stage door, her left leg stretched bare in the nightdark of the alley. She might have been waiting outside of all time, still in Ingrid's silver gown when she should have changed into a troll along with the rest. "Hey Fay," I said. "Are you all right?"

She turned her head under the yellow light from the bulb above. It rode across her face until it was only a streak along the edge of her brow. "Jones sent you? Why not do it herself?" She sucked in her cheeks, knit her brows in an imitation of Jones that wouldn't quite come off; her face would not allow it. " 'You can stay here,' " she said. " 'You have one line in the next act and I can just as well give that to someone else.' She's done it often enough before."

Then I saw that she had something in her hands. It made a flickering sound when she opened it across her lap, a small brown book with the spine ripped completely away and a metal latch in front that held the pages together. One by one they flickered out under her thumb, into the alley light: ghostlike photographs of fierce Victorian women, of men in beaver hats, stiff youths with faces like Poe, girls with vacant eyes dressed all in black, children trussed up in lace and bows. "Is that your family?" I said. "No," Sylvie said. "I just like them. Jones got it for me. It was the first month I knew her."

"Why do you try to disappoint her?" I said at last.

Lon turned out the lights from the main box beside the stage. I felt Sylvie move in the dark beside me, her curls glowing yellow, the gown rustling thick and loud as she came to her feet. She hissed at me in the dark. Her voice was not like Harlow's or Wray's or anyone else's that I'd ever heard. "I know you want her," she said. "Everyone knows. So why don't you just fuck off." And she brushed past me, a blur of silver and blue, all in a rush as if she had just remembered the costume change. I heard her snaps popping as she passed into the green room. I heard her kick off her shoes.

"Now isn't the time," Jones said to her reflected face. She pulled off an eyelash, then looked at me out of the mirror. "Or the place. We have Mister Ibsen to concern ourselves with."

I had caught her mid-way in the transformation from the princess of trolls to the seductress Anitra. The talons were already gone from the ends of her fingers, as were the squaretoothed dentures that made it almost impossible for her to speak; when her face came into the glass it was partly one thing and partly another, a face without age. "Maybe if we knew why," I said.

She lined up the eyelashes on her make-up tray, between a spidery pair of false eyebrows and six rubber warts. "Oh, I know why she does it," Jones said. "I've tried to give her some business to cover it. But she panics and forgets."

"So what can we do?"

"Live with it." She chose a brown pencil and lifted it to her face. "Sylvie's a natural actress, not a skilled one. If she were more disciplined she wouldn't be any use to me."

"But what about   "

Jones turned in her chair so that I had a double view of her profile. "Leave it alone. If you want to do something, keep an eye on the stage door after curtain. I have a feeling about this." She untied her hair so that it fell dark and loose around her shoulders. "There," she said. "Presto change-o."

In the alley I felt as if I was the one being punished. I sat alone on the middle step, scuffling my feet around in the gravel, making toy highways with my shoes. The rest of the performance had come off without a hitch, but the thought remained that Sylvie had used her anger at me as an excuse to stop the show. *Why does she think Jones keeps her in supporting roles,* I said to myself. At the mouth of the alley, distant couples crossed under the lampposts to the parking lot beyond. The whistlers never came.

When I stepped back inside, Sylvie was nowhere to be found. I had a little play that I wanted her to hear, about three drunks in plaid suits who'd come down the alley calling for her, "that Harlow one," and how it had taken Lon with a lead pipe and me with a two-by-four to scare them away. I wanted to say that if the lights hadn't blinded her, if she'd known what she was grinning at, maybe she would have thought twice. I wanted to tell her that she'd damn near started another riot. I thought it would make her laugh. At least, that was what I told myself. But she wasn't in her dressing room, she wasn't in the green room, she wasn't helping out on the stage. I didn't find her until I went out front to check the booth, and then I regretted trying.

The lobby doors were locked tight, the shades all drawn, the lights turned out for the night. When I stepped onto the invisible tile a vast, quiet sound rose up in the gloom, like a sigh in the dark of a hidden cavern. I stood there for some time, not because I liked the stillness or the lines of moonlight that came through slitted shades, though I liked both. I suppose that I had been hearing it for several seconds before I knew, before the foot-echo died completely, leaving the other sound unmasked at last.

In the booth the shades were down halfway. There was a faint stirring behind the darkened glass, a motion like black smoke congealing into mud, rising and falling. Cloth rustled against cloth on the other side of the grate. Breath in the empty air.

"Come on," Sylvie whispered. Her voice came through the grate and carried along the length of the tiled walls. "Shut up," Moscow said. I heard something rip. "Oh," Sylvie said. "Oh."

I came closer to the glass. They were a mess of rumpled clothing, bare hands floating disembodied in the air behind the counter. Moscow pulled at her bodice and then at her hair. Her throat was bent back against what remained of the light. "Uh," she said, and Moscow clamped his hand down hard over her mouth, so hard that when it came away I could still see the yellow imprint of his fingers on her cheek...

*

I met Mary on my way out through the back. She looked tired and rumpled in a light summer raincoat, the basket that she used for a purse looped over one shoulder, a fresh bottle of wine poking out of the corner. Her face was clean and bare. She said, "Did you find her?"

I shook my head. "No," I said. "Not her."

CASTING SHADOWS

I disliked Moscow because it seemed to me that he was without despair, that he lacked any understanding of it, and so was inhuman. Under pink or blue light his face would change, his body shifting and melding, building, so that one moment he could be formidable and black, and in the next become as fragile as dead leaves. On the boards he was cold as a man out of dreams commanding the forces of nature, fading again each time he ducked behind the curtain into a small man with large insincere brown eyes. I see him now in the shadows just offstage, yellow sweat beading above his brows, his black hair plastered down, ragged, his nose turned away from the light. He is re-drawing a line under his eyes; he might be picking a lock or juggling explosives for the concentration he shows as he raises the pencil to his face.

But there were parts that he could not play, a touch, a feeling that escaped him and had eluded him for so long that he knew better now than to chase it. His men were hollow — Jones used to say that in moments of great sadness or great humor you could slice open his chest and find nothing inside; only hollow metal, without mess, scraped clean.

And I suppose that she would know, because she was there through it all, she knew more of it than Lon must have, though Lon was the one who told me, early one afternoon. We were playing chess alone in the lightbooth far at the back of the theater. Waiting for him to move, I was looking down through the glass at the others as they worked on an adaptation of *Whispers*. Moscow had taken the Vitae character (against my wishes — I thought that the part should go to Templeton) and as I watched, unseen, he composed the professor into something entirely different from what I had imagined: an actual magician, a powerful lady's man, compelling in his cloak and his dark brow, passionless and so invulnerable, bringing Sylvie (in a new part that Jones had insisted on, to take the place of the boy) and all of the others, mawkish countryfolk, under his power. Watching, I must have said something; I was unhappy and so I expect it was something bad. That was when Lon told me the tale. He did not tell it to pacify me, or to bring me around to their way of thinking; it wasn't that kind of story. I don't know why he told it. It wasn't any of my business.

"This was in Chicago," he said, moving his piece, removing one of mine from the board. "Moscow had just joined us a few weeks before. Booted from another company because he'd got carried away during a swordfight and wounded someone. He'd broken the knob off the tip, see? Did it on purpose. Wanted to give someone a good scare. Wanted to make The Nose work for his applause."

"The nose?" I said.

"Cyrano. Moscow didn't have the lead. S'pose that was the problem. But listen to this..."

In five years Lon had not changed. Then, as when I knew him, he would stay late after every performance, alone in the quieting theater, packing things neatly away. Half in supernatural darkness, he would roll the canvases, coil the cables, push a mop over the dusty stage and then make one last walk through the auditorium. Listening to the echo, he said, which was different in every hall, hollow or full throated or faint like a sound from the far end of a canyon, his own footsteps bounding from the walls and windows all around.

So that at first I thought this was going to be a ghost story, of some prima donna haunting the halls, taking the boards once again after everyone had gone, perhaps holding her own head under her arm as she delivered a speech from Shakespeare. Wondering what it all had to do with Moscow, with anything, I listened as Lon described the sigh. He had already pulled on his jacket, had already picked the key from his ring when the sound came from somewhere off behind, so soft that it would not have been heard during the day, not even a sigh really, but perhaps a whispered curse. Turning back, he saw a faint sliver of light leaking from one of the rooms behind the stage. There, alone at his favorite mirror, the last of a dark, angled row, Moscow sat hunched over an open tray, putting his face on in the glare of white bulbs lining the glass.

Lon said, "Are you still here?"

At first Moscow didn't answer, did not even pause as he brushed a thick, cloudy syrup onto his chin; he only raised his black-lined eyes for a moment before returning them to the mirror. His face was darker, brown; his eyebrows had been shaved off. He was wearing quilted padding across his chest, over his shoulders. Lon thought that he was scowling. But he only said, "Trying this on for the new piece."

"You're a dedicated man," Lon said. "Lock the door behind you when you go." Moscow said that he would, and Lon turned away, buttoned his jacket up close around his neck. He had felt the evening air gusting into the theater when the others had gone; Chicago would see some frost before morning, he guessed. There was already a thin layer of crystal forming in the corners of the windowglass.

Lon went out into it, but did not go back to the hotel. He did not know Moscow then; he said that if he had it would not have made any difference. He would still have been there, shivering in the shadowed spaces on the far side of the stair, when Moscow came out.

Lon said that it was the first time he had ever seen Moscow perform. The man who left the building was several sizes larger than Moscow, bearded, and walked with a commanding, businesslike gait that carried him rapidly to the end of the block. Lon came out and stood under the light, watching the man go. He was wearing a long coat that belonged to the company; the wind caught at its hem, lifted it fluttering behind him as he went.

Lon said that the only reason he followed as far as he did was because it was on his way. The bearded man, Moscow in whatever guise, wearing whatever name he had chosen for himself that night, walked the three blocks across town to the larger, cleaner, brightly lit theater where Cyrano was still playing. He stood under the yellow lights there for several minutes, looking at the marquee or pretending to, alone in the street, his breath pushing as if driven from an engine through his nostrils, clouding up above his head. If he was looking for his own name he would have had no luck, Lon said. They had already pasted another card over it, another name as false as Moscow's neatly lettered in blue ink.

Then Lon went on the rest of the way to the hotel, three more blocks down into a darker, sooty neighborhood where the rates were not so high. I can imagine him there climbing three or five floors to a room that looked out the back of the stone building into a disused alley. He told me that what Moscow had done was no longer any concern to him, but I can't believe that he didn't pause by the window in his undershirt and slacks, and look out, and wonder.

Lon was always the last to go, always the first to arrive. The next morning, through a frozen blue sunlight that had to fight like blazes to get into his room, Lon rose an hour early, ate a quick breakfast and went straight to the theater. Even so, he only beat Jones by about five minutes.

She came into the back of the building at something close to a run, calling his name, passing around behind the scrim to find him at last as he flicked on the last of the auditorium lights. He had only just turned to her when she took his arm and led, dragged, him off of the stage and out through the back again. Her hair was uncombed, her clothes rumpled as if she had never taken them off; a large half-empty duffel bag was slung over her shoulder.

"Come on," she said; *"Hurry!"* and on their way out they passed Moscow coming in.

"And this is the important part," Lon said to me. "More important than anything, even than what he did. It wasn't the way he looked, the beard ripped off, the false eyebrows half gone, the scratches on his face, one sleeve of the coat ripped at the seam and coming off; it was the look he wore. I'd watched him come off the stage after a performance, and whenever he'd done well he always had on the same expression that you could see even in the dark behind the curtain. Stiff faced, like a celluloid mask with sweat on it and his eyes showing through from underneath, shining. Not like triumph, nothing that big. Just calm, and absolute satisfaction at getting the job done so well. This was the same look, just quiet, not saying a word, as he came up the stairs."

But Jones did not allow him any time to think. They went down to the street and when Lon had climbed into the waiting truck Jones pushed him across and slid in behind the wheel herself.

"What's happened," Lon said, holding his hands at his stomach as they came screaming over the curb, the wooden back of the truck *thunking thunking* as it spun out behind them. "What is it?"

Jones only pounded on the wheel. "Oh, come on, *come on.*" Then she said, breathing again, "It's his wife."

Lon looked out onto the road, remembering Jones and Moscow alone together behind the scrim. He said, "I didn't know he had a wife."

"She stayed on with *Cyrano*," Jones said. "I told him, Don't be a hypocrite. But he'd made up his mind, this was going to be his greatest role."

She didn't say anything more, driving on with the needle heading on up there past forty, even in the city, until at last they stopped at an old brick house that had been chopped up into apartments. There was a wooden vestibule and steps leading on up to the second floor; the door that they found there was open, and just inside, lying where it had been dropped in the middle of the floor with its cord all stretched out behind like intestines, was the lower half of a bisque lamp that had once held the figure of a long, tall lady in an orange dress. Its jagged edges where it had been smashed were flecked with blood.

The rooms probably did not smell of cake make-up and spirit gum, but I imagined them to be reeking of it, because Moscow must himself have reeked of the stuff when he had been there, at whatever hour, wielding the lamp. From beyond one blue-papered archway they could hear the woman's ragged sobbing, and when they went through they found her half-sitting in the corner, leaning on the edge of a rumpled, unmade bed. There were two cuts, and many more bruises on her face and arms; as she cried a thin ropy line of crimson spit dangled between her lips.

When Lon told me this, I could not help but look back through the glass at Moscow on the stage below. He was sitting off stage left, drinking a cup of coffee as Jones gave Mrs. Templeton some notes. He had not changed in any way, a small intense man; he did not know what was being said, thought, about him. He would not have cared.

"Your move," Lon said. As I touched the playing piece I could see Lon hefting the wounded woman up onto the bed, covering her over with a yellow blanket he found there, while Jones unpacked the antiseptic and the gauze, the cotton and the rolled wad of bills from out of her duffel bag.

Under their hands the woman stopped moaning, though her eyes were too swollen for her to see clearly who was tending her. "I told him," she kept saying, not wincing as the longest cut there at her hairline was washed clean and then bandaged. "I kept telling him that I knew him. I knew it was him all along. I said why else would I bring you back here." Then she shuddered, and wiped at the bottom of her eyes with her fingers. "That only made it worse   I suppose it was the wrong thing to say."

Around noon, when the woman seemed to have calmed some, Jones motioned Lon to go down and start the truck. She packed up the gauze and antiseptic, but left the money rolled where she had set it, there on the table next to a yellow vase with cloth flowers that had somehow gone unspilled. Back at the theater, Moscow and the Templetons and some others that I never knew were waiting in full make-up for the day's matinee, a modern dress version of *Measure for Measure*. It was their last night in town; it would have been their last night even if the schedule had said otherwise. They played one performance that afternoon, two more in the evening, and together they loaded the trucks, tied them down. Jones and the Templetons went on their way. Lon stayed late once again, with Moscow and the others who couldn't fit in the first truck, to give the keys of the theater back to the owners.

That was the first time Lon had a flat tire. His truck was three hours behind the other in arriving at the next town; the troupers that I never knew were subdued, haggard, as they climbed out and each went to check into their rooms. Lon had a small bruise on his forehead, he said he bumped himself. Moscow had to be carried in. Someone had thrown a coat over his face.

I didn't know any of this when I joined the company; even so, I had seen the passion in which he worked at changing himself: bending his body in strange harnesses, hunkering over a cracked glass, attacking putty with his thin fingers, molding it over his face, painting himself again and again until he found just the right colors. Then he would emerge wearing clothes choked with dust, and walk silently in a tight circle while Jones inspected him, until, in a different voice every time that still carried the same inflection, the same contempt, he would ask: Well?

THE SCAR PARADE

JONES as a blonde was more unnerving than anything I could have imagined, as if someone had pasted her supernatural eyes over a magazine glamor photo. She came to the foot of the stage, where the House of Marvels gathered itself in a claustrophobic semicircle. Posing so the footlights reflected off her tiara, she said to Moscow's back:

"... *we define ourselves by the things we save. What does that say about you?*"

In the center of that elegant clutter, an indoor junkyard of wheels, jars, phony mummy cases, Moscow turned his face into the blue light, and we all saw the scar for the first time.

It was nothing more than an inch-long dab of plastic above his left cheekbone, a moment's work, a scratch. But it was something he had never worn before, not for the Professor; it stood out like a lurid Karloffian thing, transforming the character in one easy stroke from a dusty shut-in to a Man of Mystery.

"Fool," Templeton said, *sotto voce* in the wings beside me. His indignant neck and shoulders were stretched out so far that I thought his shoes must be nailed to the floor. " 'Motivating' again. No doubt he's made up some 'history' to go with it. Con-*founded* Stanislavsky, 'System' mumbo-jumbo. Idiot."

When I looked at him in the afterglow his face was almost scarlet. At first I thought it was the colored gel that Lon had used in the overheads. Then I remembered the things that he sometimes said when the company gathered for meals in the little diners, or around the rug in midnight rooms. "Connie," he would say, giving a wink to anyone who would meet his eye, wearing something very close to a leer. "Connie. How's your 'tempo-rhythm' today, Connie? How's your 'psycho-technique?' " And I remembered the way Moscow frowned and gripped his silverware in reply.

"Why Connie?" I had asked Lon the first time I heard Templeton say it. It was an awful, rainy day, and he was walking behind the rest; I had fallen back and was counting on the water to cover our words. "His way of ragging on Moscow," Lon said, hands in pockets, not lifting his eyes from the damp sidewalk. His feet had started to squeak. "Thinks he took his name from the Moscow Art Theater. But Moscow just likes the way that it sounds."

I still hadn't understood. Now, for the first time, I knew what it was all about. Templeton stood rooted at the corner of the scene, jabbing at his cheek with a finger. "Trying to get the character's *soul* onto his face," he said, making the word sound like something loathsome. "Fool. Why doesn't he just *act?*"

Onstage, Jones's skin was pale blue. She halted in mid-sentence, and for a moment her face was vacant, as if she could not make up her mind whether to stay in character or to step out. Then her mouth twisted into a smile. "Um," she said to Moscow. "That's... That... That will have to go."

Which might have been the end of it, if Templeton had only waited long enough to see. Moscow frowned, ripped the thing off of his cheek, leaving a white line of unpainted skin gleaming at the edge of his face. "Fine," Jones said. She licked her fingers and worked at the spot until the make-up blended. But by then Templeton had vanished into the back, stirring up dust and a cloud of noise in his hurry to get off the stage. Lon watched him go. He looked up at me from behind the light board, gave me a nod that said *Here we go.*

At first I thought that he meant Jones and Moscow. They started again from the top of the scene, Jones coming down into the gloom. The way she held her body made it seem as if I was looking at her through a curtain of heat. "I told you no more flowers," she said, in a whisper that rose and penetrated throughout the building. Moscow stood with his fingers curled where the scar had been. He had changed shape somehow; his weight seemed to have shifted itself along the frame of his bones. Slowly, so that an audience might not have noticed, Lon let the overheads bleed one into another. In that accretion of light that formed around him (at first I thought it was an illusion), I saw something crawl across Moscow's face, something that did not belong to him; anguish. The only sound in the theater was the rasp of his shoe leather against the stage floor. As I watched, the Professor took on flesh before my eyes.

It was not the Svengali Moscow had been rehearsing for the last three weeks. It was the thing I had set down on paper, a lovesick showman on the downward curve of of his career, betrayed by his own fantasy, his own heart, still clinging to the remains, hoping, hoping...

The ghost of a person who had never existed had just materialized before my eyes. "Look," I said. "Look." Moscow touched Jones's freezing body with a tenderness, a frailty that I could not fathom or accept, that couldn't have been contained anywhere inside of him. "Not him," I said. My mouth had gone dry. Then Mary's fingers touched mine. "He can still feel it there," she said softly. "That's all that matters. A wet spot on the edge of his face. Sometimes the strangest things help him to find it..."

Now came the cutting, pivotal line from Jones: and just as if he had been punctured the Professor was propelled away from her, crying "You just... You just..." (it had been the most difficult line to write, oddly enough), declining visibly so that his clothes seemed to grow larger on him, until his hands, groping to hang on to something, anything, fell quite by chance into the mouth of the Sphinx...

This of course was one of the major points of deviation from my original story. The Sphinx, operated by Sylvie, immediately bit down on the Professor's fingers. Roaring in pain, The Professor spun, doubled over, his hands drawn under his chest. Then the physical pain seemed to stop. He looked up and saw that Jones had transformed from the woman of his imagination back into the plain, tiredlooking waitress he had hired to show his exhibits. "Jack?" she said.

Lon crept back to the board to bring down the dark. There was a silence that lasted eight or ten seconds. At last, out of unbroken blackness, Jones said, "Great. Do that every night and we have a show."

Lon switched on the worklights. He and I went out as quickly as if it were an actual performance and began to break the set into its component pieces. "Wear it, if it helps," Jones said over her shoulder. She gathered up the sequined folds of her gown, lifted it free of her legs as she came down out of the scene and turned into the cool of the wings. "Just see that it's gone by the time you come on. The professor doesn't strike me as the kind of man who gets into knife fights."

Moscow said nothing. He waited with his shoulders set, the sweatstained beaver hat clenched under his arm, until Lon set down the chairs for the next scene. Without looking at him, Moscow took three clipped steps, swirled around in his coat, and sat. That was when Lon said to me, "Listen. Here he comes."

From out of the back I heard a sound like a leper clumping around behind the flats. It grew steadily more pronounced, *thud, drag, thud,* until even Moscow had to notice. He raised his gaze from the boards…

… and Templeton came onto the stage, looking as if he'd been hit by a truck and dragged a few hundred yards. His face had been hastily smeared with gray paint, his silver hair stuck out in threatening points; the high-collared Amish suit that was his usual costume had been twisted all out of shape by a large hump set between his shoulders. He had a crutch jammed under his right arm, a prop cast wrapped close around his left. On his left cheek, a livid, blood-red gash ran in a jagged line from just below the eye to the corner of his mouth.

He shook his crutch, pointed with it like the Ghost of Christmas Yet to Come. "Connie!" he said. "There you are! I've been looking all over for you! How do you like my 'Magic If,' Connie? I think it lends considerable weight to my character's character, don't you?"

Moscow sat with his legs tightly pressed together, his fingers folded in his lap. Without shifting his gaze, he lifted his chin so that Templeton could have seen his clean cheek, if he had been looking.

But the lawyer in Templeton had set his mind on presenting its case. He jittered and shook. One by one he offered his injuries up under Moscow's nose for inspection. "*My* character's had a rough life," he said. "I want to demonstrate that to the audience. Now, *this* helped me find his subtext. It was self-inflicted. He leapt into traffic in a fit of Romantic Angst; I'll bet you didn't think he was capable of something like that. *This* helped me find the through-line. I'm afraid he was born with it; it symbolizes the burden we all have to bear, just by living life. But this" …Templeton brushed the scar so carelessly that red paint came off on his fingers… "*this* will help me to send out *rays*. It came out of a long-ago swordfight. You didn't know that my character was a swordfighter, did you? Well, he was pretty bad at it…"

"Your character has only one line," Moscow said.

Templeton smiled. "Just my point. I want to make him real. I want to lend irony to the line."

"Ho," Moscow said. "A hit. A very palpable hit. But I heal well."

For the first time, Templeton bent to look at his cheek. A terribly pinched, scowling look came over him, as if he were auditioning for a gangster movie. He stared down at Moscow under the heat of the lamps, the crutch creaking under his arm, and Moscow sat motionless as a man in a painting staring back. At last Templeton said "Honestly," and turned away. He took up his position halfway down the stage, just off-center. In his stage voice, and in his stagey manner so that he might almost have been running over his dialogue from the scene, he declaimed: "Took it off, then. Good. Good. Looked damned silly."

"And how do you look?" Moscow said.

"I think he looks terrific," Jones said. She came rustling on in a beige waitress uniform that swirled just above her knees. Her heels clacked over the boards. As she neared Templeton she laughed out loud, something that I had never heard her do before, that must have come as much from the character, from the wig, as from Jones herself. Templeton winced. Moscow's face went slack, and so, I suppose, did mine. "Like an eroded old statue with stigmata," she said. "A good Allegorical image. But not what we need for this play." Then with a harsh, red-painted smile unlike her own, her voice so blurred that the words became vaguely obscene, she added: "Here. Let's get those things off of you."

Templeton pulled the stuffing from under his coat, while Jones stood by in silence, holding his crutch. When he had cleared it all out — the bunched-up workshirt, the socks, the lumpy, understuffed pillow — and could stand up again, he gave a smile of apology all around and pulled a handkerchief out of his sleeve to wipe at the smear on the side of his face.

"No, leave that," Jones said. "I like it. The Wounded Amish. If it improves your performance as much as Moscow's did for him, than it ought to be worth something, hey?"

Templeton glowered at her, but Jones never saw it. "Just this," she said, unsnapping the cast from around his arm. Little flecks of plaster dropped out of it to the stage floor, a delicate shower of white dust. She fastened it again so that it wouldn't fall apart in her hands, then gathered up the crutch and the pillow, the shirt and socks all into her arms and offered them to me. "Take these and lose them somewhere, please," she said. "Tell Lon lights out."

But Lon heard it for himself; the stage vanished before I could even make it into the wings. It was stuffy back there, and wet. It felt as if the air was full of cobwebs strung from canvas to brick, rope to flat, holding everything together. Sylvie gave a small, pointed laugh out of the dark and was quieted by a word from the stage. As my eyes began to adjust themselves, Mary's face came swimming out of the gloom. She was wearing a simple gingham dress; her auburn hair rested in a wavy length against her neck. "Excuse me," I whispered. "Got my hands full." She gave me the sweetest smile and held herself out of my way. As I squeezed by, the lights came up onstage and I saw that her left eye had been blackened.

We were so close that I could feel her breath on my face. She was still smiling. "Mary," I said. There was no swelling, though she held her eyelid low enough to suggest it. She touched the bruise, then showed me her fingers. "You see?" she said. "It's an old wound. Don't say anything..."

The crutch slipped out of my fingers. It was Mrs. Templeton who caught it before it could hit the floor; when she straightened again I saw a mark on her face, though it was hardly noticeable, a chaste thing almost, just a tracery of blue watercolor above her jaw. Sylvie was laughing again. There were dark welts on her cheeks, as if she had been struck with a cane. She was painting Lon's forehead in the glow of the electrical console, adding bloodcolored marks to an incision that ran from temple to temple, like the stitches in a patchwork quilt. She gave me one of her triumphant looks, then came around and showed me her wrists...

Now Jones and Moscow sent their voices drifting back to us from the stage. Mary took her cue; she patted me twice on the arm, set her face into a businesslike mask. Templeton lifted his eyes to meet her as she stepped out. He said his one line, saw her, and could not suppress a chuckle.

It was a low, repentant sound that warmed me to his nameless character in an unexpected way, simple utility made human at last. Jones did not even stop the scene. For the smallest moment she allowed Constance to drop away, just long enough for us to catch a whisper of satisfaction as it passed across her face. Then Constance was back, resurrected behind her eyes, setting down plates of rubber food, moving along from table to paper-covered table...

Moscow was sulking when he came offstage, and I knew that it was more than just personal hurt. It was not like him to lose a character once he had hold of it, but I had watched the entire act, and I saw the

Professor evaporate out of him, line by line, until midway through the parade of painted scars (the scene punctuated by giggles and snorts whenever anyone made an entrance) Moscow dried up completely and was raised, empty handed and aware of that emptiness, that vacancy, from his actor's trance.

So that now he was like a drunk who just had to kick something, barreling into the wings with his face turned down, his hands jammed into the pockets of the greatcoat, the scenery billowing and trembling as he passed. Though looking down, he still managed to stumble over the pile of rags and props that I had set down well out of the way, next to a coil of rope. Even then he did not stop. He cursed once, caught himself with his palm smacking hard against the brick wall. Then, without violence and without care, he pushed through and was gone.

I caught up with him in a grey intersection of passages, where a fan pushed stale air from the alley with a sound like indoor rain. I meant to tell him that I admired what I had seen, that he had impressed me, had done something that I hadn't thought him capable of, and that he shouldn't worry about having lost the character because I was certain he could find it again. But when I came up to him Moscow preempted me. He had lighted a cigarette and he tossed the match, still flaming, in my direction. "What do *you* want?" he said. He cupped the cigarette between his fingers and smoke billowed out through his nose. "Hah? What d'you *want?*"

"Relax," I said. "They were just having some fun...."

"Shut up," Moscow said. Moisture dripped from the hem of his greatcoat, forming dark splotches on the bare unvarnished wood. He turned until he could look over his shoulder into my eyes, and I saw that his face was melting, thick black beardstubble showing through the basecoat of orange paint, a dark smudge in the place where the scar had been. He had left the beaver hat onstage somewhere, or lost it; his hair was soaking wet, curling thick and dark in the air above his forehead. He stood looking at me with his blacklined eyes half closed, his lips pulled back, his arms straight at his sides. His voice was soft and very low. "Do you know what?" he said. "Nobody gives a good god damn what you think."

Jones was laughing quietly to herself when I came to her dressing room an hour later. "Like a horror show out there tonight," I said as I put my head in the door, and she looked up into the mirror and grinned. "Regular Dwight Frye stuff," she said. " 'Mathter, *pleeth* let me act...' "

She had taken off the wig and changed into her own denim shirt and dungarees, so that now she was recognizably Jones again, beautiful and dark and a little tired around her naked eyes. I came in and sat with her; we talked about the afternoon and laughed about it together, there alone in that freezing, cluttered, greasepaint-smelling little room.

"The funny thing is," Jones said, "Moscow hasn't read a word of *An Actor Prepares*. Claude's the reader, he's been through all of the books. You're lucky not to have known him then, he was mad all the time. He knows there isn't much of Stanislavski in what Moscow does. But it doesn't matter. He takes the straightest route. Moscow takes the long way around. They're both traveling through the same forest, they both come out at the same point. But they fight like Tweedledum and Tweedledee. Over the process."

"What's your process?" I said.

Jones gave me a smile that I did not understand. She shook her head. "I think not. That would be telling everything."

Now Jones pulled herself out of the cracked mirrorglass, drawing her chair so close that her knees pressed between mine. She lifted my chin into the light. Neither of us spoke. With my face in her hands, Jones looked at me as if she had caught me out in something. Then the chair creaked under her. She dipped her little finger into a pot of rouge, bent and kissed me gently. As her mouth touched mine I felt the tip of her finger drawing a line cold and wet against my temple. "There," she said. "Now you start to fit in."

HARE

"**ONE** night," Lon said, "Jones came drunk to the edge of the fire." And I thought: This is it at last. He is warning me away.

It was one of those times when night seems to have been going on forever, the residue of body heat where the audience had been packed close upon one another with their programs folded as fans waving slowing under their chins, and the smoke from them not fading or burning off, even now, but settling over the backs and arms of the empty seats. Lon and I were sweeping the stage. Except that the dust would not be collected, only pushed and stirred; when it began to seem that we had been pushing at it, stirring it for hours, I gave up and went over to sit at the edge with my legs dangling down into the orchestra pit.

"I didn't know that she drank," I said. And soon he came lumbering up behind, settled himself heavily down next to me, and lit a cigarette.

"Well she was stewed that night," Lon said. He turned his thick face around into the light so that I could get a good look at it. He was wearing a smug expression that I had never seen on him before, the kind that says I know and I'm not telling.

Because he knew all about my imagination. He wanted to be sure that I had enough time to picture the worst: Jones on opium, dark Jones, passing out with her fingers just at the edge of the fire, her hair spreading like black water across the sand. Lon and I sat in silence before the empty house, and before long I had to ask, "Why? What, then?"

Lon dropped ash into the pit, blew out smoke. "Nothing," he said. "The open air. That's all."

Then the night was doubled. Hot black air cutting through the cab as they came the four hundred miles along from the east, hot black air rising from off of the grill, so that now as Lon turned his cigarette in his fingers and looked through the smoke he was not seeing the empty chairs at all.

It was the tiniest of fires, a faint spatter of flame; the men were nothing more than indistinct humanshapes on the grass. But Jones and Lon would have been watching them for more than an hour, and Jones alone still sitting, still looking at them through vapors from the dying charcoal when the rest of the company was off setting up tents, or stretching out on the seats of the trucks, getting ready for sleep.

Then, alone under the moon, Jones stood and crossed the road. She would have paused in the center, where no car had passed for more than three hours, waiting empty-faced with her hands straight at her sides, looking not at the figures by the fire now, but at the single half-covered truck much like one of her own, dusty and battered even in the moonlight, parked close off of the shoulder and facing in the direction from which the Jones Transportation Company had come. Not a full stop; just a hesitation between one step and the next, before she crossed the rest of the way and was swallowed in the truck's shadow.

That was when Lon, wedged into a too-small sleeping bag he had parked off in the grass, closed his eyes. One second later he was wakened by the touch of her hand on his free arm. "Shh," she said, invisible now, only her voice in the dark, and her hand still resting below his shoulder. "Come look."

Lon fumbled, squirmed, kicked the bag from around his legs, calling softly, "Wait, hey wait," because she had already gone. It was not that he was blinded, it was a bright, blue night; but he could not see her. He followed along the edge of the grass until the strangers' truck stood between him and the campfire with its four huddled shapes, and then he heard her whisper to him from across the road.

It was an old Ford pickup that had been re-shaped under the hands of its owners, fitted out with a wooden top that bulged over the sides as if it had been pushed in from above, as if it were dough, or had been stuffed too full from the inside. Jones was waiting at the back. As he came around she lifted the corner of a foul, footsmelling tarpaulin that hung from rings over the mouth of a vast, stinking black tunnel that led far into the bowels of the truck. She had picked up a flashlight somewhere; now she flicked it on.

Inside there were wonderful things. Suns, fires, hides, the pale moon. And something plaster, not quite alive, that stared back.

Jones gave over the flashlight. Lon stood shining it into the back of the truck, and watched as she went alone out to the men by the fire.

"Good evening," Jones said.

And the man on the far side of the coals, the one with the flat face and the stick with a hot dog pierced on the end of it, said "As good as any."

Now Lon could see that they were Indians, dressed in checkered shirts, dungarees, heavy work boots, but sitting cross-legged around the fire all the same, all turning now to look up at Jones except for the man with the hot dog. She said something more to them that Lon could not hear; and he could not hear their whispered reply. There was some movement, some scooting this way and that in the circle of dust. A place was made for her, but Jones did not take it, only squatted at the periphery of their group, elbows on thighs, chin in palm, the faintest trace of a smile on her as she looked from face to face.

Lon turned away, stuck his head into the back of he truck. It was the head of a buffalo staring back at him, but its eyes and horns were painted, the nose beginning to rip from age and use so that he could see the raw layer of stiffened newspaper that was the flesh beneath the varnish. It rested partly on a collection of poles that had been tied into a tight bundle, partly on a bolt of cloth. Lon could not see the rest of it.

He shut off the light, went around to the street side, and rested with his back against the jutting edge of the truck. At last there was a hint of wind, blowing up from along the west. In its touch he realized how wet his clothes were. He closed his eyes. He thought that he could smell the older man's hot dog blackening above the coals.

Then Jones came fast around from the other side. She was not drunk yet, but Lon said that she had already caught it, that it was just a matter of time. She grabbed him by the shirt, hauled him back across the road, and halfway there began to hiss at him, "Get the others up.

Get them up. It's to be *The Tall Stranger*."

So now Templeton was sitting up, straggly-headed, blinking as Lon showed the flashlight through from beyond the tentflaps. "What what," he said. "What?" And then "Jesus God!" as over Lon's shoulder one of the trucks began to roar, snapped its headlights on, and came swerving around directly at the tent.

Templeton dove over his wife and stood out in his nightshirt with his ankles exposed, shouting as the truck came up close behind Lon and honked. Lon got out of the way, and it rolled forward another few feet until the tent where Mrs. Templeton still slept seemed to glow from the inside. Then it closed its eyes and died.

"What the hell ——," Templeton shouted. "What the hell ——." Jones came down from behind the wheel and trotted away without seeing him. Moscow rose up in the back seat and put his hand on the windowglass. "What's going on?"

"*The Tall Stranger*," Lon said, shining the flashlight through into Moscow's unshaven face. "Now."

And behind him there came another roar as the second truck started up and began its wide swing around.

"There they are," Jones whispers from under orange-painted cloth. A cold breeze catches at the edge of her: she stands, I know, as she feels, like someone out of dark tales. At her feet, Lon pounds another stake well into the dirt, until he is no longer even hitting metal, until the sound of the hitting becomes a dull thud. He sets the mallet down and feels the rope. It's taut, the pole should be steady now but she hasn't let go. Canvases tied above and beside her flap in the wind like banners or flags; the torchlight flickers against her face. Lon follows her eyes: across the road, three of the tribe are standing in the dark at the edge of the grass, silently watching.

They have raised a translucent canvas box just at the black lip of tar, tied at the back to the sides of the trucks standing one behind the other. Working in the unfamiliar light, Lon manages to hang a backdrop for them to play against. Not the right one; that was buried behind the props for another show. The substitute is too tall for the job; he leaves it half-rolled on the grass and ties the top and corners. It is not like the stage, where klieg lamps reduce the colors to flat pastels. Here the firelight makes them jump, changes them into something pagan and horrible and wonderful.

Lon comes out of the light and nearly runs into Mrs. Templeton, who stands waiting almost in character just offstage. She's holding a green sweater closed at the front; it is not part of the costume. Her glasses are as opaque in this light as if they have frosted over; Lon cannot see her eyes. She has more than her own natural stillness, calm. Still, she talks in whispers: "Who are they?"

Now there are five of them, three men and two women, standing opposite the portable stage. As Lon watches, a sixth, no more than three feet tall, breaks through from their midst and sits in the dirt at their feet. "Jones says they're Winnebego. But they are a long way from home. Are you all set?" Mrs. Templeton looks from the Indians to Lon and back, smiles and nods. She and Lon can both hear her husband swearing to himself off in the solid blackness behind the trucks.

Lon finds him fumbling with the numberless black buttons on his waistcoat. "We're working without a curtain; I couldn't figure a way to rig one on."

"I know that, damn it," Templeton hisses. One of the buttons has come off in his hand. "Get that damn light out of my eyes. Shit."

So now they stand invisible to each other, Lon threading the dead flashlight through a loop in his overalls, Templeton breathing furiously close by. Dew settled long ago over the unmowed grass; Lon feels damp through his shoes as he eases between the nose of one truck and the back of the other. There behind the backdrop, where only a faint breath of purple light filters through from the stage side, Lon rifles through dimly outlined piles of junk and cloth until he finds a worn-out cardboard box that rattles and clangs as he pulls it down. It is full of tin noisemakers that have been lithographed with pictures of pumpkins and black cats and witches on broomsticks; he sets them out in a row on the grass, one by one, carefully so as not to make a sound. Taking up his place out of the light, he nods across at Mrs. Templeton; she nods back, and the sweater is lifted from her shoulders by invisible hands.

She takes the stage with her husband and Mary. Moscow comes out last. He stands posed with one hand holding the black book and the other at his chin, two fingers raised, two curled. He is Cotton Mather now, a perfect vehicle for the story about to happen, though History hasn't whispered to him about the witches just yet. He moves, reading aloud; it is all the curtain that's needed.

There is the softest rustle of fabric, and when Lon looks up Jones has appeared at his side, whitefaced, in a cloak that has been tied over with thick, loose clusters of orange and red and yellow silk. A belt of gold circles her waist; she is adjusting it on her hips so that a central, engraved pendant will dangle just between her legs. She wears blue eyeshadow, blue lipstick. She flashes a quick smile at Lon, falls into character, draws the hood close over her face so that all he can see of her is the tip of a white chin.

One of the noisemakers is a metal sheet with two clappers mounted on either side; another is a tin bell. Lon rests on one knee, holding them ready; there is one more line of dialogue from the stage. Then Jones heads out, and Lon sets up a thin, mystical clanging on his orange-painted spooks, Jacks, hags.

The characters cannot see her; they cannot even move. She comes behind Mather and touches him ever so gently, once on his face, once in the small of his back, once below his stomach. A shiver runs through him from head to foot. He begins to change.

Lon can only wonder why she has chosen this one, the single play in which she has no lines. Across the road, the Indians watch in silence, their faces expressionless, nodding softly to themselves...

I'm not only listening anymore; I'm riding in the back of his mind, just like riding in the back seat, looking out over Lon's shoulder. It plays itself out under the moon, the stranger's repeated visits, her touch that reduces people to their base elements. The Jones Transportation Company takes a collective bow and splinters as one by one its members step to the edge of the road. Jones is last. She can be seen again under her make-up, exhausted, coming down with her unaffected walk almost like a man's, bowing so that her hands touch in front of her knees, the mascara running some now and her eyes like two lightbulbs inside of her head.

Once down, once up, and the company waiting for her to come back to the line so that they can take one final bow together and then pull the plug on this production. But she does not come back. She stands by the torches with her hood down, not quite steady on her feet, as though fighting the wind. There is something going on across the road. The Indians are in motion, pushing things around over the grass, murmuring to each other, laughing.

A man in a blue coat and dungarees and boots comes alone from the other side. His beauty is of the most exotic kind, his hair runs down to his shoulders and is held in place by a purple and blue beaded band. Jones offers him her hand, and as we watch unmoving from the line, he takes it.

"That was fine," he says. His whole manner is quiet; the two stand holding hands and nodding at each other. "You surprised us. We were expecting just a medicine show, not goddesses and monsters. Thank you. Now..."

Without letting go of her hand he stoops and snatches one of the torches from the ground. Half-turning, he calls in a stage voice so that the whole road can hear: "This is one that we don't do for just the curiosity seekers. This is one that we do for ourselves."

On the far side of the road he walks in a rough square, and a line of fire springs up in his path. "There is the world of the Earthmaker," he says, "and here below it the world of Wakdjunkaga. Here is the world of Turtle, and here is our world. This is where Hare is in charge."

It has grown into another box of light, backed by a great black scrim. An unseen drum begins to tap just lightly; from out of the scrim comes a young girl and an old woman painted the color of dirt. They build a fire in the clearing, set out bits of old pottery, and the soft-voiced man whispers to us.

"There was a virgin girl who lived with her grandmother the Earth. Though she had never lain with a man she became pregnant, and only seven months later she died giving birth to a male child unlike any other. This is Hare."

Ripples in the memory-fabric. "It's horrible," Lon says, but two years later I force him to look. Her belly is already horribly swollen and growing larger by the second, her teeth exposed now, the whites of her eyes showing as she holds herself, alone, by the fire. The dung-colored woman washes her face in clear water, helps her to a pallet in the corner, covers her over. She is glistening with sweat now, unmoving, digging her fingers into the dirt. She has heard the words of the storyteller as clearly as we: she knows she is going to die.

One short, airless shriek, swallowed by the black mouth, and then she is torn apart from the inside out. A full-grown man, dripping with blood, pulls himself from out of her twitching body and stands naked, erect, laughing at the moon.

Hare covers himself in a fur loincloth, is washed clean by the grandmother in her heavy, crusted rags. Under the blood his face takes shape: it is the narrator again, looking out past where Jones is sitting, coating himself in a white powder like dust. His is an athletic style that the Jones Transportation Company has never seen before, more dance than acting, his wiry body pulled tight as if by a string through his intestines. Hare kills a buffalo and fights with himself, wounding himself so that a sticky fluid that looks like real blood drains freely from his left arm. Hare is shot with an arrow, but only pulls it out of himself. It is a marvelous weapon, but he cannot make it work, it only falls from his hands.

Hare begins to grow. He is taller than the scrim, taller than the trucks, taller than the trees. Sparks dance and sputter behind his cloth eyes. His hands might scoop up the Jones Transportation Company where they sit. But when the fingers open, arrowheads fall upon their shoulders, pelt the ground in a mile-wide circle.

Now Hare is man-sized again, though his head is false, too large for his dancer's body. Inside a crumbling old lodge, disembodied heads in shadowplay jump down from their shelves to dance in a circle about his feet. At first they seem harmless; then they leap at the parts of his white body and hang on with their small white teeth.

Hare beats them off; he escapes up a tree that has appeared where the lodge interior once stood. But the heads mill around at its base, they chew through the trunk and are upon him again as it crashes soundlessly to the ground. Hare finds a river of blue cloth and leaps it clear; the heads try to follow, they fall and rise for a moment wearing astonished faces before they are drowned. Soon they bob lifelessly on the surface; Hare plucks them out one by one and flattens them with awful crunching sounds, and casts them back.

Lon cannot now believe what he is seeing. Mere effects: some of them are even known to him, one or two he has used himself. But the man in the white powder and the others with him perform without flaw; Lon cannot see where the tricks end or begin, cannot imagine the vaprous machinery like underwebbing that they must require. Puppet heads filled with red paint, real heads shouting curses, puppet gods on invisible telescoping poles, animals that are not animals, the *undercraft*, magician's work, moving-picture stunts performed without the benefit of film. Whether out of his own concern or out of mine, he looks for us both to where Jones sits cross-legged in her gypsy robes. It has happened now: Margaret Darwin unleashed from Jones's controlling hand, drinking it all in.

Now Hare is in tears. He is half-held, dangling by the neck, kicking in the grip of his grandmother, who has swollen into a huge leafy mound with an impossibly large face painted in reds and greens. She has eight arms; Hare escapes from one only to be caught and held by another. She will not allow him to grant immortality to the humans, her leathery lips working slow, oozing sap. All things must die, she says. Even me. And a portion of her side collapses in upon itself, ancient dust rising from out of the hole, the same faint shriek of his mother being torn echoing out of the stage's giant mouth.

Now Lon sat with his hands on his knees. He drew in a load of air and let it out again1 then pulled his feet back up onto the stage. He had finished his cigarette long ago; after a careful search through his pants pockets and then through his shirt he padded empty handed off into the wings. I heard him opening the fusebox there, behind the curtain. One by one the rows of ceiling lamps went out, back to front.

I sat in the dark, and thought: *God.* I knew then that the comparison was right, that drunk would be just the right way to describe how she must have felt, but that it did not go far enough: like drinking in a church, not to set aside faith but to see it better: alone in the sacristy, belly full of wine and all the holiness of all the beliefs, until the figures in the stained glass began to move and speak. That would be how she felt.

"Come on," Lon said. He handed me my jacket as I came by and herded me out through the back, tracing a path along the blue-painted walls with his flashlight. We stood outside where it was just a bit cooler. Lon locked the back door with a key the owner had given him, then ran a chain through the handles and locked that up, too.

Out on the road, far off, there was the sound of a motor running. I heard it all the way to the rooming house, never fading from where it idled, and I thought, that will be the Indians along any time now, in their truck loaded down with magic things. My legs felt weak. I walked along slower and slower until Lon called again, "Come on." Then I decided, no, they won't be, they were just passing through, they must have already gone, and I just missed them.

Lon said goodnight and went to his room in the corner, and I went along the hall. Halfway down I saw the light coming from under Jones's door. Inside, she would be reading or making notations in her careful handwriting, sitting Indian-style in the middle of the bed or working out some bit of staging in the center of the room, the chairs and bags all pushed into the corner. Or else asleep with the light on, a single blanket pulled up over her waist, a book lying face down across her breast.

I went past, into the room that in this town, this once only, happened to adjoin hers. It was our second week, I had lived in the room long enough so that scraps of paper, empty envelopes, dirty shirts had spread over the backs of chairs, the dresser top, the floor.

There was a connecting door between Jones's room and my own that had never been opened, and every night I thought to myself, I could knock. Always to be followed by, *No. She might not even be alone; or, worse, she might simply look up and say, Yes? Can I help you?*

Now I only went to it, and sat carefully so as not to make a sound, and let my hand rest lightly against the knob. She came drunk to the edge of the fire, in her dirty old traveling clothes now and her face cleaned off, bare. Her imagination on fire. Holding first Lon and then Templeton and then all the rest, one after the other, in her arms. *Did you see...? My God, Did you see...?*

I felt so close to her at that moment. Only now, looking back, am I jealous of not having been there, jealous of Hare, who took her, and carried her off into the world of dreams.

FIRST NIGHT

THIS was in a town called Cuba, where the dry wind carried dust through crevices into every room. It was the most trouble that we ever had, for it was the only stage we ever used that did not have a trap door; and so Jones insisted that Lon make one.

He had only just drawn the curtain on our third night at the Cuba Grange when Jones announced that she was retiring *The Twilight of the Gods*, and had decided that a pair of the new dramas were ready for a trial run. One of these was *Crickle House*, a key feature of which was the discovery of a body under the floorboards at the end of act one. This had to be produced somehow; and our mannequin did not have fold-away limbs.

Set in a grand old manor house suspiciously like the one we had stayed in during our gig in Clinton, the play revolved around an ex-railroad baron played by Templeton who had lost his fortune thanks to his own compulsive ambition to acquire and control absolutely everything; now he

118

could not bring himself to tell the family, all of whom were more or less disreputable types who had hangers-on that depended on them and reasons to need a fast cash infusion. It was my first awkward attempt at placing Greek-style tragedy in a modern setting; the only notable thing about it, apart from the sort of acidic dialogue that I was developing a knack for, was the way that it marked an unspoken, unofficial, but definite shift away from the collaborative approach in favor of at least staying in orbit around what came out of my pen.

I was aware of the change, but I was two people in those days: the one who wrote, and the one who did for all the others, who ran errands and cleaned up and brought in the lunches and made sure that things were where Lon needed them to be, when he wanted them. The writer was so small. He only lived for a few hours in the middle of the night. Every morning Jones came along and for maybe fifteen minutes he had the thrill of her full attention before she moved on.

In rehearsal the company had perfected an increasing hysteria that lent some effectiveness to the piece, but it needed a better ending than what I had yet been able to supply. Jones said that it did not go far enough; she said that I had dug around the idea without ever hitting it. Perhaps, by putting it on the schedule, she meant to nudge me along. Whatever her reason, she had played the Norn for the last time; *Crickle House* was needed, ready or not.

When Jones liked an audience she would send the company out to stand at the theater doors, to receive them as they emerged from the world of the Transportation Company on their way back into their real lives. "Thank you for coming," she would say, over and over, sometimes taking their hands into hers, sometimes laughing, sometimes leaning forward with a smile. All of the company enjoyed this ritual; good feeling and happiness radiated from them in almost visible waves; they seemed to glow. Watching from inside the building I could always see the members of the audience filling up on that feeling, whether they were aware of it or not, and taking it with them as they turned away into the night.

The third evening in Cuba had been especially good, with a crowd that was just about as responsive as it got. Everyone expected that Jones would give the sign to go out. Mary and Mrs. Templeton were so sure of it that they went on ahead. They were halfway out the door before they realized that Jones wasn't behind them.

She was still working. Without waiting for the house to clear, she paced across the length and breadth of the stage, pausing every other step to pound on the floor with her heel, the black Norn gown whispering over the boards in her wake. She was not trying to find the trapdoor; she already knew that it didn't exist, had already made up her mind. "Here," she said at last, sighting her position with the back wall. "Put it here." On the far side of the curtain people rose from their seats, passed whispering up the aisle. Jones gave one final stamp. "Don't make it too big. I'll set the program tonight. We'll run through everything out of costume tomorrow afternoon."

"Why now?" Templeton said. "We've played it this long; we can play it two more nights. For gosh sakes, there must be a better way to leave your mark on this tank town."

But Lon had already started to work with a drill and a keyhole saw. "Don't think of it as vandalism," Jones said. "Think of it as making an improvement."

"Christ," Templeton said as she went off. "Christ, I hate this."

But he did not leave. He stood off to one side and gaped at Lon and I crouching like ice fishermen around the growing hole. "You know this play isn't ready," he said to our backs. "We don't need this thing." Lon said nothing. He had cut three sides in the place Jones wanted; as he started on the fourth the stage floor gave out a loud crack and began to fall against the blade. It didn't slow Lon at all. He cut until there was a final snap, and then the wood disappeared from beneath my hands. It landed somewhere in the darkness below, kicking a cloud of dust into our faces, on up over our heads.

"Get a flashlight," Lon said. Before I could move, Templeton slapped one into his outstretched hand, as if he had read Lon's mind. He draped his suit coat over the footlights and came rolling up his sleeves to join us at the edge of the hole. "Not much room down there," he said as Lon pointed the beam down into the shadows.

Like opening a Pirate Cave, I thought. I suppose I must have babbled that nonsense out loud. But the stage was built just a few feet above a smooth floor of dirt. Lon swept the light far along under the floor; there were no eruptions, no scattered bones, and certainly no iron-bound treasure boxes; only the footprints of mice swirling in a pattern back and around as if they had been caught in the middle of a waltz.

"Sorry, son," Templeton said. "If they have any booty they've buried it somewhere else."

"Dunno this will work," Lon said. He climbed to his feet and shuffled away into the wings, returning a moment later with the mannequin stuffed under one arm and his favorite box full of butterfly hinges and other metallic goodies under the other. "Take this," he said to me.

I needed both arms to hold the mannequin, and even then Templeton had to discretely cup its heels in his left hand to keep me from falling over sideways. Lon got down on his hands and knees, fished the square of flooring out from the hole and flung it to one side. "Doesn't look good," he said. "Hand 'er down. Feet first."

We angled the mannequin through the trap, first one way and then another. We tried it face up, face down, sideways, at the sharpest angle we could manage. It kept getting hung up around the hip line. The hole just wasn't deep enough to allow it through.

Lon sat back on his haunches and covered his mouth with his big, dirty fingers. "Go on out to Red and get the spade," he said. "We're goner have to do some excavating."

But when I got to my feet Jones was resting against the proscenium edge, looking at us lackadaisically. Her arms were crossed, her booted feet crossed at the ankles, her favorite tweed jacket draped freely over her shoulders. The Norn make-up was gone forever, that character absorbed at last or else set free, I didn't know which. She said, "Too stiff, is he?"

Templeton gave her a look. "If you mean, 'Does he bend?' no, he does not."

She gave us that sideways twist of her mouth that had become a familiar thing to me. " 'S okey," she said. "He wasn't realistic enough anyway. I have a better idea." Then she cocked an eyebrow, and her gaze fell on me in a way that I didn't like at all.

Lon and I didn't finish with the trap door until well after one. By then, I expected that Cuba would be cool and still as the other little towns had always been, a place of empty windows, of cars sitting motionless in silent yards, a place of cats and the occasional rush of far-distant trains. But on the landing out in back of the grange, under a yellow lamp that burned all night, I was surprised to hear music drifting up from the street below. It wasn't coming from the boarding house; it wasn't coming from anywhere that I could tell. It was all over the air.

Lon looked at me and I looked at him. We ducked between the buildings, into a V-shaped slash of shadow. It wasn't just music anymore; as we came through the grass I thought I heard soft, distant voices, the low murmur of an engine at idle. "What is it?" I said, and Lon said, "You never went out much on Saturday nights, did you?"

All the way down, as far as we could see, the main street was lined with cars and trucks caked in road dust. They were parked with their noses to the curb, windows half open, the music splashing out across their parallel hoods so at first I thought they all had radios, tuned to the same channel. Then Lon pointed down the length of the sidewalk. Among the two or three buildings with lights still burning was a modern-looking dance hall standing open to the street. People were going in and coming out, but the cars never moved. In dark seats behind the dashboards, or perched out along the row of fenders, handsome men and women sat whispering to each other in a language that I didn't know, didn't even recognize. Lon and I had the better part of the sidewalk to ourselves. A few townsfolk waved as we passed, or offered their hands as if they knew us. Lon seemed completely at ease. We strolled along the busy, peaceful lane until we came into the light of the hall.

Inside, there was fiddle music, dancing couples, and smoke. I spotted Jones right away. She was sitting at a corner of the bar, looking as if she had just come back from exploring India. She had a glass of whiskey resting in her lap, cupped in both hands. She was surrounded by men.

Lon stepped inside, paused and looked back. "Aren't you coming?" he said.

In all the racket and bustle of that place, Jones seemed contained, poised inside a bubble of her own making. She was listening closely to something that a man on her left was trying to say. As I watched, I began to sense that invisible bubble slowly expanding, to encompass first the bar, then the men standing near, and finally the entire hall.

"No," I said at last. "It's late. I've got to think about the play."

Lon shrugged, went on ahead, and I stepped back into the street. Men passed me going in. Drawn by her scent, by the prospect of her swelling to embrace them all. I went back up the whispering block, turned, and started alone to the boarding house beyond.

My room looked out on a parking space made of packed dirt, then over the backs of buildings lining the main street, out to the distant grasslands. I could just see the roof of the grange, facing south from the center of town. Every morning a man in a grey suit swept the walk in front of a dry goods store, and slowly, after that, blue and green and black automobiles would begin to drift by, covering over his work.

In the version of *Crickle House* that we had, the ex-railroad baron lost his home and his fortune and was abandoned by his family, one by one, until he was left alone onstage in an ever-narrowing circle of light, clinging to his gold-handled cane just as he clung to his last shred of dignity. I did not now have any particular insight that told me why or how this was too tame; I was thinking only of Jones and the men, and hating myself in the way that knowing her was teaching me to hate myself more than anything, more than anyone, more so even than I hated Moscow, because after all Moscow could be easy with her like all the others in a way that I still could not. I was hurting and I wanted to hurt in return, and so I thought of the people in the play and I killed them all. Without stopping to think, I scribbled:

ENTER CRICKLE in a tattered parody of his white suit, hanging in shreds around his scarecrow limbs. The derby hat is gone; his hair is unkempt, he is bruised and dirty. Only the LION'S-HEAD CANE is still recognizably new and shining. He sees his family seated in all their finery at their elegant picnic upstage and calls to them.

CRICKLE:
Jason! Myra! I've found you!
Sarah – Louise!

SARAH turns to look at him over her left shoulder, then severs a wing from the corpse of the chicken in front of her.

SARAH:
Pay him no mind. We are done with him.

CRICKLE draws nearer.

CRICKLE:
Jason! It's your father!

SARAH:
What has he brought to us but grief?

(She hands Jason the wing and he bites into it enthusiastically)

CRICKLE is nearly on top of them now. He sees their picnic and licks his lips in starvation.

CRICKLE:
Children! Don't you know me? Has it been so long? Am I so changed? Don't you know me?

SARAH distributes the food generously around the picnic-blanket.

LOUISE:
None for me, thank you. They'll be coming for me soon, I expect.

SARAH:
Pay him no mind.

MYRA:
(Tucking into her portion)
We would, father, but you see we lost everything because of you.

LOUISE:
I won't say that I'm sorry to be done with all of you, but I could have hoped for it to happen differently.

JASON:
You get what you deserve.

Now CRICKLE has reached them. He grips JASON by the collar.

CRICKLE:
Jason! Won't you share with me now?

Jason pulls suddenly, violently away. The collar rips and tears off in his father's hand. Indignantly, Jason rises and deals his father a blow to the face. CRICKLE is driven to his knees by the force of it.

JASON:
You wicked old man! You bankrupted yourself on purpose! You never gave a thought to the others you might be harming! Now look at us! Mother cooking! And I must work! Damn you and your ambitions.

He returns to the picnic. Stunned, CRICKLE scrabbles in the dust, nursing his jaw.

CRICKLE:
I brought monsters into this world. It was all I could breed. All!

SARAH:
(not appearing to speak to him)
You had a dream of Western skies, once.

CRICKLE:
Rock cannot breed flowers.
SARAH:
You had a dream of opening the world.

CRICKLE:
· Nor leather breed silk.

With the cane for support, **CRICKLE** drags himself to his feet. The picnic goes on as if he did not exist. On standing, **CRICKLE** does not stop moving. The **CANE** rises ominously above his head.

SARAH:
Oh, you had the biggest of dreams!

CRICKLE:
I brought monsters into this world!

He strikes the blow. The **GIRLS** scream. **JASON** reels, then tries to defend himself as **CRICKLE** hammers him with blow after blow from the lion's-head cane. **SARAH** grabs for the cutting-knife sticking in the chicken breast. Rising behind **CRICKLE**, she **STABS** him twice in the back.

Now, just like a silent movie, the stage begins to flicker as though a shutter is clicking open and shut, open and shut, rapidly at first, then slower and slower so that longer patches of darkness begin to fall inbetween the short frames of light. Melodramatic music flares from an unseen piano. The action takes on a Keystone comedy quality for all of its savagery. Everyone on the stage is clawing indiscriminately at everyone else; the lion's-head cane lashes again and again. Soon the motion stops entirely and all we see are isolated images of mayhem that flicker into being as the flashes of red and purple light grow farther and farther apart. Then the stage falls into darkness and silence.

Pause. A beat. Two. The lights come up on a barren gray background. There is **CRICKLE**, standing atop a **MOUND OF BODIES**. His face and arms are drenched in blood. The lion's-head cane is drenched in blood. He looks around, and sighs

in contentment. He raises himself, and shouts to the sky:

CRICKLE:
The earth is mine! The sky is mine! The seas are
mine! I win! I win!!

{CURTAIN.}

I went down to the end of the hall and doused myself in cold water, then came back still dripping. The sun was up.

It was eleven-thirty before I dragged myself down to the grange. By then Lon had loaded the thunder machine onto one of the trucks and was greasing it for the last time. His hands were black to the wrists. "You're late," he said, scooping glop out of a tin can and then vanishing his fingers into the machinery. "Turning into kind of a prima donna, aren't you?"

Jones looked as if she hadn't slept, still wearing the same canvas pants from the night before, the same blue cotton shirt with the tail hanging out, the sleeves rolled up to her elbows, gypsy-bedraggled. She circled with the others inside a boundary of chalk that marked the edges of an invisible set. They were referring to a mess of dogeared pages spread out at the foot of the stage. I recognized my own handwriting and thought, *Huh. How about that.* Jones was the only one who saw me come in.

I waited and watched off stage left until she broke away, leaving them to play out the scene in the empty space. "Hey there, stay-at-home," she said in the grey windowlight by the packing cases. "Got anything for me?"

I gave her the scene.

She read down through it without expression, slipping the pages front to back. Near the end she pursed her lips into a smirk. "Oh, somebody was angry last night," she said. Then: "She dies, they die, everyone dies. Very much in the tradition."

She punched me on the arm. "Good. We can play with this."

Did she mean Good, this is Good or Good, we'll talk about it later? I said ow.

On her way back out to the others on the stage she half-turned back to me and confirmed my fear from last night's hole-cutting. "By the way," she said. "You need to see Moscow about your make-up. I'm afraid it's not a speaking part, but even John Barrymore had to start somewhere, hey?"

*

If I wouldn't accept that I had brought it on myself, Lon would not believe that I hadn't planned it this way all along. That night, with Mary out upon the apron playing "Aura Lea" and Lon stuck with redressing the stage all by himself, Moscow sat me down in a freezing metal-backed chair and bent over me in the glare of an unshaded lamp. "Don't move," he said softly, "except when and how I tell you. And keep your mouth shut. We have just ten minutes."

His make-up case rested open on a stand that came up to the level of my chest. Moscow twisted the lamp around until it shone into my eyes, then began to mark my face with a stick of black greasepaint. "First time you've worn this shit," he said. "Does wonders for your skin."

A block of shadow decapitated him above the bridge of his painted nose. I could hear Mary in the distance and I could hear his breath sounding just like a forge nearby, just the way Lon had described it when he told me of seeing Moscow alone in the night, looking for his own name on the marquee. "Close your eyes," Moscow said. He dumped corn starch into my hair; when I didn't rub it in fast enough to please him he pushed my hands away and finished the job himself. Then a glass jar jumped into his fingertips. He prodded at the greyish-white stuff inside and began pushing it hard into my pores, cold and moist over my brow, down along my cheeks, chin and neck. "Why haven't you tried her," he said at last.

When I opened my eyes Moscow was lighting the stub of a candle, holding the narrow end of a cork into its tall flame. The base coat of make-up had already started to dry; it felt as if my whole face was hardening into a clay mask. "Tried her?" I said. "Jones? For what?"

Moscow gave out a sharp hiss of air from between his lips. "Tyro," he said. "Close them." The burnt cork was still warm as he pressed it to my eyelids, working in a circular motion that rose high up under my brow. He heated it again and painted my mouth, cheekbones and nostrils chalky black. "Next spring she'll find herself a new writer," he said. "Or she'll find herself something else to do, and you'll have missed your chance."

Moscow lifted a handmirror so that I could see reflected a withered skull-face, caked in dust with just my eyes, brown and surprised, floating there far back in the sockets. Then he picked out a crumpled cardboard box not much larger than a ring case. Inside was a set of jagged wooden teeth, brown with age, bound in curving metal braces. "This is going to hurt," he said. "Don't say I didn't warn you."

*

"How did you find your first taste of acting?" Mrs. Templeton said later that week as we rode together in the back seat with rain splashing black against black windows.

"Taste?" I said. "Not at all. It tasted like sour beer. It tasted like dust. It was almost tropical under that stage, and with all the garbage Moscow piled on my face—"

"Yes," Mrs. T said. "Yes, I did think he had overdone it a bit."

"With that on it was all I could do to breathe. Act? 'Hold your body stiff and try not to sneeze.' I didn't think I'd be able to manage it."

"Still, the play came off all right," Mrs. T said. "I knew it when that woman fainted in the third row...

A man named John Huss was waiting for us when we came through after the show. He was standing by the stage door with his hands in the pockets of a cream-colored suit, building up what was already a sizable head of steam. "Ma'am," he said when he had succeeded at picking Jones out of the group. "Ma'am, could I have a word with you?"

We all followed in her wake, a costumed retinue spreading out in a fantail shape at her back. She offered her hand and an uncommitted expression that fit over her features like thin gauze. "Of course. What can I do for you?"

It had some effect: Huss looked like he couldn't decide on the best approach. "Well ma'am, I think this is something more in the way of something that's already been done. If you needed firewood I would have sold it to you. You didn't need to chop up m' damn stage."

Jones said nothing. Her face did not change. It was Templeton who stepped in, hooking his thumb at his double-breasted chest, his eyes clear blue. "I'm the company attorney," he said, overdoing it a bit as if he thought he was playing to the back row. "If there's any problem here then I'm your man."

"Problem?" Huss said. "Well, what do you think? How about I just go out there and have my self a peek at the floor boards?"

"You can't come in here at all without our say so," Templeton said. "It's part and parcel of our contract. And you know it." He was starting to enjoy himself; Jones was giving him her Be Quiet look but he wasn't paying attention.

"I don't need to come in," Huss said. "Maybe you think that I don't go to plays. Or maybe you just think that I don't know how things are done. Anyhow, tonight you folks pulled a body up through the floor of this building, right up through a hole in the stage floor that didn't dang well exist the day before yestiddy because this place wasn't built with one."

Templeton said, "A *hole?* Listen, there's no shame in it but did you really see what you think you saw? Because we specialize in appearances."

"I believe that," Huss said. "But I saw what I thought I saw. Thought my wife was going to have a stroke."

Templeton winced and brushed that aside with his hand. Jones was letting him go and I couldn't understand that. Why didn't she cut him off? "Most of our things are made of cardboard," he said. "They fold up flat and then when we need to produce them they puff up just like a, like a Chinese lantern. There's an awful lot of trickery to what we do."

He produced a couple of cigars from his inside pocket and made a herding motion with his hand, but Huss would have none of it. He lifted a well-calloused hand and pointed it straight at me. "Uh huh. How does that one fold up?"

Much later, Templeton told me that I stepped on his best line. He meant to tell Huss that I had travelled with the Adam Forpaugh and Sells Brothers Combined Shows as a contortionist, that in fact I folded up quite well. But he never had the chance.

This was what I had been saying to Jones all along, and now I damn well was going to prove it. I knew Huss. I came from his world. He was a regular bootstraps businessman, small and solid, clean-shaven, neat, built to stand the weather. Men like him had been the everyday players in my life until this summer, this special summer had happened to me.

Before he could take his hand down out of the air I stepped forward and clasped it. "Mishter Hush," I said, and then stopped. Moscow's teeth were still in my mouth. I hadn't forgotten them but I hadn't had any chance to take them out either, and now wasn't the time.

Huss looked me up and down, then freed himself and peered into his upturned palm. A dusty grey handprint had appeared there; too late, I remembered that I'd spent the last forty minutes crawling around in the grime below the stage. "Who are you really?" he said.

"Wilshon Howe. A couble monsh agho I wash a bishnesh clergh. Now loog had me." For the part of the corpse Mary had fitted me out with a rotten old vest, a string tie and an oversized frock coat. They were as dirty as my hands; I tried to wipe myself clean and couldn't tell the difference.

"You know that almost sounds like the truth," Huss said. "Who was your employer?"

I told him about Mr. Deighton and the Happiness Home Baking Company as well as I could manage. The name was not familiar to him. I offered to show the letter of recommendation that I still carried from Mr. Deighton himself. Huss refused it. He said it sounded like a good job. What in the name of Sam Hill made me give it up?

I said, "Well shir I'm nod sure I know the anshwer do thad. Bud I can dell you thad I don' fold ub flad an' then buff ub again. Nod yed."

Now Huss frowned gave the faintest of nods. "Thank you son. There's *one* honest person in this set-up anyhow." He shot a look at Templeton, who only looped his thumbs through his suspenders and stuck his jaw in the air. "Now maybe we can accomplish something."

In the alley of canvas and paint that ran across the stage Huss's voice echoed up and down and climbed into the rafters. "Oh, my. Doesn't seem... Huh. It doesn't look the same from back here at all. Interesting."

"You shaw the show donighd, bud what you don' know ish they were worgin' vrom an unvinished scribt." He looked me in the eye and I looked him right back. "Yesh, shir. I only gave 'em a rouvh ending jush thish avdernoon. They doog a, a, a *bulb* an' made id vlower."

We took him straight to the spot where the trap door joined almost invisibly with the parallel sweep of the boards. Lon worked the mechanism a few times; with Huss so occupied Mary passed me a handkerchief, and I spit the false teeth into it, folding the whole mess away into a side pocket. "Mr. Deighton never expected me to be an expert on everything," I said. "But he expected me to know who the experts were, and to listen to them and act on what they said. Mister Huss, I tell you plain, I never met any folks who were more expert in their craft than these folks are in theirs. And if Miss Darwin says this place needs a trap door, then it needs one. I guess you can see for yourself that it's an top-notch job."

Huss watched the door work, worked it a few times himself and then shook his head sadly. "All I can see is that you understand business men all right. If that's the case, then you'll understand why I can't be seen to have been hoodwinked by an ex-office boy and a pack of mummers." He stood back frowning, sniffed through one side of his nose, and cut off my reply with a wave of his hand. "Plug it up," he said. "Plug it up, and we'll let this one go."

Jones turned her eyes from where Huss was standing and fixed them on me. She might have been smiling or frowning; her face had become a painted mask. "Thank you," I said, and again Huss brushed the air as if this too was of no consequence. He turned to Lon. "Make it good and solid, if you can."

"Don't worry," Lon said without meeting his eyes. He had his toolbox already in hand; now it hit the floor with a sound that filled the house from front to back.

Jones still had not broken her silence. "Good show, Ma'am," Huss said to her. "I liked it a lot." She offered her bandaged hand and he took it. Then with a kind of embarrassment that I had not noticed in him before, he touched his forehead and passed through us into the dark beyond the wings. A moment later the stage door opened and closed, followed by a gust of warm air washing in from the yard.

At last Mrs. Templeton stirred. "Penfold, I can't believe my ears!" She came up and rapped me gently on the forehead, on the hard crust of corpse make-up. "Is it really you? Are you there?"

When Mary and I had everything in place for the next day, I went to Lon at the corner of the stage and asked if he needed any help. "That depends," he said, looking up from a quite unnecessary mess of rulers, protractors, pencils, sawblades and nails that he'd strewn about the gaping mouth of the trapdoor. His fingers were dusted with a fine yellow powder; around his knees he had dotted the stage floor with drawings of angles, arrows, squares. "You all through playing leading man?"

I asked what he meant by that. Lon shrugged it off. He knelt there shaking his head, poking at the marks on the boards. "You've been playing yourself for her just like a character in a play," he said. "All I know is it's made a lot of work for me. Help or go away."

I went out, got my coat and stopped there cursing him, then turned around and went back. Lon didn't say anything more. We closed the trapdoor, screwed it down tight, and together sealed the edges with a thick coating of homemade glue that smelled like turpentine and looked a lot like maple sugar. When it was finished Lon sat back on his heels. He began to peel dried glue from the ends of his fingers. "You go on," he said. "We've got to let this dry, and then it'll need another coat. I'll lock up. Go ahead, it's late."

I didn't argue with him, I had had enough of that to last me a while. I said goodnight, picked myself up and this time just draped the overcoat loose over my shoulders. It wasn't a costume; it had come with me all the way from Saint Paul. Back then it always helped me to look smart. Now, in my dirty slacks and a frayed shirt smeared with make-up, I was just a shabby young man in an overcoat, and too tired to care.

I hadn't believed Mary when she told me I was going to need it, but as soon as I stepped out under that half-moon night I knew that the summer was nearly gone. I shivered, caught a glimpse of my own breath in the air, and paused under the light to push my arms through the sleeves. I was just doing up the buttons when the gravel crunched at my side and a shabby figure came up out of the dark and caught me by the elbow. "Please," it said to me. "Please, will you sign...?"

I remember jumping back, and I remember the sight of a hand gripping the air, a longfingered thing with red nails, vanishing at the wrist into a grey sleeve that extended into darkness. "Please, if you would," it said, sexless, insistent, and the next thing I knew a wad of dirty paper and the stub of a pencil were being pushed hard up against my chest. "I have all of the greats... the Barrymores, William Gillette, Julia Marlowe, Mrs. Fiske..."

Beyond the light I saw only a mass of white hair and a heavy coat piled up with layer upon layer of mismatched scarves. "I'm sorry, you've made a mistake," I said. "I'm no one whose autograph you could want." I turned away and started across the yard, but was halted midway when the hand gathered up a fistful of cloth at the small of my back. "No," it said, close at my shoulder, breathing hard. "No, I know who you are. You're Winslow Howe, the writer. You were the *body*. You're *famous*. Sign. Oh, sign..."

I tried to get away and then it held me and would not let me go, crying "Sign, please sign... sign, oh sign" but by then I had turned some and could see in the light that the face was painted and the eyes were dark brown. I took hold of his nose and twisted until it came off in my hand, and Moscow stepped back, a rough square of his own face now showing in the middle of powder and rouge. "Big playwright-man," he said and laughed out loud so that clouds poured out through his mouth and nose. "Big talker. You think we need your help? You aren't anything. You aren't piss. But you wanted to sign. You would have signed..."

I called him a son of a bitch, turned and crunched off across the cold gravel, half expecting him to follow, half expecting to hear him still shouting and laughing in the yard for the whole town to hear. Neither of those things happened, but I am not sure that I knew the difference; his voice followed me anyway, or a voice much like it, telling me that I had been warned, that I was an idiot, that Jones of course could take care of herself. If I had shut up long enough to let her speak I would have known that; if I had thought at all I would have seen why Huss had bothered talking to me. And that lady who screamed. It hadn't been anything to do with the play. It was the make-up. Only that.

At the boarding house I was admitted by a pleasant man in his forties who asked if I thought my friends would be out much longer. I said that I didn't think so but couldn't be sure, and went past him into a twisty stairwell that carried the sound of my footsteps all up and down through the building. The walls were brown and white, the paint peeling in spots above a row of oak wainscoting. My room was second on the left at the top of the stairs; I walked past it, down to the middle of the hall. Jones's light was still on.

I made the knock as small and soft as I possibly could, hoping that it would pass unnoticed. Instead it was answered by the sound of papers being pushed around, a whisper, a sigh, and her bare feet coming across the floor. She opened the door and stood blinking as if I had wakened her, her hands resting on the frame. "Hey, Doc," she said, and when I did not reply, added "What's on your mind?"

I told her about the floor, guessed that Lon must be about finished by now, that he ought to be on his way any minute. We stood in the doorway looking at each other. Far away, down in the walls, someone was clumping up in the stairwell.

"You look sick," she said.

I said I was sorry about barging in on the dealings with Huss. I said it was her company and I should know better than to try and run it. I said I would go home if she wanted me to.

Jones stifled a yawn, then stood to one side, and motioned me in. Her room was no warmer than the hall had been, no brighter, no less dusty. There were white curtains hanging against the glass. I looked for signs of her, found only her grey suitcase pushed into a corner, and a mess of paper spread out across the bed. Jones pulled a chair from beside the wardrobe and settled into it. She crossed her arms on the seat back. "You don't seriously want to go," she said.

I thought: *Yes, damn it. Of course not.*

When I would not answer, Jones said, "What is the matter with you? You had three premieres tonight, all of which went well. You should be crowing. Like Peter Pan. You should be flying."

There was no other chair; I cleared a space at the foot of the bed and sat there on the covers. "I've never crowed in my life."

"Then it's time to start. I was glad watching you tonight. It was the most talk I've heard out of you since you joined the company. I've wondered what you were like, back in your old job; now I know. You tried to keep everyone happy, and it worked as far as it could. If that isn't a successful debut, what is?"

"Moscow is right. I don't fit in."

Jones smiled. "Moscow wears his evil spirits all on the surface. It doesn't have anything to do with you, unless you happen to be in his path when he's taking them out for a walk."

I thought, *he had 'em on a short leash tonight.*

Jones looked away. She sighed, stood up again and walked over to the door. "I want only one thing from you," she said with her hand on the knob. "I want you to stop being frightened all the time."

The door opened, and then closed again before I could even get up. "There," Jones said. "You've been heard leaving. Now tell me." She pulled the light chain, came and stood over me in the dark. Her hands found my face. There was only the faintest rustle of cloth as she lowered herself around me.

"Margaret Darwin," I said.

ATHLETES OF THE HEART

"**WHAT** do you have in mind?" Jones said. "I guess we could manage a fire dance. Maybe a blood sacrifice, if you volunteered." She laughed and shook her head at the dirt. " — Why not just look around?"

The flats were light but they were long and awkward, and carrying them out was a job for two people. We made quite a parade, two by two, lifting the scenes up to Lon in the back of the truck, then doubling back to take another from the top of the pile. "Around at what?" I said.

"This. What we're doing now. packing it all away."

We stood aside for Mary and Sylvie coming through. "But this — we do this all the time."

"You asked me about a ritual to end the season. What more do you need?"

By that time I had loaded the trucks often enough so that it should have been obvious to me.

The business was one big ritual; it was ritual after ritual, raising and striking; dressing, recital, abandonment; all the tricks and methods of mummery. "I don't know," I said. "But I can't believe you don't have something up your sleeve."

Jones bent to the stack and slipped her fingers under a corner of Athens. "Not a thing. Anyway, it would be too late. The new season started an hour ago. If I were you I'd be sure that my head was well-stocked..."

There was still some light in the sky when we drove up the tarred slope from behind that last whitefaced theater hall of the season. Lon stuck his nose out into the main road, looked left and then right; then the rear axle lurched over a hump and we were on our way. Behind us, Moscow pulled out and paused as if he was having second thoughts. A cloud of grey smoke burped out of his tailpipe. He came along after us, picking up speed. It was barely half a mile before the town fell away, leaving us in open countryside dotted with a few cattle farms set well back from the road. Lon had said it was just a short hop to Philadelphia, to *Valenciennes*, our winter home. I figured he'd done this leg a time or two before.

In the front seat Jones and Lon ignored the map resting half-crumpled, half-folded on the seat between them. They talked and gestured at the road ahead; then Jones reached her briefcase from its storage place under her feet, took out a legal folder thick as a dictionary and spread the topmost pages across her lap. She never smoked in the truck, but as she read and made notes the pen sometimes found its way to her mouth. Mary and I talked about books; she admired the children's stories of Carl Sandburg, and told me all about Virginia Woolf, who I'd never read at that time; until meeting up with the Transportation Company, I had imagined my father's and Mr. Deighton's libraries to be well-stocked. She said that it would be a good thing to get home, to see her books, air out her apartment, and to learn if a cat that she knew called Monsieur Boucaire still lived in the neighborhood. He would be sure to come by, she said, as soon as he knew she had come back. He would stay for the winter. He always did.

Ten minutes later Jones looked back over her shoulder. "Hope you haven't gotten used to writing everything out longhand," she said.

I said, "That would be another one of your rhetorical questions, right?"

She handed me back a smaller brown folder with the manuscript pages of *All Hallows Eve* piled stuffed dogeared inside. "Then you'll be glad to know you'll be typing again soon. Somewhere in a box at Valenciennes there's an Underwood. You just have to find it. Been a long time since it's seen any use, but I think it still works —?" She looked at Lon, who nodded as if he knew it for a fact, which he probably did. "O.K. Start with a clean copy of this. I've made some notes, but you're free to ignore them."

"Since we take the same liberty with you," Mary said, and gave my left arm a squeeze.

"Don't spend too much time on it," Jones said. "If you get stuck just push on. We'll all iron it out together. You're a professional now; you've got a deadline."

She had announced our winter schedule more than a week before, but I still hadn't had enough time to get over the shock. Mondays and Tuesdays (and every day until *All Hallows* was ready) would be given over to the repertory productions they knew best: Ibsen, some Moliere, the odd Greek tragedy to keep the local eyebrows raised. Wednesdays the theater would be dark. Thursday through Sunday, and twice on Saturday, the Jones Transportation Company would offer all new plays. We would begin with the pieces we had worked up over the summer, the weakest of these to be sacrificed at the earliest opportunity. I was to come up with a new script every thirty days: Jones allowed one week for me to work out a general outline, one week each to rough out the two acts, and a fourth to redraft the entire project. It would go into rehearsal on the sixteenth of each month, one day after the premiere of its predecessor. That gave me four more weeks of changes and polishing with the company while I worked on the bones of the next play. There would be no room for false starts: I must get it under way, and I must get it right.

It was a definite responsibility after a long, indefinite summer, but the promise of the Underwood helped. Mr. Deighton had used an Underwood; my fingers knew it by heart. With that machine, I imagined that I could be a human dynamo.

Jones as usual read my mind. "We'll all see that you don't run short on inspiration."

"D'you know," Mary said, "He should be riding in Blue with Moscow and Sylvie. They say great plays come out of anguish and misery."

"And sometimes out of juicy gossip. Lon can help you with that." She looked down at the papers in her lap. "Hmm?"

Lon said nothing but it seemed to me that he shrank several sizes behind the wheel.

"There's always something in the air," Jones said without looking up. "Keep your antennae out and you'll never be short of material."

Then she sat back with the landscape passing by across the windowglass, across her eyes. "Keep looking around," she said. I thought she meant for ideas; I thought she was telling me that there were plays inside every house that we passed. It made sense, but after a few minutes the houses all looked the same to me, and soon I turned down to the folder in my lap, only to find that it was too dark to read. "I want Mary to look that over," Jones said without turning back. "Then tomorrow we can   wait, this is it. Pull over."

Lon eased onto the shoulder. He shut off the engine, and in the growing dark Jones rolled down her window. Cool air came into the cab. "Some night," she said. "Everyone out under the stars."

I slid across the seat and dropped down beside Mary. A moment later Lon came around the front, carrying a battered tacklebox that I had never seen before. We stood out there with the night sky looking just like a black cloak that had not yet reached the western horizon, and I thought of the myth of Morpheus that they dramatized so often in *The Twilight of The Gods*. I thought of Lon unfolding the Night Scrim, running from one end of the stage to the other with a frayed old rope in his hand, only to hurry back to the lightboard so that he could turn on the stars, one by one. "There," Jones said, pointing down across a shadowy field that slanted away from the road. Water glimmered down there beyond a row of trees: it might have been a pond or it might have been a river. I couldn't be sure.

Moscow pulled up behind us and sat there behind the wheel, unmoving with Blue's bumper almost touching Red's, his headlights on and the engine still running, until the passenger side door opened up and Sylvie stepped onto the running board. She came scuffling through the dust, into the lights, wearing a black skirt and her black band jacket with gold epaulets at the shoulders and braid around the wrists. She shielded her eyes. "Moscow says he wants to go on," she said.

"Now there's a surprise," Jones said. She set off towards the water, calling back over her shoulder. "Tell him we'll make it quick. A race, then. To the river and back. Fastest one loses."

Sylvie gave me a shove and ran laughing after her down the slope. By then the Templetons had joined us along the roadside; faced with that, Moscow at last cut the motor, but we never heard him get out.

"— You did have something planned after all," I said to Jones when we caught her up. "A ritual to end the season."

She only walked on ahead with her face turned down, cutting at the grass with a switch she'd picked up along the way. "You can call it anything you want. Just get down there and get soaked."

At the bottom of the field Sylvie disappeared into a black cluster of leaves. There was a lot of rustling and kicking about, then a white shape slanted downward from the bank. Water splashed; between the trees her head broke the surface and she shrieked at the cold. Above us the trucks waited dark and silent. Still no sign of Moscow. We fanned out along the riverside, the Templetons standing back against the slope, Lon off downstream cutting himself a pole. Jones and Mary and I went on until water squished in our shoes. We entered the brush at about the same time; I stripped off my shirt, shoes, trousers, socks, and went in like that. It was cold all right, and perfectly clear: reaching down to touch the bottom, I could open my eyes and see their distant bodies white as paper against a spillage of ink.

At the top of the hill Moscow was waiting with a wicker trunk full of linen. He threw me a towel that I caught with my face, then leaned back again and set his shoulders against the truck. He crossed his arms and kept his eyes turned down towards the water. I didn't speak to him. Still dripping, I reached *All Hallows Eve* from the back seat, and by flashlight looked at the notes she had written on the first page:

> *Funeral home and lycanthropy sequences are*
> *the most*
> *effective — Close the acts with these?*
>
> *Un Autre Monde*
>
> *1) Dream*
> *2) History*
> *3) Aspiration*
> *4) Story*
>
> *Tantalus?*
> *) a harlequin of the Devil*
>
> *Artaud: we are athletes of the heart   we*
> *make use of our emotions the way a wrestler*
> *makes use of his muscles — DON'T SHY*
> *AWAY from the darker implications of these*

stories. I trust your choice of subject and your
feeling for the characters   Try to play with
the form a bit: multiple endings, audience
involvement, music, etc...
& don't be so straightfaced and serious!!

I sat on the running board reading this, my trousers soaking wet, the towel draped over my head. I knew what most of it meant, but the way she had used it confused me. What parts of it, I wondered, should I feel free to ignore? Was it only the play that was too straightfaced and serious, or did she mean me? Could the two be separated?

"Use our emotions," I said aloud, forgetting (or perhaps not?) that I wasn't alone. "She's sure giving mine a workout."

Moscow looked at me and said nothing. Below the rim of the hill, their voices started to grow. They were coming back.

Good

Callie:

You never came around here while she was alive. Now that she's gone, you're over here every day, wanting to take things out of the house...

~~& things you nee~~

Brom:

You should talk to the ~~Baileys~~ Carvells down the road a piece. I bet they might have an interest in buying this old ~~place~~ dump. Their sister's niece...

Callie:

~~I'm not sure. Here starts this ~~ again =~~

You did nothing but take and steal from her while she suffered. You did nothing but make things worse. Now before I can even ~~make~~ sense of what's happened, you want to ——

What we (to Brom) ~~about~~ need is ~~I could not~~ grisly here ~~I could do it for you~~?

That ~~would~~ maybe Brom: yes be good. ~~All~~ poetry ~~Af I~~ ~~recall~~ you have a ~~way~~ with those ~~old fashioned~~

Always cackled

Neither ~~of you~~ are listening to me! This ~~with~~ what I ~~want~~ is I'm the only one who made any effort at all to care for her, I think ——

JONES TRANSPORTATION COMPANY

MATINEE

ADMIT ONE

14 W. Seventh Street
New York, New York
12 October 1958

Mr. George Spelvin
St. John Publishing Company
545 Fifth Avenue
New York 17, New York

Dear George;

...

If I hadn't been fortunate later on in life, 1939 would have been the beginning and the end of me, the all there was, something that I thought about on sleepless nights or dreamed about wistfully on bad days at the office. No one would remember these early pieces (and there wouldn't have been any later ones); I would not have been given the opportunity to revisit them and substantially modify their contents over the years, and you would not be collecting them between two covers (I wonder what Margaret would think about that; I wonder if she knows). Every time they were performed, I was able to cut some bits of naiveté here, lob off embarrassingly large chunks of stupidity there and replace them with more sensible material. Always, you understand, in the interest of making the piece more like itself. I could have completely remade them, and sometimes wanted to. But always, in the end, I decided that I couldn't remake the person that I was in those days, and so the work should stay basically faithful to what that dunderhead, that lovesick dolt had produced, whether or not I agreed with it anymore fifteen or twenty years on.

Likewise, there was substance in those shows that was tailored to Margaret and her "Gang of Six," content only they could have performed... and so these things were reworked so that other companies could put their own stamp, their own personality on them. The pieces became more generalized, or more universal, depending on how you look at it. I am afraid that Margaret would feel that I watered them down. I know that isn't the case. And yet, after all these years, I still worry about what she would think...

Still, if it hadn't been for this one year, this one thing, this one person, then I would never have dreamed at all. I would never have come alive. That neutron bomb would never have gone off in the back of my brain. That fire would never have been lit in my poor stupid naive heart. I don't know what life would have been like if the Transportation Company had not visited St, Paul, although I had a taste of it later on. How I survived that I don't know.

That Big Love that I craved so desperately, the all-conquering Affair that would Rattle the Bones of the Universe — I'm not ruining anything by telling you up front that it never happened. But she did love me. In the end she did. And not, not the same way that she loved everyone else in the company. Not that way. Not like that.

Valenciennes was not the name above the little theater's marquee of course; I think that was something quite ordinary like The Philadelphia. It was not located in the best part of town. When the Transportation Company was out touring it was dark. So for me, arriving there for the first time was a bit like walking into someone else's attic...

ACT THREE: THE BLACK FLAME

(SEPTEMBER 1939 — MAY 1940)

"I am thin and wasted by this consuming passion, my reason is gone, and I feed myself on dreams."
—David Garnett,
"Lady Into Fox"

ENTR'ACTE: WHISPERS
CONCLUDED

"**THANK** you for the flowers," Constance said, leading me through the grey catspace inside the walls. "They're very pretty. Did you pick them yourself?"

"Yes ma'am," I said. "They're called moonflowers. They bloom at night, just like you."

At that she halted, and looked around with a smile clear as a lighthouse beacon spreading over her face. "Wow. You're going to be quite the tomcat when you grow up."

I followed in the kerosene stench of the lamplight, while outside the wind came up hard against the House of Marvels, chilling the whole passage. "Are you sure you want to do this?" Constance said. "You don't have to, you know, just because he wants that old exhibit to work."

But I was wound up pretty well, and would not be turned back. At the inside door to the Egyptian Room, Constance took her tiara and the blue robe that she wore over her regular costume down from a hook on the wall. Even then she did not look like Isis to me; only a woman who had worked hard all day, and knew that she had still more ahead of her. "Come on," she said.

There was smoke in the air left over from the

147

first showing. We stepped around a barrier of heavy drapes, and there was the contraption standing just three feet from the wall, its two slanted wings of star-patterned cloth forming a close V around the straight-backed operator's chair. The professor had done some work since the last time I'd seen it; the chair legs had been bolted to the floor, and a leather belt nailed to the underside of the seat. A backing board covered what remained of the original machinery; the head and mouth controls were set into this very much like the controls of an automobile. And there was something new: a megaphone mounted on a swivel set right into the arm of the chair.

Without wasting any time, Constance belted me in and turned up the megaphone so that its rim brushed against my lips. "Is that all right?" she said, and when I nodded she squeezed my hand and started off around the room, lighting the braziers from a book of paper matches.

I tried the controls one last time. The right eye squeaked awfully when I worked the trigger, so much that I was sure everyone would hear it. But it was too late to fix, even if I had known how. "Just stay calm and follow the script," Constance said. "Just whisper. It'll be over before you know it."

She went softly to the main door and pulled back the bolt, then hurried to take her place behind the velvet rope. I heard her give a faint sigh. Outside in the corridor, the new group came shuffling along, led on by the professor, his voice raised in signal to us. We waited and held our breath, listening; then the doorknob turned.

"Friends," the professor said, "beyond this door is the most dangerous room in the house. Here in exact detail is a reconstruction of the Tomb of Osiris, including the mortal remains of Osiris himself, as well as many interesting and mystifying relics dug from beneath the belly of the Great Sphinx. Folks, there's ancient magic in this room, magic more powerful than anything — "

"Aw, quit speechifyin'," a man said from outside. "Are you gonna let us in or not?"

The professor drew himself up very tall. I could almost hear him do it. "Well," he said. "You've been *warned*."

How many were there? I could not tell: belted as I was behind the casing I could see only faint shapes through the cloth "wings" of the machine. They came in one by one, gathering in the little space at the center of the room, and when Constance stepped forward with a burning brazier cupped in her hands they greeted her with catcalls and nervous laughter. The professor turned it into a joke. He said, "Mister, if I were you I would not make the Goddess of Life angry with me," and some of the people still laughed, except this time it was turned on one of their own.

He walked them along the velvet rope, starting at the north end of the room and working his way around. It was the standard show, the same things I had seen and listened to half a dozen times before, a mishmash of truth and lies that sounded like truth, all done up in a calculatedly grotesque package. It went all right; no one believed a word of it, but they hadn't come to find belief; only cheap thrills, and the Professor was doing his best.

I was the last. He drew them all up in a tight little group, then stepped over the rope and gestured at me with his hands. "Now folks, here we have the most *in*-triguing piece in the room, perhaps in the *en*-tire Museum. It is the actual, the living head of an *E*-gyptian Sphinx. I say living my friends because although this head has been *severed from its body*, as everyone knows Mythical Creatures cannot be killed by the hand of mortal man. They have a life my friends that extends *beyond the boundaries* of reality as we know it, just as a fish line extends down, down into the invisible depths of a pool of black water. No, friends, this head, this *thinking and feeling creature* of the far-flung desert sands, is only laying dormant. Trapped in the metamorphosis of sleep, it breathes with distant life even now, dreaming *metaphoric visions* of the far-flung future, of other worlds that you and I can only imagine. And yes my friends on certain nights, under the proper alignment of stars, planets, mystical influences *and* celestial forces, this creature, this *marvelous freak of nature* and the gods, raises itself ever so slightly from its eternal slumber and whispers.

"Yes, it *whispers*, ladies and gentlemen. I have heard it with my own ears. It whispers in a voice from outside of time itself. It whispers from the other side, from the land of dreams. It whispers of what it has *seen* in those spectral worlds just around that invisible corner that we can never cross but once. It whispers the *secrets* of life, and it whispers them to *us*, the mortal men and women who wait here, humble petitioners violating its slumber and its tomb."

The customers fidgeted and coughed nervously at my feet. "Perhaps," said the professor, "perhaps, if we are all lucky, *tonight...*"

A woman said: "It never does. I've been here twice before, and the planets are never aligned."

That was when I moved my fingers, just lightly, and the machine's right eye gave out a faint, painful squeak. I expected someone to shout out: "Look, it's moving!" I expected someone to call it a fake. But nobody made a sound. I brushed the footpedal ever so gently, once and then again. At the second touch, I whispered into the megaphone:

eye-ssisss

"Who is that?" said the man who had wanted to get into the room so badly. There were scuffling sounds, shushing and cursing, and above it the professor trying to get some order. It didn't come, not until Constance knelt at the base of the machine, and said: "Yes?"

I clenched my eyes shut and maneuvered the controls with hands and feet. *Eye-SSISSS, I said into the megaphone. Who embraces the spurned… whose gaze enchants and poisons… Beloved of Oh-sire-isss… none other may have her… none other may taste her… Eye-ssisss…*

Much of this was not in the script. I did not know where it came from, only that I hadn't planned to say it. *He's cursing me,* I thought when the professor did not respond. But it was only acting; that, and trying to hold them back.

"Folks, this is… this is a rare moment. If anyone has—"

"Should I buy stock?" someone said. They whispered and pressed against the velvet rope. "How is my daughter?"

Too late; the Head coughed dust, drifted away back into sleep. I breathed out through the megaphone, released the controls, and said nothing more.

By the time I came around from behind the machine, Constance had her weight against the door as if the whole crowd were pushing from the other side. "Isis!" I said. She slid the bolt home, shaking with laughter. "That was great!" she said, and scooped me up into her arms…

Downstairs in the professor's office, it was like someone had lit a bonfire under the floor. "Son, I never doubted you," the professor said. He clapped his hands, scrubbed them in the air, and danced around in place. "Where'd you get that jealous god stuff, kid? Was that hot! You have the gift, I'll tell you that. Just wait 'til the word gets out, we'll be swamped here every night. Swamped. Here. Here." He turned his pockets inside out; when he lifted his hands they were empty, until the fingers came together and unfolded something crisp and green out of the air.

"Wow!" I said. "A dollar! A whole dollar?"

… and I snatched it crackling out of his fingers. Constance clapped and laughed and patted me on the back. "You earned it," she said. "Didn't he earn it, and more?"

But the professor had already forgotten me. "That's not all," he said. His eyes were like green glass under the skewed, battered old top hat. "Connie, you and I are going to celebrate. I'm going to take you out on the town; we're going to have a big fancy dinner and drink lots of wine, then maybe we'll drive down to the river. I'll take you out boating on the river! How 'bout it?'"

Constance stood half in the secret doorway and didn't answer, except to turn her eyes away. How sure he had been, how flushed with success; now it all dropped away from him, leaving the strangest expression, as if he was trying to swallow his lips. "Not the River Styx," he said to me, trying to make a joke of it, lowering himself until his eyes were level with mine and the tail of his coat settled in a black puddle on the floor behind him. He gave me a weak smile. "You go on home and get a good night's sleep. Dream metaphoric visions. I want you wide awake here tomorrow night."

He squeezed my shoulder, and I balled the dollar bill all up into a wad in the center of my hand. I said goodnight to them both, passed between them, turned back at the door, waved.

"Okay," Constance said. She rubbed her nose and refused to meet his eyes. "Just let me get out of this thing. Okay."

The next day we got rain from the edge of a big storm that had only just missed us. I came to the House of Marvels all bundled up in a mackintosh, boots, and my father's rainhat with the big brim almost as wide as my shoulders, looking like a pint-sized railroad man who had lost his way. There was no one about. I stood dripping, looking around, then went clumping down to the cashier's booth, folded my things all up into a slippery bunch and left them in a corner. The professor wasn't up yet; there was nothing unusual about that. I went into his office and made myself comfortable with an old book of his that I'd started the week before, all about an Illusion Device called the Dircksian Phantasmagoria. Learning the secrets did not spoil them, I found; the machinery was so baroque, the writing so elaborate and unfamiliar, that they carried a magic all their own, the magic of history, of lost wonders brought to light again.

I read and waited for what seemed like hours, thinking again about the voice, the true voice of the Sleeping Sphinx, encased in its brittle cylinder of wax. Rain pelted the house off and on; I felt quite alone, and perfectly content. By three thirty the professor had still not come down. I climbed up onto the desk, reached for the bronze handle that had been screwed into the ceiling. By hanging on tight and lifting my feet completely off the desktop I could just budge his hidden stairway.

Up there in a sea of clutter, of cages, bear traps, stacks of worn-out hats and shoe boxes, the professor lived at one end of the floor, close by the only window in the old house that was not shuttered or covered over. Rainwater leaked through the roof in two places, ran in a broad stream down the walls. I found him on a cot in the corner, stretched out in his undershirt, suspenders and slacks.

Seeing him like that, asleep with his mouth open, a blindfold covering his eyes and his inkcolored hair all mussed, I realized that he was still a young man. Not my father's age, certainly, though older than my schoolteacher. He couldn't have been much more than thirty five, though in costume, with his old-fashioned tie and his eyebrows that premature grey, he looked sixty.

"Perfessor," I said. "Perfessor?"

"What time is it?" he said without even stirring.

"Quarter to four. Say perfessor, you know what we forgot? We forgot the Sphinx's real voice. We forgot to listen."

Professor Vitae sat up on the edge of the cot with his face in his hands. He didn't say a word.

"Um, how did your date go? With Constance."

He pushed the blindfold back up onto his forehead; when I saw the way his red eyes looked at me I was sorry to have asked. "The voice," he said, sticking his feet into a pair of paintspattered shoes. "The Sleeping Sphinx. All right."

For a night and a day, ever since he had lifted it from the body of the Sphinx Machine, the cylinder had been resting in a side drawer of his desk, wrapped in a thick bed of tissue paper. Now he snatched it out with so little care that I asked if I could carry it myself. We went down through the building to the Room of Technological Wonders, past the Astrology Room and the Room of Teratology. There in back, in a corner that never got much attention either from the customers or from the professor himself, was the oldest, most dilapidated recording machine I had ever seen. As I watched, the professor blew away a coating of dust, turned the crank on the end; he lifted the cylinder out of my fingers and fitted it into the machine.

"Ready?" he said.

He lowered the needle so gently that I was sure nothing would go wrong. But perhaps there was a flaw in the wax that neither of us had seen. Rasping noises at once poured out of the horn, masking another, stranger sound that came leaking through as from an impossible distance of time: the sound of breathing; then the cylinder cracked and snapped in two. It fell out of the machine, shattering twice more before it even hit the floor, leaving the needle to drag across empty air...

The professor stood frowning a moment watching the machine still turning inside. He lifted the horn back over the top. "Well that's that," he said, and walked out.

*

That night I sat buckled into the Sleeping Sphinx, bumping my heels on the chair legs while Constance lit the incense, rushing from corner to corner until the room was marked off in strands of smoke. Her manner had not changed, not to me, but the professor had hardly talked to her except to say hello and ask if she was ready. It wasn't that there was any anger in him; but he acted as if it hurt something awful just to look at her.

I watched and listened to her tell about restaurant work until I couldn't hold it in any longer. Then I got the idea to make the Sphinx say it for me. It opened Its eyes, fixed her with a curious stare. *I guess maybe the professor loves you,* It said.

Constance shook out what remained of the match. She came over and stood just in front of the stand, where I couldn't see her. But I knew she was looking It in the eye. "I guess maybe," she said. "But I don't love him."

The Sleeping Sphinx blinked at her. *Why not?*

I heard a low sigh on the other side of the screen. "He's been very nice to me. But for heaven's sake, look at the life he leads. Look at the things he saves! All monsters and freaks and things. What does that say about the kind of man he is?"

Well, I'm not a freak, It said. *I like it here.*

Down in the corridor, the professor barked out his warning speech ahead of the group coming our way. "No, you're cute," Constance said. "Are you all set? Think you can give them a good show?"

Big deep voice. *Oh-Kay.* Then: *Um, Isis?*

"Mm-hmm?" She slid back the bolt, hurried to take up her pose as Host of the Room.

I love you, too.

"That's nice. Shh, quiet now!"

They sounded like a pack of elephants coming up from the first floor. They sounded like more people than the room would hold. And there was one thing that they wanted to see; one thing only. As soon as they came in I could feel them rushing the velvet rope, while down at the other end of the room the professor tried in vain to interest them in the other things Egypt had to offer. "Here we have Anubis," he said, "the dog-headed god. Ehm, and here an alter stained with the blood of a thousand sacrifices." But the word had gotten around fast: give us the Head, they said. Go on. Let's see this thing work.

"That's plaster," one man said. "You can't tell me that thing's for real."

... and the professor, showing off his vial of Nile river water, finally gave in. "You're all wondering about that Head," he said to their backs. "You've heard that we had a remarkable experience here last night. Well, folks I can't promise you that history will repeat itself. That thing never stirred in more than a hundred years, and it will probably be another hundred before it stirs again. Come on, folks, and take a look at some of these other exhibi— "

At the sound of his voice, the Sphinx fluttered Its eyes. *Ohhhh, broken man,* It said now. *Listen, listen...*

"Again," the professor whispered. He pushed through the rubes, turning up the volume with each word as if he could not believe it himself. "It's happening again... *The Sleeping Sphinx is stirring again!* Blanketed not in death but in mystic hibernation. Come on folks, press close, press close but be warned: others have come here, and have been struck senseless by the sound of the sphinx's voice. Does anyone have a question that they would like the severed head of the Sleeping Sphinx to answer?"

"Is my husband true?" cried a lady in the middle of the group. "Should we buy that house?" said another. "Where will I get that money I need?" "Leo says I must move to the city. Is he right?" "Will there be a strike?"

"One at a time, folks," shouted the professor. "One at a time."

Then a man came up out of the crowd and put one leg over the rope. I can't say that I recognized his step, but I had a bad feeling about it. I didn't know him until he spoke.

"I have a question," the man said. "Where's my boy when he should be at home in bed?"

Scuffling sounds reached me; the professor tried to push him back, and failed. The eyes of the Sleeping Sphinx popped wide open, then drooped again as I dropped the controls. "I thought so," my father said. He came on and this time the fighting sounded mean; at the end of it the professor tore backwards through the right "wing" of the machine, sprawling in the dust with his legs in the air. Through the canvas tear I could see Constance frozen in place, and a few slack-jawed customers looking in at me. My father came up with his hands raised, took hold of the machine by its molding and started to kick and pull and curse.

"Go on, boy," the professor hissed. He ripped the megaphone away, but could not help me with the belt.

I wasn't fast enough. My father overturned the Sphinx machine, crashing it head and glass casing and all at the feet of those customers who hadn't already run away. I covered my face. His hands clamped down on my shoulders, hands that weren't used to this kind of nonsense, this crazy brawling. He was so balled up that he couldn't understand why I wasn't coming out of the chair; the belt held me fast. At last he stepped back and stood puffing above the wreckage of the machine. "I'll be waiting for you outside," he said. Then he turned his back on me, and picked his way to the door.

The Egyptian Room looked like it had ben raided. Constance had withdrawn and stood rigid with her back up against a papier-mâché sarcophagus. The professor floundered in the rubble, massaging his head. A few gawkers remained behind. When they saw that nothing more spectacular was waiting to happen, they shuffled out, one by one, until the only other person left in the room with us was a tall, broad man in a checkered coat and a bowler hat. He stood in the doorway with the hall light behind him, studying the wreckage, saying nothing. A rim of wetcombed hair bordered the top of his face. He looked very uncomfortable.

The professor stood up, slapped at his trousers. Half of his moustache was missing; the other half hung sideways across his right cheek. He glared at the broad man and said, "What do *you* want?"

The big man's only answer was to look at Constance. He put a fist to his mouth and coughed. "It's all right," Constance said. "I'll be right down."

"Who was that?" the professor said when the big man had gone off down the hall. His face was quite calm. He went on brushing aimlessly at his clothes.

"My ride," Constance said softly. "Just a friend."

The professor wouldn't look at anyone. His hands stopped moving. He sniffed at the air. Constance said nothing more. Still shivering, she turned and walked out.

"Protection," the professor said, following into the length of the dark corridor. "You think you need protection from me?"

"Please," I said. "I'm sorry... Perfessor? Please," but I didn't know what I wanted and now my face was all wet and I chased after them with my hands over my ears and my voice like a little siren inside the bones of the house.

"No" Constance said. Behind the cashier's booth she took down her overcoat and I saw her turn at the edge of the light. "He's just a friend. We're going — him and the boys and I — we're having dinner."

"Perfessor," I said. "I'm suh. I'm sor." But he gave me a sharp push, and I sat down hard against the grey wall.

"Well get out then," he said. He followed her through a clothcovered arch and then out into the dripping yard. A maroon sedan was waiting for her there with its lights on. She went straight out, kicking up flecks of mud with her heels. The car opened itself and she climbed in. "Don't come back," the professor shouted. He stood hatless in the door and watched the headlights rake across the house and down onto the city road, and I sat against the wall and wept.

"You too," he said at last. "Your pappy's waiting. Go home. Get out of here." But by then I was safe inside the wall passage, running up through the house, and his voice came to me from far away. Scrabble and claw, feeling my way in the dark, I climbed to the Egypt Room, halting now and then hand to mouth holding back my breath so I could hear if anyone followed. Inside the Room braziers burned on untended, choking the air. I closed and bolted the door, turned out the lights by the switch. Darkness came down like a curtain from ceiling to floor. I took hold of the velvet rope, following it from post to post; gradually the ebon shapes of the displays rose up and took form around me. I knew them so well: here the low case with the phony bones inside, here the jade ornaments that were only painted celluloid, here on the stand a magnificent sunburst mask that the professor had made himself out of glue and newspaper and gold paint. I stood with my arms outstretched and my fingers spread and the hokum all around me. My face was all itchy where the tears were drying. It's not wrong to want something, I thought. It's not wrong to want something to be real.

Then I heard a soft sound in the dark, a soft mechanical sound like a whisper of steel, a soft whirring close, close at hand, rising from the invisible floor. It did not frighten me, but I knew that I had to see: and so I ran again and put on the lights and came back to stand nearly a yard away, looking down. The head of the Sleeping Sphinx was lying sideways in a puddle of shattered glass, its eyes wide open as in surprise. At its right was the painted case on which it had rested for so long, broken in three places so that I had a clear view of its mechanical guts. Inside, rusty wheels clattered and turned in perfect unison. A metal arm reached the end of its path, raised itself in a graceful arc, lowered again. The needle came down scraping against an empty spindle. The mouth of the Sphinx was open. It said:

ratch...

    ratch...

        ratch...

            ratch...

                ratch...

A SENSE OF HISTORY

Moscow in the truck ahead took a wide cut into oncoming traffic and disappeared between a mismatched pair of buildings. Lon cursed him under his breath. Instead of following he turned into the curb, coasting along for several yards before the truck coughed, shuddered and came to rest in front of a long, low marquee. Facing the street, square in the afternoon sun, it said in black letters:

VALENCIENNES — CLO ED

above a plain grey front broken by two glass-and-wood doors set back a few feet from the sidewalk. They were flanked by a pair of display panels filled with sepia-colored photos. The glass was cracked in two places; it had been taped over at some point, but the tape itself had yellowed and flaked, and hung peeling like dead skin from the dirty panes.

The four of us climbed down to the sidewalk

looking every bit as weary and rumpled as the truck, which stood making little disgusted sounds at us, overheated sighs and clicks, for having pushed it so hard. Mary came toting her case around from the other side and disappeared into the minimal shade under the marquee; she stood with her back pressed against brick, puffing her cheeks as if to blow something away. Lon followed, searching through his ring of keys. It was Jones who caught me looking at the faces in the display glass.

They were people that I'd never seen before, as strange and almost as stiffly antique as Mrs. Templeton and her mentors had been in the photographs she'd shown me: a dignified gentleman with a face shaped like a shoebox and heavy-lidded carbon gray eyes, wearing a harsh paper collar, top hat, and monocle; a bosomy, bejeweled woman whose mascara had run spiderlegs down her cheeks; a feral creature clothed all in dirty leaves, rivulets of black hair framing a dark pointed face with enormous dark eyes; and a dozen more of all types, though some of them must have been the same actors pictured in wildly different parts.

"Who are they?" I said when I noticed her face reflected in the glass beside my own.

"Gargoyles," Jones said. "Set out to watch over the place." She named them to me, raising her hand to each. "Cameron Watson MacTeagle. Evelyn King. Frances Garnett. Nelson Omaha. Sissy Hartley... she was almost as bad as Sylvie."

Lon coughed beside the door. "MacTeagle again," Jones said, pointing out a donkey-headed man, "as Bottom. That was his finest moment; I've never seen anyone to equal him in the part. But Mac was a mule I couldn't control."

Lon went ahead and unlocked the doors, pushing them as far back as he could against the chain looped through their handles, half an inch of black space with nothing but silence, pent-up air and a sense of disuse beyond. He coughed again; Jones said "All right, I've got it," and bent to open the padlock with an iron key that she fished out of her dungarees. A wave of heat spilled out across the threshold. "There you are," Jones said, motioning into the gloom...

I stepped into a dusky room draped in sheets of faded midnight colors, billowing half-moon shapes that hung overhead like the inside of a gypsy tent. Tassels dangled at the ends of brown cord, swaying gently now as the stale air was pressed back from the street. A canvas broadside faced the doorway, large enough that it had the effect of a picture window, although the view painted onto it was anything but natural, the Queen of Fairies cradling Bottom in her lap, stroking his long ears under a starry sky. Other, smaller pieces like it layered the walls of the tiny room: now in a slash of sunlight, now in cobwebbed shadow, I saw a circusful of powerfully exotic figures, magicians and monster men, hags and air spirits, amazons and ogres, automatons, gods, cat-women, and even a wolf baring his fangs. They peered and posed out of the steaming dusk, stirring against fresh new air. I wasn't sure whether they were welcoming me or daring me to step inside.

It didn't dawn on me that they were Mary's work until I saw her pause in the center of the lobby and turn to each as if greeting old friends. There was very little echo for such a still place; she stepped forward with hardly a sound, drew an old handkerchief out of her sleeve, and began to brush dust from the faces. Watching her, I caught Jones watching me, standing with the light at her back, making no effort whatever to hide her amusement.

Beyond the inner archway, which was just large enough to admit a couple if they were on quite intimate terms, I could not help but compare Jones's *Valenciennes* with Mr. D.'s *Regent* back home in Saint Paul. At a quick guess, I calculated that the house in front of me would hold, at most, about ninety people. It was so small that a center aisle would have robbed the place of its best seats, and so the rows were all grouped in the middle of the house, bordered by two uncarpeted pathways (they certainly were not wide enough to be called aisles) sloping very gradually down to the foot of a little stage not more than fifteen feet wide. Its bare, blue-painted walls were shot through with cracks. One of the ceiling panels had a hole in it big enough to accommodate Lon's head. Dust was everywhere; Lon had already gone halfway down the aisle, peeling filthy drop-cloths back from the seats, and sneezing at what they kicked into the air.

Jones and I were starting down after him when a murmur and a shuffling climbed out of the empty space behind the stage. It was Moscow, Sylvie and the Templetons coming through from the back with relieved expressions on their faces and a suitcase or two that they carried like props.

"Here," Templeton said to me from the apron. "What do you think of our ancestral home?"

I did not want to answer. The size of the stage alone appalled me. I had watched the Transportation Company fill some large canvases. This was a postage stamp; and one that had been postmarked and re-used again and again at that. I said, "Not what I expected..."

"What did you expect?" Jones said. She reached out and gave one of the drop-cloths a good hard whack, and then to a great burst of laughter from the stage pressed her palm roughly into my face, leaving a handprint of filth that I could feel like itching powder from my forehead down to my chin. "This is every playhouse that's ever been!" she said. "This is The Dionysus and The Globe, The Vaudeville and The Théâtre des Arts! This is every dirt arena, every amphitheater, town square, and courtyard that's ever hosted a mummer's ball. Here. Here, try it on."

Jones stepped into the nearest exposed row, drawing me by the arm after her. We flopped into the center seats. They were made of wicker and wood and the only comfortable thing about them was that the backs weren't absolutely straight. She got out her silver-capped pen and held it between her fingers, covering the bottom of her face. "All the builders of the theater, Vitruvius, Serlio…"

"I'll take your word for it," I said.

"They all, their efforts all come together right here. Look down there."

Two rows ahead, Lon folded a drop-cloth into a neat square, squinted at us, sniffed, and turned away. He went on down the aisle, lifting sheets from the chairs below. "I think he wants some help," I said.

"Don't you see it?"

I looked again. Moscow and the Templetons had disappeared into the back. They'd left their suitcases parked in a corner by the proscenium. "Nnnn-no, I don't see anything. Except—"

"Not the baggage. Look... there."

"What?"

"That shade. A whirl of silk. That's the spectre of Miss Bernhardt down there. Doomed to spend an eternity learning how to act. Listen."

"What's she saying?"

Jones drew a precise line on the air with her pen, tracing the movement of her ghost actress along the little stage. "She's reciting from *Hero and Leander*. 'When bees make wax, Nature doth not intend it should be made a torch. But we know the proper virtue of it, make it so, and when 'tis made we light it.' "

She recited the last three words with particular relish, wrinkling her nose. I whispered, "You've got good ears."

"Shh. You're not paying attention." She reached across and with her left hand covered my eyes. "What do you hear?"

The rustle of heavy cloth; soft, muffled footsteps all around; a wind from somewhere. Moscow and Templeton muttering to each other.

"What are ghosts," Jones said, "but memories of passion? And what does an actor do but evoke the passions? Think of all the spirits that must be at work here. All those nameless actors who've played out The Great Comedy of Life…"

Her hand fell away from my eyes. Lon had gone off somewhere; we were alone in the house. " 'Now, Dido,' " she was saying. Her voice was low and had taken on the mesmeric tone that she used when playing witches. " 'With these relics burn thyself, and make Aeneas famous through the world for perjury and slaughter of a queen. And from mine ashes let a conqueror rise, that may revenge this treason to a queen by ploughing up his countries with the sword!' "

Nothing in the little playhouse had changed; but Jones was so intent on the stage that I couldn't help but listen and try to see.

She pointed again, and looked sideways at me quite seriously. "Don't blink," she said.

Don't blink.

Don't blink.

Don't blink.

When my eyes had begun to water and the edges of my vision had blurred so that the corners of the little playhouse ran together and there was only the center stage, a circle of painfully burning light, she gave a low growl into my ear.

" 'I have told thee often,' " she said, " 'and I re-tell thee again and again, I hate the Moor. My cause is hearted; thine hath no less reason. Let us be conjunctive in our revenge against him.' "

"Can I blink now?" I said.

She hit me hard on the shoulder and then her face touched mine. Her hair and her breath grazed my cheek. She was laughing silently. But when I tried to look at her the hand holding the silver-capped pen came between us. She pointed again to the stage.

" 'Sweet Helen, *make me Immortal with a kiss*—' " she said. "Now. There. Look: 'Her lips suck forth my soul: see, where it flies! — Come, Helen, come, give me my soul again.' "

"Who was that?" I said. "You never said it like that…"

"Shh. Don't blink. Listen, he's playing: 'When thou cam'st first, thou strok'st me and made much of me, woulds't give me water with berries in it, and teach me how to name the bigger light, and how the less, that burn by day and night; and then I loved thee and showed thee all the qualities o' th' isle, the fresh springs, brine pits, barren place and fertile.' "

"Caliban!" I hissed, proud of myself for having recognized this one single line of dialogue. "But you'd make a better Prospero."

" 'Curs'd be that I did so! All the charms of Sycorax, toads, beetles, bats light on you! For I am all the subjects that you have, which first was mine own king; and here you sty me in this hard rock, whiles you keep from me the rest of the island.' "

It was my turn to laugh. "You don't even *need* a stage," I said.

If anything, she managed to press herself closer to me. One of her hands curled around my left knee, but when I tried to cover it with my own I found myself strangely crippled. My left hand hovered in the air, out in front of me, like a dead thing. She whispered, " 'Have I any other joy in this world but smoothing the way for you, my dear boy? You who've had neither father nor mother to turn to. And now, we've reached our goal, my dear!' "

I felt the dusty imprint of her hand again on my face. Not more than five rows away, the stage held itself in silence and murk. Its words came through her out of a far-distant past. She withdrew from me and it was just as if she had vanished into thin air, although I could still feel the weight of her eyes, of her attention.

" 'Then for you   your heart, your mind, your soul —it's the Sphinx or nothing.' "

Silence fell in the little theater. I was just about to turn and meet what I knew would be an intolerably smug, self-satisfied expression when what sounded like a shock of gunfire exploded from the stage.

It was Lon standing just downstage right, clapping. "Brave-oh," he said, completely deadpan, but his clapping grew a little more enthusiastic and began to echo and re-echo around the hall until I saw an opportunity and joined in.

The two of us clapping sounded like fifteen. Jones sat twisted sideways in her chair with her back against the armrest. She closed her eyes, nodded and scooped the air with her hands, indicating *More, More…*

"Point taken," I said. "I think."

"Brave-oh," Lon said again from the stage, and then I was clapping alone. He turned away into the wings with a show of disgust. "Now will you two stop pissing around and give us a hand?"

"He was maligning my theater!" Jones called after him. She climbed out of the seat, shoved her hands into her pockets, turned and caught me there still in the attitude of ovation.

"How will Sylvie be able to turn around on that stage without knocking something over?" I said.

"Wipe your face," she said, putting on her best cat-smile.

ROUSTABOUT

"**PUD** should have been packed and gone three weeks ago," Lon said. "But you never know." We went on along a row of lampposts and in the circles of light I could see the keyring turning 'round and over in his hands. He separated out a single nickel-plated key, then let it fall and searched through the ring again. "She leaves it a lot neater than I do. And uses more of it. Some rooms I never go into. Don't need the space, and anyway I always feel like they aren't mine to use. Funny how territory can get marked out, even when you hardly live in a place."

We passed an all-night movie house with all the bulbs burning in the marquee and the lobby lights brightening half the block. Lon waved at a redhead behind the ticketglass and she grinned and waved back. At the corner a squat newsstand sat closed up for the night, all sheathed in metal. "Where else did your family live?" I said.

The street-signs meant nothing to me. Lon did not even look where he was going. We turned left, and the brilliance of the theater was snuffed out behind us. Out of the dark Lon said, "Hell, this was just the house. We were here maybe five months of the year all told. Weekends we went upcountry, summers we had a cabin my folks rented out on Sebago Lake. This was just the house."

One time on their last night in Maine, Lon and his sister Pud waited up till past midnight and then stole out onto the lake in a wooden rowboat with a picture of Krazy Kat painted on its side. She was eight; Lon had just turned seventeen. He rowed them out over the water until he couldn't see any land anywhere, not even as a black shape against the sky, and there he pulled in the oars and just let the boat drift where it would. Pud sat up in the bow in her nightgown with the tigers leaping on it, her solemn face turned up to the stars. Lon just stretched out with his feet under the seat and his butt getting a little wet from the water in the bottom. He hung his arms over the side so that his fingers trailed just under the moonspotted surface. Then he remembered that *things* lived in there, and he got up and looked out over the water, thinking about *things* gathering under the surface, under the drifting boat, and then it was time to go.

"Do we have to?" Pud said, not whining because Pud was no whiner, even at eight.

Lon dipped the oars, pulled and raised them dripping out over the water, swinging them back in a wide arc. He pointed the boat back towards the invisible bank. "Don't have to do anything," he said softly. "Just time to go, that's all."

All that summer Lon sort of worked in a tumbledown garage close by the lake; he said "sort of" because they never did pay him anything. Pud and Lon had discovered the place during an expedition through a patch of scrub woods just down the road from where they lived. Lon hadn't wanted to go; it was too hot for one thing, and for another he wanted to go fishing or at least swimming. But Pud was determined to ferret out the Hun base-camp. She wore a makeshift helmet made of vines, and, following along behind him, she stopped every once in a while to chop at the undergrowth with her "machete," which was a switch longer than Lon's arm. "Come on," Lon would say. "What's holding you up?" and behind him he would hear *whack! whack!* and Pud would say, "Brush is damned thick, sergeant, damned thick!"

After about five minutes in the jungle they came up on a long, low rock wall half-covered in rotting leaves. "So much for your uninhabited forest," Lon said, and stepped over.

"It's a, it's a fossil wall," Pud said, poking at it, "left over by a ancient jungle tribe. We'd better be careful, sergeant, there could be natives right around here, waiting to pounce!"

But Lon had already gone ahead to the wood's edge and was looking out into the back yard of a place that connected up with the main road out front. "Say, pal," he said. "C'mere and look at this."

Pud came scrambling over and peered through where Lon held the branches apart. It was a big old box-shaped thing with the look of a hunting lodge, all logs and vine and antlers, hidden in a thicket of scruffy bushes and grass that hadn't been cut since Spring. It would have seemed like a peaceful sort of place if it hadn't been for the awful racket of poundings and mechanical rattlings coming from inside. "That's it!" Pud said. "That's the Enemy camp! I bet the place is crawling with Germans."

"You're sure about that," Lon said, and Pud looked up at him with the gravest mixture of certainty and doubt, and said, "Uh-huh?"

"Well we'd better check it out then." For her sake he went forward crouched in the manner of an advancing soldier, motioning for her to stay put. That was like telling a bengal tiger not to eat steak; before he had gone a yard he heard at his back the soft rustle of her paper bag filled with pine cone "grenades".

They came up flush to the building and went creeping along until they found a dirty window below the eaves where the pounding was loudest. Lon wiped a corner of the pane clean and stretched his neck out as far as it would go. "Wow," he said at last. "Well what do you know?"

He continued straight along the wall, leaving Pud wondering what it was he had seen. She was too little to reach the window herself, and there were no rocks or logs or anything for her to stand on, and so all she could do was go after him. When she poked her head around under the low branches of a maple sheltering the front corner, she saw Lon standing right out in plain sight, smack in the middle of a broad driveway. The whole front of the building was nothing more than two giant doors standing open to the air. Lon's mouth was open and his hands were in his pockets. He had a stupid, kind of dazed, eager look on his face. "Hey, Pud," he said. "Come on 'n' look at this."

As she stepped out into the yard something awful began to roar and scream inside. She grabbed one of her grenades, bit off the pin and spat it out; but when she came up beside her brother it dropped out of her fingers and rolled away, forgotten, to the bottom of the drive. She squished her sack of pine cones up close in the crook of her arm and put her fingers in her ears. The two of them stood looking in, and didn't say a word.

Under a high row of greenshaded lamps three men in dirty overalls worked with their hands in the stomachs of antique machines. Their arms were black to the elbow; they had streaks of grease where they had scratched their noses or wiped their foreheads. One had a pair of black-lensed goggles pulled down over his eyes. At the end of his hands sparks jumped and sputtered and whirled.

Around them the building was all dark and clutter, tools hanging against the wall, roadsters half covered under oilspotted tarps. The floor was bare ground covered over with shavings. Slowly, bit by bit, Lon went in under the lip of the building with Pud one step to the side, one step behind, so she could see in and still use him as a shield, just in case. They went ahead until they spotted a thing far in the back that was not a car. Blue cloth hung from its wings like shreds of webbing. It looked like a giant blue moth. They were standing under its nose, looking up, when the man in the mask put up his torch and peeled the gloves off of his hands. He looked right at them with his invisible eyes. "Well, partners," he said. "What d'you think?"

After that, Lon went up there every day. He started getting up early in the morning to do the sweeping and the lawn work, and then after a quick breakfast with Pud and his parents in the cabin's yellow-papered kitchen he would set off along a path that ran through the brush beside the lake. He never got more than a few hundred yards before the rustle or snap came from behind. Sometimes a branch or fern leaf might be bobbing unnaturally when he looked back, but he never did manage to catch her. He'd make a noise like an owl hooting, and before long the sound would come back to him from around the bend or behind a canopy of leaves. Then Lon would put on a face like a man having a heart attack and cry out loud: "*Injuns! Injuns!*" and run like hell.

Half an hour later he'd be working on someone's runabout with Mr. Hardaway or Mr. Sharpsteen, or anyhow handing them tools and watching to see how they did it. "Any time now," Mr. Sharpsteen would say, and sure enough when Lon looked up over the radiator there would be Pud with her bag of pinecones and her Buster Keaton expression just peeking around the edge of the garage's big door. If he was under the car, changing its oil, all he would see of her would be the rolled-up ends of her pants, her socks falling down, her overlarge tennis shoes kicking up sawdust as she came straight in with the same purposeful walk that carried her past the spare tires, past the cars, past the clutter of rusted parts that grew uncontrolled in the middle of the shop, straight through to the back corner where Lon and the mechanics never went.

It was always perfectly still back there. The only light came from pinholes in the roof above. Silk rested smooth along the wings of the sleeping thing, or drooped in pale blue folds. At the end of legs almost as skinny as Pud's, two big wheels sat inch-deep in sawdust. She would stand there in silence, the bag pressed up against her side, sometimes for ten minutes or more. Then when she thought no one was looking, and sometimes when no one was, she would climb right under the old dropcloth and up into the concealed and all-concealing secret place that was the cockpit.

Lon said he never asked what she thought she was doing in there. They never peeled away the cloth to see. But he said he was pretty sure he could guess close enough, and he guessed she was sitting just quietly with her hands on the stick and a determined look on her face. The blue cloth would have made a perfect sky. And she had her pinecone bombs all ready, just waiting to be dropped on the unsuspecting Hun down below.

Now Lon struck a match and lifted it to his face. When he shook it out there was an orange glow floating about an inch and a half from his lips. Sparks flecked away and fell to the concrete; his voice was low and steady in the night air. "That went on for most of the summer," he said. "Till just before August. Then the owner started coming down more often than anyone liked, and one day he caught her at it. Made a heck of a stink. Said he could lose everything. Pud came down out of the 'plane and stuck her tongue out at him, and he said to me you get that kid sister of yours out of here and keep her out. That afternoon Pud went out and got herself a length of clothesline. She tied one end around a tree and the other end around the bumper of the owner's car, and after that I didn't work there anymore..."

Just then we stepped out of the gloom of the sidestreet into a broad, well-lit square with a strip of parkland down the middle and a solid mass of brownstone houses all around. It had an effect like the opening of a play, black curtain sweeping away from the face of the stage, the stage itself unfolding into something huge and real yet somehow contained in the space between the fire wall and the proscenium. The park might have been cut out of black paper, all treetrunks and the shadows of leaves. On the far side Lon's house stood in the backlight, second from the corner, the smallest building in the row. It had four windows in front, each of them the size of a big man. We crossed over to a short flight of clean marble steps and stood under the overhang while Lon fumbled with his keyring one last time. "It wasn't so bad as it sounds," he said to the door. "I figure what he didn't pay me about covered the damage. Come on in."

The lock turned without making a sound. Lon put his shoulder to the door and pushed his way into the greater dark inside. "So this is Burden House," I said. "Your folks did all right for themselves." Lon said nothing. I heard him padding along a wooden floor; then a globe mounted on the wall above flared up, lighting the whole room. It was a medium sized entryhall with pale green walls and a border of painted leaves running along its edges, flaking in places down to the plaster underneath. Lon kicked off his shoes and arranged them below a cast iron coatrack. He set the keys down on a sideboard nearby. Hanging above it was an ancient, speckled mirror with a sheet of paper wedged between the glass and frame. It had Lon's name on it, written out in blue letters, in a woman's practiced hand.

Lon folded it away into his breast pocket without reading it. There was no need to ask, even if I had the nerve; there was no one else it could have been from. He shook his jacket off, draped it over his arm like a butler or a bellman, then put his hand out for mine. "Take off your shoes," he said. As I bent down to oblige, I saw him open a slanted door under the stairway and hang the old coats neatly inside.

We went stocking-footed up and around, past the second floor and on up to the third, Lon turning the wall lamps on ahead and turning them off behind so that we were encased in a bubble of light that moved with us through the solid dark. "That last night on the lake," he said from three steps above, "Pud and I heard the 'plane take off and bank out over the water. We'd turned the boat around and I was rowing back, not knowing where the hell I was going, and from the end of the lake we heard this chopping in the air, like a flapping sound above the engine noise. He was flying with his lights out. Passed right over us, close enough to kick up the water, close enough to shake us, and still we never saw a thing. Stupid Pud got right up in the bow. She sat up there on her knees gripping the rim of the boat and looked up at nothing, and I hung onto the oars and paddled for dear life. My end went up, slapped down hard, then hers went up. The 'plane went out over the far shore. After it had gone she scrambled over and gave my pants leg a good tug. 'Valkyries,' she said. 'A whole flock of them. Did you hear their wings? Like Pegasuses. A flock of Valkyries carrying all the dead Germans to War Heaven.' Can you beat that? Where the hell did she get that? Eight years old. I didn't know what a Valkyrie was until I met Jones."

When we came up to the landing Lon set his overnight bag down beside the railing. "We sank up to our ankles in the mud," he said. "A fine night. Boy, we caught it." He opened a big brass-handled door at the head of the passage and stuck his hand inside. Pale light fell out onto the edge of a braided rug. "You can stay here for a couple of days. Until they find you someplace of your own. Then get out. I need my quiet."

It was a small blue-papered room behind one of those big front windows; inside it had a brass bed made up under a fancy quilted cover, a writing table beside the window, a dresser with three shelves hanging above, and a bloated old trunk with a round top resting at the foot of the bed. It did not have the musty smell of a room that has been closed up for a length of time; there was no dust, nothing was covered over. It looked as if someone could be back at any time.

Lon stood in the doorway with his face turned down and away, leaning ever so slightly toward the invisible end of the hall. He looked at the wood, the floor, the pale, papered walls. "Pud gets the place during the summer," he said, "and I use it winter-times. We never did agree on that, it's just the way things worked out. Works fine. She and her husband and the damn kids come down every July from New Bedford. They take over the whole house. But by then I'm long gone."

He went back to the rail, stooped and then rose with the overnight bag in one hand and his ashcolored eyes raised to mine for the first time. "Can't figure those kids," he said softly. "Miniature Puds, every one of them, at least to look at. But that bastard Weymon has hold of them. They're his kids, too. Spookiest thing I ever saw. They never speak. They look like she did, but they don't have the spark. Give them a sack of pinecones and they wouldn't know what to do with it. And Pud seems to approve."

Now the fatigue of the whole summer settled down hard around his shoulders. A sound came out of him like a weather balloon slowly deflating. His bones seemed to turn into lead; his face lengthened and took on the color and texture of flour. He shook his head, turned away. The light passed out of his eyes. "Not a god-damned thing *I* can do about that," he said. "Good night."

He went off down the hall, and I stood a while just inside the little room, listening, before closing myself in at last. The door would not quite shut; a steady stream of cold air blew under from the hall. I opened my bags all in a muddle on the floor, and was half undressed before I realized he had given me Pud's room.

She was in the papers still spread across the desktop, the letters poking out of their envelopes. She was in the summer dresses hanging up in the closet, and now as I pulled back the bedcover I thought I could even smell her on the sheets. She was in the row of silver-framed pictures looking back at me from the shelf above the dressing table. She was not what Lon had described.

Prudence was her name. She had light brown hair with thick curls that licked at the sides of her face. She wore plain skirts and bulky, unattractive blouses, and very little make-up, except around her eyes. She looked as if she was forever being caught unawares by the camera, a pleasant, smiling, slightly distracted woman who came into focus only in relation to the people she posed with: the three sullen daughters lined up before a fence; a rumpled old man in glasses that reflected too much light; a bland, fatfaced man in a business suit, standing with one arm curled awkwardly around her waist.

Where was Pud, then? Not in there; not inside that woman, not anywhere. Pud standing barefooted on a gravel road with a bucket in one hand and a fishing rod in the other, Pud on her knees in the Krazy Kat boat, under the stars; Pud on long walks all alone through the woods, venturing into clearings far back from the lake, where the stones spoke in whispers and the ragged ends of a thousand myths blurred and came together, just beyond reason; Pud peeling a back curtain of leaves from the face of a make-believe stage in the yard behind the cabin; Pud saving the free world from the back of a winged horse; always with the same intent straight face framed in the same severe haircut, the same overlarge eyes with the same non-expression of fierce gravity and calm and purpose like an indignant store mannequin with a go-to-hell attitude.

"Jones," I said aloud, and still I did not understand. How could I? It was two in the morning and I was standing thin and naked and cold in a stranger's room with all of unknown Philadelphia looming wonderful and black at the window. *Lon would follow her anywhere,* I thought, and I did not even know who I meant. Perhaps Pud and Prudence were the same after all; perhaps Pud just got washed away. *Whatever,* I thought. *For Lon, she is someone else, now.*

The bed was cold, well-pressed, crinkly. I turned out the light, slipped in under the freezing weight of the blankets, and turned away from the wall where the pictures looked out over me. It was darker inside than out.

ALL HALLOWS EVE

ON my third night portraying a demon ticket-taker in the *Valenciennes* booth, Mary brought me an early edition of The Inquirer along with my usual jam sandwich and coffee. It was set out neatly along the edge of the tray, folded open to the entertainment page. *'All Hallows' — Trick Play a Treat for Those Not Faint of Heart*, it said right there in cold print. I suppose they expected to hear me whooping it up all the way into the back. But I hardly had time to notice; the phone was ringing off the hook, and people had already started turning up at our door. It was time for me to go into my act.

Every evening at six-thirty Mrs. Templeton zipped me into a suit made of muslin and leather and fur, topping it off with a papier-mâché mask that fit right down over my head. It was a good theatrical gimmick, if an old one; as the men and women came in from the street I lurched up at them out of a sudden rush of blood-red light, raking the bars with my wooden claws. It provoked more laughter than fright, as we intended; they came to my booth knowing they were in the right place, and left it ready to have a good time. Once inside the hall, they met up with yet another nightmare figure: Mary, dressed in a shroud bound all in rusted chains, waiting in the shadow behind a table set out with bloodspattered programs and a row of paper cups. "Here, drink this," she said to all who filed past; and before their eyes the cups were filled with wine flowing thick and purple from the tips of her fingers.

I never saw the reaction to that, never even heard it there in the booth, under the diving-suit head of the demon. For half an hour the folks came in a steady stream, so many that I had to keep my red light on all the time. I snatched at their money, ripped two or three tickets from the paper "tongue" that drooped between my mask-lips, and hurried them on. By seven forty-five I was turning them away. Curtain time was eight; it was eight fifteen before I was able to close up.

So even then I didn't have a chance to look at the article, just time enough to slip out of the demon outfit, dump the cold coffee into me and grab a half of the sandwich to eat on the way. But the heading I'd seen was too encouraging to ignore; on my way out I scooped the paper up, and with jam running down from the corner of my mouth I scanned the length of the column until I found my own name. *The play, by Winslow Howe, is an effective bit of Halloween trickery, it said, drawing on...*

Backstage was the usual blur of painted faces, the attentive silence with everyone poised all at once, ready to move, Templeton working alone for the moment inside the box of light. His voice came over the backs of the scenery, rattled in the wings...

... and it came to me suddenly that he was not changing anything, not ad-libbing. This was a first. It was my voice that powered him, my words being spoken so beautifully, sounding much better than they had ever sounded in my own head. "Listen," I wanted to say. "Hey, listen to that."

I held the newspaper so tight that it crackled in my hands. Off in the dark, waiting to help them, I spoke the words along beside him, not making a sound, only his voice rising from my mouth into the rafters above and then on, into the house.

We were an odd group coming out of the alleyway, the Templetons in their street clothes and phony age lines drawn onto their faces; the corpse-colored woman towering over them, Mary and Moscow and Sylvie following along, their eyes sunk deeply into black-painted sockets; and Lon and I, an oversized day laborer and a youth shivering in a frayed summer jacket. We walked in the descending cold, alone in the street with our shadows lengthening from lamp to lamp. Jones came between the Templetons, linked her arms in theirs. Her breath rose into the city night. "What was his name?" she said.

"Edward Moran."

"Hah! Well bless his heart."

"Maybe we should send him flowers," Sylvie said.

"Calla Lillies!"

"No," Jones said. "The time to do that is when they give you a bad review."

We went to a little restaurant just a block from the theater, up on the second floor of a building that I passed every day. There were no signs to mark the place, only a three-by-five card saying CLOSED TUESDAYS tacked into the wall at the top of the stairs. The owner said that we sounded like the entire Russian army, but he didn't seem to mind. Somehow he'd managed to squeeze six tables and a bar into a room no bigger than our stage; it was late enough that most of the chairs were empty. He gave us two tables next to the row of windows overlooking the street, and we sat around them in a figure eight and passed the newspaper from hand to hand.

" 'Those with a taste for the unusual,' " Jones read out loud, " 'will not want to miss *All Hallow's Eve*, a melodramatic bit of work by newcomer Winslow Howe.' "

" 'ray!" Mary said, and Lon whistled and Templeton said "Here here" and everyone clapped and thumped the table. Jones motioned for silence. " 'By turns amusing, ghastly and absurd...' "

"Absurd?" Templeton said. "Not our Mr. Howe."

" '...the play draws on some very ancient horrors and succeeds in making them effective for a modern audience. It has been given lavish treatment most in keeping with the season, including some Grand Guignol stage effects not for the squeamish.' "

The owner brought us wine and said that it sounded like we had had a good night. He took orders from all eight of us without writing anything down; somehow in the middle of all that, Templeton got hold of the newspaper.

"Second paragraph," he said. " 'Connecting story concerns an awful old man who...' Hmm." He read on, or pretended to, in silence, making a show of steadily building anger until I thought steam would pour out of his ears. "Why, that's horrible! Outrageous! I'm going to see to it that this show is banned!"

"Oh, stop it," Mrs. Templeton said. "You *are* awful." She snatched the paper out of his hands and peered at it over the top of her glasses until she found where he had left off. " '...an awful old man who weaves tales around all who have the misfortune to come in contact with him. First, a night nurse finds herself embroiled in serio-comic reworking of the Saint Winnifred legend, in which a decapitated woman wreaks terrible vengeance on her killer; next, his own granddaughter enacts the leading role in a nightmare vision of a child terrorized in the workroom of her father's funeral home.' It does sound gruesome, you know."

"That's all right," Jones said.

My face hurt from all the grinning, but I couldn't seem to stop. Only half a glass of wine and already I was lightheaded; I blamed it on my empty stomach, the sandwich four hours gone. I felt tired and warm and happy. Mary had the article now; her voice rose from the next table, and she made it sound like music.

" 'Second act features tales of a priest who can see into hell and a society woman who becomes a rabid hound by night. In these stories Chaos is suppressed or masked by Order, only to come bursting to the surface, stronger than ever, and with an even greater power to terrify. Much of what could have been offensive is deftly handled here, though it should be stressed that *All Hallows* is not your church Sunday-school meeting...' "

"Ah, you see?" Templeton said. "Close the sinners down!"

Then the newspaper found its way into my hands. It had been folded into a fly swatter shape. I had to open it again to read down into the lower half of the column. "Shh, shh," Moscow said. "He's going to speak."

" 'The production...' "

"Louder," Moscow said.

" 'The production allows greatest possible leeway for bravura performance, and its cast does not fail to take, uhm, to take advantage.' " More table-thumping. " 'Claude Templeton as the tale-spinner gives a grand performance but is nearly surpassed by the deft Margaret Darwin, cast here as the socialite hound woman...' "

"Socialite Hound Woman?" Sylvie said, and everyone had a good laugh over that.

" 'Ruth Templeton, Mary Eckert and the beguiling Sylvie Lindstromm all contribute first-rate work.' "

A chorus of wolf whistles rose from around the two tables before I could even finish the sentence. Sylvie actually turned red. "All right," Lon said. He cleared his throat. "Don't get us thrown out. Acting like kids. Here, look at this: 'Peter Moscow's turn as the priest plagued by demon visions proves once again that he's as big a ham as they come.' "

"Give me that," Sylvie said. "It says, 'one of the most strenuously physical turns of acting in this or any season.' " She glared at Lon. "My public," Moscow said. Sylvie ignored him and went on reading to the bottom of the page. " 'Mounted in settings that awaken thoughts of the melodramas of the '90s, *All Hallows Eve* makes for a festive and chilling seasonal treat for those with strong hearts and a taste for the macabre.' "

The owner and his wife carried in two big trays of food and began setting it out around the tables. Jones sat back in her chair. Black hair spiraled over her brow and shoulders. In the soft restaurant light the heavy paint around her eyes made her look like something out of The Arabian Nights. She lifted her wine glass. *"Sursum corda,"* she said. "I'm proud of you all."

After dinner we walked back up to *Valenciennes* and stood in the cold under the marquee. It was past time for us to be saying our goodnights, but we paused there for ten or fifteen minutes before the chills set in deep enough to make it happen. Then Jones took out her key and turned to twist it in the lock. "I'm going in for a few minutes," she said. "No rest for the deft."

I was tempted to tag along. But I would have been the only one, and anyway they hadn't gone to the trouble of finding me a "writer's garret" as they called it just so I could follow around after her like a puppy dog with its tongue hanging out. I knew better than to make myself a fair target. And so the goodnights were finally said; we went off our separate ways, and when I looked back the sidewalk was empty, the theater standing dark and strange against the street with Jones alone somewhere inside, cleaning away the remains of my "hound woman" from her face.

The "writer's garret" was one and a half rooms looking out over a private garden bordered on all four sides by brick houses. I had a bed, a writing desk and a couple of shelves for books; Mary said that she'd help decorate the place, but I had only just moved in and she hadn't yet had the time to do anything more than hang a star-patterned curtain across the front of my closet. Even that was more than what I needed. But Mary said there was a trick to living alone, and part of it was to make home a place that you liked coming back to.

If that was the case, I had a long way to go. When I came in that night I was too restless to sleep, too unsettled to work. There were a couple of books I should have been reading, but I didn't feel up to that, either. I was used to having the rest of the company just down the hall. Instead of undressing I sat in the little half-room and read the clipping again and again, wishing that I hadn't drunk so much wine, feeling exultant and a little bit sinking, too, a little down in a way that I didn't understand. At last I got up, threw my jacket back on and went down to the pay telephone on the landing. I fed it as many dimes and nickels as I had. And I dialed my parents' number.

Waiting for the call to go through, I marveled at how fast these things worked, how something like a signal carrying voice could travel all those hundreds of miles down the black wires. It found their house and shot into the receiver beside their bed. My father answered after two rings. He said, "Do you know what time it is?"

"Sorry, Dad, it's, it's me! But — I had to tell you. It's good news. We got a, we got a review in *The Inquirer* today, and, and wait till you hear it..."

"Son, it's one in the morning. Couldn't you just send it? This is costing you money."

"A, a few cents. Listen, I think this is going to work out. Jo— uhm, Miss Darwin, she says that I'm getting better with every act. Hey, you should see her as the Angel of Death. I, I really think it's going to work out. Listen, Dad, to, to what it says…"

"That's a good thing," he said. "Did you hear about your Mr. Deighton?"

I thought: *How could I?* "No," I said. "No, I, I didn't."

"He passed on last week. Went into the hospital with a pain in his chest, and died that night."

The hall was so cold that I was afraid I'd left the door open coming in. There was no place for me to sit down. The wall was bare, and covered with handprints. I felt as if he'd swept away the entire evening; there had never been a play of mine, we hadn't had any cause to celebrate. Jones and I had never laughed together. "If you could only see her the way I do," I whispered into the mouthpiece. "He did. He knew."

Far, far away in St. Paul my father sat up with his back against the head of the bed. "Whatever assurances he may have given you are no good now," he said. "You've burned your bridges."

I wanted to say: *good.* Instead I apologized again and told him to get some sleep. I went back to the room with my hands clenched in my pockets. It wasn't until I went to lock the door behind me that I saw what I had done to the review.

STAR WITNESS

ONE *night,* Templeton said, *a voice from out of the ether called me to the stage.* For a time that was all he would tell about the start of his career; whenever I asked it was always the voice bubbling out of nowhere, out of the air, some legless ghost or deity leading him to his fate. It was the only concession to mysticism he ever made, an ordinary man with a long dignified face who at any other time seemed perfectly happy with facts, and with making sure that other people stuck to facts as well. Onstage he specialized in brash, fast-talking types and in dignified eccentrics, though lately he found himself playing grandfathers or retiring gentlemen caught in the process of looking back. It did not seem to disturb him that, more and more, he was playing old men. He was not given to thinking about his parts, or about the effect that they had on him.

And so there was always this mystical moment (though he would never have seen it that way) when Templeton came off of the stage, tossing aside his character as if it were an old robe. He would be in the light and then out of it, one foot down and then before he completed the stride it would be gone, and as Templeton again he would meander on into the back. But it happened sometimes that a kind of invisible residue of the character would remain floating about him, and once when the character was evaporating, looking back, I caught Templeton looking back as well.

It was not more than a shift in the pattern of his breathing, a slight *push* of air that might have been a laugh, or might have been a sigh. When I looked over at him his black-lined eyes were fixed on something close, something in the air that had already started to fade away. He looked out onto the glowing stage, and it would have vanished completely if I had not said:

"What?"

He only shook his head and pulled a grey handkerchief out of his back pocket. When it came away from his face it was smeared with orange paint, a swatch of color cut out of his brow. Then he saw that I was not going to let it go, and said, "The buzz would always come just as I was getting to sleep. It was never any other way."

So I had no idea at first that he was talking about the voice. He said it as if it had made perfect sense, and he offered nothing more. In the end I had to ask again:

"What?"

This time Templeton made such a discomforted face that I knew he was wishing for another cue to draw him away. "All right," he said, whispering so that his words wouldn't carry out over the boards. "It wasn't from out of the ether. It was over a wire. At three thirty in the morning the effect is the same, believe you me."

He pulled himself to his feet and turned away into the back of the building. I watched him disappear, then followed after, tracking him first by the shuffle of his shoes and then by the gurgle and clatter as he filled the company coffeepot and set it out on our hotplate. It had already begun to heat up by the time I came through into the back room; he sat there in the dark with the exposed coil glowing red above the table top, the water starting to rumble and groan against the pot's tin sides.

"Jones told me that you were a discovery of hers. She said that she found you practicing thaumaturgy in an unappreciative little town."

"Margaret only tells the truth as far as she knows it," Templeton said. He raised a silhouetted finger and touched it to his nose. "And what she does tell is pretty well colored with show paint. There were no miracles about what I was doing. And she was a few years late to claim any right of discovery."

I remember feeling disappointed at that; I had always assumed that the voice was hers. Nothing could have been more interesting than what Jones had said, or so I thought. Then I remembered what he had said about the buzz.

"Yes," Templeton said. "The first came while I was still at school. I was taking my degree at the University, and at night I ran the switchboard in a basement room in the administration building. It was tedious work for the first two or three hours; after that I could unroll a sleeping bag on the floor and stretch out. There was never much in the way of light, but I managed to get some studying in, always keeping one eye on the board. Sometimes it would buzz, and then I would have to scramble. But sometimes I could sleep straight through from three o'clock to about five.

"In the winter it was terribly cold down there. So if I wanted to sleep I really had to work at it. And I was just drifting off one night, oh about a quarter to four, when the machine lit up over my head.

"It was a woman. She didn't sound tired at all. 'You've got a nice voice,' she said, 'but it's not the one I called to hear.' She gave the name and number that she wanted and I connected her. We let it ring a long time. It didn't bother her that there was no answer. She thanked me for trying and rang off.

"The same thing happened the next night and the next and the next, the call always coming through just as I was fading out. And it struck me at last that I didn't mind. On the fifth night I even tried staying awake. But she still managed to catch me napping. That was the night she said, 'You know, maybe yours is the voice I'm calling to hear after all.' I was still pretty groggy and not thinking well, so I went and put her through anyway. But at the first ring I could hear her laughing, and knew that I should stop.

"I wouldn't say that we talked until dawn, but in those hours even a short talk seems like forever. She said she was an actress, the leading actress of the Baxter Company down in town. She said her name was Ruth. And she invited me down to see her.

"I went in secret the very next night, and took a gander at her from the wings. She was very much the prima donna, already skilled in the art of upstaging. She must have frightened other young men my age. I suppose that she frightened me. But I gave up the switchboard job so I could go down to the theater every night. I was fortunate. They paid me to lug some scenery around, and in time I was introduced to the great Theodore Baxter, a king in his profession, the most mannered of all actors. I was given some small parts in his shows, not for money of course, just the experience; and I played everything as if I believed in it absolutely.

"After the shows, we took walks together across the park and back. Ruth would be in an exultant mood. She wore dresses that whispered when she moved in them. In those days women dressed in a way to feed a man's illusions. None of the things belonged to her; costumes were her delight. It was a chaste sort of courtship that I had very little control over..."

"That was Mrs. Templeton," I said, grinning. "You married her and joined the Baxters, and years later the two of you were rediscovered by Jones."

"No. I asked her, of course. But I was still two years away from my degree, and anyway she would never have left the company. For my part, I had squatted with them long enough to see how actors lived. Baxter had a mansion outside of town, but none of that wealth ever trickled down to the rest of the company. And so one day I stopped coming down. I was not irreplaceable; I doubt Baxter even noticed. I worked at the University, took my degree and inherited a position with my Grandfather's firm, from which I looked back only rarely. Though oftentimes in later days Ruth was to remind me that my few parts with the Baxter Company had made for excellent training in my profession."

The pot had long since begun to boil, and now Templeton found his mug and poured it full to the top with steaming black water. I could not see his face. He was standing with his back to the emergency light, had posed himself that way on purpose. He said, "The law, son. That's how I know this new play of yours isn't any good. Full of legal improbabilities."

He let that one go and just stood there waiting for it to take effect. It didn't take long. "I don't think so," I said.

"Ha! Which part of it are you having trouble swallowing? Don't bother." He slurped, made a face, and set the cup down. "Come on."

I followed him into the cramped maze of rooms that filled the back of the theater building. "Of course, Ruth and I still saw one another," he said, clumping on ahead, "in a fragmentary way. Sometimes after court she would meet me at our place in the park. Always with a silk flower in her hands, always wearing those old costumes that would have made anyone else look overdressed. But she still could not see herself as the wife of a lawyer, even after old Baxter finally closed down the theater. That was a terrible day for her. She came to me in tears, in plain dress for the first time ever. We stood together in the park, and she wept, and I held her. But the answer was still no."

Templeton's dressing room, like all of the others, was an eight by seven windowless box furnished with a cloth screen and a vanity with a mirror up above that took up much of the east wall. The rest of it, bare of paint or wallpaper, had been covered with photographs, none of them of stage figures, banners and framed newspaper clippings that looked like reviews of stage shows but were not. Their headlines were brash and hinted at murders and extortion; in the small print the same name recurred again and again, sometimes underlined in red ink. There was an old American flag with not enough stars on it draped across the frame of the big mirror. In the dusty glass I saw Templeton wrestling with something behind the screen, and as I watched he pulled a battered trunk into the center of the room and stood puffing over it.

"There you are," he said. "Rummage to your heart's content. There's nothing to incriminate me." He turned away as if I did not exist at all, stripped off the blue frock coat that had worn onstage, settled into the thickly padded chair before the dresser. There were several open packets of cigarettes laid out among the tins of make-up; Templeton selected the most crumpled of these, took one into his mouth and lit it.

And so I had to open the trunk myself, aware that I was poking into someone else's memory-box but eager for all of that, too much drawn into his play to be bothered by the niceties of private property. It was clean inside and lined with pale blue paper, stacked full of old newspapers that had yellowed a little, had curled at their spines. They gave off a pleasingly musty smell like attic furniture, so that when I lifted out the leather binding that rested on top it seemed that I was handling something impossibly old. It creaked as I opened it; inside was a diploma embossed with *Indiana State University* and Templeton's name.

I set it carefully to one side, moved on into the stack. Now Templeton shifted in his chair. He leaned forward almost to the edge of the trunk. "You see," he said as I touched the brittle pages, "I saved the whole newspaper. Not just the clippings. It's hard to keep the true memory that way, and impossible to keep perspective. The standing one has. There, you see? Not page one. Page three."

I opened to page three and saw *acquittal* before he snatched the paper out of my hands. He had joined me now, was kneeling uncomfortably beside the trunk, rifling through the papers. "They're stacked just as I bought them," he said, half grinning. "The latest on top. Here, look at this one."

He lifted away the four latest issues, and there in big letters I saw **BAXTER PLAYHOUSE THEFT.** "There, you see? You see that? The crime, now that's front page material. The acquittal, my achievement; that ends up on page three. perspective; you could never know that if I just kept clippings."

"Who were you defending?"

He parted his hands in a theatrical gesture that might have belonged to Fagin. "Read on, MacDuff."

Under the big letters, less bold but still a part of the headline, it said: ***5,000 and Props Stolen; Actor Held in Custody.*** Then: *Actor Lon Burden was held for questioning last night after theater manager Jack Moran notified police of a break-in that left more than $5,000 missing from Moran's office safe. Moran claims that Burden, member of a vaudeville company playing here during the past week, has been behaving suspiciously ever since his arrival. Moran's office occupies one room at the back of the playhouse building; the famed Baxter Collection of theatrical props, costumes and memorabilia (several pieces of which Burden is also accused of stealing) occupy three rooms on the floor below. Burden was apprehended just after 1:00 AM on his way out of the theater; witnesses claim he was carrying a golden crown worn by the late Theodore Baxter in his production of King Lear, but no money was found on his person. Margaret Darwin, spokesman and secretary of the Jones Transportation Company players, refused comment. No trial date has been set. Burden will be arraigned tomorrow on charges of unlawful entry and theft.*

I looked quickly through the rest of the paper, then checked the date. February 9th, 1934. "I thought you were the Grand Old Man of the company," I said. "You've only been part of it for five years?"

Templeton ignored me. He climbed back into the chair, crossed his legs, folded his hands. In that position, dressed as he was, he looked legal indeed. "Now then," he said. "point to the factual errors in that article."

"Jones was never just a spokesman, " I said. "One. This isn't a vaudeville company, two. Lon isn't an actor, three. He didn't do it, so he couldn't have been carrying the crown, four."

"Well the number is right," Templeton said. "But he was carrying the crown. Claimed to have found it lying in the middle of the stage. Of course the vaudeville part is hogwash. The company had been playing to empty houses, but the next night the Baxter Playhouse was packed. I was there. What I saw was no vaudeville.

"It was Margaret's first season out. They were doing a little number about the witches from *Macbeth*, a sort of sequel. The idea was that the witches were immortal, and still around in 1934 mucking about in the lives of men. The sort of thing she likes. That was the first time I saw her. The second was the next day, when she walked into my office.

"She was dressed... almost like a tramp, in a man's workpants and a torn jacket. My secretary thought her terribly rough. And I must say neither my partners nor I were ready for her theatrical bluntness. She insisted on meeting us all you see, insisted with that attitude she has of... of boredom and... and foreknowledge, standing there with her hands in her pockets. I said to myself, this is a woman of true composure. Then when we had all gathered in the senior partner's office — my grandfather's old office — she sat down and gave us the same story that she'd given the papers that morning."

That was my cue; it was meant to send me to the next edition, to see what I might find. "Can't you just tell me?" I said.

Templeton only leaned forward and snatched the paper out of my hands. He unfolded it so the back page crackled and shook in the air above me.

It said: **ACTORS CLAIM BUILDING HAUNTED.**

"No," I said. "She didn't."

"She did. Mind you she made it clear that she thought it all hogwash. But this was what she had heard from the members of her own company, and talk around the local bars and such like had gone a ways towards confirming it."

Now I could even see her in the chair opposite the lawyer's desk, her face stone calm, her voice low and ordered, telling about the shadowy figures that some stagehands thought they had seen, about the head that floated across the stage on a levitated sword, about the vaporous madwoman in the first box whose mascara had run over her cheeks, who cried in perfect silence...

"Hasn't any of this disturbed you? Why haven't you left the theater to its ghost?" (a partner of Templeton's might have asked.)

Jones only moved her left shoulder a bit. "Things like that don't frighten me. Even if I had seen them, which I haven't. Lon stays late, so he's the one to ask. He only claims to have heard scuffling sounds, and then to have found the crown center stage. If I were you I'd ask Moran about it. Now, my head man is in jail. I have all his work to do. I'm sorry, but I can't spare you any more time."

"My partners thought she was a fool," Templeton said. "But I was convinced that this Miss Darwin absolutely knew what she was doing. She had played a very theatrical turn in the papers. The town was all up with it. It was my kind of case."

So Templeton was alone when he went down to the jailhouse and spoke with Lon for the first time in a grey cell with a lopsided table in it and three chairs. Lon would not have said much for himself under any circumstances; but when Templeton came down he found Lon so taciturn as to be almost frozen, sitting up at the table with his back slightly hunched, his thick hands folded and his lips sealed.

"He would not even look at me," Templeton said. "He would not even say hello. Have you seen anything, I asked. Have you heard anything, even if it was just scrabblings, rats in the walls. No, he said. And then his grip tightened; the most disturbing thing of all. No change in his face. Just the noticeable pressure as his fingers closed in on each other... and then the cracking. Like he was breaking the bones in his hands.

"So there I had this client with a case of lock-jaw worse than a snapping turtle, his people babbling about ghosts and lust blinding my judgement."

"Did Mrs. Templeton know this?" I said.

"Lust for the boards, son. For the spotlight. I had nothing to go on but I could hardly wait to get into court. Miss Darwin had done such a fine job of promoting that I was assured of a full house. Under the circumstances, the only thing I could do was follow with more promotion. I called a friend of mine down at the *Herald*, Jameson Tripp, announced my intention to spend the night in a haunted theater and asked if he would like to tag along."

I had leafed through the next day's paper back to front and then front to back. "There's nothing here..."

"I keep it to mark the occasion," Templeton said. "What happened that night did not belong in the newspapers."

"This reporter, this Tripp, he agreed to that?"

All Templeton did was smile. "He was a strange duck. Plain faced, shaved smooth without ever once cutting himself. He didn't smoke, and except for that night he didn't drink. Style meant nothing to him, but form did, the Form that he set up for himself. Fifty dollars wouldn't have bought him off of this story if it had come from anyone but me.

"We spent the afternoon getting our provisions together, all the right gear for a haunted expedition. He'd heard that spirits chilled rooms as they flitted through, so he brought along two raccoon coats, one for each of us. I bought us some flashlights, and I got a baseball bat for myself because I kept thinking about some of the things that this Jones — Miss Darwin — had said, and even though she had been skeptical they had set down black roots in the back of my mind. Build-up. I knew it for what it was, but sometimes seeing the labels on things doesn't keep them from working.

"Well he and I went down to a little restaurant I knew and talked about things. Not about the theater; a newspaperman and a lawyer, we had bigger fish to fry. But I could see that it was working on him, too. I had a flask in my hip pocket and long about midway through the meal he asked if maybe we hadn't better break it open.

"It was mostly gone by the time we got down there. The girl in the box office wouldn't let us in unless we paid for tickets, even though the show was nearly over. So we went around into the alley that ran alongside the building, and we finished the flask and waited. Well before long we had a feeling like as if we weren't alone. And sure enough when we looked up, there was Margaret just standing in the stage door. She was still in costume, her face still painted so it looked longer, sharper. Her eyes looked like gleaming glass. Jameson turned stark white. He wasn't used to women with power any more than he was used to drink. Then she smiled, and that was worse.

"He was stricken with love, the way you can only love a woman you know is out of reach. You understand."

He looked at me like a prosecuting attorney. It was a good job. I mumbled back, half-heartedly, "Speak for yourself."

" 'Come on,' Margaret said. 'I'm not the ghost. Do I scare you that much?' And we all went inside.

"It was not my first time in the hind end of a theater, pulleys and sandbags didn't awe me. Jameson was craning his head all around, had a hard time keeping his eyes in. We talked to a few of the company as they went around; none of them had seen ghosts, though Mr. Moscow did himself look haunted. 'There's your ghost,' Jameson said, and a few other things not so polite. He was out of his element and it showed.

"Now, what we should have done was search the theater from top to bottom, and the office and storerooms in back. But our expedition had become rather more companionable and less scientific. We climbed from the stage into the orchestra pit — Tripp would have stayed there if he could have, he felt hidden there — and went on, oh, about halfway back along the aisle. We made our camp in a row of seats there, and talked some more and waited. And this is where Jameson surprised me. I felt sure that he would be the one to razz me about this whole "ghost" thing — he had started as a sports writer for the *Herald* and I had him figured as a man who didn't believe in anything he couldn't catch or throw. But he turned out to have quite a secret history of tracking spiritual manifestations. Swore his old house in Kansas City was haunted by the soul of a murdered rum-runner; said he'd met a widow in town who was being terrorized by a pernickety gentleman ghost who wouldn't let her sit on any of the furniture. He would appear, blue in the face, beside her as she sat, bloating himself up like a liver-spotted old bullfrog, and hurl her off.

"So in the end I was the one making objections. We argued about it for half an hour before Miss Darwin appeared on stage — out of costume — to tell us she was locking up now and would it be better if she were to leave some lights on. No, I said. It must all be just as normal. And she gave that best smile of hers — I could hear Tripp's heart flopping about in the chair beside me — wished us a good night and went off. A moment later the lights above began to flick out, one row after another from back to front, until only the stage was lit, and that in the flat, clear light that the public never sees; then the entire hall went black. We heard her go out; the big door in back made a soft click that echoed through the whole building. And we were alone.

"Well, Tripp thought to start in with more of his occult tales. Silence, I said. We're here to investigate and not to babble. And so we sat quietly in the dark, watching for what would happen."

Templeton paused, leaned forward and snapped his fingers in the air as if calling a bellhop. "Now, take a peek in the left back corner. There should be a little box. Open it up." I did as he said, found it far down in the bottom of the trunk, packed in a wad of tissue paper. Inside, under a square of cotton, was a beautiful silver-cased pocket watch. It felt cold and comfortable in my hand; the back and sides had been well polished and cared for, but the glass was missing and the face was worn and smudged. "I have that from my grandfather," Templeton said. "It was his idea that I should become a lawyer. He ended out his life as a blind man, and doctored this watch so he could feel the time. I had it with me that night, for the same reason. Tripp and I sat in the dark for forty minutes, and then another forty, and nothing at all happened. I did not even feel as if we were being watched, didn't feel any sort of nasty presence as it were. I sat with the liquor dying in my stomach, felt of the time every few minutes and wondered about Mr. Burden's honesty. Jameson had fallen asleep beside me. And I was just about to perpetrate a bit of mischief on him when I saw something there, down on the stage.

"At first it was nothing more than a soft blue glow, rising and growing steadily as I watched, until an odd form began to take shape in its center. By this time I had wakened Tripp. He sat up and gaped. Because it was a face appearing there, slowly from the eyes, white, crazy eyes, outward to a ring of blood-spattered hair and a curiously wide jaw. Blue fire flowed under where its neck should have been; then

I saw that the head was resting on the flat of a sword.

"I believe that Tripp had still not left his seat. I was halfway down the aisle, and the eyes were watching me come and they looked upset. I had seen a few magic shows in my time and this was the oldest trick in the book.

"The head was floating at about waist level, and as I approached it made three little jumps backward. It made an awful racket on the floor for something that was supposed to be suspended in air. That was when Tripp started shouting. The head worked its lips at me; I managed to get hold of a length of cloth that was so black as to be invisible, and I gave a good hard yank.

"The sword was not even real; it bent in six places as it hit the boards. As for the ghost, it was the oddest apparition you could ever hope to see. Its face was painted deathly white, save for the lips, which were black. The tangled mass of hair fell well below its shoulders. It was wearing an old-fashioned man's nightshirt. It was in fact a man."

"Don't tell me," I said. "It was Moscow."

"Ah, no. No, it was a man you never met named Cameron MacTeagle. Of course Tripp came clambering up over the lip of the stage and said, 'You see, I pegged him from the start. I told you he was your ghost.' He practically danced. 'Doesn't look so hot for your man Burden,' he said. And he went out. I knew where he was going.

"The ghost could hardly contain himself. Of course he'd been hitting the bottle like the rest of us, only more recently. By giving the spirit angle a little substance he was honestly trying to help. I would have told him that he had helped his friend right into twenty years in the pokey, but just then I had more important things to do.

"Because I had seen something else as I came down that aisle. Someone had been sitting in the box up above, and the blue glow had provided just enough light for me to catch a moving shape as it rose and ducked behind the drapes there. I was now certain of what I had suspected all along: someone, some tramp, was living in the theater, and Burden was protecting him.

"But in the end it was not quite that," Templeton said to the wall. A kind of settling came over his bones; I heard it in the sounds that came from the chair. "There was a place where the wings connected with a maze of old passages. When I got out there I could hear that ghost running hard into the back, into the museum rooms where the old Baxter collection was kept. Kept," he said, "not cared for. I ran along flicking lights on behind me, so pretty soon that whole end of the building was lit up bright as day. Finally I came to a room that might have been a mausoleum. It was not just dust, but *layers* of dust, cobwebs, mold; everything had a solidified look just like a crusty mass of coral, dead coral on the hull of a sunken ship. Except for this one clear path, this one trail worn through it; clean because it had been walked over so many times. It cut straight through from the door to a rack of old costumes in back. So you'd think I would have known. But it was...

"They were all so clean that they seemed to glow. All those nights in the park. Pressed. It was such a little room, and I stood there in the center of it, shaking. I still had on that raccoon coat, see, and underneath it I was wringing wet. I breathed, and listened to the other breathing. And all I could think of was how old I was getting.

"Then I heard a little, sad little voice rise up and out from behind the dresses. 'I always brought them back,' it said. 'It wasn't really stealing.' Then they parted themselves, and she looked as if she felt as old as I did."

Now Templeton lit another cigarette. He closed his eyes, and would say no more. There was only the most recent edition of the Herald, dated two weeks later, with its modest letters almost whispering *Acquittal in Theater Case* there on page three. Mr. Lon Burden freed following testimony of an important new witness; police seeking former manager Jack Moran on charges of embezzlement. I could not reconcile such a soft ending to the headlines Templeton had taken me through. The room fell very quiet, Templeton's smoke drifted down over my head, and from under it I said, "It does look as though you were working wonders."

Templeton blew a ring of smoke, watched with some satisfaction as it dissipated. "The morning after the trial there were blossoms out on the dogwood bushes. It was a glorious day, but my office didn't have much of a view. I spent the morning going through the mail, starting a new brief. Miss Darwin came down to see me around eleven o'clock. She had a carnation in her lapel. She was carrying a purse."

"Jones?"

"Mm. I thought she was going to pay me. Instead she walked around my office, touching things, pulling the curtains back. She said it looked awfully grey. I kept watching her gloved hands moving about; Tripp was convinced that the Jones Transportation Company was a lot of vagabonds, and though I hadn't agreed I found some of that feeling washing off on me.

" 'You have a very dramatic manner in court,' she said. I said sometimes it helps and sometimes it doesn't, and she said, 'I'm told that you considered a theatrical career.'

"Then she pushed aside some of the trash I kept on my desk, opened her purse on it, and took out a thick, folded piece of paper. It was a contract, beautifully hand written, drawn in the simplest of language. And she said, "Do you think that you might consider one now? I don't usually make contracts with people, but I thought it might make you feel better.' "

I folded up the final *Herald* and set it at the top of the stack. "That voice was not from the ether," I said. "That voice was not even over a wire."

Templeton smiled. It was not more than a tug at the corners of his mouth. "No. That voice was an echo. When I speak of the voice that called me to the stage, Margaret always assumes that I mean her. But she was just my second chance."

BLOCKING

I parked with the house in my rearview mirror. It was a grey and white Colonial like one I'd imagined in a story several years before, a huge silent thing with a well-kept yard, a brass nameplate beside the door and windows with flowered curtains that were just heavy enough to keep me from seeing inside. "Drive on down the block," Sylvie had said. "Don't wait here." Then she went alone up the stone walkway and knocked on the door. She had been inside for almost an hour; how long did it take? When would it be time for me to start worrying?

"*Watch her,*" Jones said. "*All right? She comes down here to the rail, stands looking out over the ocean. Don't take your eyes off her.*" She'd been talking to the Templetons, guiding Sylvie (who was standing in for Jones herself) through a complicated floor pattern of masking tape intended to represent the nonexistent set; but now as I waited alone in the truck, I thought that she must have known, must somehow have meant something more.

They had spent the better part of the morning

190

working together up there under the ungelled light, blocking out act one of the new play. It was not a rehearsal for character or plot; my dialogue was tossed off in a casual manner where it was spoken at all. Ranging from the front row to the back of the house to the stage itself, Jones moved them about like figures on a board, searching for the right combination of action and inaction, the certain balance that would move the story along, increase its dramatic impact and also please the eye. By ten fifteen Sylvie had disappeared (now when Jones needed someone to fill her shoes it was Mary up there, taking the calls, shifting a little this way or that), and I was far in the back of the house, sniffing the air, calling out numbers to Lon in the booth above. We'd been getting a distinctly smoky smell from the lights all morning; Lon said that my nose would stand a better chance than his of tracking it down.

"Not that," I said. "Try number twelve." Lon squinted at me through the glass, then turned down to the board. Overhead another row of lights winked out.

That was when Sylvie came back onstage, dressed for the cold in a green coat that came down to her ankles, an outdated cap and a knotted paisley scarf. At first I thought she was playing a scene, a whimsey of hers, the small frightened figure peeking around the curtainedge like a child that had just found its way in out of a snowstorm. It was a thing she did sometimes, sudden flights into fantasy, into other unnamed, unknown characters, when the process of blocking had finally and completely bored her and she could no longer stay inside the lines of tape. Sometimes I wondered why Jones allowed it, how Sylvie could get away with so disrupting a rehearsal. But whenever I asked, Jones would only say that it was just something we had to put up with. "No one else complains," she'd say. "Why should it bother you?"

Sylvie came lightfooted across the stage and whispered in Jones's ear. She had a purse gripped tight in her fingers; while Mary and the Templetons stood patiently by, she took out something that looked like a business card and slipped it into Jones's hand.

"Well?" Lon said. "Is that it?" Jones wrote something down. She handed back the card, gave Sylvie's arm a squeeze, and I sniffed the air. "Yes," I said. "Yes, I think that's the one."

Up there in the booth Lon looked like the pilot of a rocketship. He reached across a soft field of colored light, pulled down a battered old cardboard box and began to rummage through the jumble of fuses and switches and wire. I told him I'd fetch the ladder, but he shook his head no, then gave that faint nod I'd seen often enough before, the one that meant *Don't look now...*

When I turned, Sylvie was standing in the aisle right behind me. Her hands were gloved and folded; yellow hair curled under the edges of the cap. She gave me a bright, unforced smile, and said, "Will you drive me?"

"What?" I said. Her eyes were pale blue. She was using them on me again, and I couldn't understand why. Not for a ride...

"It's a dentist appointment," Sylvie said. "Jones said we could take one of the trucks if you or Lon drove."

I looked up one last time. Lon was pretending not to hear; he had turned his back to the window. "All right," I said. "Let's go."

It was a clear freezing day with the sun coming in a slanted line along the alley wall. The two trucks were standing end to end, rustcolored and empty as derelict tanks, in their places far back from the street. As we came down from the stage door the broken ground crunched under our feet. Sylvie unlocked her side and tossed the keys to me, and I pulled away the blocks that Lon kept around the wheels, just like an airplane in a hangar.

Inside, the trucks were bare and green and cold. I had never driven either of them before; the seats were adjusted to accommodate Lon, and at first I couldn't fit my long legs into the cramped space under the wheel. The seat didn't want to move, the door didn't want to close; the gearshift was a thin, yard-long rod with a bend in it and a knob on top with the numbers worn completely away. Sylvie sat shivering beside me. "Choke," she said as I was about to turn the key. She pointed to a place under the dashboard, and when I still couldn't find it she reached over and gave it a good hard tug. Then the truck coughed and roared; I watched in the mirror as the alley began to fill with blue smoke.

"It must be an important dentist appointment," I said. I pushed it into what I hoped was first and began to edge out toward the street. "If it were me she'd say take the bus. She'd say, do it on your own time." At the end of the alley the world came alive. I poked our nose out so I could see all the way down the avenue. "A company truck and two of us on rehearsal time. Your mouth must be all rotten. Right or left?"

"Left," Sylvie said, and added, "Rotten is right." She showed me her perfectly even rows of teeth. "See? I may need falsies. Seems I've got something that has to come out..."

It was a long drive across the bright, heavycoated town. She guided me straight out toward the suburbs, but would not give me the address. We had been gone for maybe fifteen minutes when Sylvie drew her purse up close against her belly and unsnapped the clasp.

Inside was the book that Jones had given her, the tattered album filled with tattered photographs of tattered people, spectral families she had never known, in whose faces Sylvie seemed to find inspiration. It was not that she studied them, or used them as models: Sylvie was not that conscientious an actress, and in any case the ingenue parts that she played for us bore no resemblance to the people in the book. It appeared most often in the nervous moments before a show, or when she had lines that needed to be memorized quickly, or when she'd had an argument with Jones or Moscow, and could not get her own way. Now, as we left the last cluster of warehouses behind us, Sylvie drew the book out of her purse. She held it tight, unopened like a bible, in her gloved fingers.

The sign in the shadow of a leafless maple said *MD*. With the truck paused at the gate and Sylvie climbing down to the street, I'd made a point of looking at that strip of brass: *MD* in curled letters cut deep into the metal, not *DDS*. For half a moment Sylvie stood unmoving in the street with her hand on the doorframe. She looked up at me from under the edge of her cap. "I'll probably be a while," she said.

I nodded. "Will you be all right?" I said in the rumble of the engine. "Is it — do you need help?"

Sylvie pushed hard on the door until it clicked, stood with her face framed in the window. She gave me her best ingenue smile. "You can, if you want," she said. "You can hold my head..."

She had waved with the hand that held the book. She had turned her back. *Drive on,* she had said. *Don't wait here.* Now I sat alone in the truck with my shoulders hunched against the cold and my knees pressed together, and hated her for the whole affair; for the necessity of it, and for dragging me into its midst. In the cracked glass of the rearview mirror a patrol car came slowly down through the neighborhood. They passed me at a crawl, the blue-suited men inside turning their faces up to mine. They had long, cleanshaven jaws and eyes like broken glass set well back under their brows. They looked up at me as if they knew it all, as if they thought I was the one responsible.

Shortly after one there was a fluttering behind the iron gate. She appeared at last at the bottom of the yard, standing with her feet in the leaves and the edges of her coat stirring against the cold air. From a distance she was unchanged. She waved as I fired up the engine; I backed into someone's driveway, spun the wheel around, and Sylvie waited on the white sidewalk. She lifted her eyes as I brought the truck looming over her. She was trying not to look wistful, and failing.

I was so foolish; I knew so little. I half expected to see blood running down her ankles. At the very least, I thought, the color will have drained from her face. But in the afternoon light she looked fresh and just a little bit pale; she even laughed when I raced around the front, around the warming grille, and offered to help her up. "Star treatment," she said. "I like that." She pulled herself up over the running board, into the cracked seat, her hand sliding down over my forearm until the tips of her fingers rested lightly in the palm of my hand. "Well now, Jeeves," she said. She looked down at me, bit her lip and took hold of my index finger. "D'you think we could stop somewhere on the way back? D'you think you're up to buying a girl a strawberry frappe?"

I would have agreed to anything to get out of that neighborhood. The houses all seemed to have black glass in the windows; apart from the police car nothing had stirred but the leaves beyond the silent yards. It reminded me of home.

We found a white-fronted pharmacy on the edge of the city that had a soda fountain in back, past rows of patent medicines and cheap celluloid toys hanging from hooks above the dusty shelves. In a corner by the restrooms was a poorly installed booth that we took even though the counter seats were empty. They had strawberry ice cream, so Sylvie was happy. I'd been hungry when we left the theater; now I only ordered a cola.

"You're kind of quiet," Sylvie said when our glasses came.

"I think doctors are the most frightening things going," I said. I hadn't really thought about it before, and wasn't sure if I meant it, but I had to say something. "Was it very frightening?"

Sylvie licked around the edge of the froth, swirled thick reddish ice cream around her spoon, tasted it and made a face. "Nothing compared to forgetting your lines," she said. At first I thought she was trying to keep up the charade, the non-existent dentist appointment that kept things nice and did not fool anyone. But there was none of her usual coyness in the way she said it, nothing of the happy distraction that signaled one of her fantasies, her wanderings. She sat with her fingers curled around the ice cream shaped glass, her eyes sometimes averted, sometimes not, and talked to me as if she was not even an actress, as if I was not even male.

"You've never been in a position to have it happen to you," she said, "so you couldn't know. It's the worst when you've done something a hundred times, so you think you're safe and you don't worry about it. Then you get up under that light, in front of hundreds of people and you don't remember what to say, you don't remember how to move or what to do or where to go, only you know it's your line next and you're supposed to do something. That's the worst. That's when I just bat my eyes. There's always someone out there who knows how to whistle."

There was too much ice in my drink. "So you get prompted," I said. "It's no big deal. It happens to everyone sooner or later."

"It doesn't happen to Jones," Sylvie said. "Anyway, it's how you feel before the prompt comes that counts."

She had spooned out about a third of the frappe when something dark passed over her face. "Maybe this wasn't such a hot idea after all," she said, looking down into the open mouth of the glass. She dropped the spoon clattering into her empty plate, pushed the frappe away in a long wet line across the table and fumbled in the seat with her hat and purse. Her hands and cheeks had turned white; I thought she was going to vomit all over the booth. "Can you take me home, please?" she said. "I don't feel very good..."

Sylvie lived in one room on the fourth floor of a decaying old brownstone house not more than ten minutes walk from the theater. Beyond her narrow door the walls were so covered with theater programs, discarded costume sketches, magazine covers, circus posters and fragments of antique dresses that the room seemed to be made entirely of paper and cloth. In the dusty light from a single iron-bracketed window the roof made one-half of an inverted V over a childsized bed covered neatly with a black and red patchwork quilt. It was maybe three steps from the door to the bed; between them was a wooden hatstand with a dark robe on it and a man's pajama bottoms.

Sylvie looked half asleep when I sat her on the bed. I took off her cap and hung it with her purse on the hatstand, then unbuttoned her coat. She let me pull her arms through the sleeves, but she thought it made a pretty good blanket, and wouldn't let go.

She seemed better now, her color had returned, yet she was acting as though she had been drugged. I unlaced her shoes, and Sylvie hummed softly to herself with her head lolling backward at a strange angle, her hair against the curling edge of an unframed watercolor. I recognized Mary's hand in the brushstrokes; it was a swirl of maroon and purple tacked into the descending slope of the roof, a costume plan of Sylvie as a dancing Cossack.

"Stop pretending," I said. I pulled her feet out from under her, and she sank back flat onto the little bed. There was an aged, satiny pillow that crinkled as she rested her head upon it. Sylvie gave a sigh as if she were just waking from a trance, and opened her eyes. She looked like she'd never seen the room before, but decided soon enough that she liked it. Her breath came in long, relaxed whispers. "Thanks," she said, quiet almost beyond the level of hearing. "Moscow would never have helped me. He's an old poop."

I didn't like the way she was smiling. She ran her fingers along the wall of silk and textured paper, turned her head on the pillow and looked up at me from under her lashes. Something was tugging on my collar. It shunted my tie all out of place, drew me down until I could feel her breath against my cheek. The bed creaked under her. Our noses almost touched. She lifted her jaw, and still could not reach my lips. "Why are you fighting me?" she said without opening her eyes. Then her fingers came up around the base of my neck, and her tongue found its way into my mouth. She let out a sigh that seemed to completely deflate her beneath me. She tasted of strawberry ice cream.

I wanted to touch her and I wanted not to touch her. I wanted both of them a lot. I kept my hands straight at my sides. I tried not to breathe. There was a laugh and something else in her eyes when she finally let me go. I lost my balance in getting away from her, from the bed. I nearly fell over. "She doesn't love you," Sylvie said. "Not the way you want. She never will."

I looked around for my hat, realized that I hadn't been wearing one, and Sylvie remained with her head on the pillow and giggled. "I know," I said. I went out into the rank stairwell, into the cold air; I tried not to slam the door behind. I could see my breath.

The sun had already passed over when I came backing down the alley. I had to turn the lights on to keep from bumping into the truck behind. Jones was standing nearly invisible in the shadow of the stage door. "Well?" she said as I climbed down from the seat. "How did it go?"

It was so cold out now that I could not keep from shivering. Jones was only wearing a light work shirt; how could she stand it? "She wasn't feeling all that well," I said. "I don't think she'll be coming in tonight."

Jones shrugged. "I told her not to bother." She took the blocks from where I'd piled them, handed me a pair, and together we fitted them around the dirty wheels.

"Do you know what she was having done?" I said when we came into the bright, warm rooms in back. I could hear Mary singing somewhere close by; out on the stage, Templeton was practicing his lines.

"How do you think she got the address?" Jones said. "I couldn't have her going to the neighborhood butcher." She turned to me and smiled. She didn't seem to mean anything by it. "You saw her to bed?"

"Yes," I said.

"Good. Now I need you onstage. We're blocking out act two; you'll have to take Sylvie's place for now."

THE LIMITS OF NATURE

ONCE, in interval between two strenuous shows, I asked Mary if she could tell me what an actor sees. She didn't have to guess at what I meant, but she wouldn't tell either, not right away. She didn't get back to me until after the second show, and then I had the feeling that she needed to say it in a hurry, before the answer got away from her.

She said that all the stories about actors losing their sense of reality could never have come from anyone who had done the job, that stage magic was something that had to summoned by force of will. Painted flats only resembled a setting from the audience's perspective and then only if the actor could convince them; when you were inside the shadow-box, in costume, the best that could be hoped for was to believe in that moment and that moment alone, but in the end an actor could never really, truly forget that it was all repetitive play, reflex, at best a shared trance, and so impermanent. But she also said that when she looked at an actor's face under colored light and paint, when they were all working together to achieve the same lie, to cast the same spell so to speak, the actor and the character did sometimes seem to blend into a third creature halfway between reality and fiction, the faces of the people you knew and worked with and perhaps even socialized with transposed over the well-rehearsed and mutually agreed upon fantasy. Even that, she said, did not last beyond the closing of the curtain.

There were curtains in my apartment, but when I closed them it did nothing to vanish the Jones that I saw in my mind. Dreaming had become my stock in trade, an occupational hazard, abetted by the sense of unreality that had never left me since those first days seven months before, by the exhaustion I would never have admitted to, by the success we were having, and, perversely, by my parents with their weekly calls urging me back towards respectability. It was only natural and expected that I should get notions of all kinds; the one that occupied me all through that Christmas didn't raise any eyebrows when I finally trotted it out in front of the whole company. Even so, it was the most ill-founded notion I ever had. Perhaps if I'd been just a little less exhausted, a little less hungry, I would have been better able to see it for what it was, and could have tossed it out with the rest of the mental garbage that flowed through the Underwood on a daily basis.

But I suppose not. I suppose I knew that it was a bad idea, and craved myself into it, worked myself up for it, by coming up with An Angle. Oh, those Angles are Dangerous Places. In the angles there is light and hope. The idea, and the danger, is that they will lead you on to attempt something greater. Angles, Jones said, must always be explored.

CHRISTMAS MORNING, Valenciennes. 11:30. Snow blowing under the curtain. Thumping sounds heard.

SYLVIE
(from the dark)
God damn it!

Lights rise gently as the curtain is drawn away. It is a pale, whitewashed scene, the theater's side alley piled high with snow. Centerstage two trucks stand one behind the other, crusted with ice, looking like sightless trolls. A narrow path cleared to their right recedes to the street at back.

Downstage right, **SYLVIE** in a green knee-length coat, wool gloves and a knitted cap stands fumbling at the stage door, kicking snow from her shoes, trying to keep hold of a heavy paper sack, in which the tops of several Christmas-wrapped packages are visible.

From the back, a young man's voice:

Ho Ho Ho! On Dasher On Dancer!

Enter **PENFOLD** along the little pathway from the street. He's wearing the wrong kind of shoes for this weather, grey trousers, and a heavy coat marked with the wrinkles of several previous owners. He, too, is struggling with a package: a brown box, not too heavy but oversized and cumbersome.

Sylvie sees him, waves and flops against the door.

SYLVIE
Oh! Winslow! She's locked us out!

PENFOLD
Don't you have a key?

SYLVIE
No. Don't you?

P shakes his head. Awkward pause.

PENFOLD
Maybe she doesn't trust us.

SYLVIE
Shit. She's in there. I know it. But try to raise her. You'd think she was wearing ear muffs.

She pounds on the door three more times, then in a sudden fury brings her feet into play; she looks as if she will either knock the door down or slip and hurt herself.

SYLVIE
(under her breath)
Jonesey, you... damn you, if I...

PENFOLD
I'll have a look around front. Wait here.

SYLVIE
(still sparring with the door)
If they find me here in the Spring frozen into a
block of ice, it'll be your fault.

P starts back through the snow. Behind him the scene
rotates soundlessly away; he seems to be walking in place.
At the edge of the busy street he turns under a row of
icicles dripping from the marquee, which has taken on a
look much like the entry gate to a Winter Carnival.
P sets down his box, raps on the door and then peers in
through frosted glass. He gets no answer, sees nothing
but the empty lobby, his own reflection and the reflected
street at his back. Out of that mirror image a figure takes
shape, dressed in green; at first he thinks it is something
emerging from the dark inside – then with a start he
turns to face the street.

MARY has entered stage right and picked her way gingerly
through slush and traffic. She is carrying a cardboard
suitcase and a wreath wrapped in velvet ribbon, and looks
as if the long walk across town has only just got her warmed
up. At the curb P offers to take something; instead she
steps up and into his arms in an enthusiastic but awkward
hug that's all crunching paper, pine boughs scraping on
cloth and the suitcase flopping against his backside.

PENFOLD
(muffled, with unexpected feeling)
Hey there... it feels like I haven't seen you in a
month!

MARY
(stepping back)
Winslow! Happy Christmas. Where is everyone?

PENFOLD
Jones is inside. We can't get her to open up.
Sylvie's out back, working herself into a state.

MARY
Oh well, I can help that.

From her coat pocket she produces a ring with two keys on
it. As she bends to unlock the building its facade breaks

neatly into two halves and is withdrawn, followed closely
by the lobby doors which separate magically to admit them.
Snow washes into the space beyond. It is a place like a
flatwalled cave, lined with painted canvas and tile. MARY
and PENFOLD set their things down on the cold floor and
stand clapping snow from their clothes, unwinding scarves.

PENFOLD

How was your holiday?

MARY

I worked on my walls, that made it good. Max ate
Christmas pudding with me. Otherwise...

P says nothing. A distinct battering, banging sound filters
through from deeper within the building...

MARY

Sylvie. I'll go.

PENFOLD

You're brave.

He follows after, not wanting to be left alone. Again the
theater splits; painted play-figures are vanished right and
left. Laughter is heard; not P or MARY, but something
cutting from the further dark. Gradually, as though our
eyes are adjusting to the change in light, narrow rows of
black seats begin to take shape. Cigarette smoke curls in a
wispy arch above them. In the middle of the house JONES is
sitting, slumped well down into her chair. She is not alone.
PENFOLD has fallen back, halted by something, by the
voices below. Mary pauses halfway down.

MARY

You _are_ here.
Why wouldn't you let them in?

JONES shows her face for the first time, backlit from an
invisible source, one hand raised to her lips.

JONES

I'm sorry. I didn't hear. We've been...

The banging is louder than ever. MARY climbs to the stage

202

and disappears behind the curtain. JONES turns in her
seat to face the man beside her. She lowers her face almost
to his, and the soft laughter rises out of her again.

The man looks around over his shoulder. A handsome face
darkened with beardstubble. It is MOSCOW. He catches
sight of P, smirks and turns away.

Lights dim ¾ on all but PENFOLD and the seated figures.
The striking of a GONG is heard.

A low, mechanical humming rises slowly to fill the air like
bloodrush pulsing greek chorus funeral murmurs.

Out of the shadows behind PENFOLD, a BLACK HAND at
the end of a five-foot-long puppet ARMATURE swathed in a
decaying shroud reaches out, curls almost lovingly around
him and then clutches at his stomach. A mocking VOICE
made up of many voices and coming from all directions
begins to make a CHUFFING sound, and then intones:

>   UGLY VOICE
> —Forget not that they have a Past—
> —Think of them together—
> —And don't imagine that you can compare—

>   PENFOLD
> He got here before us, that's all.
> They've been telling jokes.

The hand TIGHTENS. Using P's STOMACH for leverage, an
ENORMOUS BLACK SHAPE drags itself up from behind him,
heaving into view above his head. It is fully eight feet tall, with
batwings of gauze depending from skeleton arms. SNAKES
and WORMS writhe where there there should be hair. The
eyes are liquid, blood-red, and draining. An gash of a mouth,
full of razor-teeth, grinning. It paws and caresses his face.

>   WHISPERER
> —Jokes, yes. About you.
> You thought he was with Sylvie.

>   SYLVIE
> (offstage)
> God damn it, it's about — oh, hi.

PENFOLD
(trying to brush away the hands, the gauze, without success)
She knows I'm in love with her. I think she knows.

WHISPERER
—You're a child to her.
She wants something that won't break in her arms.

PENFOLD
(with some anger)
Break! I've gained some ground here! I'm not —
WHISPERER
—What ground have you gained?
Tell me how have things progressed since Cuba...

PENFOLD
She hasn't got time for that!
She's Jones.

WHISPERER
—I see. It all fell neatly back to place, just the way it had been before, yes? The Mistress and her Pet?

PENFOLD
No! We're more intimate than ever...

WHISPERER
—Like that?
Look at them together.
—She's not inhuman.
That's what you make of her.
Look at them.
—How many times have you been to her bed?

PENFOLD
She is the company!
There's no time!

WHISPERER
How many times?

                    PENFOLD
Once. Just the one time.

                    WHISPERER
—And was it the stuff of legend?

Pause. The hands roam. The face turns down to grin at him.

                    PENFOLD
No. I was — I was —

                    WHISPERER
—Frightened. Inept. Unable to finish it.
—Idiot. <u>Say</u> it.

                    PENFOLD
Go to hell. It wasn't so bad.

                    WHISPERER
—It was pity. Idiot. She pitied you.

                    PENFOLD
She said...

                    WHISPERER
—She's an actress. Idiot.

The thing STABS Penfold with its pointed fingernails.
Penfold goes pale; blood spatters in the aisle.

                    WHISPERER
—And you never tried again?

                    PENFOLD
There was never — she never I never

                    WHISPERER
—Idiot. She goes where she needs to go. To
someone who can please her. She's not interested
in your Love.

P cannot say anything more. He can only listen.

                    WHISPERER
—And now, <u>now what of your present to her?</u>

                    LON'S VOICE
(low at first, as from a distant radio station, growing steadily clearer)
Children. They won't hold the trains just to suit your Christmas Spirit. Let's go.

Lights up suddenly. Lon has entered at the back of the house, carrying a monstrous picnic basket roughly the size of a steamer trunk. Below, MARY, SYLVIE and MOSCOW crowd each other in the left aisle. Much laughter and gabble, all of it indistinct. Sylvie has placed herself square in the middle of the group; the only trace of her former anger is the determination with which she seems to be putting on a merry face.
Between Lon and the Company, Winslow stands alone. The puppet **WHISPERER** is gone, but it is clear from P's manner that he still feels its presence.

                    LON
(to Jones)
Unless you've got a friend at the Transit Authority that I don't know about.

                    JONES
(hooking an arm over the seat back)
Would that surprise you?

LON frowns and shakes his head.

                    JONES
Then I don't. Hoicks and away, everyone.

                    LON
(exiting, with his basket)
I'll wait for you if you put a wiggle on.

The players start to amble out, squeezing past Winslow still frozen in the aisle. Sylvie and Moscow do not even acknowledge his presence; Mary tries to speak to him, but is put off by his miserable look. Jones is the only one to pause as she comes abreast of him.

                    JONES
Take a break.
(taps his forehead)
You're writing again. It's one of your more

endearing qualities but just now I can smell the
smoke. Remember, this is the only Holiday you get.

She goes on. Penfold brings up the rear.

                    PENFOLD
          It's not something you can turn on and off.

                    JONES
          (off)
          Of course not. It's something you have to work
          for.

At the door, P looks back distrustfully into the corners of
the theater. Silence. If he expects mocking laughter to rise
from its shadows, it does not come. Scowling, he turns and
walks out.

LIGHTS DOWN.

SCENE II: Passenger car of the 11:45 train out of
Philadelphia. Windows covered with frost, but for a spot
in the center of one that someone has cleared away,
through which we can see telegraph poles rushing by, the
occasional white-faced building, the frozen city getting
smaller in the distance. The car is quite full, Jones
and her company of players occupying a section in the
approximate middle. In the aisle, Lon stands balancing
his picnic basket in the carrier overhead. To his left,
Mary and Sylvie seated together, chatting animatedly.
To his right, Jones and Moscow. Across the aisle, behind
Sylvie, Penfold sits apart from the others, trying to keep
from looking at Jones, and failing. Steam pouring from
his nostrils. Beside him, a man in grey clothing sits
reading from the front page of a folded newspaper.

Due to the noise of the train, none of the separate groups can
hear what the others are saying. Only LON, standing between
them, can listen in on any or all of his fellow players.

                    JONES
          (with humor)
          —can't see your interest in this. You're too young
          for the lead, and the other parts are too small to
          appeal to you...

MOSCOW
It would make a change from what we've been
doing.

JONES
(Laughing, light)
What we've been doing was meant as a change
from Henrik and Father William!

THE TRAVELER
(suddenly; not looking up from his paper)
She doesn't talk with you that way.

P turns and looks at the man in disbelief. The traveler does
not move, except in the rhythm of the train. He does not
look up. Nothing more is said. P returns to his previous
occupation of brooding and staring.

SYLVIE
We never had anything like that.

MARY
Oh, always a puppet show at Christmas. My
grandfather...

MOSCOW
(at ease; flirting with Jones)
I'm getting bored with Mr. Winslow Laconic and
his minimalist plays. He's no poet; just moves us
in and lets the settings do all the work. I don't
think he knows how people talk.

THE TRAVELER
(whose name is Walter Plinge)
Look, be a man. Buck up. They can feel you
sobbing all over the carriage.

JONES
All clipped, pinched sentences with his
characters trying to squeeze in more meaning
than the words will carry? He knows exactly
how people talk.

PENFOLD
I haven't said anything.

FREDER.

PLINGE
Christ, you don't need to say anything. You
radiate it like an overstuffed coal burner.

JONES
Besides, there's a kind of strangled poetry to be
gotten out of not being able to say what you wish.

PENFOLD
All I want is to feel like I'm a part of things.

PLINGE
Liar. And anyway, you're very much a part of <u>this</u>
scene. Why do you think they're ignoring you?

MARY
... had a little portable puppet theater that I
think he'd made himself. He kept it in a smelly
old suitcase, and he kept the suitcase in the
attic, and he only brought it down once a year...

MOSCOW
Oh, please. All this nonsensical mumbo-jumbo
he comes up with. Whole families slaughtering
each other.

PLINGE
How can you be honest on paper? You can't even
be honest in your own head.

JONES
(without malice)
You should like that. Lots of leeway for you to
chew the curtain up.

SYLVIE
Your Christmases were so elaborate. It wasn't
like that with my folks. Stockings and apples
were about all we got up to.

PLINGE
How can you even say that you know her? What
d'you really know <u>about</u> her? Where was she
born? What kind of family did she have? What've
you bothered to learn of her?

PENFOLD
I know her.

PLINGE
Oh. Mysticism. Soul Connection. Telepathy.
—What a load of hogwash!

MOSCOW
(laughing)
I don't need him to give me that kind of a chance.
I do perfectly well on my own.

JONES
I think you're afraid of him.
PENFOLD
I can't help it. She's in my dreams at night.

PLINGE
You're writing her. Giving her all these powers.
She's only half real to you; one of those inbetween
characters Mary was telling you about...

PENFOLD
Eidolon. I think that's the word she used.

PLINGE
No wonder you can't start with her. Have you
ever thought that she might just be Human?

MOSCOW
(teasing)
Peer Gynt — a Troll! You're on the wrong scent
altogether.

JONES
(sly grin)
I'll let it go.

The train is slowing down. Through its one clear window
we can see snowy rooftops, the eaves of well-to-do houses
dripping with icicles, all blotted out suddenly by the bulk
of the station looming into view.

SYLVIE
Did you see their house?

MARY

No. It's a block or so down, back from the corner.

PENFOLD

She can play any role. You've got me all wrong.

PLINGE

Do I. Do I.

The train lurches to a halt. LON lifts his picnic basket down from the rack. Much confusion in the aisle as approximately half of the passengers (Jones and her Company included) all rise and try to exit at once.

LON

(to Penfold, over the noise)
Hey. Who're you talking to?

P, in the aisle, turns his face away. He gathers up his brown box; he was the last one on, and will be the first one off.

PENFOLD

Nobody.
(louder; to the company)
—Which way are we headed?

JONES

Left out of the station. I'll catch you up.

They file along and out onto the ramp.

LON

(exiting; to Penfold's back)
Well if you don't want to tell me, don't tell me.

P is long gone; if he replies we do not hear it. As soon as the doorway is cleared, new passengers begin to trundle aboard. The traveler, Plinge, sits alone beside his window, reading his paper, moving only to turn the page. He never looks up.

LIGHTS DOWN.

Stacatto tapping in a quiet room. Only by running it through the Underwood, a black-faced, steel-gutted device, can I see it for the comedy it was, not high comedy but a kind of emotional slapstick complete with pratfalls, played matter-of-factly by the rules of engagement, much like the long, straight-faced battles between Laurel and Hardy and Charlie Hall. From the station we turned onto a silent, wintry street bordered on both sides by cast iron fences. Two and three-story brick houses loomed behind the gates; they had broad flat roofs and cupolas buried in snow. "Do they really live here?" I asked Mary. Because I knew pretty well what their income from the company amounted to; it would not have been enough to buy even the smallest house in this crisp, historybook place.

"Just the top floor," Mary said. "Can you manage with that box? It's a bit of a climb."

The Templeton's house fronted on a yard dotted with half a dozen bare-branched trees. Candles burned in every window, a wreath edged with frost hung from the front door. The walkway, shoveled maybe half an hour before, was already covered with a dusting of snow deep enough for us to leave a muddle of tracks. Jones had Moscow by the arm. They moved side by side as in slow motion, falling back through the Company until they lagged well behind, framed in winter and treeshadow, wavering some against the blue wind. "Remember," I heard her tell him. "You promised to be good. No scenes."

SCENE III: First: a tree, brightly lit in the dark at the foot of the stage.

TEMPLETON
(offstage)
I'm not saying there is and I'm not saying there isn't. But mainly I'm not saying there isn't.

Next: a rush of well-fed voices, all talking at once. Slowly, the room begins to grow brighter.

TEMPLETON'S VOICE
(above the racket)
It's brainless, that's all. 'Oh Rhett Rhett' and 'Oh Scarlett Scarlett' and 'Oh Ashley! Oh Ashley!" — ad nauseam.

JONES
I don't disagree with you. But audiences are going to be so blinded by the spectacle they won't notice.
Laughter, mixed with sounds of clattering silverware. By

now the lights have come up ¼ on a well-furnished living room, decked out for Christmas. The tree, downstage left, shelters a circle of presents; beyond it, a monstrous sofa rests slightly off-center, surrounded by a mismatched grouping of chairs borrowed from other parts of the room. Large windows in the wall stage left, admitting moon and stars. At the back, an archway opening onto an entry hall. An open door stage right, filled with light from the dining room beyond, is the source of all the voices. As Templeton finishes his speech, PENFOLD appears there and stands backlit as though unsure what he should do next.

> MRS. TEMPLETON
> (off)
> Left, Winslow. Then left again.

> PENFOLD
> Thank you.

He moves into the room, but instead of following her directions, comes down to the tree and disappears behind it.

> MOSCOW'S VOICE
> Gable's nothing more than a smirk with greasy hair.

> SYLVIE'S VOICE
> Oh I don't know.

> TEMPLETON'S VOICE
> Honestly, Margaret, if that's what passes for drama these days, we are in trouble.

Rustling sounds heard from behind the tree. A couple of the packages are pushed aside by an unseen hand. Penfold appears again, working his way on hands and knees around from the back.

> PENFOLD
> (sotto voce)
> Crap. Where did they hide it?

> JONES'S VOICE
> It doesn't affect us. I'm more concerned about the spectacle.

>TEMPLETON'S VOICE
>And that ending! It's a good thing I never read
>the book! I'd have thrown it across the room!

Rummaging through the packages, P grows more excited
and careless.

>PENFOLD
>Shit. Shit. Shit.

>SYLVIE'S VOICE
>What do you mean the spectacle?

>TEMPLETON'S VOICE
>I think she means that when you dazzle an
>audience on that level, our box of tricks begins
>to appear quaint by comparison.

Now P finds what he's looking for, a Christmas-wrapped
box, eight inches wide by eighteen inches long. Removing
it carefully from the bottom of the pile, he begins to fumble
with the tape.

>PENFOLD
>Come on. Come on.

>JONES'S VOICE
>We'll be all right. Stage productions will need to
>become less realistic, more stylistic. And more
>intimate. And that's just what we do.

Sounds of agreement.

>TEMPLETON'S VOICE
>As soon as that pair produced a child I knew that
>it was doomed.

>MRS. TEMPLETON'S VOICE
>What's keeping Winslow, I wonder?

P cannot seem to open the box. His fingers claw at it
without success, as if they have gone numb, as if they are
receiving mixed messages from his brain.

PENFOLD
God. Come on!

MOSCOW'S VOICE
Maybe he fell in.

TEMPLETON'S VOICE
... for the sake of argument...

Mrs. Templeton appears in the doorway. Behind her, the after-dinner chatter diminishes to a murmur. She starts in the direction of the bathroom, then pauses, listening; in the darkened room, P has frozen in place, but his breathing is clearly audible against the stillness of the scene. Hearing it, she turns and takes a step towards the tree...

MRS. TEMPLETON
Winslow? Are you all right?

P. shrinks into the circle of packages. Seeking darkness, he succeeds only in knocking over a small stack of the boxes. It is more than enough to give him away; Mrs. Templeton comes straight forward and finds him set aglow in the blue, green and orange of the Christmas lights.

MRS. TEMPLETON
(stage whisper)
Winslow! What's got into you?

PENFOLD
Just – just curiosity. I couldn't wait.

MRS. TEMPLETON
Now you're telling stories. You're the most patient young man I know.

PENFOLD
You don't know me at all.

Silence. P sighs, bows his head. He hands the package up to Mrs. Templeton.

MRS. TEMPLETON
I don't understand. This is your present to Margaret.

PENFOLD
I have, I have to take something out of it.

MRS. TEMPLETON
It's a bit late. Whatever for?

PENFOLD
You need to know the audience that you're playing to.
(Pause. Harsh silence.)
This is no different. What am I to her? What am I to her? How can I give it to her, even like this, without knowing?

MRS. TEMPLETON
(uncertain)
Don't be silly. What is it?

PENFOLD
(gripping the package)
A, a ring.

MRS. TEMPLETON
Oh.

PENFOLD
Not a real one; I wouldn't have dared. It's imaginary. See, that's the angle: it's an imaginary ring. It's a play. Just a stage piece I found. A moon and a star. It doesn't mean anything.

Pause. A beat.

MRS. TEMPLETON
I think it does.

From the dining room, the other members of the company enter silently one at a time, taking up places in the chairs around the tree. TEMPLETON, dressed as ST. NICHOLAS in a peaked cap, fur-hemmed greatcoat, beard, and carrying a shepherd's crook, is last to appear. Ignoring the scene taking place in front of them, moving in a kind of stately pantomime, they begin to open the packages that Templeton has already begun to pass around.

PENFOLD
Anyway, it was a bad idea. Now I think it had better come out. I'm rewriting this scene. I have that privilege. I have it until curtain time.

MRS. TEMPLETON
You thought she might accept it, if you could make it into harmless fiction? She might at that. Then what?

I thought about that. Under the canopy of pine, it occurred to me that the kind of marriage I wanted so much was, to a certain extent, already mine. I saw my jealousy for what it was; I saw the fool that I had been playing all morning. It didn't change the way I felt. It didn't change anything. But it helped me to understand the thing that she said next.

MRS. TEMPLETON
(releasing the package into his hands)
Never mind. The thing to do is give it to her.

PENFOLD
You think so.

MRS. TEMPLETON
Yes. And so do you, or you wouldn't have wrapped it up tighter than Fort Knox. You knew you'd have second thoughts and saw to it that there wouldn't be any last minute rewrites.

PENFOLD
(laughing softly)
I guess you're right at that.

MRS. TEMPLETON
Then it's settled. Now come back in to dinner. There's dessert yet. Baked Alaska. I made it myself, and I expect a full display of sensual enjoyment from you all.

Lights and sound rise on the scene behind them; Mrs. Templeton turns and settles into it like a piece into a jigsaw puzzle. SAINT NICHOLAS has given out more than half of the presents, the floor is littered with Christmas paper, tissue and empty parcels. PENFOLD stands outside of the scene, looking in with some trepidation.

> SYLVIE
> (holding a silk robe against her body)
> You dog! Where did you find it?

> MOSCOW
> Little place in Provincetown. Thought of you...
> stepping out of it.

Laughter. Penfold makes his decision. He stuffs the package into St. Nick's empty hands, and attempts to enter the scene, only to find his place taken by a **HUSK**, a **DUMMY PENFOLD** dressed as he is dressed, with a face painted into an expression of fixed anticipation. He takes up a position just behind the mannequin's left shoulder, looking on as the scene unfolds. When others address him, they address the **DUMMY**.

> TEMPLETON
> (approaching Jones)
> Well. I have something here for a very good girl
> indeed.

> JONES
> Can't be me.

She shakes the box. A dull rattle sounds from somewhere deep inside.

> MARY
> Open it!

> JONES
> Can't be a pony.

> MARY
> Open it!

> SYLVIE
> It's from Winslow.

> PENFOLD
> (anxiously; to the dummy)
> Say something!

FREDER.

A hush falls over the group as Jones rips the paper.

JONES
Somebody didn't want me to get in here.

MOSCOW
(to Templeton)
How much more do we have?

TEMPLETON
Hold your water.

JONES
Say!

From the box, she lifts out a full-face **BLACK MASK**, made of papier mâché and decorated with occult symbols. She turns it under the light...

JONES
Oh, say. That's fine...
(presses it over her face)

JONES
One flows from Two,
Two Rivers are One.
One is Three,
And Three is One.'

Laughter. By now half-contorted into a witchdoctor pose, Jones peeks over the top of the mask.

JONES
Why is the right eye taped up?

PENFOLD
(as before)
Tell her!

Jones shakes the mask gently; the same rattling sound is heard, louder than before.

MRS. TEMPLETON
There's something inside.

> **PENFOLD**
> (to the dummy)
> Why don't you <u>say</u> something?

Jones peels black tape from the front of the mask. Holding it flat in her hands, she peers inside. Puzzlement and curiosity settle onto her features, then vanish, leaving her face a masklike blank.

> **JONES**
> That 's...

> **PENFOLD**
> —Speak!

> **JONES**
> ...that's...

Stepping forward, she lifts the mask chalice-like, offering it up in a swirling circular motion as though panning for gold. Something small and hard as a pebble can be heard rolling around in the eye socket.

> **PENFOLD**
> —<u>Speak!</u>

Jones approaches until she is standing over the dummy Penfold, wordless, her eyes fixed on the thing in the socket. Without wasting any extra motion or emotion, she tilts the mask over him...

> **PENFOLD**
> <u>SAY SOMETHING!</u>

... spilling the ring so that it falls like water into the dummy's lap. At once the mask is clapped back over her face. As she turns away, the ring, a beautiful fake all of emerald and gold, rolls out of his lap and drops to the floor.

> **JONES**
> (through the mask)
> Thank you. It's perfect. Perfect...

The Company, more or less unconsciously, bows as a unit to peer at the thing on the floor. Moscow starts to laugh.

Sylvie bolts out of her seat. Mary turns to the dummy with some concern, then looks away. Moscow cannot stop laughing. Nothing is said. Templeton fishes under the tree, comes back with a present clasped in both hands.

TEMPLETON
And now one for you...

CURTAIN.

"You've been going around with a long face for more than a week," Mrs. Templeton said one afternoon during a matinee of *The Questing Season*. It was not a casual encounter, though she was careful to make it seem one; Mrs. Templeton knew the play as well as any of us, knew where I could be found at any given moment, knew to the instant the amount of time we would have alone before the end of the scene. She came straight back to me from the stage, dropping her character not all at once but in bits and pieces as she handed over her handbag and parasol. She was wearing her standard stage face and a gown that looked like silk under the stagelight, though it was really painted muslin. It crinkled as she moved. "You mustn't think that you have to hold it all in," she said softly. "If something's wrong you just let it out for some air."

I said I was fine, but Mrs. Templeton went on ahead as though I hadn't spoken. She unscrewed the Thermos, poured out two mugfuls of stale coffee. As she passed mine over she gave a furtive lowering of her head. She looked as if she'd caught me out in something. "Could it be difficulties with your Muse?"

"Not at all. The new play is going fine. Duck soup. Writing itself."

"Well that's good to know," Mrs. Templeton said. "But it isn't what I meant. I meant your Muse. The one who leads you on. Margaret."

Just then the audience laughed at something Moscow said, something I'd written a month and a half before, far enough back so I could no longer remember whether or not it had been intended to get a laugh. The sound came back to us from beyond the proscenium, a faraway thing that made me feel once again like the detached arm of the Company.

"Relax," Mrs. Templeton said. "I think it's charming. Not many men take a mythological approach to love. She does have that quality. I'd be surprised if you weren't taken with her — I was taken with her myself at one point. I think our Mary still is. So it's nothing to be ashamed of. Eventually you'll find that she can't read minds or walk on water; the powers she does possess are formidable enough."

Neither of us had touched our coffee. "Why are you saying all of this?"

Mrs. Templeton pushed her mug aside and made ready to go to the stage. The scene was about over. "You're fretting so because you've seen how its all going to end up. That's good: forewarned and all of that. But it doesn't mean that you shouldn't see it through. Keep after her anyway. The pursuit itself will raise you."

I had to hand it to her: her timing was perfect. She picked her way back through the muddle of props, and was in the wings when her cue came out to her from the boards.

TWELFTH NIGHT

ONE night when I couldn't hold it back anymore I went out for a walk, taking with me a jumble of loose pages that I thought might come in handy as an excuse. I told myself that it was just another midnight walk to clear my thoughts, that I didn't know where I was going or what I was doing.. This was just another fish story. I told myself to turn back, but there was a light at the end of the block, and another at the end of the block after. It was a simple thing to follow the lights all the way down into a neighborhood where no one lived, where no cars broke the darkness, only the silhouettes of empty storefronts and the hum of a factory in the distance. I didn't stop until I came to a low brick building with catwalks and a fire escape in back like exposed ribs. On its left side, facing the street, was an unpainted metal door, dented in three places where someone had tried to kick it in. A plastic holder mounted over the buzzer had a piece of paper wedged inside. It said, in the ghost of faded ink:

Darwin.

The whole city seemed to be blowing off steam. It felt like the longest night of the year, like a horrible Norwegian night that had been going on for six months. I hugged myself in the frozen air; somewhere far off in the lower blocks a machine was working overtime, banging methodically on a hunk of metal. Nothing happened when I pushed the buzzer. I waited for a long time. "Go back," I said to myself. "Take a shower. She doesn't want to be bothered. Not by you."

The front of the building had 707 carved out in granite characters over a boarded-up window. Up on the second floor, orange light hit the panes of a sloping casement. As I watched, a shape appeared against the glass in slow, oblivious motion.

When I went back to try it one last time the door was standing ajar. Darkness from inside leaked out into the street; the handle burned my fingers. I stepped through into a grey-walled stairwell that was as hushed and still as the empty theater. At the landing the same orange glow spilled through an arched doorway, between a pair of secondhand curtains. Beyond this proscenium, center stage in a circle of light, Jones paced back and forth at the end of a long black cord. Behind her the wall was dotted with painted faces, animal and human alike: glowering demons, wooden elk and wireframe wizards, samurai and demigods. I recognized the hierophant Templeton had worn for the Halloween show, the badly shattered child-face that she had found during the summer, and the witch-doctor I had made her for Christmas. They regarded me with a mixture of welcome and hostility. They dared me to come inside.

It was a studio occupying the entire top floor. She had partitioned it off into an arcane arrangement of "rooms" with a series of folding screens, some made of wooden panels patterned in blue leaves, mystical symbols, painted stars and moons, others of simple black or green cloth stretched across a ramshackle frame. In the largest open space a woven runner stretched into and back out of the light. Jones was using it as a track, vanishing and reappearing, the receiver cradled between her chin and shoulder, the cord twining snakelike around her ankles.

After a time she caught sight of me beside the curtain. She wasn't in the least bit startled or surprised; she waved and settled onto the rug in a smooth melting motion like mercury falling that ended with her cross-legged in the exact center of the apartment. She talked for a minute more with her eyes lifted unblinking to mine, but for all I caught of her words she might have been speaking in Cherokee. There was something that needed to be made clear; whether to me or to the man on the other end of the line I wasn't sure. At last she lowered her eyes and said into the mouthpiece: "All right. Yes, you too. Goodbye."

Jones held the receiver out for me to take. She gave me a sort of tolerant smirk as I lifted it out of her fingers. I thought: *This is it. Say something.*

It took me some time to find the telephone, off at the end of the cord, resting on a low table in a corner made from screens. She was still sitting, facing the hall, when I came back onto the long rug. "Isn't it past your bedtime?" she said, not turning. "What brings you out?"

"Characters," I said. "They were making an awful racket under my bed. They wanted me to dress them, but they didn't like what I had in my closet."

"So you came to look in mine? Well. Did they follow you over?"

"What do you think? They're in here." The new play didn't have a name yet; it didn't even have a shape. It was twenty pages of feeling around in the dark; the characters were just asking questions, and that's never a good sign, because it means you don't know what to do with them. Just now it was stuffed all anyhow into a leather folder Mr. Deighton had given me three years before. "Wouldn't forget my pretext," I said, and offered her the whole mess.

"I've never known you to need one," Jones said. She waved the folder aside, and with both hands slapped the bare floor. "Sit down. Tell it to me."

A whole summer spent trying to sit Indian style and I still hadn't quite got the hang of it. Now I managed a reasonable fake without hurting myself, and took out page one. Jones at once covered it with her hand. "No," she said, "that's not what I mean. Don't just read it; come on! *Tell* it to me."

"I wouldn't know how to sum it up. I wouldn't know where to start."

"It doesn't have to be in fifty words or less. Give me the full treatment."

"There isn't any full treatment. What I've got is the literary equivalent of pushing food around on a plate. There isn't anything to treat."

"Well, try. How many acts?"

"I don't know."

"How many characters?"

"I don't know."

Pause; a beat. Heavy sigh. "All right," she said. She took the folder, opened it across her lap and set the covering page aside. "*The Bone Tree?*"

"An all-purpose title. Until I find something better. It doesn't mean anything."

Jones made a sound like a whisper. "You say nothing means anything but it always does." She read on. The pages settled one after another into the beginnings of a white mosaic across the floor. "It had to come from somewhere," she said after a time. Then she looked up. "Why don't you go look in the icebox. Get us something to drink."

I left her alone. At the end of a short maze of screens, in a corner dark enough to have belonged to another room entirely, was a grey, old-fashioned box with a pan underneath it and a lid in the top for the ice. There was nothing inside but an open bottle of red wine tilted against the back. Six glasses with long crystal stems were half buried in excelsior inside a packing crate on the floor nearby. I wiped out two of them, and went back to find Jones still reading, motionless but for her hands turning the pages, adding to the growing pool of paper.

I was standing there looking at her when she said, quite suddenly and with some excitement, " — Do you know who this is?"

"Which one?"

"The woman on the train. Helen, you call her. She appears on page fifteen and..." she rifled through the remaining pages "...I don't see her again."

"What about her?"

Jones looked at me over her shoulder. "You don't recognize her? *'I've come some distance, Mr. Sallis. I won't be staying long. If we're to be friends it must be with that understanding.'* Think about it. Where have you met her before?"

It was a line from the new piece but the voice she used belonged to another character entirely, a female con artist named Rebecca who appeared in *The Questing Season*, our December play. She was nothing more than a Deus Ex Machina designed to bring about the fall of the hero — Jones said I was hard on my heroes and I guess she was right — but when Jones lent her form and force, audiences held their breath. They stomped on the floor, blew through their fingers and sometimes called for her to come back. Jones said it was because Rebecca had something behind her that they recognized. I just thought it was a hell of a performance.

"All right," I said. "I'm repeating myself. I'll take her out."

Jones held out page fifteen, gathered the rest of the play into a neat bundle and tossed it aside. "Don't be an idiot," she said without malice. "*That's* the stuff you need to take out."

I stood there with the glasses warming in my hands. "Sorry you don't like it," I said. "Do you want one of these or was that just a goose chase?"

"What do you think?" She accepted one of the glasses, took a big unhurried drink and set it down half empty beside her knee.

"I only came by to ask your help," I said, not drinking.

"Liar. You came by to force an issue. Well, now you're here. Let's see what you've got."

"You've just told me I've got a load of crap."

The tips of her fingers found page fifteen and turned it against the rug. "You've got Rebecca. Obviously you're not done with her yet, or she wouldn't be here."

"That's no help. She's a cypher."

"Yes," Jones said. "The Bone Tree. But she's riding on a train. Going somewhere. She must have a reason."

Silence came down over the room, perfect silence but for the wind outside and the floorboards squeaking under my feet as I paced around her. Jones never moved from her place on the rug. If she followed me with her eyes, I never noticed it, or felt it. Now for a change I didn't pay any attention to her, to the masks, to anything.

I saw Rebecca as a child of seven might have seen her looking back from a seat just ahead and across the aisle. She had aged a few years since *The Questing Season*; she looked more like Jones than ever. She was wearing a dusty ankle-length dress not meant for travel, a dusty frock coat the color of faded olives and a dusty straw hat encircled with straw flowers. That would have to go.

Coming off the train she had the manner of a woman who didn't care where she was so long as she did not have to go any farther. She walked with the bearing of a lady, head up, eyes roving, carrying with her an expensive calfskin bag. Her free hand held the coat tight at her breast. She ignored me, and went instead to question another man. He pointed down the street to a pawnshop squatting at the corner; she shook her head. What, then? The lady could not say. Wouldn't say... because what she really needed was a mark...

"How about this," I said at last. "She's tired. She doesn't want to move around anymore. But there are too many places where she's known, and the places where she's not known aren't very likely to welcome a woman with her background. So she has to re-make herself. That works; she has all the skills. But she can't do it alone."

Jones frowned. "As a subtext it's fine, but that's all it is. It's not anything more than re-stating the title."

"What title?"

"The Bone Tree," Jones said again. For a moment I had the uncomfortable feeling that she had already written the play, had it mapped out clear in her mind, and was only prodding me along, waiting for me to catch up with her. "She's something of an actor. She does what an actor does: pack flesh onto an empty framework, a different set of bones each time. She doesn't deceive her victims so much as enter into a conspiracy with them. A conspiracy of imagination..."

I thought of Jones offering her hand to Mr. Deighton, in that dim, well-ordered office where she had seemed so out of place, and so at home. I'm your tenant player, she had said. I thought of his words to me: *If I was your age, I would already be lost.*

I said, "Like us."

Jones let it go by. She turned page fifteen against the floor.

"She'd have to find herself... someone well off. And frustrated. So that she could be the bomb, ready to drop on him."

Jones said, "I still don't see any drama in this." She felt through her pockets for a cigarette, found one, and tossed it away with the discarded pages of the first draft. "You're still thinking about her effect on the man. What about the man's effect on her?"

"Does he have any?"

Jones waved that one aside. "Think about their marriage. She'd have to marry him, in your scheme of things. The ultimate con job, because he'd be making of her something that she isn't, and for a while at least she'd have to be a willing participant. I give it two years, at the outside. Then watch the fireworks."

I stopped my pacing. Jones and I looked each other in the eye. "Act one," I said.

"Two years later."

"Something to chew on."

Around and around, watching Rebecca grow in my mind. The floor went on complaining every time I passed over a spot mid-way behind her. I should leave now, I thought. A gentleman would: mission accomplished, inspiration restored. No excuse to remain. No pretense if I do. In the end, the only thing I can do is nothing. Constipated from not wanting to make the wrong move, not knowing how to make the right move, nor even if the time for moves has come. Go, write. Get back to the typer. No, stay.

It felt like I had lost the script, like the lines had been written for me and I had neglected to learn them. I said, "That's some Santa get-up Templeton has. Does he do that every year?"

Jones looked up and smiled and shook her head. She said, "You always do everything the hard way, don't you?"

I said I guess I did, and sat down cross-legged on the rug opposite her. I said it wasn't something I was proud of, but after all you can't fight genetics. That got me another smile. I gave myself a pat on the back.

Light fell through her glass, spilling red circles on the MS. She tilted her head in what might or might not have been a calculatedly wistful angle. "What am I going to do with you?" she said. "I can't make up your mind for you. You're going to have to write this thing yourself. You want me to open the door to a golden room. All I can do is dump fertilizer on your head. I shouldn't even be doing that."

I leaned forward and kissed her on the mouth. She didn't kiss me back, but she didn't pull away. I took that as a sign of encouragement. She smelled of cake make-up and powder. I opened my eyes enough to see that hers were closed; that encouraged me more. I took hold of her by the arms. Her wine glass floated between us, cradled in her unmoving hands.

"Look at yourself," she said when I let her go. "You could be the mascot of yearning. You could be its prophet." Her face had not changed; it was fixed in that same feline expression, the disclaimer, behind which anything she said could be truth or fancy, take your pick. She emptied her glass, turned it sideways in the air. Then she raised herself in one easy motion, leaving the folder lying there flat across the moat of paper. "Come on. It's getting pretty thick in here. Let's you and I walk it off..."

Jones beside me was nothing more than a shadow, a black ghost wrapped in her bulky sailor's coat, the collar turned up to conceal all but her eyes. We went along an iron fence slanting back from the sidewalk, black lines across the blue snow, snow-covered obelisks growing out of the opposite ground under leafless branches. Inside the cemetery the snow was three feet deep, covered with a thick crust that made sounds like muffled gunshots under our feet. It was the only sound for miles and miles.

Jones told me about another Jones, who on Twelfth Night produced a masque recreating the structure of the entire Cosmos. She told me about seeing Venetian and Dominican revelers going masked in the streets, about a Swiss festival she'd heard of in which whole towns reenacted events from history, about a family of puppeteers and the cycle of plays that took them seven years to perform. She told me about a greek actor named Polus who carried his son's ashes in a production of Electra, parading his genuine grief before an audience that suspected only craft. Not very professional, Jones said. But who could argue with that kind of dedication?

We came up through the churchyard under trees folding their fingers across the luminous sky, past stone angels with wreaths of dead vine looped around their ankles. An uneven row of raised humps bordered the grounds like mosscovered igloos. A few of the saints were missing their hands. In a narrow alley beside the chapel we paused to admire a row of cast-iron markers. Above the names, Jones's flashlight picked out the Angel of Death, a black skull spreading black bat-wings. "There you go," she said. "Put your tongue to that."

I said No thanks. We went on to a rock wall that ran across the rear of the yard; Jones climbed up onto it and laughed and said nothing. "All right," I said when she offered her hand. "I'm all bleary-eyed. That doesn't make me stupid."

She gave the laugh again that could have meant anything, a sound not much more than a whisper or a sigh. On the other side of the wall the sidewalk was clear and dry. We continued along without speaking, straight to the end of the neighborhood and then out past a row of clubs that were just closing down for the night. Their colored lights flickered out one after the other, as if Jones was drawing off their current and diffusing it in her wake. When we had passed them all, and entered into another neighborhood of silence, I looked at her and said, "Mrs. Templeton thinks I should stop worrying myself about endings."

"She's right," Jones said. We walked with our shoulders almost touching, and I waited for her to deliver the killing stroke. That it didn't come was no consolation; there was always another time. "I see why it worries you, but endings are a writerly thing. The essence of theater is in the process of arriving. It's in the doing."

"But endings are important. It's where every line has to be focused. It's what gives the characters purpose."

"No," Jones said. Smoke came out of her and rose up under the lamps. She made a fist and knocked on her chest. "Their purpose comes out of here. The ending is what happens when all the conflicting purposes and cross-purposes are put into action. Rebecca wanted security, but the security frightens her. What does she do? Her husband fell in love with the gypsy in her, but in marrying her he's bled the gypsy out of her. How does that make him feel? For two years this has been building up. Now something's going to happen. The ending is just an effect."

"What about playing out all the different endings we can think of

— and let the audience decide?"

"We'd be there all night. Anyway you're jumping the gun. Hadn't we ought to get the cast in place before we start to think about endings?"

I knew what we had to work with, and approximately what was needed. I improvised: "I see Templeton as the husband. A man named Record. And — Moscow as Sallis, the man she was talking to in those pages you trashed."

"How does he fit in?"

I thought about that. I didn't like the answer. "He's Rebecca's lover. He's a painter; Record hired him to do a portrait of his wife, that's how they met. This was maybe six months before the start of the play, a year and a half into the marriage. You can't say there isn't any drama in that. The irony is..."

"Go on," Jones said. "A little irony is never a bad thing."

"The irony is that taking a lover was probably her attempt to hold the marriage together..."

"And Ruth?"

"Sister of the husband. Who finds out about the affair, and takes her knowledge... no, to Rebecca. That's, I guess that's pretty ordinary stuff."

"We'll work on it."

"How about this: Mary as the housemaid, this crazy housemaid who keeps stealing things right out from under their noses: candlesticks, silverware, flowerpots, mirrors, anything she can get her hands on until finally all that's left in the place are a few sticks of furniture and the painting of Rebecca! And everyone too preoccupied to notice!"

Jones laughed. "All right. That leaves Sylvie."

"Another complication," I said. "A student of Sallis's. In love with him, of course. That ought to be drama enough for anyone."

Jones's boots clacked against cold pavement. Her hand pressed into the small of my back, then withdrew. "It's coming along," Jones said. "That's what I hired you for. When you're needled enough, you begin to think fast."

We rounded another corner, and I saw that we had come in a wide circle back to the building with the catwalks and the casement window. Jones drew up beside the battered door and stood with her hands in her pockets. "You'd be fine, if you ever learned to relax," she said. "Have you ever bothered to notice the change since you started? You're not running around pestering us anymore about how the performance went. You're not asking them what kind of parts they want to play. They're asking you."

I looked at my feet. I thought of Shakespeare and the others who made it look so easy, whether through intervention of the gods or natural magic, just a few graceful words, and then the **CURTAIN** at the bottom of the page, underlined in black ink. I felt so heated in the cold air that I thought sure I would crack and break open. At any moment she would say goodnight and disappear behind her door. In my confusion of hope and despair, inspiration and writer's block and lust, there was nothing I could think of to stop her.

Jones drew her key out under the blue streetlight. "It's not how I want it to end and it's not how you want it to end," she said. "It's how it ends. Now, are you ready to go in?"

Halfway up the stairs our silhouettes appeared on the wall beside us, tilted crazily like a scene from a mystery play. There was still the rejected MS lying all anyhow in a wedge of darkness; Jones threw her coat down in the midst of it and disappeared into the maze of screens. "Do you want anything in your hot water?" she said from the back. I said a little tea would be good.

I settled down without taking off my jacket, and turned over the pages to use their backs. *Rebecca Painting Sallis*, I wrote. I drew a heart shape, crossed it out. I bent to the paper.

I had scribbled five pages by the time Jones came back with a pair of mismatched cups, trailing steam. She had changed into a black robe that fell to her ankles. Her feet were bare. She settled onto a small trunk resting against one of the room's few genuine walls. "Hard at work," she said.

"Don't think you're going to like it."

"Maybe not." She sipped from her cup without lowering her eyes, studying me over the far rim. "Let me see."

"It reads a little melodramatic," I said. Jones didn't answer. "Handwriting's kind of messy. Can you make it out?"

"Mmm. Fine."

She read it through in silence, then turned back and read it again, faster this time, but pausing more often as if to confirm something she already knew. "So?" I said when she had finished.

Jones ignored me. She rested her chin in the palm of her hand, the little finger curled against her mouth. "Recite," she said.

"You are old Father William..."

She fought that one, but finally relented and grinned at the floor. "No," she said, pointing with her foot. "I mean that. Take Record."

"Starting where?"

The voice that answered me belonged to Rebecca. It was more remote than I'd ever heard it before, almost hollow in the way it picked over my words. "What are you doing home?" it said. "What have you done?"

She had started about mid-way through the scene. I found the place, cleared my throat, and made my attempt at something resembling a dramatic style. "I've just come from the Board of Directors. They've agreed to —"

"No," Jones said. "No. This isn't Major Bowes. Just read it in a normal tone of voice."

"Sorry. They've agreed to grant me an early retirement. Tomorrow we'll go down to the Agency and register this house. We'll put everything up for sale. Then we'll go. It will be a new life for both of us."

Silence, the script said. Jones accounted for it. There wasn't any acting in what she did; it was strictly a test of the timing involved. At the proper moment, she lowered her eyes. "Please," Rebecca said. "You've got to go back. For your own sake. You must beg them to give your job back. Please. I'm not angry, but you've done the wrong thing. If I leave, I can't have you tagging along..."

"It wouldn't be tagging along. I would take you anywhere. I would adapt to any kind of life you wanted. I'm showing you that I can change. I can be everything this man Sallis is to you, and more. I can be anything you want."

"You don't know what I want. You're using me as a mirror. You look into my eyes, and see your own self reflected."

"If that were the case, I could never have loved you. You would only have bored me. When we first met you had the eyes of a wolf. I knew I had found someone who could set me free..."

"It was written all over your face. I've seen it before. It's the same look Sallis gives me. I can't carry you anymore, either one of you..."

"I'm not asking that. I never have. I only want you to let me in. I only want to meet the wolf, to *finally meet her,* after all this time."

"You mustn't try."

"But I must. I love you."

"It's not a question of love. We've painted ourselves into a corner. Now we're both working at cross-purposes, trying to get out."

Out beyond Jones's window, a car or truck sounded its horn. The sky was not so dark as it had been when we came inside. Jones got to her feet. Her eyes raked across the wall of masks, then settled on me. "I'm glad we had this little conversation," she said, and vanished.

I knocked over my cup and had to mop the spill with my dirty handkerchief. "She's not you," I said to the floor. "I didn't mean you." There was no sound. I might have been alone. "Meg. Jones. I didn't mean you. Rebecca isn't you."

Rebecca's voice came over the walls like a machine of the gods, a voice from on high. "Of course not," it said. "She's your vision of me."

I followed it to a little room at the end of the passage, furnished only with a folding bed and a cardboard bureau, strewn with clothes. An unshaded bulb hung from the ceiling. "I'm not imagining you," I said from the doorway. "There wouldn't be any point."

Jones hung her bathrobe on a closet peg and turned to face me. In her bare feet her eyes were level with mine. "I don't mind," she said. "I'd even play the part. But these things have a way of sticking to my bones. And where would that leave us?"

I stood there trying to stuff the handkerchief into my coat pocket. I felt as if she had twisted me into a knot, so that facing north I could only walk south. *To finally meet her,* Record was saying, over and over again. I fought the words, and lost.

"You've had us married and divorced in your mind," Jones said. "You've had us growing up and growing old together. That's all right. 'Magician, priest, maker of myths, manipulator of signs and hieroglyphs.' That's us. That's you."

"But I must," I said. "I love you."

"Come on," Jones said. "It's after five."

When I opened my eyes an angle of sunlight cut halfway across the ceiling. I was alone in the bed, wrapped in a cocoon of sheets; outside the building there was streetnoise and motion, but in Jones's room it was perfectly still. I pulled on my pants and went from the bedroom to the kitchen. There were no notes, no dirty cups, no sign of her. It would not have surprised me to have found the room stripped bare, the trunks missing, the tent pegs pulled. I took it as a reassuring sign that everything, down to the last mask, was still in place.

I dressed while the water was boiling, and drank my coffee at her casement window, where sunlight took off the morning chill and the people below gave me something to watch. When I thought about the things I had said and done the night before, I felt like such a clown, a Chaplin tramp gone out of control, spouting a kind of brazen pathos in the streets. But the thing that shamed me most was the little voice in the back of my mind that whispered, *never mind — it worked.*

The walk back to Valenciennes took half an hour. It wasn't until I got there and found them well into a technical rehearsal for *Vanishing*

Breed that I realized how late I was running. It didn't seem to matter; at that stage words are the last thing on anyone's mind. Mrs. Templeton was busy fitting Sylvie into a costume, Mary and Moscow were having difficulties moving a piece of scenery, Templeton sat looking sullen and neglected in the front row. Lon had come down from the booth to consult Jones about the lighting design. They stood whispering to each other at the foot of the stage, making notes in a spiral-bound planbook. If she was feeling any effect of the long night, it didn't show; she looked fresh and alert. I tried to catch her attention, but she would not meet my eye. It was like any other day.

THE UNBROKEN LINE

"**SHE** was just a girl who came out of the night," Lon said suddenly. "A girl none of us had ever seen before, who seemed to know everybody. Jones old Hirsch thought of himself as quite a sharpster, but I don't think he would have let her through the door if he'd known he was looking at the future."

It was a Monday afternoon, Valenciennes was supposed to be dark, but Lon and Mary and I were there, giving the place its weekly beating. There were the seats that needed to be cleaned, aisles that needed to be vacuumed; while up on the stage Mary had a backdrop that was showing some wear. Of Jones there was no sign. Yet none of us asked "Where is Jones?", whether out of self control or lack of interest or in my case because nobody else was asking (was it a point of honor not to show any curiosity?), until I couldn't hold it back any longer and it popped out of me somewhere in the middle of the third row.

Lon didn't answer for a time, didn't even give

me a look or a shrug as if to say "How the hell would I know?" Instead, he continued along the maroon aisle with his face downturned, his hands in constant motion against the seat backs. At first I thought he was forming a reply; then, that he might be punishing me for some unknown reason with his silence. It didn't occur to me that he might not have wanted Mary to hear, that he might simply have been waiting until we worked our way a little farther back from the stage. Whatever the reason, it was ten minutes before he finally spoke, still without turning or looking up from his work, about the girl.

"Hirsch?" I said. "I don't understand."

"He was the Jones before Jones," Lon said. "And he wasn't the first. He'd swindled this place or blackmailed it or anyway taken it from a man named Jones who built it and owned it up until around 1924. Or so it goes. All I know is, he kept the name, wore it as a kind of joke trophy." Now Lon dipped his cloth, wrung it out, and scrubbed the red wood until the whole seat rattled and pitched against its moorings. "That was just one of the things I didn't like about him."

Lon said that when Hirsch hired him to watch the stage door three nights a week, he didn't think it would cost him his day jobs. But there were actresses back there in bright colors who knew just how to tease him along, and a man called MacTeagle, who acted under the name of Harry Shelby and made of Lon "a much better drinking companion than old Hirsch"; given that, it wasn't long before his day bosses found out and asked him to make up his mind where he wanted to work.

And so nearly every day now from two in the afternoon until almost midnight Lon sat alone by the stage door, turning away men with the names of dancers on their lips, or drifting in the anesthetic effect of boredom mixed with the sad, distant echo of the melodrama playing on the other side of the scenery. He was allowed half an hour off during the early part of the evening; instead of leaving the building he would unwrap a chicken sandwich that he had made himself the night before, and wander away into the back of the theater, chewing carelessly, drinking in the mysteries of the wings, the traps and marks, the whisperings of the girls as they came and went through the gaudy shadows.

Then on a crisp November night, just on the edge of winter, the girl came to the door for the first time. Lon was leaning back in his usual spot, half asleep, half wondering if the act was about to end, when he heard the distant crunch of boots on gravel. It was too early for a Johnny, too late for a bill collector; it wasn't even the same kind of sound, an assured stride not quite like a man's but very much unlike the clipped, posed walk of the actresses. Lon had to drag himself hard out of the thick haze of almost-sleep. It was still gripping at him when the footsteps ended on the other side of the door.

There was no knock. For what seemed like a long time Lon stood with the door between him and whatever it was, fighting back a terrible feeling that he should warn the company, clear the building, get everyone out the front entrance. "If I had," Lon said to me across the intervening years, "it would have saved her a lot of trouble."

At last he got his nerves up and opened the door just a crack. She was standing with her face half under the yellow light, quite calm, her hands buried in the pockets of a battered old aviator's jacket. Her eyes lifted to his. She could not have been more than about twenty two or three, but already there was the edge of something inhumanly patient about her, in her face and the set of her shoulders. They studied each other for a moment, Lon still standing with his body blocking the way, as if she were a drunk or a cop, as if she might get violent. "Nice night," she said, in a voice that held every possible variance of frost and thaw. "What's your name?"

Lon answered her without even stopping to think. Then he remembered having a job to do, and said, "I'm sorry, but you can't —"

"Margaret Darwin," the girl said. She slipped a hand out of one of the zipper-edged pockets, and held it straight out under the light. "I'm not here to sell anything, and I'm not here to audition."

Lon could not even be sure that he was awake. He took her hand — warm where he had expected it to be cold, a bit calloused where he had expected only softness — and stepped aside. He didn't have to ask himself why he did it; the answer was there in the way she drew herself up into the entryhall, the jacket creaking against her, and stood just inside looking around with her profile sharp against the night light and that curious smile around her eyes. "Can I see Mr. Hirsch?" she said.

Lon didn't know where she got the name. It wasn't listed on any program or sign; as far as the public knew, the place was still owned and managed by a man named Jones. He told her to wait, then went and left her there alone, thinking all the while about something Pud had once said about vampires, and that he had been the one who invited her in.

Hirsch kept his office up on the second floor. Lon said that it might have been a nice room once, but by that time, with its broken paint and broken plaster, it suited its owner pretty well. He said that he didn't like to go up there, even at the best of times, because he was never quite sure what he would find: back then the measure of an actress was how well could she swoon, and Hirsch liked it best if they did their swooning on his lap. But this time Lon found Hirsch alone at his desk, posed in a circle of lamplight, copying something out into the margin of a yellow legal pad. There was a mess of scrap paper spread out across the blotter, a shotglass half filled with amber liquid sitting close by his wrist. "Jones," Lon said. "There's a woman downstairs. But I don't think you want to see her."

When Hirsch looked up Lon could tell from his expression that the only word he'd caught was "woman." A stocky, well-groomed man, he was wearing a grass-green suit that fit him too tightly around the middle and a bow tie the color of mud. His mouth turned up at the corners. Without haste, he lifted the edge of the blotter and slid the papers under. "Nonsense," he said. "Where is she?"

They found her at the edge of the stage, looking as if she belonged there, her arms folded, her eyes fixed on the actors passing close under the light. She was whispering something into the stagehand's ear; Lon said he wondered about that for months after. "Hsst," he said to her. "Miss Darwin."

She turned so that her face fell half in shadow. "Mr. Hirsch," she said, and gave Lon a look that made him feel uncomfortably like a conspirator. Her hand came out of the pocket again, pointed straight at Hirsch's gut. "My name is Margaret Darwin. I'm a Natural History major down from Miskatonic University. I'm an admirer of yours..."

"Jones," Hirsch said. "You call me Jones. Just like Mr. Wimpy — a heh — I'm one of the Jones boys."

Lon watched as he shook the girl's hand. "Poor bastard," he said to me. "Poor sap. He didn't have the slightest idea..."

Then it was back to his chair by the door. He supposed that he could have stayed and listened in, but it wasn't any of his business and after all he supposed he would hear about it anyway. Show folk sometimes tried to have secrets, but they never managed to keep them very long. This time Hirsch couldn't even manage it for ten minutes. Because it wasn't that long before he and the Darwin girl passed Lon on their way out, walking side by side and close together. Hirsch pretended not to notice Lon sitting there, but Lon noticed how they hushed themselves up. The Darwin girl nodded goodnight; Lon couldn't say what he saw in her eyes. He touched his forehead, and they were gone.

Then Lon thought: *What the hell*. He opened the stage door very carefully, and stuck his nose out into the cold. There, halfway up the blue alley, he saw the two of them walking almost in step, not too slow, not too fast. The Darwin woman laughed. As he watched, she reached down and patted Hirsch on the ass.

I was at the point of asking Lon to please shut up, but he wouldn't give me the chance, wouldn't even look up from the last of the chairs. "I'd just gotten settled again when MacTeagle came around," he said. "We were pretty well into the comedy portion of the show, so he had his coat on with the red candy-stripes running down it. He was all hot and bothered. 'Who was that?' he said. 'That beautiful woman.' I told him everything I knew and everything I thought, and he just stood there for a while with his jaw slack. I was afraid he would miss his cue. Then he said, 'Well by God. This calls for a drink.' "

Lon laughed softly to himself on his hands and knees in the row above. He sank his rag into the brown water, looking down into the pail the way an oracle might look into a glass ball. "Oh," he said. "This was the winter of '28."

In that season, sometimes two or three nights a week, Lon and MacTeagle would wait until the actors and the stagehands had all gone their various ways ("Out there," Mac said, "into the night"); then, meeting as if by chance in one of the storage rooms beneath the stage, they would build a little speakeasy out of a cluster of unused and half-forgotten props. It was nothing more than a miniature table cast off from an ice cream parlor, a metal lamp with a metal shade, and two mismatched chairs; while Lon set them up, Mac would pick out a scene from the rows of faded, peeling flats, and then with a Paris sidestreet for a background, or a forest or a crypt, they would sit and drink from a fresh bottle of bootleg that Mac had concealed in an inside pocket of his comedian's jacket.

"Listen," Mac would say when they had reduced the level of the whiskey, dark powerful stuff, by about half. "I think she's made another move..."

And he would whisper the latest of the secret news, lowering his face across the table like a spy whose job it was to track the sightings of the Darwin woman's progress, the ripples she made as she passed through the company. Lon already knew the bulk of it: when he walked through the wings with his chicken sandwich half unwrapped, there weren't the crowds of whispering actresses, or of stagehands standing around doing nothing; in any case, it would have been hard for anyone watching the door not to notice the number of people who left and never came back. But that didn't matter. Mac wasn't telling it just for the sake of being informative. He was telling it so that he could share his disbelief, and his wonder.

Three days after Miss Darwin came out of the alley, Hirsch had fired the stage manager and installed her in the job. For a short time there were no further signs of motion; the shows went on in their usual manner, though perhaps more efficiently than before. But Lon didn't dare believe that that was all she had wanted.

"No," Mac agreed. "No, she's only getting her steam up." His voice rose into a lyrical, shivery singsong as if he were reciting sonnets to a house full of maiden aunts. "You should see her at work; she's charming, but alert to every little thing. She never turns on the lamp over her stand — doesn't need to. She has the book memorized to the smallest detail. Never has to look away from the stage. It's something, to be playing and to feel her eyes on you, to know that she's there where you can't see her, watching, and waiting, and putting on steam."

"That much waiting, that much steam," Lon said.

Mac filled both the glasses and knocked his back. "Nothing less."

"She has a way of making her wants belong to you," Mac said on the night of the first big firing. She had replaced the magician, a man named Henry Arnaud, with one of her own choosing, and though Henry had been liked and the new man was what Mac called "a certain prick," everyone agreed when they saw him perform that the right choice had been made.

"You aren't afraid?" Lon asked him three weeks later, after seven more dismissals.

"I thought I would be," Mac said. "But this is too interesting. D'you know what she's up to now?"

Lon thought he did, but he said no anyway.

"She's incorporated that magician of hers into the melodrama. He's the hero now. Instead of getting run off to the hoosegow, I'm vanished in a circle of flame!"

"That could be dangerous," Lon said, "with all the alcohol on your breath."

Mac let that one slide by. He had white showing all around his eyes. His face and hands were wet. He told Lon about all the changes creeping into the show, peculiar shifts of emphasis, sudden flights of fancy, including a new sketch about a drunk whose best friend was a thing called a hippogriff. "Never heard of a thing like that," Mac said. "But she made it sound wonderfully funny. All these additions she wants to make, and there she is jettisoning people right and left."

Lon said, "What does Mr. Jones-boy Hirsch think of all that?"

"I don't think he knows," Mac said. He waved his hand so that whiskey slopped over the lip of the glass. "Or if he does, then she's found the way to make him like it..."

The next time they got together, Lon saw that Mac had drained a quarter of the bottle before they even sat down. "She's done it," Mac said, more as if he was beholding a miracle than announcing the dismissal of a friend. "She's fired old George. Him that played straight man to me for going on six years. And d'you know who she replaced him with? Herself! She herself! Imagine it! She puts on a white wig and an evening gown and sucks in her cheeks and throws back her shoulders (lovely white shoulders she's got), and then d'you know what? She starts ad-libbing on me! And I that never recited a word that wasn't writ for me just has to chase after — until I realize of a sudden *I'm* the one playing straight to *her*..."

Lon imagined it as he'd been ordered, and couldn't help but give a soft laugh.

"And that's not the most of it," Mac said. He was going on just like an engine that had finally reached full speed. "She's good! She's bloody marvelous!"

Lon said, "That surprises you?"

It went on like that for some time, well into the night. By the time they had finished the bottle, Lon could feel the world warming and turning to liquid light all around. He could look off down the broad painted avenue towards the Seine, and almost believe in its reality.

One night, just as they were setting up their bar parlor under the floor, a soft laugh almost like a whisper came at them from the slantwise shadow of the stairs; when they looked around, there was Margaret Darwin, a tall thin shape descending into the light from the gloom above. "Well hello," she said. "The two Opera Ghosts."

Lon stood there with the table still in his hands and didn't say a word. If he had known her better he might have guessed from her words that they weren't in any real trouble, but she was still just The Stranger to him, and there was nothing in her tone to say whether she meant it as a joke or a threat.

Mac's eyebrows had climbed half the distance to his hairline, but when he put the smile on it didn't look so much like surprise. "Miss Darwin!" he said. "It's good of you to come by. Welcome to The Mask and Paint. You'll find it's the most exclusive club in town, I think. Will you join us?"

"Margaret," she said. When her face came into the lamplight she was wearing the same knowing expression that she'd used that first night, in the alley. "I might. If it's my kind of club."

Mac said, "Set it down, man, set it down. Fetch the chairs." From the corner he began leafing through the row of flats, peering into each scene as if they were the pages of an enormous book.

"There's a view of a Viennese garden somewhere in there," she said. "If you could find that..."

Mac stopped looking at the pictures. He walked his hand spiderlike over the pencilled notations on the frame edges, and at last gave a low whistle. "So there is," he said; a moment later he had drawn the scene straight out of the row so that it cut off more than half of the room. "Would that be the one you were looking for?"

Margaret Darwin stood half in the light and half out of it, hands in pockets. "The very one," she said.

Lon had set out a third chair for her, a blackpainted thing with curling metal legs that almost matched the table's, but as they were all settling down she lifted it aside and sat crosslegged on the dusty floor. Lon said he had an uncomfortable moment trying to decide if it would be rude not to join her there; Mac didn't seem even to notice. He sat with his palms flat on the table as if he were going to try a magic trick. "Now then," he said. "What's old Jones doing leaving a lady like you all alone on a huge, enormous night like this?"

"Oh come on," Margaret Darwin said, chin on fist. "You know exactly what he's doing."

"Ah," Mac said. He drew out the new bottle, pulled the cork and sniffed it, then raised it to the level of his eyes. "Yes. A toast then to Mr. Jones née Hirsch, without whose tireless efforts we could not gather here this evening. Eh, you wouldn't happen to have brought an extra glass, would you?"

"'fraid not," she said. "Just pass it around."

Lon said that Mac's eyebrows began to climb again, and this time he couldn't raise a smile to cover it. Margaret Darwin took a long pull straight from the bottle, wiped her mouth on the back of her hand. "Tell me," she said. Her face was such a changing, flickering mask that it tired Lon just to look at her. "What do you two gentlemen think of Shakespeare?"

"That depends," Mac said. He poured out a shot or so into the bottom of the paint-stained tumbler he'd been drinking out of ever since the "speakeasy" had opened. "Which play would you be talking about?"

"*Twelfth Night*," Margaret Darwin said from the floor. "I'll be taking Viola. I've talked to a handful of people in the company, and some others I know of have agreed to take part, but I still need a Toby Belch."

Lon sat with his knees together, watching the two of them and saying nothing. He said for a moment it felt as if he and the bottle, the table and lamp, the painted Vienna, had all turned invisible.

"I see," Mac said at last. "Typecasting. Still…"

Margaret Darwin flashed a smile like a lighthouse beacon cutting through solid banks of fog. It hit Mac full in the face, puffed him up and set him aglow; Lon thought it was pretty funny until she turned and aimed the same look at him. "And you," she said. "I've seen how you spend your lunches. You must know the works by now."

"More than that," Lon said. "I know how it doesn't work."

"Then you can't really want to sit by the door all summer. Or can you?"

"There doesn't seem to be much point. You've fired all the girls who used to bring them around."

Margaret Darwin laughed. "They were coming around for the wrong reasons," she said; Mac handed her the bottle, and she raised it in a toast. "We start rehearsals next week. In the meantime, can I trust you boys to keep it under your hat?"

Oh yes, Mac and Lon said together. Absolutely. The bottle went around one more time. Then in one smooth motion as if that magician of hers had been standing behind the scenery, levitating her, she rose to her feet and started over to the edge of the dark. With her head half bowed, half turned, she regarded the fading backdrop. "The Mask and Paint," she said. "Yes. It's my kind of club exactly."

And she vanished outside the circle of light. A moment later, Lon and Mac heard her climbing the stairs, then a few soft footfalls over their heads, then nothing more. That was when Mac turned back to Lon, blew out a gust of stringent, whiskey-soaked air, and poured himself out a good tall one. "Any time now," he said.

But it didn't happen in the next week, or the week after; it didn't happen until Spring, and by then Lon and Mac had grown so complacent from waiting that it came as a surprise even to them. The rehearsals for *Twelfth Night* began in secret, with a cast of fourteen players, strangers and friends, crowding themselves into the little room under the stage, so that The Mask and Paint had to fold up and save its business for another night. Mac said he had never been involved with anything that moved so painfully slow; once a week was too little rehearsal time for anything, he said, and Lon had to agree: Miss Darwin allowed the readings to drag on for what seemed like months, and nothing at all was done in the way of blocking until the winter was more than half gone. But Lon could not help but think that he had the worst of it. "Just watch," Miss Darwin told him. "There'll be much more for you to do as we near the opening, but for now all I want you to do is listen, and watch." Which was all fine and dandy, Lon thought, even as he tried to keep awake through endless dronings of nays and doths and fertile tears. But what did she want him to see?

By the end of April the topic had come up at The Mask and Paint that perhaps this Miss Darwin was not perfect after all. Here at last, Lon and Mac decided, was something that she did not do with complete assurance. Even if she grew into the job — and they knew that she would — how did she expect to mount a play without props, without costumes, without scenery? And how to make Hirsch swallow it if she did?

They had just decided that her *Twelfth Night* was doomed never to open, and had made up their minds to withdraw from any part in it, when the posters announcing its premiere appeared, yellow and gold and black on the lobby walls and across the rainy facade of the theater, in such quantities that they overlapped, bearing her name and Mac's and the twelve others in fancy letters so fine and bright, and dates, actual dates so close at hand that it chilled them to think it would happen so soon.

At first Lon and Mac did not even notice. They came to work through the side entrance as usual, taking their usual places, Lon in the swaybacked chair by the door and Mac in his dressing room, fussing with collar and make-up for the first show, sipping now and then from the bottle he kept in the bottom drawer of his dresser. Mac said he would never have found out if a stagehand hadn't gone by making an awful racket just outside his door. "What is it, blast you," Mac shouted, and the fellow burst in with a scrap of curled poster paper and a look on his face like a mackerel in the claws of a black bear. Mac said he took one look at the thing and grabbed it and pushed the boy out of the way. He went charging out to the stage door, his collar undone, shirttails flying straight out behind, crying for Lon to "Look! By God, look!" and at that exact moment Hirsch came in from the street.

He was wringing wet from his shoes to his bowler hat. His shoulders were bowed up high against the back of his head, as if his neck had retracted itself into his body. His face was hard and blank. In his left hand an open umbrella was hanging upside-down, an inch of rainwater in the bottom, its metal tip scratching up the floor in his wake. In his right hand was another copy of the poster, ragged-edged and mottled with a pattern of glue on the back where he had torn it away from the wall.

"You're fired," he said to Mac.

Then he pushed his way past, and from the back rooms they heard him repeating the same words, over and over, to everyone he met. "Come on," Mac said. "She's struck."

All they had to do was follow the trail of water. It ended in a puddle beside the stage, where Jones sat relaxed but unmoving at her stage manager's post, studying the pages of a well-worn ledger book, her back turned on the big wet man in the big wet coat standing there trying to bore a hole through her with his eyes.

Lon and Mac never heard what he said. But he was holding the soggy poster as if he wanted to beat her with it, as if by the power of thought he could turn it into a baseball bat and knock her brains out. Margaret Darwin did not even look up. She said something back at him, of which Lon only caught the one word, "read."

"Bitch," Hirsch said. "Whore. You're fired."

Margaret Darwin only closed the ledger book and held it up for Hirsch to see. From the look on her face it was obvious that she thought it would end the matter, that by doing it she had already won. "Go home," she said softly. "We'll talk about this later."

Pausing now in the aisle above, and with a hard sort of puzzled look on his face, Lon said, "Then, uh... then... well, it didn't have to happen this way. But Hirsch made a grab for the ledger book and that started it. He dropped the umbrella and the poster and went after it with both hands; got it, too, or would have if it hadn't been for the other one, the man who came out from behind the curtain."

Lon said he had never seen the man before, and hadn't let him in. But he recognized the gun, an old military surplus revolver that belonged to the company. It was pointed at Hirsch. "You'd have thought that would have been enough," Lon said, "but he had to go and make a speech, too. Got Hirsch's back up even more. Hirsch said he wasn't afraid of any cheap shitfaced hood, and tried to prove it. There was a struggle. I was just heading over there to break it up when the gun swung around at me and went off."

"Christ," I said. "What did you do?"

Lon looked at me with his dark sad eyes and his mouth set in a frown. "What the hell do you think I did? I died."

He said he'd practiced the fall until he was afraid the bruises would give the whole thing away, but it hadn't been enough. He hit the floor hard, knocking the wind out of himself and spraining his wrist in the process. He didn't even need to bite into the gelatin capsule Jones had given him; it broke in the impact and spurted a gooey red froth from the corners of his mouth.

The plan called for Lon to die immediately, but his inability to stop gasping for air put a damper on that, though Lon said it must have added some realism to the scene. Four or five of the company regulars came around and started fussing and shouting for an ambulance. They were supposed to keep it up until Jones, Miss Darwin, gave the signal, but Lon was just readying himself to take the final breath when one of their number gave an unrehearsed yelp and leapt aside. The shouting melted away. Lon was afraid to open his eyes; he felt terribly alone, and knew he was being watched.

Then the toe of a shoe poked him in the chest, about where the bullet was supposed to have hit. "Get up," Hirsch said. "Out of everyone I thought I could trust you. Come on, get up."

Lon said he could feel the words hitting him. He said they packed such a wallop that he couldn't even laugh when he saw the look on Mac's face. "All right," Hirsch said to Jones. His voice was soft and low. In the stillness of the moment he could be heard in every corner, against every brick, on out to the back row. "Fine. You want it so bad, you can have it. It's just a money hole. It's nothing to me..."

And Jones said, "That's why I had to take it."

That night, as Lon was walking home, he became aware of a grey truck that paced him for more than a block along the broken sidewalk. It had no markings other than a patch or two of rust; inside, someone was trying to drive and roll down the side window at the same time. Lon turned onto an empty sidestreet, and a moment later the truck came lumbering around after. When it passed under the lamplight he saw Margaret Darwin at the wheel, aiming the front bumper in his general direction, making signs at him with her free hand.

She pulled up beside him at the curb, opened the passenger door and lowered her face out of the gloom. "There's life in you yet," she said. "How about a drink?"

When he had climbed in under the dashboard's green eyes, into the spartan, unheated cab, she spun the wheel around and headed back the way they had come. "You were quite wonderful," she said. "All that wheezing and heaving."

"Sorry it didn't work."

"Nonsense. It worked perfectly."

Margaret Darwin shifted up, crunching the gears. They rode through the empty streets for what seemed like a long time, and at last Lon said, "How do you figure that? He saw right through me."

In the blue night Jones shot him a look from the far side of the cab. "True. We never thought he was stupid. But it saved me from having to carry out a threat."

Lon sat back and watched the dark storefronts crawling by. He didn't know where she was taking him. He thought of the green ledger book and what Hirsch had given up for it, then pushed it back out of his mind. "I won't ask you about that."

Jones looked at the street ahead. "I liked you from the start," she said.

Now Lon came around the back row. He straightened and tried to stretch the kinks out of his back. "That was her first big production. D'you know, of all the people who saw it, the only one fooled was Mac. It wasn't that he believed my performance. But he wouldn't have put anything past her."

He gathered up our dirty rags, dropped them in the bucket, wiped his hands on his knees. "You hungry?" he said.

We went rattling up onto the stage where Mary was repairing the trick painting for act two of *A Prophet of Yearning*, the one from which Jones emerged every Wednesday and Friday night, and twice on Saturdays, bloated, paint-smeared, dripping with color, as the ghost image of Rebecca. "Winslow and I are going to hunt up some chow," Lon said as we came over her. "D'you want anything?"

"No thanks," Mary said. She dipped her brush into a jar of clean water and splashed it around until a purple cloud rose to the surface. "I'm almost done here. I've got to get back home and feed Max."

"Suit yourself," Lon said.

He went off into the back to get his coat, and I remained looking over Mary's shoulder. The painting was Sallis to the letter, just as I had imagined him in the extreme edge of his Cubism, all layers of blocklike figures, slashes of blue and black. "That's beautiful," I said, and meant it.

Mary said thanks. She looked up at me, and her smile vanished. "Are you all right?"

I made a face. "It's just Lon airing the laundry again. Some stuff I didn't particularly want to know."

"Like what?"

She was capping up the jars. There were fresh droplets and smudges of paint on the stage floor, even though she had set down newspaper; we scrubbed at them with rags soaked in turpentine, but it was no use, they were just new additions, another series of marks that the stage would carry forever. "Well, you were there," I said. "What was Jones like when you first met her?"

Mary wrinkled her nose. "She had a lot to prove. I barely knew her;

I heard it said that she was like a chess player moving pieces around on a board, but I never saw that myself." As she was speaking, Lon came out of the wings zipping himself into a light jacket. He came over to where Mary and I were kneeling and poked me with the toe of his boot.

"What happened to Mac?" I said as we crossed through the lobby.

Lon's footsteps made no sound on the tiled floor, but the keys rattling against his hip echoed as loudly as if he had dropped them into an empty water tank. He broke through the speckled windowlight, unlocked the left door and let in a flood of cold air. "She fired him about three years later," he said. "He'd finally learned how to ad-lib, and was an important player in those early days, but after prohibition was repealed he was drunk all the time. She put up with him longer than I would have."

We went out under the marquee. On both sides of us the facing rows of yellowing, old-time photographs, the forgotten actors that guarded Valenciennes, lined our way to the street. I looked straight at them, into their fading eyes, and knew them for the first time.

MARY'S ROOM

EVERY morning Mary came on foot all the way from the grey, chimneysmoked neighborhood where she lived alone with a stray tomcat called Max. She was never later than seven-thirty, even on stormy days; she was always in a cheerful mood. She would come breezing in through the stage door with the same chilled, good-morning smile and pause to shake the snow out of her hat and mittens. Then she'd head straight for the coffeepot, to spend a few minutes planning her day with Jones or Lon or both. "Aren't you awake yet?" she would say to me, shivering with the mug in her longfingered hands, the steam rising up into her face. "No, dammit," I'd say. And she would squeeze my arm, returning to her conversation with the same relaxed, obscene alertness, to ask about the proper size of a window, the right color for a cloud.

Mary spent her mornings kneeling over muslin backcloths, which, when spread out to their full length, looked to me like windows in the stage floor opening down into Athens or the Black Forest. She crawled over them with pads strapped to her knees and feet, a kerchief tied across her brow, a tin tray filled with a dozen or more paint-jars, a rainbow-smeared rag and a camelhair brush that she held far down the handle like a pencil, re-painting the spots where a leaf or a cobblestone or a bit of trompe l'oeil masonry had flecked off or cracked. She always worked from left to right, top to bottom, covering the whole length of a scene in an hour or two. From time to time the damage might be greater than usual, might lead her astray across the face of the canvas; that was when she might whisper to herself, so softly that you would have to be with her on the scene just to hear it:

There'll come a time, now don't forget it
There'll come a time, when you'll regret it
Some day when you'll grow lonely
Your heart will break like mine and you'll
want me only
After you've gone, after you've gone away —

with her once-white gloves brushing away loose flecks of dried paint and her face downturned, following the crack, as she mended the summer's wear.

Around noontime, Mary could sometimes be found sitting alone in the back row of the house. Who knew what she was dreaming? She kept a black book, nothing more than a leather cover stuffed so full of sketches that she had to keep it bound with rubber bands. There in her favorite chair, where the only light came from the stage down below, she would open the book and unfold the pages one at a time into her lap. "She'll be working on the designs for the new show," Jones would say. "Go on up. She'll want to ask you about some things..."

By the time I reached her, she would already have the beginnings of a scene sketched out in blue pencil, the book balanced on the back of her knees, a draft script and a page of Jones's notes in the seat to her right, a raft of old drawings splayed out all anyhow and three sharp pencils held in reserve in the metal ridge of the armrest. "Well hello," she would say as I settled into the row in front of her. I would hear the pencil scratching in the dark. "Sit down and tell me more about this..."

When Mary was needed in rehearsal she would carry the black book up close against her breast, even if it was late in the process and she had to be in costume. Sometimes she wore her calm, attentive face, and sometimes the closemouthed smile. From time to time as the other actors moved around her, she might think of something and make a quick sketch, though she was not a caricaturist. "Wait," she might say, and we would all see the lightbulb over her head as she came down and handed the drawing over the footlights. "Why don't we do it this way?" When that happened the scene always played, because Mary always got the picture right.

Who could tell what she was dreaming? When Mary was not rehearsing with the group she was hiding herself out back, either to work on the new scenery or to practice on dulcimer, guitar and piano. That was my favorite time of the day. If it was scenery, she would sometimes let me help with the base coats. Painting flats with her was like painting in the numbers; I had my own cloth and cap, my own brush that didn't want to stay in my hands, and the afternoon would pass like nothing. If it was practice, then the music of the plays would come seeping through to us, torch songs and classical melodies, a half-heard snatch of an Irish jig, modern dissonance and always a bar or two of *After You're Gone* or *Reaching for the Moon* to warm herself up. It worked especially well on the coldest, most miserable winter afternoons: dusk would already be coming down and the slush would always find its way into my boots; I would come into the little theater with fresh sandwiches for all, into light and warmth and activity and best of all the piano sounding wistfully from the back room.

When the rehearsals wound down at about four-thirty, Mary walked all the way back across town to feed Max and herself and to sit for a while (so she said) with a cup of hot chocolate on the table at her side. But by six o'clock she would be back, setting up the dulcimer in her corner off of the stage, and by seven she would be changed and made up and ready to go out.

Mary approached acting with great enthusiasm, but never once made me believe that she was anyone other than herself. She played crafty artisan women and bubbly girls fifteen years younger than true age, bluestockings and peasantry and fairies, and filled in wherever a feminine form was needed. Everyone in the company played multiple parts, but Mary had it worse than the rest, for when she was not on stage she was playing music to keep the action flowing along, and during intermissions she would appear before the curtain, guitar in hand, to play Hoagy Carmichael tunes for those who cared to listen. She never had a break, and apparently never needed one; the only sign of tiredness she ever showed was when she came around the dark side of the curtain, smiled and blew a loose strand of hair out of her eyes. Then without a word unless it was something about how well the play was going she would take up her next position and set to work, masquerading under the light or turning her face down to the shadowed keyboard.

Mary always stayed late after the show, helping where help was needed, hanging costumes on the one rack if they needed to be cleaned and on the other if they could get through another performance. The picking-up done, we might decide to meet and relax in a little bar down the street; Mary always came along. She drank only red wine, and then only one glass; she talked about other plays she had seen and clothes and movies and Max. She sat in the open end of the booth, well back from the table with her legs crossed and her back straight; when she laughed, she turned her face downward and touched her nose. When the time came to say goodnight, Mary was careful to acknowledge everyone at the table, sometimes taking each of us into her arms. Then she would be off, alone, picking her way over the icy sidewalks with her carpetbag draped like a knapsack over one shoulder and her long coat catching in the night air, whipping around her ankles as she went away down the block.

Then one day Mary never came in. It was a quarter to nine and no Mary; Lon spread the backdrop out for her (it was a place by the sea) and still no Mary. Ice broke and fell away from the windows, Lon and I swept out the lobby where the canvases she had painted rippled like broadsides at a carnival sideshow — donkeyman, catwoman, shining knight — and by noon she had still not turned up.

Jones spent the morning on the pay phone out by the dressing rooms. Between calls to the cleaners, the printing company, the papers, she dialed Mary's number and stood tapping the dial with her pencil, letting it ring perhaps ten times before she hung up at last without talking to anyone. Then she fished out the nickel and waited, dialed again and waited, and hung up.

At eleven fifteen Lon and I began to set up for the evening show. We worked around the painted puddle of seaside as long as we could, then without a word between us we rolled it up, and carried it over to join the others stacked in a rough pyramid-shape against the back wall. Lon would not even meet my eyes. He set out the furniture for scene one with his face closed up, his mouth tight and the keyring jangling at his hip. "Maybe she had to take Max to the vet," I said as we pulled the flats she had painted into place. Lon only looked away and said, "Maybe."

When it was almost time for the afternoon reading, Jones took me aside. "I think you should go down there," she said, scribbling the address out on yellow paper. "Here. Call me if there's any problem. If she doesn't answer the door just get in any way you can. I don't have a key anymore; I don't think Lon does either. Ask him on your way out."

"Why me?" I said.

Jones tore off the sheet and pressed it into my hand. Her face was hard and reserved. "Because you're the only one I can spare."

I went out into the alley just as the Templetons were coming in. They thought I was hunting lunch and beamed at me expectantly; I only crushed the yellow paper in my hand and went slagging past them to the street. It was a bright springlike day. The city was turning into brown water, trickling and gurgling all around. I went on across the avenue, following the distant rumble of the freight-yards to the crest of a long hill lined with brown and red apartment buildings. Far down by the river a horrible brown factory with spines and smokestacks sticking out of it loomed over the roofs of the houses. Islands of ice broke in the street. The cars kicked up a shimmering brown spray from under their tires; a little river carried the remains of last year's leaves down to a brown grating.

The number had fallen off of the building where Mary lived. It was a three-family house at the end of a sidestreet down at the bottom of the hill. There were three white porches one on top of the other and a flight of stairs that ran all the way up one side of the building. A ground-floor window had been knocked out and covered over with a hunk of cardboard. All the other windows were black; the house looked empty and cold and unlived in.

I found her name hand-lettered onto a card above the mail slot, *Marilyn Eckert* in curls of black ink wedged between *Dubonnet* and *Hogan*. The inside door was standing open; beyond it was a bare skyblue hallway that creaked when I came in, a plaintive sound that climbed all through the building, top to bottom, walls and floor and ceiling. It was clean enough, the paint was almost new. I went up to the second floor and stood there worrying about what I knew I had to do next.

Her door had two shallow holes where the number had been taken off. It had the battered look of a broom closet. But somewhere on the other side there was a tinny, fluttering recorded band playing, and a recorded voice that whispered at me through the keyhole:

> ... *when you'll regret it*
> *Some day when you'll grow lonely*
> *Your heart will break like mine and you'll*
> *want me only*

After you've gone,
    … after you've gone away

I held my breath; I knocked, and knocked again. The little voice cracked and faded with the music. I waited in the sudden silence, knocked once more and never got an answer.

I was in the middle of counting to twenty when the music started up again, soft on the heels of a rasping needle sound and the shuffle of footsteps. I took hold of the knob and gave it a good hard twist. Like the door below, it was not locked. It scudded over a high spot in the sill where the paint had been rubbed clear. Music spilled out into the stairwell. There wasn't even a chain to keep me out. The door swung open. I said, "Mary?"

It was a barewalled room with rag rugs thrown across the floor and a stool in the corner with a grey-and-white-faced tiger cat sitting on it. A gramophone resting on an upended orange crate sang *After You've Gone* loud enough for the entire house to hear. Of the room's three chairs, two were filled with books. The only other furniture was a ramshackle blue table with a bowl of fruit, a patchwork napkin and a pear cut into wedges on a tin plate resting at its edge. I spotted Mary right away. She was sitting in a muddle of paint jars and brushes spread out on a spattered dropcloth in the corner opposite Max. Her legs were crossed, her back straight. She wasn't moving at all.

She had been painting her walls. From the hall I could see that the room was awash in color, but it wasn't until I stepped inside that I noticed the dozens of painted panels, canted at opposing angles and connected by a tapestry pattern of moons and planets and stars, a mural encompassing the whole apartment, doors, windowsills, cupboards. I saw a Punch and Judy play in the wall above Max, a Santa Claus riding a goose, a crucifixion scene and a night city. In one of the panels the Jones Transportation Company was putting on a play; the figures were so small that I recognized us only by the painted curtain. In another, factory workers were rioting. I saw crows in human dress and haunted art galleries and a farmer slaughtering pigs. There was too much to see it all. It bled into the other rooms, into the dark.

At first I couldn't tell if the empty space in front of her was a section she had whited out or the only place she hadn't yet covered. Blue paint had dribbled into it from above. It would have been a simple thing to clean up; it surprised me that she hadn't. Max curled his tail around his forelegs, looked at me and said nothing. "Mary," I said again.

After you've gone away, the gramophone said, and wheezed into the final chorus. Max closed his eyes. I went over and knelt on the sheet beside Mary. Her eyes were open, but she wasn't seeing the empty wall. My hand found her shoulder. "Mary," I said. "Everyone's worried."

She tore herself away from whatever was on her mind and gave me a weak little smile. "I'll be fine."

I did not know what to say. I did not know what to do. All I knew was that when she sang from high on the stage sometimes everyone in the company, even Moscow, stopped to listen to her voice. All I knew was her talent. I was crouched in a stranger's room with the record scratching in the background and a thousand painted faces watching. In the end all I could do was ask "Are you sure? Is there anything I can do? Is there anything I can get you?"

Mary thanked me and shook her head. She looked at the floor, then back up at me. "Tell Meg not to worry," she said. "I'll be there in time."

I was shaking when I came out of the room. Halfway down the stairs I heard the singer start in again, wistful as the rest of Mary's room,

> *After the years we've been together*
> *Thought joy and tears, all kinds of weather*
> *Someday blue and downhearted*
> *You'll long to be with me…*

before I lost it finally in the vestibule and the brown yard outside.

I went back through the premature thaw. By the time I reached *Valenciennes* I was so nerved up and angry at myself that I could hardly speak. I told everyone she was fine and would be there in time, but I dragged Jones off into a dark corner alone and hissed and whispered at her "What was I supposed to do? Why did you send me there? I've never seen her so unhappy. How could I help her? What do I know about her? She was she was — "

"She's not a Martian," Jones said. We were standing behind the cyclorama; her face was all blue. "Use your head. What do you *think* it could be?"

"She wouldn't tell me. But it had to be something big."

"It's been a perfect little season," Jones said.

I swallowed hard and thought about Mary in the painted room. "What the hell is that supposed to mean?"

"I told her. I'm telling you. The rest will know in a few days."

"No," I said.

*

When Mary finally came in it was just as if she was coming back after feeding Max his dinner. There was a slight edge of redness around her eyes, but she gave us the same chilled, good-evening smile and paused to knock the slush off her boots. Nobody mentioned the afternoon, or broke out of their usual pattern: when Lon came by with his case of sound effects he just said "hey Mary," and grinned and kept on walking. I was the only one who gave her a second look, and even then I did not say what was on my mind. She went around to hang up her coat and hat, and as she passed through again on her way to the stage she took me by the arm, gave me a squeeze and smiled. And that was that. She set up her dulcimer in the corner off stage right, and by seven she was changed and made up and ready to go out.

CURTAIN

WHEN in the summer of 1941 I told this part of it to Bill Schor, with whom I collaborated on the screenplay of *The Crime Annihilator,* he gave me an astonished look and said "Gone? Just like that? And you let her go?" I had to laugh. "*Let* her?" I said. "Billy, you haven't been listening to me at all."

The light booth at *Valenciennes* was nothing more than a six-by-six cage overlooking the stage floor. Like every other part of the building, it was jammed with boxes and gels and junk, leaving barely enough room for the light board and a chair to sit at. From below, no eye could penetrate its built-in defense of darkness and clutter, except during a performance when the face of the man at the board would be lit in a soft, green glow. But by then, everyone was too busy to look.

"Still playing rabbit," Lon said, climbing headfirst through the hole that served as the booth's only door. "Is it only Jones or are you mad at all of us?"

I turned away from him and concentrated on the empty pad of paper in my lap. Lon frowned. He crawled under the board and made a show of fussing with some wires, but it was nothing more than a kind of free-matinee performance, a bit of stage business while he worked up to the next line. "All right," he said at last. "You're mad at all of us. Guess I can live with whatever share of the blame you seem to think happens to be mine. Not fair to the others, though."

I got up to leave. When I couldn't squeeze past the combined bulk of Lon and the light board, I said "Excuse me." Lon only gave me a backwards look and went on doing nothing. I had no choice but to settle back into the chair, and wait.

Before long a big sigh came out of him like a steam engine slowing on the tracks. "Jones doesn't have to account herself to you," he said. "She doesn't owe any of us anything. Maybe it's the other way around."

But he wasn't going to make me feel guilty. I was determined in that. I didn't say anything.

Lon had already begun to sweat. "Okay, maybe we've had more time to get used to the idea. She was ready to leave at least a year ago. If she hadn't found herself a writer to play with she'd have been gone by the end of summer. So look at it this way: you bought us another eight months of her time."

"You're a liar," I said. "You could talk to her. You could get her to stay."

"Sheee," Lon said. "Maybe Pecos Bill could rope a cyclone. I sure as hell can't."

I hadn't liked the sound of my voice when it finally came, but now that I'd started I couldn't seem to stop. My ears were ringing. I said, "She's all that's holding it together. If she goes it's all over."

Lon cast a look back at me, then fixed his eyes on the board's underside. "There've been other Joneses before her," he said. "There'll be others after she's gone. She wouldn't have it any other way."

Three nights a week (and twice on Saturdays) we burned the stage in black flame. It never failed to catch the audience by surprise, though I couldn't understand why: Sallis painted so obsessively throughout the play's two hours, so much that I wondered how he found the time to talk, much less participate as a viable character, until there was only Rebecca hanging on the walls, Rebecca swamping the tabletops, Rebecca and Rebecca and Rebecca looking out from every corner, in oil, watercolor, chalk and charcoal, dressed and undressed, warrior woman, enchantress, ingenue and citizen, until it should have been obvious that with so much combustion going into the work a little of it must break free and take it's creator on a quick tour of the afterlife. So how could they not see it coming, I thought, when it was virtually preordained from the start?

All unsuspecting, out beyond the curtain, they watched and listened as Templeton and Moscow quarreled under the light. "I know it's only a dream," Sallis said. "A ghost of perfume rising out of an old book. But I won't put it aside. Not until I hear it from her own lips. And perhaps not even then. Because I would still have to know Why not."

"You must stop this," Templeton said. "Your early portraits of her were fine, there was no doubt but that she ignited something in you. But now you must learn to shine that light in another direction. This won't get you anywhere. You can't alter the fabric of reality itself."

"Can't I?" Sallis said. In the blue, shadowed space behind the scene, Jones made ready for her entrance, her wig and nightshirt so encrusted with paint that they crinkled and creaked as she moved. Bone-colored in her fresh coating of make-up, she already looked like a ghost; it was my job, and Mrs. Templeton's, to make her look like a nightmare.

She took her place without a word or a sign, empty of expression, her hands crossed over her breasts, her eyes shut tight. There were three trays of paint resting on a stand at her side. Mrs. Templeton and I each had a brush, fat things meant for house work. Holding fast in our most professional backstage silence, we dipped them and began throwing paint into Jones's face.

"Watch me," Sallis said. Grabbing up his palette and brush, he attacked the canvas with such violent strokes that the whole set began to shiver. "I'm conjuring her now. Freezing her place in reality. In my reality."

"That horrible thing," Templeton said. "That isn't her. It's the work of a madman."

Red, purple, yellow: the Rebecca that haunted Sallis's mind was a creature of paint, and from paint she would come to him. "Your imagination has betrayed you," Templeton said. "She doesn't love you. Not the way you want. She never will," and there I was hitting Jones with the paint, as if my hands had gone liquid, as if the colors splashing her forehead and cheeks were growing from within; actual welts, actual blood. "You could at least have warned me," I said out loud, shaking now with anger that had passed out of my control. "God. You could at least tell me why."

Jones opened her eyes. They were blue glass in a dripping mask of paint. She did not look at me. She did not look at anyone. If anything her attention was drawn inward. She said nothing.

My voice climbed in pitch and volume. "It's no good if I talk to you. It's no good if I don't. Why don't you just go?"

Mary looked up from her dulcimer. She didn't miss a note. I felt Mrs. Templeton pry the brush out of my fingers, and realized that I'd been flailing away with it all this time, long after it had gone dry. She dipped it, then dipped her own and set to work with both hands. Jones shut her eyes.

"A hazard of the profession," Moscow said. A bit distracted; he'd heard it too. He's going to kill me, I thought, the moment he walks off the stage. He'll still have Sallis kicking around inside him and together the two of them will take me apart.

It was nearly Jones's cue. Templeton had already withdrawn, helpless and defeated; all that remained was a bit of rough action in which Moscow, Sallis, smashed up some paintings, fought back the tears, and lost. We could not even see his shape against the flats; he had moved downstage into the darker light, so close to the front row that they could have reached up and touched him, had they dared. Only a moment now.

"What are they offering you?" I said weakly. "You couldn't even tell us that much." Moscow made a futile gesture of wiping his face. Still weeping, he moved upstage into the shadow of the rigged painting. He raised his brush. "Now," Sylvie hissed from the corner.

Jones turned and thrust her right arm into the canvas. It burst through under the stagelight and was met with the usual rush of gasps and whispers from the house. Mary drummed out an eerie glissando across the face of her dulcimer. "Listen to me," I said to Jones's back. I was thinking about the man on the telephone, that time in her room. I wondered if she was going to him. I wondered who he might be. "Why did you bring me out here?" I said, but she was far away; with her free hand she broke the canvas a second time, clawed the air, and began to force her way through the painting. "Hush," Mrs. Templeton said, drawing me back out of the gash of light that poured through in Jones's wake.

She guided me into the shadows like a samaritan walking a drunk around the room. My hands touched cool brick. There was an awful crash from the stage as Moscow stumbled against a worktable and fell backwards into the mess. A low sound like a cough came up out of him; I heard the canvas tearing and I heard the clatter and splash of the turpentine jar spilling its contents over the floor, the flats, everything. "Look at me," Jones said, leaking paint, "if you can remember how.

Look at me. How can we dream together in this room you've made? How breathe?"

Not a sound from the audience. "Leave me alone," Sallis said. "You've ruined me." His right hand closed 'round the handle of the kerosene lantern by which he had always painted. He pitched it so hard that I could hear it cutting the air. It broke at Jones's feet and enveloped her in a nimbus of fire.

It was nothing more than a couple of shuttered spotlights, a sound effects machine cranked by Sylvie, and a fan beneath the stage that blew yard-long shreds of black and yellow crepe up and around her body. It caught and spread like real flame, the audience sometimes yelling out loud now, though never loud enough to drown out the cries that Moscow gave as the Rebecca thing, eyeless, shockheaded, a siren in paint, grasped him and held him in the blaze, in her fatal embrace. For a moment only: just enough to drive it home. Then without a curtain the scene ended in abrupt darkness, in silence that filled the house.

Before they could recover from its sudden descent the epilogue would be half over. I called it the King Kong scene, because it served the same purpose: "It wasn't the flames, it was beauty killed the beast." But by then, I thought, I'll be dead: Moscow will have come and bashed my brains out against the proscenium. For talking out of turn. For ruining his concentration. For being heard.

Instead, he walked straight past me into the dark. He did not even look angry; only tired and a little bruised after the performance, a machine winding down and badly in need of an oil change. He waited quietly at the back for the final curtain, the slow rise of applause; then he dragged himself back to the stage, walking past me again without even looking, without as much as a flicker of awareness from his owlish eyes.

All right, I thought. It will be Sylvie then. She has better reason to say it than anyone, after the talk I gave her that last time she broke character, when she used the same words I'd just given to Templeton. I thought, Now she can make me eat them. Now...

But Sylvie ran off like a character in a fairy story, rushing through the woods; just a shimmer of white and she was gone. I stepped out behind the closing curtain and the line broke around me: on the other side I could hear the audience filing out, chattering to themselves in the way that always depressed me, because I could never tell if they were saying good things or bad. The company shed their characters inside our empty set, and went on about their business, ignoring me. And I thought, Well, come on! I disrupted the performance! Isn't anyone going to yell at me? You have that right.

I waited and waited and nothing happened. Finally Mary came by and rested her hand on my shoulder. She squeezed me, smiled and let go. Is that all? I thought. Has it come to that point? Am I speaking for us all?

That night when I climbed up to my apartment, Jones was there waiting for me. I was fumbling for my key when I heard a motion like breath against the walls; then her voice came out of the corner, as from an empty stage. "Help me out here," she said softly. "Give me something. One of your purple images."

When the overhead light came on I saw her posed at the farthest edge of the landing, legs crossed at the ankle, the collar of her greatcoat turned up for no reason at all. "Not me," I said. "I'm past it. All it ever gets me is grief."

Her hands appeared out of bottomless pockets and floated at waist level, palms up in a gesture of innocence. "Nothing up my sleeve. Thought I'd save you the walk to my place."

It had been nearly a month since I'd been to the room behind her casement window, that window that glowed orange and held silhouettes like a shadowplay screen. It surprised me to realize that I had no intention of going back. Looking at her there, at her face under the light, her neck framed by the coat and a mass of dark hair, I knew that it was not because I wanted her any less. But I was too upset; and by the time it had passed over I felt she would be gone.

I turned my back to her, pushed open the door; Jones rustled past me into the little room beyond. She circled for a moment without speaking, parted the curtains with two fingers and peered out into the black yard. "You kick like a mule," she said then. "Slow to wind, but when you finally get good and coiled, look out."

From the hall a narrow oblong of light cut the room into unequal halves. "I don't want you to go. No one does."

"That can't be helped," Jones said. She drifted around the foot of the bed, her shoulders squared, hands sunk into her pockets. "It's long past due. Time everyone got a change. Time for *you* to stand up and walk on your own two typing fingers."

When I didn't answer, she took my hand by the fingers and shook it playfully. "I can't help that, either," she said. "Come on. I'm not leaving because of you or anyone. I'm just moving on."

"To what?" I said. "Everyone seems to know but me."

She fell silent. In those rapid moments I could have believed that the apartment house, the city outside, and the world outside the city had all dropped away from around us. Some elemental passion, some fireball, soared and sparked behind her mesmeric eyes, yet on her face there wasn't the tiniest stir or ripple, only the stillness of silvered glass, her own, her perfect Darwinian calm. "Venice," she said, unblinking, her voice level and serene. "It's not an acting job. I'll be doing restoration work. As an apprentice."

Whether by instinct or design, she had taken the best dramatic advantage of the room and its light: the moon falling through the window framed her head and shoulders in a soft backglow, while the hall light brushed her left cheek, leaving half of her face in darkness. 'So you see there's nothing to be jealous of. What you imagined would only have been a step to one side. I won't be leading anyone, for the moment. I have too much to learn."

She had kicked the stool out from under my anger, and I knew it; still, the only thing I could think of to say was, "We need you here."

"You need a Jones," she said. "It doesn't have to be Margaret Darwin. That's the other reason I'm here. To make you an offer."

She floated over to my writing table and clicked on the lamp. From an inside pocket she withdrew a long, cream-colored piece of paper, folded into thirds. Gently, as if the paper were a thousand years old, she smoothed it out under the light. Without looking back, she said, "You ought to recognize one of these."

Did I not. It was a Bill of Sale, written out in india ink, in her own graceful hand, and adorned like a college diploma with a purposeless red ribbon affixed with sealing wax. Of course it would have to be theatrical, I thought. It offered up *Valenciennes*, its contents, the Jones Transportation Company and all of its property for the purchase price of one dollar.

"It will mean changing your name," Jones said. "At least in spirit. But I'm prepared to sign it over to you now."

I stopped breathing. Out came the silver-capped fountain pen that she carried over her heart. She held it up against the light. "One buck," she said. "And your John Hancock."

And I suppose a part of me wanted to grab and sign fast, before she changed her mind. But not a very large part of me, and not the part that mattered. Vaguely, I felt as if I'd seen a car wreck about to happen. "Put it away," I said softly. "Go on. I can't do this."

Jones looked straight up into my eyes. "It's the right choice. For everyone. You know it is."

"No," I said. "Sorry. But I'm not interested."

Something turned over behind her eyes, then sank again beneath the surface. She leaned forward in the chair, as though trying to reach me with her mouth. "Just imagine. Not having me reshape your ideas for you. Not having to write in some gaudy part for me to play. You'd be master of your own imagination, with a full company of players at your disposal. Consider that."

I did. The idea frightened me, but that wasn't what held me back. I could have done those things that the Jones needed to do. Given time, I could even have learned to do them with finesse. But I couldn't see myself providing the glue needed to hold the various members of the Jones Transportation Company together. I couldn't see myself replacing Margaret Darwin.

I turned away. There were no stars in the window, and the moon had passed behind a cloud; all I could see there was a reflection of the room, of my own shadowed face, and of Jones at my back. " 'Get your mind fermenting,'" she said. " 'Give your imagination free play; and invent the real limit of human daring. Show us how to fly to the moon; direct the way to Mars; point the signboards down the roads of human daring. And I for one will go.' "

I could hear the quotation marks around her words, but couldn't identify the source. "What's that from?"

"Not a play. Octavie LaTour said it once in an interview. You wouldn't know of her. She looped the loop in a circus act. Defied gravity. What about you?"

There were several things I could have said to that, but I didn't like any of them. I kept my mouth shut.

"Don't think that by turning it down you can force me to stay," Jones said.

"I wasn't. I wouldn't. I'm not an idiot."

There was a long pause from her corner of the room. At last her reflected image stood up and flowed ghostlike towards me, turning the bill of sale gently in its fingers. When it spoke again, it wasn't quoting anyone. "Listen," it said. "Just now we can go along pushing our hopes ahead of us, into the future. But at some point we'll start looking back, and find that our hopes have slipped past us. I don't want that to happen to me. And I don't want it to happen to you."

I felt like saying, If you're so concerned with my dreams then why are you going? But it wouldn't have done any good. Lon was right about that; you can't argue with a cyclone. The best you can hope to do is stand firm, and hang onto your hat.

"I'm grateful," I said. "But I won't change my mind."

Jones bowed her head and gave me a sad smile. "No. Well, I

didn't think you would." Her hand passed over my shoulders, paused, and withdrew. She folded the paper away into her breast pocket, alongside the silver pen. Her shape broke into the doorlight. She said "Good night," and went through without looking back. Her footsteps descended into the building. The vestibule door opened and shut. Then I was alone.

I didn't bother about closing the door to my room. Still in my shoes and socks, I flopped down onto the bed and lay there with my feet spread, my head propped up and one hand draped over my mouth. There was nothing in the room worth staring at. I sat there frozen in time, and felt Jones moving away in the night.

When I told all this to my friend Bill Schor he frowned and would not meet my eyes. At forty-seven, Bill was a paunchy, balding man working his way down through the studio ranks; two years before he had co-scripted a feature for Ernst Lubitsch, and now he was writing serials. I didn't know why this had happened to him, but I knew he could always be counted on for an honest answer.

Which is why I can still feel the difficulty of it, looking back at him from a distance of seventeen years as he scooped a cigarette out of the remains of what had been a fresh pack just an hour before, shook his head and at last gently said, "I gotta tell you, bud, I think you made the wrong decision."

At the time I did not know how to answer him. If I had to answer him now I probably still wouldn't be able to come out and just say it, just the simple "Of course now I think you're right. But at the time it was the best I was capable of." Instead, I'd probably answer him in the style of the Ancients: indirectly, and with a further puzzle. "You know," I'd say, "much as I couldn't talk about anything except in euphemisms or symbols, I think Jones was the same way. It's the reason why everything she said had three or four different meanings. I guess it's the reason I loved her."

And Bill would say "Oh Christ" and turn back down to his work. But then in Hollywood terms I was still just a kid. I brushed his words aside. "Now you sound like Lon," I said. "Only Lon understood the why of it, even when he lit into me."

"Maybe he didn't know what you were going to trade it in for," Billy said.

Our office at Republic Pictures didn't look out on anything, because it didn't have any windows. Under a yellow ceiling lamp we sat with our desks pushed together, facing each other across our typewriters and piles of paper and pens. Sometimes we banged out forty pages a day between us, other times we did next to nothing. When we weren't actually writing we made diagrams of the characters and the places they had to go, charts of their progress to paper the walls. It had been exciting work for the first three months, but even at its best I wouldn't have called it glamorous. I never saw the actors, except at a distance, and then they seemed more like automata than anything I would have recognized as actors: they worked only in fits and starts, wind them up and let 'em go for a fleeting moment, repeating their stock motions seven or fifteen or twenty times from five different angles; they never had to sustain anything for more than five minutes at a time. And yet it was a skill. Jones couldn't have done what they did. It would have driven her mad.

Billy's typewriter clattered into life on the opposite desk, hauling me back up out of my thoughts like a fish out of black water. I waited him out through three pages of fistfights, car chases and grim heroics; then he paused to light another cigarette, and before he could start in again I said, "The day that she left us, Moscow wouldn't even come out of his dressing room."

Billy scowled and ignored me. He threaded another page into his machine, posed his fingers over the keyboard as if to write something and then flopped back in defeat, blowing out smoke. "All right," he said. "All right. I'm going to have to sit through it sooner or later. Might as well be now."

This is what I told him, in that burning room, on studio time:

It was a Sunday near the close of May. Behind the heavy shades blanketing the ticket window I sat in my own personal spotlight, trying to count the draw, thinking only of sleep. Outside the booth the lobby was dark and silent, empty but for the painted figures hanging there, motionless, looking out of the gloom with fixed anticipation, *Valenciennes* presenting a closed front to the street. Three times I'd counted, and each time gotten a different total; the coffee might have helped, but by then I was so tired that I'd forgotten to drink it.

I had just put my head down when I felt Lon's shadow fall across me. He jingled his keys. "Hey," he said gently. "Better hurry up if you want to say goodbye."

I said, "What?" The clock said one-fifty. I'd been asleep more than half an hour.

Lon started to repeat himself but by then I'd left the chair and was stumbling bleary-eyed into the lobby. It had been two weeks since Jones had come to my room to offer me the company; two weeks since anyone had mentioned the possibility of her going away. In that time I'd almost managed to convince myself that it wasn't going to happen. Now here I was, roused out of sleep like a child wakened early to bid a visiting relative goodbye, only worse, because I knew the permanence of this, and knew that I'd wasted my last weeks in hope.

She was waiting for me down on the empty stage, looking like a dockworker, travelworn and a bit disreputable in her blue jacket, a lightly-packed duffel bag resting in the dust beside her. She had combed her hair and tied it back behind her neck, but there were still faint smudges of stage make-up along the edge of her brow, around her eyes and cheekbones. She didn't look sad at all.

"It's not too late," she said as I came down to meet her. "Mary would be happy to stand aside for you. She told me she's not sleeping nights."

I rested my hands on the stage floor. It was all I could do to keep from grabbing her by the ankles, in a crazy attempt to hold her there. "Come quick!," I would shout. "I've got her!" Instead I tried to raise a smile. "Anyone would get butterflies, trying to fill your shoes."

"She'll need your support."

That was something I could promise easily. Jones said that was good. She sat on her heels at the edge of the stage, and for the first time looked at me the way a lover might. Her eyes were bright and full of warmth. "It's too bad," she said at last. "In ten years you'd be perfect."

No, I thought. In ten years there would still be better than a decade between us, still that gulf of experience, and she would want something else.

Jones took my hand. She said, "Keep your eyes open. I'll be there." Then she rose, slung the duffel bag across her right shoulder and started out.

— "And that's it?" Billy said to me. "That's all?"

"Almost all. As she walked away I asked her to keep me in mind if she ever needed a writer. I think she heard me: she turned her head. But if she said anything I didn't hear it. She went straight out into the back, into... an unhappy silence. Then the stage door opened and closed. That was it. When I finally got up the courage to go back I found them huddled together like a losing team, holding each other. All except Moscow; he could weep in front of a house full of strangers but not in front of us. 'She's gone,' I said, and they opened a spot for me."

Billy gave me one of his big contemplative sighs. "Kid, if you tried to sell that one here they'd laugh you right out of the studio."

Which made me kind of angry. "If I was selling something you'd be right. I'm telling you what happened."

Billy grinned. "This is Hollywood, my friend. As such I feel obligated to point out what your story is missing. The hero has to stand up for himself. For love. He has to follow her out into the alleyway, make some speeches, win 'er back. Then she has no choice but to fall into his arms. Boom! A triumphant clinch for the fade-out. I don't understand why you didn't try."

"It's not that I didn't have it in me," I said after a time. "I did. But she would never have allowed it."

So now it was my turn to go through the motions of lighting a cigarette, even though I'd never learned how to smoke. I did it for the same reason Billy did: it gave me time to think. "I guess I never did find the one right word to describe her," I said when the thing was blazing away in my fingers. "Pilot, explorer, pirate, gypsy, lion tamer. She was all of those things. It wasn't sex that got her through. It was assurance; the quality of having been places and seen things that most people only dream about. The quality of Time."

"That Jones woman?" Billy said. "That Margaret Darwin?" He shook his head once again. "I still don't understand."

"No," I said. "I guess you don't."

EPILOGUE:

MASKS OR FACES?

IN the fall of 1940 I accepted a job writing chapterplays as part of a team at Republic Studios. It was fun dreaming up the oblique situations and hairbreadth escapes, but the constant fight scenes (although simple to write) left not much room to "grow" a character, as Mrs. Templeton would say. In 1941 I was lucky enough to have a typewriter handed to me instead of a gun; I rode out the War Effort working on training films with a crew of animators whose only previous qualifications for mayhem were Bugs Bunny and Donald Duck. I spent some memorable afternoons with them in hot screening rooms watching rough cuts of Private Snafu cartoons. It was from them that I learned how to simplify the most complicated things, and how to sweeten the inedible with entertainment, like putting an envelope of chocolate around a laxative. When the war department animators built their room-sized maps of Japan, I was one of the few writers present. They filmed flight paths over this incredibly detailed miniature continent, and used them to brief their pilots. I helped write the narration. When they bombed Hiroshima the pilots were, in part, following my directions; that about killed writing for me.

So when all the surrenders were signed and done I took the advice of a friend and used the letter of recommendation that Mr. Deighton had written for me nearly seven years before, back at the beginning of that short, confusing summer. It got me a job as salesman for the Eagle Novelty Company, based out of Clear Lake, Iowa. I spent the better part of a year driving from appointment to appointment in a rented Chevrolet, listening to baseball games over the radio and keeping my mind on the business at hand, the business of roads and selling. The long miles from city to town sometimes reminded me of similar trips I had made with the company of players, similar towns visited, but for the most part I was not plagued by Shakespearean ghosts. I did not think about theaters or actors; I did not think about writing. I didn't even carry a typewriter. At night, in the little motels that were springing up along the highways, I kept myself well lubricated.

It was in the offices and back rooms of retail stores that I began to understand Moscow for the first time. There, waiting in some awful corner for the buyer to see me, I learned how to wear my face like a mask, and how that made-up face, though invisible, could put over a sale and still protect my own insides. What will it be this time, I thought, imagining a combination of Templeton's straightforward nose, Moscow's jawline, Margaret Darwin's reflective eyes, all fitting snugly over my own features, so that when I extended my hand it was like walking onto the stage, not even my own hand anymore, but the hand of a new character sewn together out of the parts of corpses. It was not enough to just take a deep breath, put my mind away and follow the script; when the clock started ticking and the samples started coming out, I had to **BE** The Salesman.

Then on a hot afternoon in the back of a little five and dime outside of Boston, my face almost came apart. I don't know what set me off; I'd been with tougher customers in my time. I never went back and thanked this one. But I feel that I owe him a debt.

He was a hard-faced man who refused all small talk, leading me straight through into an "office" that was nothing more than a painted desk crammed into the corner of a storage room. Three planks straddled a pair of beams overhead, loaded down with so much stock that they had bowed into a threatening U above us. He dragged a painted chair over for me, then sat at the desk with his arms folded and his knees pressed tightly together. "Fifteen minutes," he said. "That's all you've got."

I had fortified myself in advance of the call with several swigs of scotch whisky from a flask that I carried with me most everywhere in those days, and so now for some reason I lost a few of those minutes just getting my cases open. Inside, packed neatly into their own snug compartments, were the whimseys and toys that I sold: false-bottomed boxes painted with crude oriental symbols, silk scarves that could be made to change their colors, bouquets of paper flowers that sometimes popped open on the long rides, false thumbs of varying sizes, a jack-in-the-box in the shape of a camera, a ten cent box of marbles, pamphlets with astrological symbols arcing over a purple background, Halloween baskets shaped like cats, pumpkins, devil's heads, skulls; a grey hare of not very astonishing realism made all of wool, old-fashioned optical disks picturing horses or ogres in motion and usually a mouse or cat dancing around the hub, a wooden egg with a hole drilled in one end (for vanishing kerchiefs or paper money), a metal bird that sang in its cage, a crystal ball complete with visions painted on a canvas roll concealed in its base, make-up kits and simple costumes of a sikh or clown, a wizard's peaked cap (folded flat) covered with moons, stars and ringed planets; three different tarot decks (French, Hindu and British), and Jugglehead, my own favorite, "the quick change toy; makes many funny faces."

I laid it all out before his empty eyes, remembering Moscow as he peeked through the curtain. *"Look at them,"* he said, turning away from the slit of light that separated us from the house. *"Farmers, shopkeepers, a banker or two. To them we're freaks. All of us, even you."* And with my suitcases full of cheap tricks, of junk, I felt the same way.

"How now, Spirit," I said aloud. "Wither wander you?"

"'Scuse me?"

I couldn't remember where I had heard the line before; only that it was Shakespeare and I should know it. I nearly repeated it to him, until I saw the confusion on his face. "Sorry," I said. "I came all the way up from Philadelphia yesterday, and Baltimore before that. 'Next Week East Lynne.' " I had to laugh at that. It was an old theatrical phrase meaning I'd better have a sure thing. "Um, where was I?"

The man sitting with his hands behind his elbows gave me a blank, solitary look. "The Eagle Magic Set," he said. "Number ten."

"Ten?" I said. "That has a wonderful device. We used a larger variation of it, once. It went over big." I fumbled through the sample case until I found what I wanted. It was a plain hand mirror with a molded stem, and a deck of cards. "Patter's included with the instructions, but we won't bother with that. If you'll just pick a card..."

I riffled the pack and my client stuck out his finger. "Three of hearts," he said.

Holding the mirror at arm's length, I asked him to place the card face down against the glass. He tried not to look at himself, and failed. "Now what?" he said.

"Pause for effect. Not too long. All right, take it down."

But his fingers were too thick; the card dropped away and fluttered to the ground. Instead of picking it up, my client looked into the glass. I knew what he was seeing: the image of three ghostlike hearts floating one above the other, superimposed over his own reflection in the silvered depths of the mirror.

"The hearts are printed on celluloid," I told him. "Elastic bands hidden inside the frame snap them into position when I touch a button on the handle." I pressed it to demonstrate: Click, and the hearts withdrew in a sudden rush, Click and they rose again before his eyes. "Simple. But kind of elegant, don't you think?"

"No thanks," he said. "What else have you got to show me?"

Then I lost another few seconds of my fifteen minutes. All right, I wanted to say to him, here. Here's some plastic shit, startle your neighbors confuse your parents. Here's some plastic vomit, just add water, is that the stuff you like? But I grappled and managed to pull my face back into place. It didn't fit as comfortably as it had earlier in the day, but I swallowed it all and just went on and finally got a small order out of him. When I left him I said to myself, Take a bow. I felt I'd earned it.

I went down to a cafe at the end of the block and ate dinner there with the street at my back and the remaining sun crawling across the orange wall of the booth. The meal tasted all right, but I was feeling too distracted to enjoy it. Instead of getting a start on my paperwork, I dumped scotch into my coffee and sat in a daze, thinking about Jugglehead, the three hearts, about magician's secrets, cliffhangers and *Twelfth Night*. It wasn't the kind of thinking that led anywhere, or accomplished anything. But it was the best I could manage.

In that strange, wistful mood I took myself back uptown, riding in a crowded car with my sample cases pressing on either side and a straw-haired lady at my elbow complaining that I took up too much room. When I came up out of the subway there was just enough light in the sky to blot out the glow of the streetlamps. It was three blocks to the parking garage where I'd left the Chevrolet; I didn't get more than half way before I noticed the lighted marquee glowing from an adjoining street.

It took me three or four seconds to decide that I wasn't going to stop, but by then my body had made the decision for me. The cases swung so heavily in my hands that I set them down on the sidewalk. Loitering there under the gathering night, I peered down into that street and argued with myself over whether or not I should go. Perhaps the box office would be closed. Perhaps I was too late, had missed the start of the show, or perhaps I would be too early. A steady flow of passersby broke and drifted around me; at last a traffic cop noticed me and beckoned me on. I picked up my cases, crossed over and kept on until I came to a row of glossy pictures. There were people sounds coming from inside, but no one in sight. The doors were open.

I entered into a lobby done up in dark blue paper, smaller than it seemed, relieved only by the light of the ticket booth and a brightly glowing candy stand. I bought a ticket and lugged my cases over to the cloakroom. The girl there laughed when I hefted them up onto her counter. "What've you got in those things?" she said. I said props, and added that it had been seven years since I'd seen a show as a paying customer. She was a hawk-nosed girl with dark eyes like an Egyptian. She said it was about time I saw what I was missing.

On the other side of the candy stand her twin sister was waiting for me in an ugly red usherette's suit. "Go on ahead," she said. "Take any seat. Curtain's going up."

The house was pretty well packed. By the time I found a seat, in an awful balcony overlooking the stage, the lights had come up, the music was swelling in a nervous, atonal chorus, and a large cast of actors was beginning to draw itself out from the corners of the theater. They came from the aisles, the exits, from out of the walls, waving their arms and calling aloud as if this was Market Day.

A handful of them passed under an iron grate hanging directly below me. Among them I saw a burly, shockheaded man who looked as if he had lost his way. He crawled up out of the orchestra pit, turned his face up and back and scanned the house with eyes like brown searchlights sweeping the night sky.

It was Moscow. He was twenty pounds heavier, covered with dirt, graying and crow-footed, but I recognized him and I saw that he recognized me. For a moment, the rest of house, the players, the play itself, all dropped away: he stood alone in the hard light above the pit, in a scene of terrible silence, looking up at me, as though waiting for the words that only I could give him.

—*New York City,*
October, 1958

FOR SALE

One slightly used theatrical building, well–loved, complete with settings, props, costumes... entire worlds for the taking and making. Exceedingly reasonable terms to the right customer.

Inquire in Person: 1182

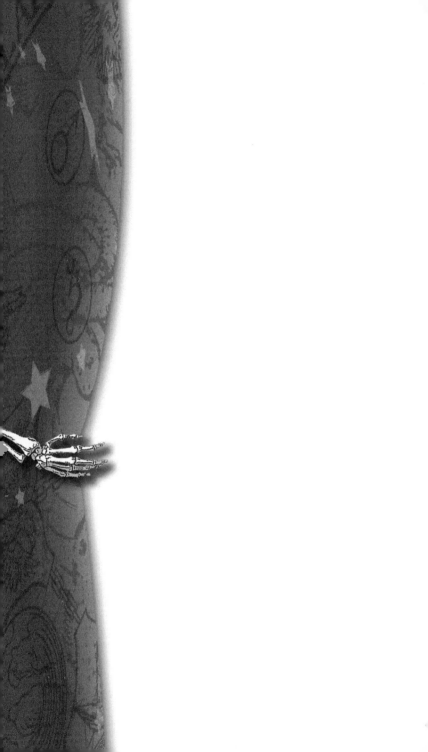

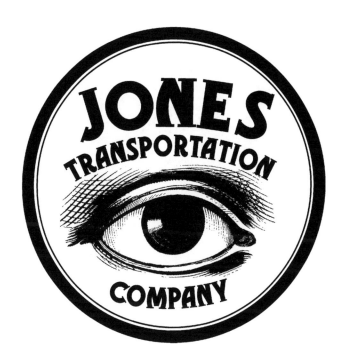

featured

Mary Eckert • Sylvie Linsdtomm
Peter Moscow • Ruth Forsythe Templeton
Claude W. Templeton

and

Margaret Darwin
Lon Burden, *Stage Manager*

assisted by Winslow Howe

—ACKNOWLEDGMENTS—

The play described in chapter nine is based on Winnebago Trickster and Hare cycles as recounted in Paul Radin's book *The Trickster: A Study In American Indian Mythology* (Schocken, 1972).

The following people all contributed to *Persephone's Torch* in ways ranging from advice and/or criticism to financial support to ideas and inspiration:

Mr. & Mrs. C.R. Bachmann, Bruce Canwell, Alyson Hagy, Cathryn Hankla, Leif Peterson, Douglas Thornsjo Sr., and Robley Wilson Jr. My thanks also to everyone at Stonecoast '88.

In Loving Memory
Barbara Jean Thornsjo
1927 – 2010

Manufactured by Amazon.ca
Bolton, ON